NEVER

FOR AN ANGEL

NEVER

fall

FOR AN ANGEL

Dedicated to all the women with a broken past who used to dream of a knight in shining black armor, full of chinks and scuffs, who could chase away your demons. I hope you found what you needed.

AUTHOR'S NOTE

Dear Reader,

This book is NOT a clean romance. It is dark. It is very sexy (*cough* Ferris wheel *cough*). It also has very real moments that (unfortunately) happen to many people. While the story itself is purely a work of fiction, the pain is not, and I stand wholeheartedly beside anyone who has can relate.

Christian and Mila's story spans the course of five years. Because of this, they have a lot of history together and their story is longer than all the others in this series. I felt it was imperative to give these characters the time they needed to heal and flourish, and I stand by that decision.

Please read through the trigger warnings carefully before you proceed. I have taken the liberty of listing them, so they are easy to read. Your mental health matters.

- Rape (flashbacks)(Not carried out by MMC)
- Forced body mutilation
- Explicit sexual scenes in great detail (like, a lot of them)
- Graphic violence and gore
- Psychosis
- Torture
- Medieval torture
- PTSD
- Vivid nightmares
- Anxiety and panic attacks
- Murder with handyman implements

- Murder with medical equipment
- Just plain murder
- Vehicular homicide (he deserved it)
- Mentions of sex trafficking
- Mentions of parental abuse
- Mentions of the loss of a parent/sibling
- Forced Marriage
- Someone is burned alive (he also deserved it)
- Stalking
- Improper handling of a firearm
- Mental abuse
- Physical abuse
- Body part removal
- Forced spontaneous relocation (kidnapping)
- Use of sedatives for kidnapping
- Crude and obscene language
- Mentions of cancer (Not MCs)
- Strangulation
- Someone gets stabbed
- Spanking
- Handcuffs
- Slight breeding kink
- Praise kink
- Fingers (IYKYK)

"They say love makes you a better man, but . . .loving you just made me fucking ruthless."

—Christian Cross, *Never Fall for an Angel*

PROLOGUE

I'm drifting in a sea of open water.

The tide is strong, carrying me away from land. Away from people. There's nothing but me and the endless blue ocean.

Waves roar around me, lapping over my bare flesh, but the cold doesn't bother me. Not anymore.

"You fucking deserve this, bitch," *he* grits under his breath, growling as he thrusts inside me. The pain is blinding, like hot coals melting me in two until I'm nothing but a mass of burnt flesh and blood on the stained mattress beneath him.

His knife cuts my skin. The ache is unlike anything I've ever felt. Cold, hard steel against my skin being flayed open, like flames lapping at my broken flesh.

He digs in deeper, carving the brand they will remember me by. Five little letters arranged to destroy the person I was before I was brought down to this basement.

Where am I?

Who am I?

I scream behind the dirty gag in my mouth, but nothing comes out. No sound reaches my ears. Tears seep from my eyes, blood oozes from the cuts littering my body, and the man between my legs? He couldn't be happier to watch me die.

And everyone will remember me as the girl who never screamed despite my voice rattling the rafters in this cold, decrepit hell.

"Mmm . . . you look so pretty covered in all this blood."

My stomach turns, bile rising in my throat, but I can't vomit. The sensation gets stuck in my lungs, drowning me until I feel my head tightening, the room spinning in circles around me.

My vision goes, and all I can think about is my mother.

What will she say when she learns what I've become? Will she ever know?

Will they find me, or will I rot here in this purgatory, my spirit lingering to watch my body decay until there's nothing left but bones and matted hair on broken concrete and a dirty mattress?

Please . . . I say, but the sound doesn't come out. Not that it matters. Pleading won't save me.

Nothing can save me.

"You love this shit, don't you? You like being used like the whore you are?" A hand connects with my cheek, but the pain doesn't register. I'm full of pain. His slap means nothing. "Your pussy's fucking soaked. You just had to fucking do it, didn't you?"

That's all I am, right? Pussy for a man to use until he's decided he's done with me. When he'll either kill me or leave me here to bleed out.

Why am I not dead? Why am I still breathing? Was the act itself not enough? When does this hell end?

I hope my mother doesn't cry. I hope she knows I didn't mean all those horrible things I said to her. That in my last moments I couldn't stop thinking of her. Of my brother. My sisters . . . him.

God, don't let me think of him. Don't let him know what became of me after he left.

My vision blackens at the edges, the waves pulling me under, and I can't breathe. The pain fades. The light above me blends into one striking white light. His grunts fade, leaving a ringing silence that hums in the air.

I blink up at the sun above me, feeling its warmth on my skin. That is . . . the sun? Right?

White fades to black. The hum fades to nothingness.

And that's when I learned silence is the loudest sound in the universe.

Is . . . this it?

Is this what the end feels like? A flash and then . . . emptiness?

Am I dying?

God, I hope so.

CHAPTER
One

CHRISTIAN
ARKANSAS, JULY

I f the Arkansas's Best Inn is the best they have to offer, this state is well and truly fucked. The place is in serious need of a maintenance man—or a flame thrower—and judging by the sleazy motherfuckers that keep going in and out of room A-7, I'd say a couple cops, too.

She always chooses places like this. Somewhere she thinks I won't search for her. As if I'm stupid enough to believe she'd use her credit card.

This is the closest I've gotten since *that* night, and my dick aches to move closer.

Perfect little body. Blonde curls, wild in a messy braid. I can't see her eyes, but I know if she were to look up and spot me, they'd be a striking, soft gray, like moonlight on the lake or some shit.

She's as beautiful as I remember, save for the hollowness behind her smile.

Mila Carpenter was made to ruin me. Like the devil himself handed her to me on a silver platter because God would never give

I've been trailing her for five long, long fucking months. Just watching. Waiting for the perfect time to strike. Every time she thinks she's gotten away, I show back up to remind her she will never escape me.

Especially not since she shot me.

I hate that the light in her eyes was stolen. What struck me like a thousand volts the moment I laid eyes on her. That sweet fucking innocence *I* stole from her when I made her mine.

—The crushing reality I forced on her when I gave her back.

Unfortunately, there's a part of me that lives in her, and not a single person on this fucking planet could cut it out. Not even me.

She's burrowed her way into every one of my thoughts. Every one of my fantasies. My fucking soul . . . and now all that's left are the charred remains of what used to be my self-control.

Diagnosis? I'm fucked.

I sit in the front seat of my car parked at the gas station across the street, watching her while I pull on the end of my cigarette. She doesn't realize the curtains to her little motel room for the night are sheer, and I can see her, even if she can't see me through the tint on my windows.

Nearly every night is the same.

She runs.

I find her.

She runs again when she senses my presence.

I find her again.

This time in Arkansas will be no different. The states are only so big, and she doesn't have a passport to get to either Mexico or Canada, and I'm running out of patience. Soon, there will be no more running.

She will be my greatest revenge.

She pulls the curtain back, peeking out into the night, and pauses, her gaze lingering on my car as if she can sense me.

Unbeknownst to her, we stare at each other for a long moment.

She's scared.

Finally, she lets the curtain fall back closed and slips back on the shitty motel bed.

Cutting off the lamp, she turns away from the window as if she can hide. Softly, I let out a dark chuckle when a shiver rolls through her.

Silly fucking girl.

I'll always find her.

The devil doesn't just give up what belongs to him.

And I don't plan on starting now.

CHAPTER *Two*

MILA
ARIZONA, MAY

Fuck off, asshole.

The man watching me from the other side of the platform hasn't looked away since I sat down, and I can feel his gaze roaming across my skin like a thousand little cockroaches.

I glance at him.

—Still watching.

I glance at the clock hanging on the wall.

—Three minutes until my bus is set to arrive.

The back of my neck feels sweaty, but it has nothing to do with the sweltering dry heat of the Arizona weather.

I tug the brim of my hat lower to cover my eyes. Slipping from my seat, I hoist my bag over my shoulder and walk in the other direction.

Careful. No need to draw attention.

Slipping through the crowd as casually as I can, I make my way down the platform, passing through families and people speaking on their phones.

I feel eyes on me everywhere I go, but I force a shallow breath through my lips and keep walking at the same leisurely pace when all I really want to do is run as fast as I fucking can.

I'll leave and come back later. I'll call an Uber and get to the station a few towns over.

I knew I was overstaying my welcome in this town. I should have left two nights ago when I was sure I felt someone watching me.

Heat trickles up the back of my spine, and I know, without turning around, that the mystery man is following me.

They're all the same. Every man they send is just as dangerous as the last. Men twice my size, trained to deal with nasty little problems like me.

With my stomach in my throat, I approach the bathroom, slipping inside. The moment I'm out of sight, I let out a deep breath.

Great, now I'm trapped.

I scan the room, looking for anything I could use to protect myself. I can't alert the security at the station. They'll call the police, and then I'll be a sitting duck in a jail cell, waiting for one of their big, bad Mila-killing machines to find me and put me out of my lonely misery.

Fuck that. I'd rather die in a dust bowl bathroom in southern Arizona than in a jail cell surrounded by shitty, corrupt cops.

Think, Mila.

While scanning the bathroom, I spot an air vent in the back of the large stall.

Guess it's better than being dead.

Internally gagging at the crusty toilet paper beside my left shoe, I sink down and pull out the small screwdriver I keep in my backpack.

"Are you fucking kidding me?"

There aren't even any screws. It's just painted shut with years of cheap five-gallon bucket paint from the hardware store clearance section.

I try again, a desperate attempt to pry it off, but it just scratches off the top few layers of paint.

"*Fuck.*"

A pounding at the door causes my heart to lurch in my chest, and I fall back into the wall, toilet paper-covered floor be damned.

"Just a minute," I call out, my voice shaking as I scramble to my feet.

I only have one option.

It's not one I like.

When the door opens, I move further back in the stall, pressing my back against the wall. The sound of heavy boots on scuffed tiles fills the empty bathroom. At three o'clock in the morning, there aren't many of us in the station, and those of us who are here are almost always running from something.

I'm no exception.

Climbing on top of the toilet seat, I lift my legs and clap a hand over my mouth to silence myself from breathing too heavily and pray to God someone else will come in the bathroom.

"Here kitty, kitty . . ." a man sings, voice low and menacing. And *I know* it's the man that was watching me. "Come out, come out wherever you are."

He pauses in front of my stall, his boots coming to a halt, sending ringing vibrations through my chest.

Okay, scratch that. Maybe I don't want to die in a dirty bus station bathroom.

"Aww . . . Come on, sweetheart. Don't be scared. I won't bite."

Fear seizes my chest, and silent tears slip down my cheeks to my fingertips, covering my mouth.

There's no way out of this.

I let out a squeak when he pounds at the door, clenching the screwdriver tighter in my palm and scampering back on the toilet.

Fuck, fuck, fuck . . .

"You find her?" another voice asks when the bathroom door

opens.

The man outside my stall turns away, facing whoever else has just walked in.

"She's hiding out in there."

You fucking bet I am, asshole.

"Boss told you not to scare her."

"I'm not going to scare her. I'm just playing with her a little bit."

"Well, stop," the other man says. I watch his boots come across the floor, a slight drag to his step.

"Come on, Mila." *Tap, tap, tap.* "I'm sorry if ol' Jerry scared you. He ain't a bad guy."

Jerry can go suck a dick for all I care.

"Let's stop playing these games now."

The soft lilt of his slight southern accent would be comforting—if there wasn't already dried blood on the toe of his boot.

And, you know, if he wasn't here to kidnap me.

"Come on out, now," he says gently like I'm a scared dog hiding under a bed.

Right now, I feel like it.

Fuck.

"Ain't no one going to hurt you."

Double fuck.

I have to get away.

Slipping from the toilet, I stand on shaky legs and face the door. When I open it, I keep my gaze trained on my toes.

"There she is," the one with the gentle voice purrs.

Never mind that he already has rope in his hand.

So, I stab him with my screwdriver.

"Fucking bitch!" he roars. Even if the screwdriver didn't fully penetrate his skin, it still sliced him open, and that's enough for me.

I dart for the door, swing it open, and get out before either can grab me as they clamber around each other in the tiny bathroom.

"Fucking bitch, stabbed me—"

Not so pleasant, now, are we?

I throw my full weight in the door, jamming the screwdriver through the handle in a brief moment of pure genius that surprises even me.

They crash against the door, the thud of their heavy bodies sending a shot of panic through me.

Hoisting my backpack up higher, I dart for my bus.

Pennsylvania, here I come.

The doors are just starting to close when I push through them, earning me a dirty look from the driver. I'm sweaty, and my legs are shaking as I make my way through the bus to a spot in the back.

I don't let out the breath I'm holding until we pull away. And when I look back, the door to the bathrooms finally burst open with the men **sent to kill me.**

CHAPTER
Three

MILA
KANSAS, JULY

I'm pretty sure someone's died on the very bed I'm sitting on. Or, at the very least, a dozen children have been created on it.

There's not much to Kansas. At least not in this area of Wichita. From New Mexico to Arizona. From Arizona to Pennsylvania. Then, a brief stop in Ohio—hated it. Another in Illinois—nothing but corn and beans as far as the eye could see. Then down to Arkansas—bizarre street names.

Now, I've made it to Kansas in *Mila's Fantastic Fifty State Journey.*

At least . . . that's what I'm calling it. It sounds a lot more glamorous than saying I'm on the run from a bunch of men who want to kill me.

My stomach growls uncomfortably, and I glance at the clock. It's still early. The sun hasn't even set yet. Way too early to go to bed, but way too late to try and skip out on dinner for the second night in a row.

Damn.

Tossing the pamphlet left in my room about STDs to the dusty motel comforter beneath me, I slip off the bed and cross to my bag, sitting on the small table near the door.

Someone's definitely snorted a line or four off this table.

"Well, shit," I grumble under my breath. I'm out of granola bars. I'm out of canned ravioli.

Out of freaking patience . . .

Moving to my wallet, I check through the cash stashed there. If I don't find a job soon, I'm going to be fucked. Life on the run is expensive, and I think it's an epidemic in America that we don't talk about enough. You should be able to disappear without a trace, without starving yourself to death.

I count through the few twenties I've and the three one-dollar bills. Sixty-three dollars and a *Chuck E. Cheese* token from a little place out in New Mexico. That's one more night at my motel before I'm totally fucked.

I chuck the wallet back in my bag and start pacing. It helps me think, even if it's a pointless waste of precious calories. I'm afraid to weigh myself. I know I've lost weight while on the road, but I don't know how much. Living off motel room ramen and dollar store granola bars will do that to you.

I push the noise of my growling stomach to the back of my mind and focus on the plan, which is . . . I don't know. I never thought I'd make it this far.

It's been a month since I've seen any sign of them. A month since I've had any contact. Six months on the run and a whole lot of sleazy motel rooms. I'm surprised I haven't picked up any extra *friends* since I've been away.

The scent of something fried and delicious wafts through the vents from the restaurant next door, and my mouth waters involuntarily.

Fuck. I'm starving.

I look back at my bag on the table.

I continue pacing.

The scent grows stronger, and I contemplate jobs that I could possibly find in Wichita, Kansas, that will pay me under the table so I can afford to eat.

I could always dance. I had a friend who put herself through college that way.

Callie *also didn't have scars covering most of her torso.*

My stomach grumbles again, and my wallet beckons me like a bad friend.

I'm going to regret this.

"Fine."

I'll eat tonight and skip eating tomorrow. I'll ask if there are any positions open for the back of the house, next door, and that will at least be a start to the job search.

I've done it. I've made a plan.

—Even if it's only for the next twenty-four hours.

Grabbing my wallet, I peek out the curtain to my rented room. Nothing. No new cars. No men lurking in the shadows waiting to sell me off to the sleazy psychopath that wants to hurt me.

Slipping out into the evening air, I pull my denim jacket tight around myself and lock the door. Wichita is about what you would expect from a Midwest city. It's calm. Less crowded than LA, and everyone's been overly friendly. Where people would walk by you if you were on fire in the streets of LA, here, they would use their last bits of water to put out the flames.

I could stay in a place like this. Somewhere . . . different. Before I ran, I'd never been to half the places I've stayed, and if nothing else good came from my time on the run, then at least I got to see a different side of the world than the party dresses and wealthy socialites I'd grown up with under my stepfather's reign of terror.

I peer through the windows of the diner attached to the motel before I step inside. It's empty, save for a few older men sitting at the counter, a family down the way, and a dark-haired man sitting near the back, reading the paper.

"Hi, I'm June. What can I get for you?" An older woman, around my mother's age, with brown hair and bright purple eye shadow, slides up to my booth when I take a seat. I jump when she speaks because I hadn't seen her approach, but her gentle smile never moves.

"Sorry," I murmur, my cheeks flaming as I stare down at the menu. Everything's cheap, but I am still Broke, with a capital B. "Can I just get some toast, please? And a water."

She eyes me like she wants to say something, but I'm thankful when it's just to ask me white or wheat.

"Wheat, please."

"Wheat toast, coming right up," she smiles and takes my menu.

In probably one of the most embarrassing moments of my life, my stomach growls as loud as possible, like a hostage trying to alert the police that I'm starving it.

Asshole.

"Sorry," I chuckle, brushing my hair over my face to hide the scar at my hairline. It's not that noticeable, but I know it's there. Unfortunately, her eyes catch on the mark, and now she knows it's there too.

"Sure you don't want something more than toast?" she grins, flashing a knowing smile at me while my cheeks feel like they're going to melt at any moment.

"Nope," I lie. Someone has bacon, and I'm *this* close to selling a kidney for a bite. "Toast is great."

I hate toast unless I have strawberry jam.

"Alright, that'll be out in a jiffy."

She heads back to the kitchen, and I twist my fingers around in front of me. I don't have a phone—it's too easy to track. I left the only book I have back in the room, and besides, I've read it probably six times in the last six months.

So . . . with nothing to do, I look around. The diner is old and rundown, but like most places like this, it seems to be a favorite among the local elderly population. That means they have good coffee, something I haven't had in months because I'm too afraid to use the motel coffee makers. I've heard the horror stories about urine.

"Here we are," June returns, but instead of the toast I had ordered, she sits two plates of scrambled eggs, hashbrowns, and bacon on the table with two glasses of soda.

I just stare at her when she slips into the booth opposite me.

"Well, aren't you going to eat?" she asks, reaching for a fork.

God, it smells amazing.

"I ordered toast," I whisper as if she hasn't realized what she placed in front of me.

"I know," she nods. "And I brought it." She points to the piece of wheat toast on the edge of the plate. "Don't make me eat alone. I'll feel like a pig."

"June, I can't pay for this."

She fixes me with a bored stare.

"Robby cooked up scrambled eggs instead of sunny side up," she rolls her eyes as if Robby fucks up eggs all the time. "That means it's free. More for us, I guess," she shrugs and dives into her matching plate.

I really, *really* shouldn't.

My stomach grumbles again, and June looks at me, clearly judging me.

"Fine," I grumble, grabbing my fork.

"What's your name?"

"Casey," I lie. I've used a different name for every city I've gone through. My last name was Matilda.

When no one knows who you are, who's to argue if your name is believable or not?

"No one's going to take it from you," she admonishes when I shovel the eggs in my mouth.

God, I could die; they're so good.

"How long's it been since you've eaten?"

"Oh, I had a granola bar yesterday," I say, not even realizing what I've just told her about myself in a single sentence.

I pause, fork halfway to my mouth.

Fuck.

"Girl's got to eat," she chastises. "Otherwise, you may as well have just stayed with whoever gave you that scar." She points to the scar on my forehead, and instantly, I move to cover it with the brim of my hat. She reaches out, pulls my hat back, and inspects the mark. "Fucker got you good, didn't he?"

I don't bother to tell her it wasn't a lover like she's probably thinking. Just a psychopath who caught me when I was in the wrong place at the wrong time.

"Did it hurt?"

"Well, it didn't feel good."

She points her fork at me, and for once, it's nice to have someone to talk to. Someone who doesn't know who I am or what I'm running from. Like having brunch with an old friend.

If I had any of those.

"You know, my first husband, Francis, was an alcoholic. Used to beat me black and blue."

"I'm sorry to hear that," I grimace, biting into the toast.

Everything here must be laced with cocaine because it's fucking delicious.

I guess it could also be the fact that I haven't had a real meal in weeks.

"No use being sorry," she shrugs. "I shot the bastard. Didn't kill him, of course." She rolls her eyes, stabbing at a potato. "Did divorce him, though. Then, I met a real nice man named Steve and had my two kids with him."

"I'm glad it all worked out in the end."

"It didn't. Steve up and died. Asshole was a gambler. Got in with some bad people," she grumbles. "Died when my kids were only

17

ten and twelve."

"God, I'm sorry."

"Nope, then I was stupid enough to get back with Francis," she waves. "That's the first husband. Then *he* died, and I started to think I had a voodoo cooch."

"Voodoo cooch?" I pause, and she nods.

"It's where all your sexual partners start dropping like flies," she explains. "*But* then I met Robby—the one who can't cook eggs—and I realized I just needed a strong man." She waves, and I follow her gaze to where a tall man is watching us out the kitchen window. He grins when she smiles and waves back at her. "He's dumber than a box of rocks, but he's sweet. And the kids love him. And he'd probably survive a nuclear blast with all the grease he's been around his whole life."

"You've lived quite the life, June."

"I'm telling you all this because I want you to understand life doesn't have to be over just because a man hit you. I know shit probably seems bleak right now, but sooner or later, everything's got to work out." She pushes her empty plate away from her. "It's the law of physics or some shit. I don't know. I didn't pay attention in school."

"I don't know," I breathe, finishing the last of my food. I look out the window beside us to see the sun slipping behind the trees north of us. It'll be dark soon. "Sometimes, I wonder if it would be better to just stop running."

"Give yourself up, you mean?"

I nod because I can't say the words out loud.

I've been running for six. Fucking. Months. I'm no further away now than I was three months ago or even the month before that.

She shakes her head. "Nope. Fuck that. A man who hits you isn't a man," she waves her hand. "I've been trying to teach my daughter the same thing. She's your age and well . . ." she shrugs. "No, that ain't a man. A man is willing to die for you. Willing to break his back to keep his family safe. But . . . you've got to be willing to do the same for him. It's how it works."

"What about Robby?" I can't help but smile when she does, looking back to see him whistling away at the kitchen stove, completely oblivious.

"Robby's a good boy. He'd do whatever he had to do to protect our little slice of Wichita heaven."

The door opens behind us, and the bell above chimes. For once, the sudden noise doesn't cause me to nearly jump out of my skin.

"Thank you . . . for this," I gesture to the table in front of us. "Can I at least leave you a tip?"

"No," she rolls her eyes, but I don't miss the hint of a smile on her lips. "I'm just happy I didn't have to throw it away. You know, Robby's fuck-up, and all."

"Right," I chuckle, sliding from the booth. June moves to grab our plates, but something in me tells me I need to show her how much she saved me. Even if not for the food, but for the normal human conversation. It's been a long freaking time.

Against everything in my head, screaming at the thought, I pull her into a hug.

"Thank you," I whisper, and she tenses for a second before she finally concedes and hugs me back.

"Sweetheart," she whispers in my ear, patting my back. "I hope whatever you're running from, you kick it in the balls and get your life back." She pulls back to look at me, and for a moment, something else flickers in her eyes. Something that has my heart beating a little faster and my skin growing clammy. "Trust your gut."

Awareness trickles down my spine, and the distinct awareness of being watched slides over me. I look around the small diner, but there's no one else here besides the people that were here when I arrived. Whoever came in a moment ago is nowhere to be found.

Something's not right . . .

Slipping from the diner, I scurry back to my room, locking

myself inside and pressing myself flat against the door behind me.

My heartbeat thuds painfully against the inside of my chest, sweat beading on the back of my neck.

They're here. I don't know how I know; I can just feel it.

"Fuck," I grit, jumping towards my bag to start throwing my stuff in.

Only, I pause to check out the window and look around.

Nothing.

Am I being paranoid?

"Probably," I answer the question out loud.

I'm exhausted. It's been a week since I've had more than a couple hours of sleep wherever I can get it. I can't keep doing this. This running. It's been a month since the incident in Illinois and three since they almost caught me in Arizona. For all I know, he could have given up by now.

In the darkness of my bedroom, I can't help but laugh.

Who am I kidding?

I've been running on borrowed time for almost a year.

I spend the entire next day looking for under-the-table job opportunities in my tiny little corner of Kansas. Short of blow jobs for truckers or selling coke for my neighbor three doors down, I'm well and truly fucked. Every place I visited wanted my social security number and real name.

How's a fugitive supposed to feed herself in this country?

Now, I'm walking through the dark and desolate streets of Wichita at night to make my way back to my motel room on the outskirts of town. I've been walking all day, and I'm exhausted and hungry. Luckily, June stopped by my room this morning with a bagel and told me to come see her before I went to bed. I genuinely don't know what I'd do without her. It feels like it's been forever since I've spoken to someone who doesn't want to kill me, and I'm eternally grateful for her feeding me. I can't help but wonder what her life would have turned out had she had someone like herself as a young woman.

Everyone thinks innocence is lost when you become a woman. They're wrong.

It's lost the first time you catch a glimpse of how the world really works. The first moment, you no longer feel like the center of your mother's world. The moment the veil starts to lift and that crushing disappointment starts to wash in, replacing the whimsical wonder you'd once viewed in the world around you.

Like the little girl in front of me. Old enough to run and play on her own. Too young to do so without her mother. They just visited an old ice cream parlor for some late-night ice cream, and she runs to catch back up to her mother from petting a stray cat. Her mother is on her phone, not paying an ounce of attention in a world that would love to rip her daughter from her in the blink of an eye.

It happens to the best of us. We get comfortable in the mundane and forget that somewhere, someone is always watching, ready to take until there's nothing left to give.

When she finally catches up, she grasps her mother's hand tightly, and the mother jumps, surprised that her daughter wasn't with her this whole time.

I can't help but wonder if that's what got me into the situation I'm in.

Comfort.

"Mommy!" the little girl squeals, laughing when the cat runs to catch up with them. I smile softly to myself, taking the next street and finally separating from them.

Unfortunately, I'm not paying attention until I'm alone on the street with a group of men on the sidewalk across from me.

Instantly, a chill slips down my spine when they stop talking, their eyes following me as I hug my jacket tighter around myself.

It's wrong to assume. Maybe they're nice men. Not all men are rapists, but . . . not all men *aren't*, either.

—A fact that's solidified for me as soon as one of them wolf-whistles.

The rest of the men snicker and a sinister silence sweeps through the air, the only sound my accelerating pulse in my ears.

"Hey, beautiful . . ." one calls, but I keep my head down and my gaze pinned on the sidewalk beneath me, hoping they think I can't hear them and leave me be.

But who am I kidding? I'm never that lucky.

"Come on," the man says, whistling again under his breath as his footsteps sound on the pavement behind me.

He's crossing the road.

My heartbeat hammers in my chest, my throat running dry as the burn under my skin starts.

The hands. Him. The knife . . .

"Please leave me alone," I manage to croak, but the man just laughs, joined in a chorus by the other men across the street.

"Oh, don't be like that, darlin'. I just want to talk. You're so pretty."

I know that voice.

The man I didn't *stab in Arizona.*

Fuck.

More snickers. More panicking as my mouth fills with saliva and my entire body feels like it's been dipped in acid. My chest aches, my lungs seizing up as I hear him getting closer.

I start walking faster and he jogs to the sidewalk as a car comes down the road from the opposite direction. Part of me wants to lunge into the street and beg them for help. The other half is worried they're just as bad as he is.

"Here . . .kitty, kitty, kitty . . ." He sniffs loudly and chuckles.

"Mmm . . . you smell like the prettiest flowers."

One . . . two . . . three . . .

Just as I'm about to run, I turn back to look over my shoulder and find him closer than I thought, and the panic that was inside me turns to full-blown terror.

"Just let me talk—" he's cut off by the loud screech of tires on the pavement. Both of us pause just as the man's hand lands on my shoulder, and I look back, wide-eyed and frozen in fear, as the car barrels directly toward us.

And . . . doesn't stop.

I have only a second to react, falling to my ass on the sidewalk when the car plows right into the man, sending him flying.

Or I guess . . . *through* him, is more like it.

My assailant flies into the air, his body crumpling on the street a few feet away as the elegant black sports car comes to a stop right in front of me.

The door opens, and death stares back at me in the face of the most handsome man I've ever met.

Broad shoulders, sharp jawline, deep blue eyes.

It's him.

"Get in."

Then

CHAPTER
Four

MILA
LA, JUNE, 5 YEARS AGO

My stepfather is fucking my older sister.

I can see it in the ways his eyes follow her. The sneer underneath the perfectly poised smirk on his face. How she throws back another glass of champagne as if she can chase away the feeling of his hands on her.

My stomach is sick, knowing there's nothing I can do. There's no handbook for how to navigate life. How do you save your sister when you know she's being abused? She doesn't talk about it, but I see the bruises on her when she comes home sometimes. How I'll catch them in a quiet, heated discussion. How she seems like just an empty shell now, covered in ice and thorns, compared to who she used to be.

I feel guilty. I'm disgusted that he could do that to her. Do that to our mother, who's never done anything but stand by his side. I know that's part of why Savannah keeps it quiet.

Telling someone would do nothing but piss Marcus Parker off. Our stepfather has more money than God and a history of violence. All the cops in LA are in his pocket, and all the guards work for him.

Telling someone is pointless.

because that's the only choice women in our world have.

Whether you're thirteen or nighty-two, the men in our society control everything, right down to the fake smiles we plaster on our faces.

"Mila? What are you doing?"

My spine stiffens from my spot on the ground, and I tear my eyes away from Savannah.

God, smite me dead right here.

Drew Marshall, my oldest sister Bailey's boyfriend and soon to be fiancé—unfortunately . . .

"Misplace your personality?" I ask, and he snickers, his posse of limp dicks that follow him around like lost puppies smirking from behind him.

"You're missing the party."

I look around us. I wouldn't call it a party. It's Bailey's graduation party, but Mom heard word the party and jumped at the chance to show off Marcus's money. Every celebrity, wealthy socialite, or influencer in the vast LA area is here.

Boring.

"Bummer."

"You know, Corbin was going to ask if you wanted to dance." He nods to the guy beside him. I look him over. Lush hair. Blue eyes. Louis Vuitton shoes.

No, thank you.

I turn back to the Gameboy in my hand. Bailey gave it to me earlier today, and forgive me, but Mario is far more fascinating than any of Drew's "friends".

"I don't dance."

Drew has always gotten on my nerves, and I do everything I can to get on his. He's condescending, using his father's money to get whatever he wants. He treats Bailey like shit, though she refuses to see it. He cheats, he does drugs. He works for Marcus.

If you ask me, a squirrel would be a better boyfriend than Drew fucking Marshall.

"Come on, sweetheart. Put the game down and be a big girl."

I grit my teeth. I'm not a fucking child who needs coaching. I'm twenty, for God's sake.

"Hey, Drew?" I ask, my voice as sweet as arsenic.

"What?"

"Is it true that you're struggling with erectile dysfunction? I overheard you and Bailey arguing the other night, and I was concerned." I wasn't concerned. I actually think it's hilarious.

"You're a mouthy little brat, you know that?" His friends are still chortling over my little E.D. comment. No shame to anyone who actually suffers from E.D. I just hate Drew, and I hope his dick falls off from gangrene sometime in the next five minutes.

I shrug at his comment. I have no desire to impress Drew Marshall. In fact, I would go as far as to say it's the exact opposite.

Letting out a sigh, I slip to my bare feet. The cobblestone terrace is cool on my toes, and my lavender heels lay abandoned at the foot of the statue. I hate shoes, especially ones with heels.

"This has been a lot of fun, but I think I've had my fill of frat tonight."

If Mason, can skip out on this party, then so can I.

I'm turning to walk away when a hand darts out and grabs my wrist, dragging me to a stop. I jerk back from Drew, but his fingers remain steadfast, a sinister smile tugging at the corner of his lips.

"Did you forget who I am, little sister?" Drew steps closer, pushing the hair off my face. I wince when I pull in his grasp, and his fingers tighten, cutting off my circulation. "Like it or not, I'm going to be your brother-in-law," he murmurs darkly. "Imagine what Bailey will say when she finds out her little sister sucked her husband's cock."

"Nothing, because the only way your cock would come anywhere near my mouth is if I were slicing it off to feed it to you for cheating on my sister."

His eyes flash wickedly, his fingers digging into my skin harder. I bite back a wince because I refuse to show him that he's hurting me.

"Make no mistake, when I marry your sister, you and Savannah will be at my mercy. Whether it's on your knees or your back, I'll find a use for you."

"I'd advise you to drop your hand," a cool voice says behind me.

Drew pauses, eyes narrowing before he looks over my shoulder.

He must not like whatever he sees there because he drops my wrist like I'd shot flames from my nipples.

I turn, my heart pausing unsteadily in my chest, when I meet the dark blue gaze of the man standing beside the statue.

He, on the other hand, looks as calm and collected as he would be walking down the street. His gaze sweeps over me, a quick assessment to verify I'm not hurt, and my skin heats under his stare.

He's . . . otherworldly. Dangerous.

Dark hair. Dark blue eyes the color of the Mariana Trench. His suit stretches over muscles so thick, I'm sure he could crush a watermelon—or my head—in his giant hands. Broad shoulders. Slacks stretched over strong, impossibly long legs.

This isn't a man at all . . .

—It's the devil in an Armani suit.

I fall back a step, and finally, his gaze leaves mine. He turns to Drew.

"I'm just having a little conversation with my favorite sister-in-law, right, Mila?"

I glower back at him, but before I can respond, the mystery man speaks up.

"And now, you're not."

"Who the fuck are you?" Drew asks, cocking his chin back like he's prepared for a fight. I don't know why. He couldn't even fight a wet paper bag, much less the man standing before us who's at least a foot taller than he or I and a whole lot bigger.

"The man telling you to get out."

The silence in the air is so thick, it steals my breath away. All of Drew's friends are still, no longer snickering now that the mystery man has arrived. A shiver rolls through me, and I wrap my arms around myself as a chill settles in my veins at the look he gives Drew.

It's as if he's death himself, come to collect the soul of an innocent and just stopped off for a quick appearance at this party.

"I'm not leaving," Drew argues, and I don't miss the little flash of fear in his gaze hidden beneath that cocky exterior.

Under different circumstances, I would laugh.

Mystery man steps closer, between me and Drew, and I fall back until my shoulders are pressed into the statue behind me. He peels his suit jacket open, and Drew's eyes widen at whatever he sees. I can't see what it is from where I stand, but I can guess.

"I've been authorized to remove anyone I see fit, and . . . as it stands, I see fit to remove you."

"Under who's order?"

Mystery man cocks his head. "Mr. Parker."

"I'm Parker's assistant."

"Not for much longer."

When Drew doesn't move, he cocks one dangerous brow at him as if daring him to refuse, and finally, one of his friends speaks up.

"Come on, Drew. This shit's boring, anyway," one of the guys says, his gaze refusing to meet the man. "Let's go."

Drew glares at me over tall, dark, and devastating's shoulder but falls back into his posse. With a dark look, he slips around the mystery man, albeit awkwardly, because the man doesn't move to let him by. Drew's friends scramble, and Drew shoulder-checks him on his way. I watch them go through the party on the terrace until they disappear up the sidewalk.

"Are you hurt?" the man asks as soon as they're gone, voice

gruff, as if he swallowed sandpaper.

I force a breath past the growing lump in my throat, shaking my head.

"No . . . thank you. He's just a dick," I grumble, rubbing the sore spot on my wrist. I fucking hate Drew, and I'll celebrate the day he takes his last breath. "I don't know what my sister sees in him."

"Everything happens for a reason. You can't control the evil in the world. You can only remove it."

"Maybe so, but then someone will just step in to take its place."

"You shouldn't allow people to treat you that way," he murmurs, straightening the cuffs of his shirt without looking at me. "You'll never be anything if you continue to let people walk all over you."

"I . . ." Ouch. Talk about tough love. "Who are you?"

He smirks, his gaze filling with dark amusement. When they finally meet mine, it feels like staring down the loaded barrel of a gun. I get the feeling this isn't a man who stumbled upon a college graduation party for fun.

"Your new bodyguard," he smirks devilishly. "And you've got a lot to learn, little devil."

CHAPTER
Five

CHRISTIAN
LA, DECEMBER, 3 YEARS AGO

W here are we going?"

"You are going to bed."

Mila giggles, stumbling along beside me like a baby deer walking for the first time. It's cute, the way she grabs onto my arm to steady herself.

Oddly enough, I've never found anything cute a day in my fucking life.

"I'm fine," she argues, right before she trips in her ridiculous heels and falls to her ass on the marble floor.

She gawks up at me as if I'd pushed her, and a laugh passes my lips.

Luckily, her mother is just as drunk as she is. I can only imagine the hell she'd raise if she knew I'd let her daughter get sloshed at the Christmas gala that we were all forced to attend for Parker's social status.

"Still haven't gotten your sea legs, I see." I reach down and slide my arms under her. I lift her and hold her against my chest, carrying her down the hall towards her bedroom.

Carrying her inside, I kick the door shut behind us and move to the bathroom, sitting her on her feet by the sink and pinning her to it with my body. She sways, her eyes hazy and unfocused, while I slip off her heels.

"I'm surprised you left these on all night," I murmur, tossing them to the floor behind us. In the three years I've been working for Parker, chasing after his three stepdaughters, I've seen Mila barefoot more than I've seen her in shoes. The heels left her feet red in spots, and I massage the skin absentmindedly. She lets out a quiet moan, and I pause, the sound going straight to my cock.

That's new.

Then, she tugs her foot away, snickering because she's ticklish.

"Take these," I place two painkillers in her palm and hand her a bottle of water. "All of it," I tell her when she tries to put the half-full bottle back down.

While she drinks, I grab a washcloth from the cabinet by the sink, wetting it with warm water before I start to work on the makeup on her skin. Her mascara and eyeliner have melted under her eyes, and her lipstick is long gone, save for the slight pink hue on her lips. Her hair, once straight, is starting to curl around her face, and I'm glad. I don't know why, but I've always liked the wild, unruly blonde curls.

"How the fuck do you get this shit off?" I grumble, and she laughs when the makeup just smears like fucking molasses. Why do women bother with this shit? "Industrial cleaner?"

I laugh with her because I can't help myself and know she won't remember this in the morning. I've never done this shit before, but I know enough that sending her to bed with a face full of makeup is a woman's nightmare. I've also never put Mila to bed before, but there's a first time for every obsession.

"Makeup remover," she slurs, her heavy gray eyes opening to meet mine.

Fuck, those eyes . . .

All the while I'm cleaning her up, her hands are sliding up my button-up, over the ridges of my abs, before slipping higher. My cock protests when I continue to ignore it and gently pull her hand away.

"Mila," I warn, and she lets out a breathy sound close to a hum. That's also new.

"Christian," she breathes, blinking up at me, and the air between us hums. She tugs at my hand, but I hold her wrist in mine, refusing to let her go.

She's just drunk and horny. She doesn't know what the fuck she's doing. I mean, this is Mila. Young and innocent. Sweet with her soft heart and even softer soul.

In an act of defiance, she stands up on her tiptoes, pressing her lips to mine, and a deep groan rumbles up my chest.

Fucking hell.

Why the fuck did I decide I needed to take care of her tonight?

"Why won't you kiss me?" she asks, falling back with a frown. My cock is so fucking hard it hurts, pressing against the zipper of my slacks.

The asshole in me says to do it. Kiss her back and let her have what she wants. The idiotic gentleman in my head tells me to do what I came here to do. Stick to the plan.

Unfortunately, the plan doesn't involve little twenty-one-year-old Mila Carpenter.

"Because you are way too drunk, and I am way too old for you."

"I'm twenty-one," she argues, her tongue darting out to lick her lips. Despite everything in my head telling me to get the fuck out, my hand has other ideas, lifting to tug her bottom lip from between her teeth.

So fucking soft.

"I'm twenty-eight."

She rolls her eyes, tugging from my grasp.

Roll your eyes again, sweetheart. I'll make sure you don't stop.

"You know what I think?" she asks when I reach for her hairbrush.

"I'd love to hear it," I murmur sarcastically.

Really, the only thing on my mind right now is the thought of burying my face between her thighs until they tighten around my head, and she's screaming my name, but I ignore it.

"I think you're afraid to care about people," she mumbles, her eyes holding a challenge.

I know what she's doing. Egging me on. It's working, but I won't act on it. Not with her. I mean, this is Mila, for Christ's sake. She's too sweet. Too innocent for a man like me. She hasn't experienced the world and all it has to offer yet.

But fuck if the idea isn't there, taking hold like poison ivy on a fallen log.

"You care more than you like to let on. I think you're just afraid to get too close to me," she continues, and the little thread holding my patience snaps.

Sinking forward, I press the front of my body against hers, my hands on the counter on either side of her, my cock digging into her stomach. I lean into her, my lips hovering over hers, but I don't kiss her. When she leans up, attempting to close the distance between us, I back up, just out of her reach.

"Is this close enough for you, little devil?"

Her cheeks flame, and her tongue darts out to lick her lips. All the while, I can't help but wonder what she tastes like. Will she taste just as sweet as she smells? Like vanilla and honey and everything that makes me want to ruin her?

And then she shocks the hell out of me.

"No," she breathes, her back arching against the counter behind her.

I search her gaze, giving myself an out before I allow the thoughts swarming in my head to go too far. She's always been the unobtainable. Perfect for me in every way.

And that's precisely why I can't fucking have her.

I'll ruin her. Steal the light from her eyes and replace it with my darkness. Until all she can feel is me. Until she's as deep in this obsession as I am.

"Time for bed."

I stoop down, lifting her back into my arms. I need her in bed where the scent of her perfume and those pretty gray eyes aren't fucking with my head.

She huffs, her eyes fluttering closed and her head leaning against my chest. I place her on her bed, reaching behind her for the zipper of her dress. I unzip it, pull it up to her waist, and slip it over her head, ignoring the fact that she's got nothing on but a black lacy thong and bra underneath.

This is about taking care of her. Something I've done half a dozen times in the last three years. Nothing else.

I lift her, placing her under the covers while she clenches her eyes shut at the head rush. I pull the covers up over her, and I'm about to walk away when her hand reaches out to catch mine. I turn around, finding her smokey eyes running over the bruises still healing on my knuckles.

She doesn't know what they're from, and she probably never will. Not if I have a say in it.

She'll never be a part of that life. Never.

"Thank you for taking care of me," she whispers.

Her words catch me off guard, and I freeze. She blinks like she can see multiple of me when I lean down, pressing my lips to her forehead.

Vanilla and honey.

Fuck me.

She won't remember this in the morning. Unfortunately, I will, and now that the thought's there, I have a feeling it'll never leave.

Looking back, I don't think I understood, even at the time, the impact that moment would have on the rest of my fucking life.

Standing from the bed, I cross to the bedroom door before turning back to find her eyes shut and breathing soft.

"Sweet dreams, little devil."

CHAPTER
Six

CHRISTIAN
LA, MAY, 2 YEARS AGO

There are two things I know for sure in life.

One: I'm not a good man. I'm crude. Chaotic. I've killed more men than I can count, and the list of unfortunate souls will probably get longer.

Two: Mila fucking Carpenter is going to be the death of me.

Fucking Carpenter women. I've gone toe to toe with some of the most sadistic motherfuckers in this country. Ruthless murderers, Bratva mob bosses, secret CIA "special" agents.

None of them measure up to the three LA princesses I've been charged with protecting.

Like wild rabbits, once you get one in the cage, another slips out behind you. In this case, I'm the idiot trying to wrangle them in, and Mila Carpenter is the fucking Houdini bunny rabbit that keeps escaping.

"I need a break, Mom," Savannah snaps. "Mile gets to go to college. Why can't I?"

This is the fourth time Savannah has had this same conversation with her mother this month.

The unfortunate part?

Monica doesn't even remember. She's usually halfway through a bottle of wine by this time of the night. Tonight is no exception.

"Because you chose to dance," Monica says, her words slurring as she takes another sip of the dark berry wine in her glass. "So, now, you'll be a dancer."

I'm supposed to be dropping Savannah off at the dance studio in half an hour, but judging by the current conversation, I'm guessing she'll ask me to cover for her again while she sees that little shit, Spike.

Spike is everything you don't want your daughter dating, complete with a spiked collar—the irony is fucking stupid. I don't believe Savannah's actually interested in him, though. If anything, she found the shittiest man she could, just to piss Monica off.

It definitely worked.

"So I'm stuck with it for the rest of my life?" Savannah grits, cheeks burning brightly. "It's exhausting."

"Hard work never hurt anyone."

"Then you do it," Savannah challenges, and Monica just fixes her with a bored scowl.

"The answer is final, Savannah."

"What about the apartment you said I could get?"

"When you're ready," Monica waves a hand, dismissing her.

"I'm ready now."

"Are you still sneaking off to see that little trollop? Spam, or whatever his name is?"

"His name is Spike."

His name is stupid.'

My phone buzzes in my pocket when they launch into the top five reasons why Spike is the biggest dumbass I've ever met. I pull it out, gaze narrowing at the name on the screen.

Stepping out of the kitchen, I lift it to my ear.

"Mila."

It's been three months since I brought her home and three months of pure fucking torture. She's fucking everywhere, and I can't get her out of my head.

What makes it worse is Monica has convinced her to see that little prick friend of Drew's, Corbin. The kid pisses me off. From the way he touches her to the way he looks at her. Honestly, his being in her presence is bad enough.

A spoiled rich kid—Daddy's money—who's never been told no a day in his life. What she fucking sees in him, I'll never know.

Not that I'm fucking bitter or anything.

He can have her. I can't. Ironic, isn't it?

My gaze goes to the family photo painted above the mantel. Mila's light gray gaze stares back at me, a smile on her face. There's a sniffle on the other end of the line, and I pause.

She's crying.

"Where are you?"

"Umm . . ." she breathes, her voice shaky. I step outside into the night and go straight to the Bentley, idling in the drive, waiting for Savannah.

Looks like she'll be getting her wish, after all.

"I don't know, but . . . I want to go home."

I swear, every time I see him, it gets a little harder not to put a bullet in his head.

I pull up my phone, opening the app that tracks her and her sister's phones. Don't hate me. Hate Monica. It was her idea to put trackers in them. Not that I'm arguing.

Like I said—Houdini bunny rabbit.

"I'll find you."

Mila's in a house down in Oakwood, and when I pull up, a house party is in full swing. She's home from college right now for Spring break, and I can't help but wonder why the fuck she would end up in a place like this.

Mila fucking hates parties.

I don't believe for a second she cares for the little shit. Like everything, It's just another way to please her mother.

I park at the curb, and before I can even text her to tell her I'm outside, she rushes out the door. Climbing in the back seat of the car, she wraps her arms around herself, refusing to look at me.

She never sits in the back seat.

"Mila."

Over the years, I've learned how to read other people's body language. It's good to know what someone's true intentions are, even if they're not willing to share them with you.

She doesn't look up at my voice, and irritation climbs up my spine. My palm itches on the steering wheel. My chest burns.

Stepping out of the car, I open the back door, gripping her chin and forcing her eyes to mine. Soft silver moons stare at me from red, tear-filled eyes.

"Can we just go?"

"We aren't leaving until you tell me why you're upset."

Her teeth graze her bottom lip, and a shiver rolls through her.

"It's nothing." She attempts to pull back out of my grasp, but I hold her there, forcing her to face me. She blinks, a tear slipping down her cheek as those soft gray eyes work their way into my chest.

"Unless you want me to go in there are forcibly remove the dicks from every boy at this party, I suggest you tell the truth."

She huffs, gaze narrowing on mine, but I don't care. She can be mad all she wants. No one touches her.

"It's stupid," she grumbles, averting her gaze. "Corbin is drunk, and he tried to get me to do stuff. I didn't want to . . ."

A deathly stillness falls over me.

"And?"

"And he tried to . . . *feel me up* in the bathroom." She shakes her head, sawing her bottom lip between her teeth. "I'm fine. Just embarrassed."

For a moment, my ears ring in the silence that follows. I swallow the burning rage, a pit forming in the center of my chest that threatens to swallow me whole. Red creeps into my vision, blood drumming in my ears like war drums on a battlefield.

I'll fucking kill him.

"Christian, wait!" Mila yells, scrambling to open the door when I slam it shut and start towards the house.

I don't even look back.

"Get in the car, Mila."

She makes no move to follow me, and I storm inside, ice slipping through my veins as the scent of weed and cheap beer fills my lungs.

I step through the front door of the house party, ignoring the gazes of the people nearby who stop to stare at me.

"Corbin Luck," I tell the kid beside me at the entrance, and he just stares like a fucking idiot, trying to blink his way back to reality from whatever shit he's fucked up on. When I turn to stare at him, he jumps.

"Upstairs. Second door on the left."

I don't stick around to hear what he has to say, making my way towards the stairs and weaving through a sea of bodies. On my way, I grab a beer bong from some kid's hand, beer sloshing all over his face when I do.

"Hey!" he shouts, coughing and sputtering, but one look over my shoulder has him shutting the fuck up.

I take the stairs, ripping the funnel off the top of the hose and tossing it behind me before I stop in front of door number two.

Inside, grunts and moans are muffled by the door, and when I try the handle, it's locked.

"We're busy!" Corbin hollers, followed by the giggles of whatever poor, unsuspecting girl he's got underneath him.

Not for long.

Grabbing the handle, I step back, shoving my shoulder into the door and splintering the wood when it busts open.

Pity.

"What the fuck, man?" Corbin grinds, pulling out of the little brunette underneath him and jumping to his feet. He shoves his dick back in his pants, and I nod at the girl, who takes the hint, wrapping her clothes around herself and running out underneath my arm.

Now it's just him and I.

"Look, man, whatever she told you, I didn't do it. She wanted to come tonight."

I cock my head to the side, a cool, dark clarity slipping through me.

"You put your hands on her," I say, stepping into the room, and Corbin backs up until his ass is pressed against the far wall. Not surprisingly, a roach climbs up by his head.

"She wanted it," he explains, his voice filled with the fear I can feel him trembling with. "She keeps trying to get me to fuck her. I thought tonight would be the night."

I snicker low under my breath.

"Do you have medical insurance, Corbin?"

"Y-yeah."

"Good." I nod, slipping the hose between my hands. "You're going to need it."

The moment he darts for the door, I'm there, grabbing him by the back of the head and shoving him to his knees. He struggles against me, but I've got at least six inches and a hundred pounds on him. Struggling is pointless.

—That's evident when I tug his arm back, breaking it with a sickening crunch of bones.

"I know that has to hurt like a bitch."

He cries out in pain, the despair in his voice music to my ears.

I don't give him time to even register what's happened before I shove him forward onto the dirty vinyl flooring underneath him, wrapping the hose in my hand around his neck and tugging his head back.

Kneeling over him, he chokes from the lack of air, his screams silenced.

Good. Maybe he'll learn to fuck with someone his own size from now on. Not a little five-foot-three blonde with the sweetest fucking smile I've ever seen.

He'll learn not to fuck with what's mine.

"Wrong girl, Corbin."

"Are you okay?" Mila asks when I slide into the driver's seat five minutes later. I'm pleased to see she's made her way to the front.

Again, Mila doesn't ride in the back.

I don't look at her because I know if I do and I see even a hair on her head out of place, I'll go back inside.

"Never better."

"You're bleeding," she gasps, reaching for my hand. Her fingers dance over the blood on my knuckles, and her eyes widen, brimming with tears.

"I'm fine, Mila." I tug my hand back from her. Most of it's not even mine.

"Did you kill him?"

"He'll live," I murmur darkly. "Put your seatbelt on."

She swallows thickly, buckling her seat belt, and we pull away from the curb. The lights of Los Angeles flash around us as we make our way out of the city, down the road that will take us toward Malibu, where Parker Estate is located.

She's quiet, staring straight ahead as we drive, and I can tell something's on her mind. In the years I've been with the Parker family, I can't even count the number of times I wished I could take a peek inside her mind. See what the hell's going on in that pretty little head of hers.

"He doesn't deserve your sympathy, Mila."

"I know," she says quietly, hugging her arms around herself. "I don't feel bad for him."

"Little liar," I chuckle humorlessly, pulling through the front gates of the Parker Estate. The mansion sits back from the road on a cliff overlooking the beach below. It's huge. Way too much for one family. A real California castle where the walls scream with the voices of all the people unfortunate to ever find themselves in the presence of Marcus Paker.

She shakes her head, wrapping her arms tighter around herself. She's got a soft heart. Breakable.

"His breath smelled like bad cream cheese," she says out of the blue, so quiet, I almost don't hear her.

I pause before a laugh slips free.

She looks at me, and that soft gray gaze does something stupid in my chest. Something that'll only cause problems in the long run. I can never act on it but fuck if it isn't fun to fantasize.

Pouty lips, covered in drool as they slide down my cock. Soft hair wrapped around my fist, the little ringlets glistening in the moonlight on my pillow. Sweet, throaty voice moaning *my* name. That same soft heart in the palm of my fucking hand.

Fucking hell.

I brush the thoughts back, my thumb rubbing over my lip to hide the grimace there.

I put the car in park, and Mila unbuckles her seat belt, the scent of vanilla and honey in the air enough to steal my fucking breath away. I expect her to get out, but she doesn't, her gaze coming to meet mine.

"I'm sorry I didn't listen to you. I know you didn't like him."

You want the truth? I don't like any of the little shits she brings home.

I almost laugh. *Almost* because now that she's in my space, the air is thick. Hard to breathe. Her breathing is shallow, matching my own.

It'd be so fucking easy to close the few inches between us. Press my lips to hers and get a taste of her. That's crossing a line, though. One I swore I'd never go to with her.

Mila Carpenter wasn't made for me. As much as it feels like it, there's not a world where I could ever deserve her.

"Mila," I murmur, my voice dark. I should tell her to go inside. I should get out of the fucking car, but her pretty eyes hold me captive.

"Christian," she breathes, and I swear the sound goes straight to my fucking cock.

"You're upset."

She shakes her head, her gaze slipping down to my lips with uncertainty before coming back to mine. "I'm not."

Her eyes lock with mine, half-lidded and hazy and so fucking pretty, shining in the dim lights through the front window.

"Do you really have a thing for Bailey?"

To be honest, her older sister is beautiful, but I've never seen her that way. I did my part, letting her think so, and even playing into the role a little bit to get closer, but it was just that. A role I was meant to fill.

Now that she's flown off to New Orleans and found a decent man, that ship has sailed. Not that I'm not happy about it.

One thing about working for the FBI is they will use whoever they have to, to get what they're after. Me. Bailey. Fuck, they'd use Mila if they thought they could.

I've done what I can to protect her from that in the last three years, but it's times like these that make me forget the job I'm here to do, and how easy it would be to forget about it all, just for a little while.

"And if I said I never have?"

Her hand rests over mine on the center console, her fingers soft and delicate against my rough and calloused ones. She feels so good. So soft and warm. My cock throbs with the need to bury myself inside her and not come up for fucking days until she's mine.

"And me?" she breathes. "If I asked you if you had a thing for me, would you tell the truth?"

"The truth?" I chuckle darkly. "The truth is a dangerous thing, little devil."

"Thank you for saving me."

She leans forward, pressing her lips to my cheek. She pauses, only an inch from my face, and time stands still when she turns her eyes to mine. I meet her gaze, both of us dangling on the edge of a cliff neither of us is prepared to climb out of.

For a year, I've been dreaming of the way she tasted, and now she's dangling it in front of me like a caged animal.

"*Mila.*"

Her tongue darts out to lick her lips, and my cock pulses.

Fuck me. What the fuck am I doing?

"Go inside."

She pauses, and I swear I almost say fuck it and pull her into my lap when I see the disappointment flood her gaze.

Temptation never looked so fucking sweet.

"Did I do something wrong?"

She did everything right. And that's the fucking problem.

I reach up, brushing my knuckles down the side of her face, but she turns away from me, her cheeks burning red under my hand.

Carefully, she falls back in her seat, refusing to look at me. When she reaches for the door, something hot and unpleasant settles in my chest.

"Mila."

"Goodnight, Christian."

CHAPTER
Seven

MILA
LA, JULY, 2 YEARS AGO

My mother keeps trying to whore me out like a prized breeder pig.

I can't say I'm surprised. Just pissed off.

That's how life is for women in our world. You're to marry who they want because it's good for the family. Connections are formed, and business booms.

Never mind what kind of man you're married off to. It's your duty to obey his every command because he's your husband. He's in charge.

If he beats you, it's because he's tired or stressed, or maybe you aren't doing enough. If he cheats, you should have been sexier. Tried harder to fulfill every one of his desires so he wouldn't have to find someone on the side who would. Unable to bear children? You may as well be worthless.

You are to remain twenty-five until you reach the age of fifty-five. You are to always look your best but never like you're trying too hard. You must be a five-star Michelin chef or have some other skill

secret stuff he asks you for in the bedroom, and never, ever show your emotions. Men like softness. Men like sweetness.

It's your job to be all those things and more.

—Sounds like a load of bullshit to me.

"Not enjoying the party?"

"I prefer séances."

I lay back in my lounge chair on the terrace overlooking the ocean, and Christian chuckles, stepping closer, hands shoved in his pockets while I try to calm my racing heart.

"Your mother is looking for you."

"Pity," I grumble. "I don't want to be found."

"You and I both know you know where to hide if you don't want to be found."

He's not wrong. I know every inch of this property. Mainly because it's been my prison for the last eighteen years of my life. I've explored every secret passage. Every hidden room. Every spare nook and cranny until there's nothing left to find anymore since I was four years old.

"I think my mother is trying to marry me off."

I'd overheard her talking with one of her fancy Pilates friends, stating they were in the process of arranging a meeting between me and one of Marcus's business partner's sons. The idea that they could just sell me off sent a bout of nausea through me, and I had to escape.

"And how do you feel about that?" I don't mistake the bite in his voice, and my heart beats just a little bit harder.

It's useless, of course. He's made it clear from the start he doesn't want anything to do with me. At least not romantically.

I'll never be anything more than a job to Christian Cross, and that is a hard pill to swallow.

"I won't do it."

"And what would you do, instead, little devil?"

I fix him with a look when he stands in front of me, watching me with his hands in the pockets of his suit. The familiar nickname sends a rush of heat through me, settling in my core.

At this angle, he's daunting. I shift in my seat, and his dark blue gaze slips over me, down the soft pale gold silk of my gown. Over the light curls in my updo that fall around my shoulders. The pink lipstick on my lips. I've never felt so seen as I do when his jaw clenches.

I'm not crazy. This man thinks about me a lot more than he lets on.

Interesting.

"I'll run," I murmur.

"And what makes you think you'd get far?"

"Would you catch me?" I muse, my heartbeat strumming in my throat. "If I ran, would you find me and bring me back?"

"Find you? Yes," he murmurs, his voice so quiet that I can barely hear it. "Bring you back?" he pauses, and my heart stalls in my chest. "Not until I'm done with you."

It's demeaning, the way he says it, as if I'm nothing more than a toy for him to play with until it breaks. It still doesn't stop the warmth from gathering between my thighs.

Sliding off the lounge, his eyes catch on the silk of my dress as it cascades down my legs, and the heat hidden in his blue eyes makes my stomach dip awkwardly.

His dark gaze follows me when I saunter over to him, his eyes licking a path of fire over my skin when they slip over my hips, up my waist and breasts, before they finally meet mine. His tongue runs over his teeth, but his hands remain in his pockets.

"What would you do?" My voice is barely above a whisper. His jaw tightens, and though I step into him until my front is pressed against his, he doesn't step back. I can feel every hard inch of him against me, his cock sitting heavily between us.

I blame the three glasses of champagne I've had for my

boldness, but I know it's him.

With my gaze trained on his, I down the rest of the champagne in my glass. Call it liquid courage. Call it the plain stupidity of a naïve young girl. I know I'm playing with fire. This is farther than either of us has ever gone with one another, but now that I've started, I'm not sure if a nuke could get me to stop.

I place my fingers on his chest, feeling his heartbeat just a little bit faster.

The intoxicating scent of leather, whiskey, and the forest washes over me, stealing my breath and going straight to my head.

Walking my fingers upward, his eyes never leave mine, and my heart flutters with their intensity. He smirks devilishly, and for the first time since I've known him, I can see that carefully constructed steel control is in danger of collapsing.

"Would you punish me?" My tongue darts out to lick my lips, and his stare follows the movement, his gaze warmer and heavier than the brush of my tongue.

For the last two years, this cat-and-mouse game has been the only thing that's kept me sane. This innate desire to garner a reaction from him to let me know I'm not going crazy on my own. That there's something there, despite his incessant need to fight it tooth and nail.

A twinkle of something dark and repressed flashes across his gaze before it's replaced with a calm clarity that stirs something unsettling inside me. He steps closer until my back hits the balustrade stone behind me, arching over.

God, he's tall.

At this angle, I'm barely grazing his collarbone as he looms over me. His gaze burns into mine, and my thighs grow slick with my own traitorous need.

Maybe I do have a death wish.

"What do you know of the world, little devil?" he asks, his voice dark and low, sending a tingle up my spine as his breath fans across my face.

"I know men like you are dangerous for girls like me," I breathe before I can stop myself.

Carefully, he reaches up, his fingers brushing a curl off my forehead. Tingles erupt from the smallest of touches, the heat from his fingers slipping through me as he watches for my reaction.

I swallow past the lump in my throat when he leans closer, inches away from my mouth. I can taste the mint of his toothpaste and the rawness of the whiskey on his breath, and my mouth waters. I force myself to meet his gaze, the deep blue depths dragging me down into the pits of the Mariana Trench.

"Do you know what I would do to you when I caught you?"

Pressed between him and the stone railing, a dangerous heat spreads through me.

Dangerous because even if I know my fate, it's nice to pretend that even if just for a night, I didn't have to be Mila Carpenter, the daughter of a wealthy socialite. I could just be Mila. His.

Yep, he's definitely the devil.

"I'd break you," he murmurs, leaning forward until his nose is traveling up the column of my neck, his warm breath sending a shiver down my spine despite the warm May air. "Shatter you into a million little pieces, and when I put you back together, you'd be too addicted to what I can do to you to ever leave." His lips press to the shell of my ear, and my heart beats a little faster. My body feels like it's been dipped in lava, my core warm and my nipples straining under my dress that's pressed against his chest. "You'd be obsessed with my fingers . . ." His fingertips trail up my forearm, over the goosebumps on my skin. "My mouth . . ." He presses a kiss so light to the side of my neck that I barely feel it. "My cock . . ." I can feel his erection digging into my stomach at this angle. "You'd be mine to do with as I please, and not even death would allow you to escape me."

I let out a shaky breath, my eyes screwed shut as I fight the tingling sensation in my veins, begging me to move closer. Forget about the world, my mother's plans to marry me off, and the fact that inside, dozens of million-dollar people are milling about at another one of Marcus's parties and just feel him.

Against my own will, my head tilts to the side, granting him better access where his stubble drags against the smooth skin of my neck.

He presses the lightest of kisses to the bare skin of my throat, where it meets my shoulder. The sensation goes straight to my core, and a need unlike anything I've ever felt before throbs between my legs.

He chuckles darkly, lingering against my skin for a moment longer until I feel like I'm either going to spontaneously combust or faint from the electricity vibrating in the air between us.

His lips brush mine in the lightest of touches, but he doesn't kiss me. My head spins, a quiet sigh slipping free when his tongue glides along my bottom lip.

"Remember that the day you decide to run."

He lingers against my skin for a moment longer until I feel like I'm either going to spontaneously combust or faint from the electricity vibrating in the air between us.

And with that, he steps back, allowing a wash of cool air to meet my skin.

I shiver at the loss of him, straightening against the balustrade and glaring at him just as the door behind him opens.

"Mila," Mom snaps, but her eyes land on Christian, and she falls silent. Then they land on me. Then on Christian again.

Busted.

My mother's gaze is unreadable. I hug my arms around myself against a chill that seems to have slipped into the air. Christian's eyes never leave mine.

"Dinner is about to begin."

Christian raises a brow as if he's giving me a choice. Follow my mother or stay here and make my own decision.

I want to stay. I want to feel that burn in my veins, I only feel when I'm with him. I want to spend the night looking at the stars while his lips cover every inch of my body.

But . . . life's not that simple.

"Coming," I reply to my mother and push off the railing. Christian chuckles under his breath when I walk by. The asshole thinks he won.

A shiver rolls through me, and I cross the backyard, following my mother to the house. I pause once I step inside, my hand on the door to look back at him.

You'd be too addicted to me to ever leave . . .

"Goodnight, Christian."

His eyes glint with dark amusement when he brushes a tattooed thumb across his lip. "Goodnight, little devil."

The FBI agent my mother hired to bring my stepfather down is in love with my sister. I'm not surprised. Savannah is beautiful. *Otherworldly* beautiful. He'd be a fool not to fall for her.

I'm not jealous of her because he wants her. Just jealous because no one wants *me* in that way.

I can see it in his eyes, the way they follow her, watching her every move. My mother doesn't think anyone has her figured out, but I do. She hired Logan Prince because my stepfather is part of a human trafficking ring, and this is the only way we'll ever be free. If we bring the system down from the inside out.

Can't say it's going to be a whole lot of fun, but neither are boring benefits, expensive dresses, and sitting through luncheons with all the other rich women in my mother's circle. It's just life.

My sister Bailey is the lucky one. Out of all of us, she's the furthest removed. She lives in New Orleans and has her own life with her fiancé, Charlie. She's no longer required to play the perfect little doll, dressing up in expensive gowns and doing her hair in pristine curls after a blowout at Santelli's Spa.

Mason, the oldest of us all, is so far detached in his garage, that belonged to our father, it's like he doesn't exist most of the time, and then . . . there's me.

Just Mila. Always just Mila.

A hand lands on my shoulder, causing me to jump and spin around.

"Fuck, Corbin, you scared the shit out of me."

He holds up his hands in self-defense and places a much-needed step back from me.

"Sorry, I didn't mean to scare you."

He looks like shit. He's got bags under his eyes, and I know he's using that weird drug again. Black Dahlia or whatever it's called. A mixture of ecstasy and absinthe that gets you so high you can't remember that your toes aren't little finger sausages.

"I came to chat."

I shake my head. "I don't have time."

"Make time," he demands, grabbing my hand when I move to pull away.

Are you kidding me?

Instant heat trickles through me, and I know it has nothing to do with the man standing in front of me. It's the one watching me from a table near the back of the room with dark blue eyes that haven't left me all night.

I resist the urge to look that way and force a smile to my face when I really want to pour my drink in Corbin's face and storm out like every dramatic scene I've ever wanted to reenact from television.

"Please, Mila . . . just a couple minutes."

"Fine. Five minutes." I tug my hand away from him and cross

my arms over my chest. I said he could have my time, not my hand. Besides, his is clammy.

"I wanted to apologize for the way things went down during spring break."

"Oh, you mean when you tried to force me to sleep with you and got mad when I wouldn't?"

"It wasn't like that," he argues, his cheeks burning red.

"It never is, is it?"

"Look, this isn't about that. I had to have surgery on my arm from your big ass bodyguard dislocating my shoulder."

Oh . . . oh my God.

I knew whatever Christian had done, it hadn't been pretty, but I never knew he did . . . that.

"I guess you've learned a valuable lesson about keeping your hands to yourself, then?"

Corbin lets out a heavy sigh.

"Can we move on? I have to talk to you about something."

I glance down at my phone.

"Three minutes left."

"Listen, this is serious."

"I'm listening."

"Something's coming."

I pause, staring at him and waiting for him to continue.

When he doesn't, I concede and take the bait.

"Summer? The election? The rapture?"

"Just . . . something," he says, lowering his voice. "You aren't safe. Not for long. You need to get out of LA."

I don't like the look in his eyes. Like he knows more about my life than I do right now.

"You're scaring me."

"I'm only telling you this because I care about you, but Drew overheard Marcus speaking about marrying you off a few months ago. I don't know why or to who, but I know that Marcus is in some deep shit, and you're on the chopping block if you don't get the fuck away from him."

Marriage?

Like a ring and husband and wife? Titles? Boring scheduled sex once a week while my husband goes out and fucks around with every coed under twenty-one?

No, thank you.

"I can't just leave my family, Corbin." I take my drink, moving to walk away from him, but again, he grabs my hand.

"I'm serious, Mila."

"I am, too. No one's going to force me to marry them." I leave out the rest of the truth. That I will never marry anyone because it doesn't matter.

Marriage is a contract, and I'm anything but willing to be a tamed show pony. I've spent years of my life making my mother happy, and that's why I chose a school a thousand miles away in Texas where she couldn't reach me. Mom may love the glitz and glam of her life, but I'd rather be completely alone in the world than marry a man simply because it's expected of me.

"There's something else?"

"What now?" I groan.

"Cross. He's dangerous."

Instantly, my cheeks heat, my stomach doing a backflip.

Men like you are dangerous for girls like me.

"Is this because he broke your arm? Because that's kind of his job. Protecting me and all."

Corbin's jaw tightens, and he looks away. "He's in love with you."

Right.

"Who wouldn't be?" I joke, but the humor is lost on him, so I let out a deep breath and swallow some of my drink. "Look, Christian's just looking out for me. Not that it matters, but I was spiraling after what happened at the party."

Even if the butterflies in my stomach say otherwise, there's not a world in this Universe in which Christian Cross and I are in love. "

"I'm just looking out for you, Mila," he says, glancing over my head. I don't have to turn around to know Christian's watching me. He's been watching me all night.

"From what? The boogeyman or your bruised ego?"

He fixes me with a dark stare, and instant guilt washes through me. I'm not normally a mean girl, but there's something about being stalked, being told your stepfather is going to marry you off to the highest bidder, and being corralled like a guinea pig your whole life that just really tests your patience after a while.

"You're smarter than you act, Mila."

I step back like he'd slapped me.

"Okay, wow. Fucking rude. Time's up."

For the third time, I turn to stalk away, but again, he catches my wrist, this time, his fingers digging in tighter. I only go because I'm not about to have him suing for another surgery because he can't keep his hands to himself.

"I'm just telling you to be careful. He's not who he says he is. He's dangerous."

Jesus Christ, if he says that one more time . . .

I yank my hand away, stepping back away from him.

"So is butter."

I storm away before he can say anything else and search the room for my sisters.

I mean, who does he think he is? Showing up here and telling me Christian is dangerous. He's the one that tried to force me to fuck him in a dirty, *occupied* bathroom.

Stay away from Christian.

As if I have that kind of choice. He's always there. Always watching.

Right now is no different when I storm up to the table he and Logan have occupied all night. He's watching me with a hint of amusement in his eyes while Logan is nowhere to be found.

Cocky asshole.

"Come dance with me."

His gaze flicks up over my legs, to my thighs, then over my breasts before, finally, his eyes meet mine.

He doesn't move.

"What did Loverboy want? Another alignment?"

"Let me rephrase," I try again. I'm in no mood to talk about whatever he did to Corbin. "Please, come dance with me.

He chuckles as he stands to his full height in front of me.

Why does he get to be so damned tall?

My pulse flutters, my thighs clenching from the tingles that shoot through me when the familiar scent of leather, whiskey, and the forest washes over me.

—and attractive?

"I don't dance."

Rejection is a harsh mistress.

Of course, he doesn't.

"Fine," I grit, my cheeks burning hot. "Have it your way."

I down the rest of my drink and place it on the table in front of him before sauntering back to the dance floor. I don't see Bailey, but Savannah and Logan are in the center, doing the devil's tango with each other.

I almost roll my eyes. I wish they'd just sleep together and get it over with.

No, scratch that. I wish I could get *him* out of my head so I could move on with my life and stop waiting for something that will never happen.

Looking back at the table, I see Christian there, his arms crossed over his chest and his gaze trained on me, daring me.

Fuck him. Fuck Marcus Parker. And fuck whoever *unknown asshole number one* is.

Shooting him a glare, I slip into the crowd.

I *feel* his gaze burning a hole through my back as it follows me through the room. Instantly, I'm engulfed in a sea of bodies, and someone's hands find my hips, moving me along to the music.

Breathe. You can do this. It's just dancing.

I suck in a deep breath past my lips, pushing those old familiar feelings of disgust to the back of my mind, and force myself to exist in the moment. No Christian. No Corbin. No masked men or scars.

I let myself get swept away, feeling the beat of the music and the shot of liquor coursing through my veins while the man slips his arms around me, our bodies moving together.

"You're so fucking sexy," he slurs in my ear, and I push a smile to my face when I really feel like I want to vomit.

"Thank you."

His hips grind against mine, and people swarm around us, immersing us in a sea of bodies until there's nowhere to go.

It's dirty. It's sexy. It's also disgusting, but I don't allow myself to think about that. I'll worry about it later when I'm scrubbing my skin raw from the touch of this man's hands, but right now, I need to do this.

This is what people my age do. We go out. We party. We have a good time despite the ramifications of our actions tomorrow because we're young and have our whole lives to figure shit out.

The man's hands on my hips venture higher, over my ribcage, and I almost pull away. Then I imagine they belong to a certain broody someone, and heat blossoms in my core, my pussy growing wet when I imagine his rough words at my ear.

Is it wrong? Probably. Is it creepy to picture him in another man's place? Also probable. Do I care?

Absolutely not, because for the first time in nearly a year, I feel like a real human being and not a defective replication.

Then, the man behind me lets go completely, and before I can spin around, new hands slip into his place.

. . . Bigger, stronger hands that cover half my front. My hips are halted and I'm forcibly pulled back into the hard chest of the devil himself.

Fuck.

"You're going to get someone killed." His voice is darker than sin, his hands sliding down my hips to my thighs, pressing me closer against him until I feel his erection digging into my lower back.

So Christian Cross can't ignore me, either?

His hands guide me to move, swaying against him to the slow, heavy beat of the music. It's more like sex than dancing. My ass grazes his erection, and my body tightens with a newfound need.

"I thought you don't dance?" I taunt over my shoulder, my voice breathy and soft. Pathetic.

I know what we're doing is wrong. Any one of the other employees could see us. That's all I need. More ammunition for them to say I'm getting special treatment. First William and now Christian.

—Just call me the whore of Babylon.

"What's the matter, little devil? Afraid Corbin might catch you grinding on my cock?" he rasps in my ear.

I don't even try to deny it. I am grinding against his cock. I suck my bottom lip between my teeth, silencing a moan when his hands slide down my front, over my thighs, and then back up to my ribs. Like he's memorizing every curve of my body.

"He's just a friend," I challenge, my voice breathier than I'd like it to be.

Christian chuckles dangerously at my words, leaning down until his breath is tickling the curls at the back of my neck.

It's a lie. Corbin maybe my friend, but he wants so much more than that.

"Does he know that?"

"Sounds like you're jealous." His hands slip lower, brushing over the smooth skin of my inner thighs. A shiver rolls through me when he slips even closer, his lips at my ear and his rough stubble scraping against my skin.

"Territorial."

My heart flutters, but something hazardous lurks beneath the surface. This high I get from what I feel with him is addictive. I can't even hug my own mother without feeling like I'm going to be sick, yet with Christian—someone I've never met until he rode into my life in a shining black murder machine—I *want* his hands on me. I want his touch. His rough words in my ear.

I want him to challenge me. In fact, I crave it.

—Just like he said I would.

"I thought you wanted Bailey?" I taunt.

He chuckles low in my ear, his lips brushing against my skin.

"Unfortunately, that spot's reserved for her little sister."

Against my own will, my arm comes up, wrapping around the back of his neck. His lips skate over the racing pulse in the side of my throat and I arch my neck to grant him more access, shivering when his lips brush against my skin. I find myself getting lost in the feeling of his fingers digging into my skin through my dress.

When I open my eyes, his are right there, inches away and burning with lust and something else so possessive, it steals my breath away.

As if he's daring me to do it.

My tongue darts out to lick my bottom lip, and his eyes follow the movement, nearly black under the blue and purple lights of the club. Time hangs in the balance for a single second that seems to last a lifetime while neither of us moves.

And then, without allowing myself to think about it, I close the small distance between us, pressing my lips to his.

He doesn't move. Even his hands stop their exploration of my body. Rejection coils through me when he doesn't kiss me back. Swallowing, I pull away, and a low growl slips from his throat.

"Sorry," I breathe, attempting to step away from him, but his fingers fist in my dress pinning me against him. "I—"

He pulls me back harder, locking me in place. His lips seal over mine, a rumble vibrating through his chest and into my spine. His tongue licks into my mouth, whiskey and mint on his breath.

It's the most intoxicating thing I've ever tasted.

I get lost in him, letting him own me for those few brief moments. My thighs grow slick with need, my heartbeat throbbing in my core with the beat of the music. His kiss is everything I imagined it would be. Rough, consuming, demanding, and it's with some dismay, I find, I could kiss him for hours.

His tongue dances with mine languidly. It's as if he's got all day when all I want to do is slip around and touch him.

With a rough noise, he nips my bottom lip, forcing our mouths apart. He leans his forehead against mine, his breathing as ragged as the heartbeat in my chest.

The sound of his darkly deranged chuckle sends a shiver down my spine.

"Mila," he rasps, my name like a threat on his tongue.

"Christian, I—" I try to pull away from him, but his arm locks me in place. His breath is warm against my ear, and goosebumps rise on my skin.

"Good luck."

He releases me, brushing the curl back from my forehead before he steps away.

"Be ready in half an hour. We're going home."

CHAPTER *Eight*

MILA
LA, JUNE, 1 YEAR AGO

"On the felony count of rape and sexual assault in the first degree, the court finds the defendant, Marcus Wendell Parker, guilty."

"On the felony count of distributing sexually explicit content including rape, murder, and assault for the intention of financial gain, the court finds the defendant, Marcus Wendell Parker, guilty."

"On the felony count of trafficking illegal substances with the intention of financial gain, including, but not limited to, methamphetamine, cocaine, heroin, and fentanyl, the court finds the defendant, Marcus Wendell Parker, guilty."

"On the felony count of fraud, including tampering with official United States documents to swing an election, the court finds the defendant, Marcus Wendell Parker, guilty."

"On the felony count of two-hundred-and fifty-eight claims of trafficking a human being for the intention of sexual slavery, the court finds the defendant Marcus Wendell Parker guilty in the first degree."

Especially when there's a camera trained on your family the entire time the judge is reading off the guilty verdict of your former stepfather.

I keep my face blank, my mind empty, save for the sound of the judge's voice as she reads off all the charges that Marcus Parker is being convicted of. If I had my way, I wouldn't have come today. None of us would.

What's done is done. We can't go back and change the past, but we can create a better future—one without men like Marcus in it.

For the last eighteen years, I've watched him hurt the people I love to the point that we were all almost murdered for his political gain. I've watched my sister, Savannah, live through his torment when he raped her, pimped her out to his friends, drugged her. I've watched my mother become a shell of who she once was. I almost lost my brother.

As far as I'm concerned, the only thing Marcus deserves is a death sentence, and I'm ashamed to live in California, knowing he won't ever get one.

"The court has gone into great detail over this case in the previous months leading up to this sentencing," Judge Higgens says, laying her glasses on the stand in front of her. "I, myself, have had trouble sleeping at night knowing what you have done. Most of your victims will never see their families again, and the fact that you were almost elected to be mayor of my city makes me sick to my stomach."

Marcus doesn't respond, simply staring at her with that same look of cocky indifference he always has. I hate that they let him wear a suit. Orange would suit him better.

"I can only hope that there will come a time when you will see the consequences of your actions and have remorse in the eyes of your maker for the men, women, and children you have hurt, though I do not know that repentance is possible for someone as quietly violent as you." She stares him dead in the face. Mom squeezes my hand so tight, my fingers ache. Someone pops a piece of bubble gum in their mouth. "May God have mercy on your soul."

If he had one . . .

"The court imposes the following sentencing," the judge says, and everything goes silent. "In the case of Marcus Wendell Parker, the court has reached the following verdict. Marcus Wendell Parker, you are hereby sentenced to five consecutive life sentences to be served at the California State Federal Prison without the possibility of parole. You are to serve your sentence immediately following this hearing, with a credit of one-hundred-and-twenty-two days time served in the Los Angeles County Jail."

Where I expected chaos in the dusty LA courtroom, silence follows instead. No one moves. No one celebrates. I'm not even sure anyone breathes when Marcus is hauled to his feet by the officer standing next to him. He murmurs something quietly to him, and Marcus places his hands behind his back. The officer handcuffs him, and he's led towards a door off to the side where he'll go to prison for the rest of his sorry life.

He's going to die behind bars, anyway. Why not save the taxpayers some money and deal with him now?

Frustration bubbles up inside me, but I have to push it back down. There's no use being angry. The decision has been made. My only hope is that by some stroke of luck, someone shanks him in his dirty prison sheets in the middle of the night and lets him bleed out for what he did to all those people. Women and children. Men, too.

Marcus smirks, looking back at us, his gaze lingering on my sister sitting beside me. She meets his gaze with her ice-blue one, finally unafraid of him after what he'd done to her for all those years. Her fiancé, Logan, the special FBI agent who brought Marcus down, places his arm around her shoulders and stares back at him as if daring him to even blink in Savannah's direction.

Marcus's gaze turns to my mother, and he stares at her long and hard. The divorce was finalized a month ago. She owes him nothing, but in true Marcus fashion, he still feels some control over her.

I pat Mom's hand, and she lets out a shuddering sigh, tears brimming in her eyes. However, she doesn't look away.

"Come on," I whisper, tugging on her hand. "Let's go celebrate."

Mom grimaces at me but nods softly, and I get the feeling that maybe I'm the only one happy about this day.

I lead Mom out of the courtroom to find my brother, Mason, waiting in the lobby, leaning against the wall. He's barely been a part of our lives since Mom married Marcus, but he's making an effort, and I'm proud of him.

The moment Mom sees him, he pulls her into a hug, and she cries on his shoulder. Logan holds Savannah, and I stand awkwardly, unsure of how I'm supposed to feel.

On one hand, I'm happy the fucker's going to prison. I hope it's filled with cheap one-ply toilet paper and moldy shower stalls.

On the other hand, I can't help but feel like it's not over. Like there's still something lurking in the shadows, waiting and watching, planning to strike when we least expect it.

Mom and Mason discuss the court hearing, and Logan and Savannah whisper amongst themselves, so I press myself against the wall while the courtroom clears out, turning my phone on.

It's been a long day, and my phone's been off this entire time, so it floods with messages from well-wishers and people who just want the inside scoop the moment it powers up. I roll my eyes at half the people who reached out. They don't actually care. They just want to know all the gritty details. It's been the same for months.

Since Marcus was arrested, we've dealt with reporter after reporter and paparazzi trying to take pictures through our windows. Average citizens throwing insults at us in public because of who we're related to.

I can't wait for a day when all this blows over. When peace isn't just a foreign concept, we can move on without ever having to hear his name uttered again.

As I scroll through my phone, deleting messages, only two stand out to me. I click on the first, my stomach filling with butterflies as I reply.

The second fills me with complete and total dread.

Unknown: Sweet, sweet freedom.

I grit my teeth and delete the message, shoving my phone back in my bag. My skin prickles with awareness like someone's watching me. If Mr. Unknown knows that Marcus was sentenced, then that means he's here.

I scan the crowd filing out of the courtroom, but no one's paying any more attention to me than it takes to shoot me a dirty look or a tear-filled glance.

I'm watching the doors swing open with each group of people that exits, and my eyes catch on a man inside the courtroom beyond, a hood pulled up over his head, casting shadows over his face so I can't see anything more than his chin and mouth.

My heart lurches in my chest, coming to a halt. My palms grow sweaty, and everything fades away as we stare at each other.

Slowly, his lips tip up in a smirk.

"Mila."

I jump when Mason's hand lands on my shoulder, letting out a quiet squeak.

"You alright?"

I look back to the courtroom door, but the door's shut.

"I forgot something," I murmur, hurrying back towards the doors. I push through, stumbling into the large, empty room, but it's just that. Empty.

I look around for any signs of the man in the hood, but I'm met with nothing but the quiet hum of the air conditioner and a fly buzzing somewhere in the room.

"Did you find it?" Mason asks, popping his head through the door.

He was right fucking here.

Right here.

"Y-yeah. It was in my purse," I lie, gaze trained on the two doors in the back of the room. One that Marcus went through and one that the judge used. Surely, he couldn't sneak out that way.

"Let's get going," Mason says, completely oblivious to the eerie feeling that hangs in the air. "Mom's tired. It's been a long day."

Slowly, I nod, and when he holds out his hand, I place my fingers in his, letting him lead me from the room.

That feeling never leaves, though.

The feeling of being watched from the shadows.

I've always loved the way waves from the ocean crash against the sand at night.

In March, the water is chilly. Freezing, to be exact, but I don't care. I'm standing at the edge of the surf, letting the water wash across my toes and erase today, along with the heat still trapped in the pristine sand of Venice Beach.

I can look out over the water and imagine a life where I'm a nobody. No one knows I was related to the man who was just charged with heinous crimes against humanity. I'm not the girl who's sister was used in some sick elitist cult. I'm not the girl getting stalked.

I'm just Mila, lost in the ocean and feeling the sand beneath my toes.

"You're going to catch a cold."

I don't have to turn around to know who it is. I feel the awareness travel up my spine from his gaze.

"Would you take care of me?" I joke, turning back to him over my shoulder. His eyes bore into mine, stealing my breath away, and my toes curl into the sand in the water from just that simple glance.

"Depends," he murmurs, rubbing a hand over the stubble on his jaw. I've always loved when he doesn't shave every day.

I turn to face him, the bottom of my skirt I'd picked up on a trip to Romania last year dripping from the water.

"On?"

He cocks his head to the side, his gaze slipping over the loose, flowy skirt billowing around my legs, up to the piercing in my navel that I did in secret two years ago with a clothespin—not recommended. The same one he had to take me to the doctor to get medicine for when it got infected so my mother didn't find out. His eyes slip over my tank top, then finally meet mine, and my mouth goes dry.

God, he looks handsome in a pair of jeans and a button-up. It should be illegal.

"On how long it takes you to get the fuck over here."

My stomach dips at the growl in his voice, and I can't fight the blush on my cheeks. Slowly, I step out of the water and step across the sand, stopping right in front of him.

"Is this better?" I breathe, looking up at him through my lashes.

"Get the fuck over here," he bites, tugging me closer by a hand on my waist.

The moment his lips crash against mine, the world melts away. My stomach takes flight with butterflies. My core heats to a sweltering five thousand degrees, and all the problems of the day just don't seem to matter anymore.

Christian Cross tastes like late nights and sneaking out. Like melted caramel dripping over vanilla ice cream or whiskey tinged with a hint of honey. Like everything I want to let ruin me if it means I can still be his.

"Fuck," he grits, pulling away and stooping to press his lips the inside of my neck. "Miss me, little devil?" he purrs against my skin, slipping his teeth over my racing pulse. My eyes clench shut at the heat that slips through me, and I wrap my arms around his neck.

Christian's eyes twinkle with mischief when he pulls back, and my stomach does a backflip at the devil-may-care grin on his lips.

"How was the hearing?"

"As good as could be expected."

He cocks a brow. "Meaning?"

I push away from him, my stomach in knots. I cross the sand to the little blanket he's set up for us and sink onto it, falling back to look at the stars.

He follows, sitting down beside me and hovering over me, forcing my gaze to his when he blocks out the moon overhead.

"Talk to me," he murmurs, brushing a thumb over my lip.

I shake my head.

"I just feel like this isn't the end."

His gaze darkens, his jaw clenching. His thumb strokes my cheek, then slips down to cup my chin.

"It's over, Mila. You don't have to worry anymore."

I haven't told Christian about Mr. Unknown. I don't want him to worry. Things are finally starting to slow down. The last thing everyone needs is to be worried about my little stalker problem.

—Because that's all it is. A little stalker issue that will eventually come to an end. I'm not that interesting. Eventually, Mr. Unknown will tire of following me around, and I'll never hear from him again.

And, then, I can't help but wonder . . . when will Christian tire of me, too?

"Is it over for you?" I ask quietly, my heartbeat thrumming in my ears.

"Stop that," he murmurs. His thumb strokes over the tear on my cheek. I hadn't even realized I was crying.

Fuck. I grit my teeth, hating myself for even feeling this way about something that I knew was transient from the moment it started six months ago.

"Stop what?" I whisper, lifting up to press my lips to his. If he's kissing me, he's here, right? And if he's here, he's mine, at least, for now.

Christian lets me kiss him for only a moment before he pulls back, pressing his forehead against mine.

"Mila."

I shake my head. I can't tell him how I feel.

How longing glances across crowded rooms and secret dates in the back of blacked-out Surburbans or darkened beaches at night aren't enough anymore. Holding his hand to release it the moment we pull into the driveway at my mother's new mansion or how falling asleep in his arms after he snuck into my room only to wake up alone guts me.

I don't just want him. I need him. The irony is almost laughable.

"Please, just kiss me," I whisper, needing him to chase the racing thoughts out of my head. He searches my gaze, an expression I can't read on his face. My heart stretches out for his, begging for his touch, and tears sting in the backs of my eyes. I push all my emotions away and focus on what I can control.

He and I, in this very moment, where no one is demanding anything from either of us and we're free to fall in love, even if it's only for a moment.

"Please."

He nods once and slowly closes the gap between us, his lips feasting on mine and a groan tearing up his throat that renders my heart immobile in my chest.

I love you . . . I whisper in the back of my head because I can't say it out loud.

When he rolls me over, my legs straddling both of his, I reach between us for his zipper and pull him into my palm. He's burning hot, searing my skin when he groans and pushes inside me with a shudder. My head falls back, my gaze locking with the moon, and everything feels complete.

It may be toxic . . . this need I have to feel him. It may be pathetic.

Nothing matters as long as we're together in this moment.

"Fuck, Mila," he groans against the side of my throat. My nails scour the back of his neck, my heart racing, and my thighs slick when he moves me over him, my skirt bunched around us while he uses his hands on my ass to drive up into me.

"Please don't stop," I whisper, my pussy clenching around him and the impending orgasm drawing closer and closer.

"Never, baby," he rasps, and I capture his lips with my own, my heart soaring.

He's never called me baby before.

"Grind on my cock, sweetheart," he rasps, his groin brushing against my clit, sending my eyes rolling. "Show me how bad you need me, Mila."

"I . . .I . . ." the words get caught in my throat, and before I can release them, my entire body seizes with the force of the pleasure rippling through me. "Christian," I moan into his mouth while he spills inside me with a rough growl.

The moment we both float back down to earth, I lean my forehead against his, and he wraps his arms around me, falling back on the blanket and holding me to his chest.

I wish, for a moment, that we could stay like this forever. Completely intertwined. Unable to discern where one of us begins and the other ends, but I know, eventually, this will end.

"I'm here, Mila," he says so quietly I barely register that he'd spoken. "Do you trust me?"

Raising my head to meet his gaze, he stares back at me with a look in his eyes I can't process.

"Always."

The problem with clandestine love affairs is, eventually, someone gets hurt. Usually, the person who's more invested, and I'm afraid, judging by the warmth permeating through my veins, that person is me.

Jessi Hart

CHAPTER
Nine

MILA

It's been one week, six hours, and thirteen minutes since I've heard from Christian.

Not that I'm counting or anything.

Mom says he had some family business to attend to, but she doesn't know anything else. After that night on the beach, he kissed me until I was panting and took me home. We snuck in, and he held me in my bed until I fell asleep, wrapped in his arms.

He was so . . . gentle. Like he was worried he was going to break me.

As I'm fragile.

Looking back, I can't stop the sinking feeling in my gut. It's like there's a pit where he was, and now it's swallowing me whole. I'm worried. He's never *not* answered me before. Even when he was just a guard.

I've tried calling. They all go straight to voicemail. I've tried texting him, but the messages go unread. It's like he's a ghost, and I'm the unlucky woman who is unfortunate enough to be in love with him.

haven't spoken to him much in the past few months he's been working with us. Christian took me anywhere I needed to go.

Of course, he was also making me come on most of those trips, but that's beside the point.

Tomas pulls to a stop in front of the apartment building, standing tall against the clear blue skies. It's only April, but the weather is warm today, and I took advantage of it by wearing the sundress I know he likes and my hair loose with my natural curls.

"I'll wait right here, Ms. Mila."

"Thank you, Tomas. It'll only be a moment. I'll text you if anything changes."

He nods, gaze trained on the road ahead. I climb out of the back of the Bently, pulling the key Christian had given me out of my purse and heading through the front doors.

The front desk clerk smiles at me as I pass but makes no move to hang up on her phone call, so I don't bother. I've been here enough times now that they don't question me when I enter the building. I take the elevator, my heart thudding uncomfortably in my chest all the way to the sixth floor.

I guess a part of me is hoping that he's up there in his apartment. The other half is dreading the knowledge that he's just avoiding me if he is.

Does he regret . . . us? Did he have second thoughts? Saliva pools in my mouth, nausea bubbling in my stomach at the thought.

Maybe he thinks I'm just another clingy virgin, pining after him because he was my first.

Bitter tears sting in the backs of my eyes, but I refuse to allow them any further.

I'm sure there's a logical explanation for all of this. Christian Cross doesn't just up and disappear.

Stepping off the elevator, my heartbeat grows louder with every step toward his door. I stop in front of it, doing the polite thing and knocking.

No answer.

I try knocking again after a few moments, but not even a shuffle comes from the other side.

"He's gone."

I jump, letting out a squeak at the voice behind me. An older woman stands in her doorway, her hair in curlers and an old chihuahua in her arms. A cigarette hangs out of her mouth, smoke billowing from the end, but it's not what makes my stomach drop to my toes.

"What?"

"He's gone. Left about a week ago. Moved out in a hurry," she mumbles as if the concept of someone leaving so fast is in poor taste.

"M-moved?"

Her gaze narrows on me.

"Are you hard of hearing?"

Turning away from her, I shove my key in the lock, the tremble in my hands making it difficult. She continues to stand there and stare at me like she's the neighborhood watch when I push the door open and rush inside.

Empty.

It's completely empty.

A shaky breath leaves me, my heart cracking with tiny fissures as I look around the living room and kitchen area. The furniture is still here. The chair and coffee table. The couch where he made me come on his tongue for the first time.

I step inside, shutting the door on the nosy woman out in the hall, and make my way on shaky legs through the apartment. I stop at the bathroom, flipping the light on. All his toiletries are gone. No soap. No razor on the sinks edge. Not even a speck of lint or a roll of toilet paper.

A quiet tear slips down my cheek, and I'm powerless to stop it, heading instead to his bedroom.

The California king bed still sits against the wall, a lamp on one end of the table and a clock on the other. The curtains are partially open, filling the room with an eerie glow. I push open his closet door and nearly fall to my knees.

All his clothes have been wiped out.

He left. He really fucking left.

I step back into the living room, a numbness taking over me, and I stand in the center for what feels like ages, just staring at the couch.

He left.

My phone buzzes in my pocket, and I know it's Tomas asking if I'm okay, but I ignore him. I'm too busy spiraling.

A quiet sob wrenches from my throat, and I sink to the carpet on shaky legs.

He really fucking left.

As if I never meant anything to him.

You need to forget about me, little devil.

My eyes stay glued on the mantel, my heart cracking in my chest, and that's when I let myself cry.

"Mila, please wait up."

I continue walking, ignoring my sister.

I was doing so well, ignoring everything that happened. It's been three months since *he* left, and yet the moment his name was mentioned tonight at the family barbeque, all the pain I've been burying under a mountain of numbness came crashing back in.

I want to forget him. I want to erase the memories that he exists in from my brain so I don't have to be reminded that while I may still be in love with him, he doesn't feel the same.

"Please talk to me? What happened between you and Christian?"

Anger swells in my chest, and I scoff. I turn around, nearly forcing her to run into me.

"I'm sure you'd love to know all about that, wouldn't you."

She falls back like I'd slapped her.

"What?" she barks.

Bitter resentment coils in my chest that's completely unfounded.

Bailey's married. She just announced she's pregnant. Christian literally told me he didn't want her, but people lie all the time. Why should he be any different?

"And me?" I breathe, my heart thudding awkwardly in my ears. "If I asked you if you had a thing for me, would you tell the truth?"

"The truth?" he chuckles darkly, and my stomach drops to my toes. "The truth is a dangerous thing, little devil."

I shake my head. Whatever he said, it doesn't matter now. He proved he didn't mean it when he disappeared without a word. "Nothing. I'm sorry. I just want to be alone."

"But Mila—"

"I'm *fine*, Bailey," I snap, stepping into the darkness of my bedroom. "Go back to the party."

I shut the door on her before she can say anything else because, quite frankly, I just want to be alone.

I can't explain the visceral reaction my body had to hearing his name. It's like he reached a hand into my chest and ripped that pain back to the surface, and now, I'm right back at square one.

Just a girl desperately in love with a man who doesn't want her.

Gritting my teeth, I throw the phone on my bed and rip out the clip holding my hair. Kicking off my shoes, I start towards the bathroom.

I'm going to take a shower and go to bed. Screw dinner.

Only the moment I turn around, I come face to face with a pair of deep blue eyes that are so intense, they burn me to a crisp on the spot.

If I thought hearing his name was bad, seeing him live and in the flesh may as well be an out-of-body experience.

I fall back a step, nearly crashing to the bed when I stumble into it. My heart bottoms out, my skin tingles, and heat slips through my veins.

It's really him. He came back for me.

And then, as quickly as the aching desire filled me, it's replaced with anger.

"Oh . . . it's you."

If Christian's surprised by the iciness in my tone, he doesn't show it.

He steps out from the shadows, his eyes dark. My heart threatens to somersault out of my chest when the familiar scent of his skin washes over me.

God . . . is it possible to miss someone's scent?

My chest aches with a pain I've never recognized. Remembering the way he used to hold me. So careful, but like I was his to break if he pleased. I've never felt so adored . . . cherished.

Then he left, and I realized it was all a lie.

Every. Single. Word.

"What are you doing here, Christian?" I have to work to keep my voice indifferent when all I really want to do is fall into his arms.

Pathetic, right?

I can feel the carefully constructed façade threatening to crumble. Three months with no word. Not even a fuck you, Mila.

He doesn't answer. Instead, his gaze continues to linger on me. Like I'm nothing more than a ghost lingering in the void. Tears well in my eyes, and I desperately try to force them back. Unfortunately, he notices and something flashes across his gaze before it's replaced with a look of indifference.

"Why are you here?" I snap, venom coating my voice. "We're done, right?"

His eyes flash dangerously in the moonlight, streaming through the window. He doesn't answer, and as each second ticks by, my heart shatters a little bit more.

When it becomes clear I'm not going to get any answers, I shake my head and close my eyes against the burning sting, blurring my gaze. Unfortunately, a tear slips down my cheek from beneath my lashes.

He doesn't deserve to see my pain . . .

"Go away, Christian. I don't ever want to see you again."

I attempt to stride past him, but before I can, he catches me around the waist, spinning me around. My hand comes up, but he catches my wrist in his fingers, preventing me from slapping him, just as my lips crash against his.

The moment our lips meet, it feels like coming home. A desperate whimper slips from my lips, and he lets out a rough growl, releasing my wrist to fist my hair, tugging me closer to him. His other hand grips my ass, holding me against his front, and I melt under his searing touch.

It's angry and violent. Caustic and so perfect, my toes curl against the soft rug beneath my feet.

"Mila," he murmurs gruffly when I reach for the button of his jeans. "This isn't about that."

"Then why are you here?" I breathe against his lips.

"Because I couldn't stay away."

"Please," I whimper into his mouth and he lets out a gruff sound—a mix of pain and desire that goes straight to my chest and walks me backward towards the bed.

My family is right outside, but I couldn't care less. All that matters is the aching desire building between my legs and the feel of his skin against mine.

The moment my back hits the comforter, my nails fingers fist in his shirt, tugging it up, and he rips it over his head. My dress comes off, then his jeans, and finally, he's falling over me, gripping my hips, and hauling me down to meet the thrust of his cock.

The moment he pushes inside me, no barriers or foreplay, I let out a shaky moan, my body sucking him in greedily.

"*Fuck*," he grits between his teeth, a shudder rolling through him.

Tears burn in my eyes from the sting, but I don't want him to stop. It feels too good. I need this. Need him more than I ever thought possible.

"Christian," I mewl, my eyes fluttering closed.

"Christ," he says huskily, his head kicking back and his Adam's apple bobbing with a heavy swallow. "I've been starved for you."

Rearing back on his heals, he spreads me so my thighs are resting over his, his eyes locking with where he's slowly slipping in and out of me. His grip on my hip tightens with each thrust and I'm sure I'll have bruises to remind me of him in the morning.

He rolls his hips, stirring his cock inside and pulling down onto his length. I let out a gasp at how deep he is, my hands digging into his, and my core tightening as if I can keep him here.

"You and I will never be over, Mila," he rasps, punishing me with harsh thrusts that only drive me towards the precipice of coming.

"Oh my God," I groan, my head falling back and my eyes rolling from the heavy wave of pleasure when he brushes that sensitive spot inside me. I've been so lonely, aching for him, that I'm powerless to stop the orgasm as it rips through me. "*Christian!*"

"There's my good girl," he rasps, and I swear, I imagined the smile in his voice.

Flipping me over, he grabs my hips, dragging me back, and I whimper at his fist in my hair, a tingle slipping through me at the rough groan that leaves him.

"Why did you leave me?" I ask through clenched teeth when he continues to fuck me. He's got my hands pinned to the mattress on either side of my head while he drives inside me like he can't stop. Like he's as desperate for me as I am for him.

"Feel me, Mila. I'm right here."

"You left," I choke out, burying my face into the comforter below me.

"I'll never leave you. Trust me, Mila . . ." he rasps, setting up a steady pace while I feel like the world is floating away around us. Nothing else matters right now.

"How can I trust you when you won't even speak to me?" I whimper. He reaches beneath me, circling my clit with his fingers, and I jerk in his grasp.

He presses his lips to the side of my neck, nipping my flesh between his teeth. "Feel me, sweetheart. Feel how bad I need you."

"You . . . left . . ." My body tightens, my orgasm threatening to steal my breath away.

He lets out a pained groan, burying his head into the side of my neck.

"It's not forever," he says, voice dark and hoarse. "You and I will never be done, Mila."

My heart flutters, but before I can speak, the orgasm rips through me, leaving me shaking and wet while he continues to fuck me from behind. His hand comes over my mouth, silencing the cry that leaves my lips, and my legs give out underneath him.

He flattens out overtop me, continuing to pump inside me, and it feels so good, my eyes cross, and I swear I see stars.

"That's it, baby. Come for me," he rasps, pulling me tighter against him until his back is pressed to my front completely. He continues to fuck me, the sound of our skin meeting filling the room, and his arms band around me, holding me tightly like he can't stand the thought of letting me go.

"You're so fucking pretty, it hurts to look at you," he groans in my ear. His face nuzzles into the side of my neck and goosebumps break my skin. "I'm going fucking crazy without you. I couldn't stay away. I had to see you."

"Why are you doing this to us?" I ask, a choked sound breaking through my voice. "Why are you punishing me?"

"It has to be this way, Mila . . ." he bites out between rough breaths.

"You're tearing me apart . . . I can't live like this, Christian."

"I know. Just trust me, Mila." He presses soft lips to the side of my face. "Trust me," he whispers in my ear.

The night passes in a frantic blur. When he's not fucking me, he's feasting on me. I punish him with my nails, my teeth. He takes it all, groaning at the pleasure and pain we unleash on one another.

When both of us are too tired to continue, he finally cleans me up and climbs into bed behind me, his arms around me while he holds me against his chest.

I don't know what time it is when we stop. I'm too tired to open my eyes and look at the clock, but I can feel him. He's here.

My skin is chaffed, my body sore and vibrating for how many times he made me come.

"Stay," I whisper, even though I told myself I wouldn't beg him.

The last memory I have is of his lips pressed against my cheek.

And when I wake in the morning, he's gone.

CHAPTER
Ten

CHRISTIAN
WITCHITA, JULY, PRESENT

G*oddamn, she's beautiful.*

"Get in the car, Mila."

Poor thing is fucking terrified, which could have something to do with the man I just ran over—I didn't buy this car with a special reinforced steel bumper for nothing. Dear ol' Jerry's going to be feeling it if he wakes up from his little nap in the middle of the street.

It could also be because the man she's been running from for nearly six months finally caught up to her.

"W-what?" she stammers as screams erupt from across the street to where the dipshit's body crumpled. I'm sad to say he moves, meaning he didn't die.

Asshole.

"Unless you want to wait here."

Sirens a few blocks away is what gets her moving. She stumbles to her feet, clutching her backpack and hopping in the car. As soon as the door shuts, I'm peeling away, watching a few men try to chase r us in the rearview.

"Y-you—"

"Seat belt," I order, not taking my eyes off the road. I'm going faster than I should be, especially with her in the car. She sucks in a wheezy breath, and I side-eye her. "And breathe."

She's shaking and a tear slips down her cheek, but she reaches for the seat belt, clasping it around her.

"Mila."

She sucks in another breath, laying her head back against the seat and closing her eyes as if when she opens them, I'll be gone.

"You-you hit that man," she croaks, her hand resting over her racing heart.

Should have backed back over his ass, too.

Pulling up to a curb, I cut the lights, reversing right between two buildings in a narrow alleyway on a deserted street.

"Water."

She stares at my open hand for a moment, still in shock, before I give up and just take the water bottle from her.

Exiting the car, I go to the front and pour it over the hood. When It's finished, I toss the bottle in the back before going to the trunk and grabbing a new plate. When I return, Mila's still jittery, though she's breathing, at least. She stares at me with wide gray eyes when I fall into the driver's seat like she can't decide if she wants to run from the man who tried to kidnap her or run from me.

"Changed the license plate."

"And . . . the water?"

I shrug. "He got blood on my hood."

"You hit him."

I look at her, my gaze sweeping over the dirt on her leggings, her hair in a wild array of tangles, and the tears still drying on her cheeks.

"He deserved it."

"Is . . . he dead?" she asks after a moment.

"Hopefully."

"How did you know I needed help?"

Because I know everything about you.

There's a moment of silence when an ambulance passes, undoubtedly going to help Mr. Handsy where the tension is so thick, you could cut it with a butter knife. Mila shivers and even though I know it's probably not from the cold, I turn the heat up.

"I would say watching a man chase you down the sidewalk was probably the first clue." And the fact that I've been following her all day. "Where to?"

She stares at me.

"Mila," I say calmly. "Where to?"

"What are you doing here, Christian?"

"Saving your ass, of course."

"Asshole," she grumbles, looking away from me. I watch another tear slip down her cheek, and she hastily wipes it away.

"I guess some things never change."

"If you're here to take me back, I'm not going."

Another moment of heavy silence rings in the air between us. Five years of memories. A whole lot of fucking trauma. A .9mm bullet and the wound to prove it.

I cock a brow at her, a rush of tension flowing through me. Honey, vanilla, and fucking *her.* The combination that's going to be the death of me someday.

I'd once told her to forget about me and move on with her life. I never expected her to actually fucking try.

Fucking poetic, isn't it?

"Where are you staying?"

She stares at me as if the concept is foreign.

"Mila. Where have you been staying?" I ask again, and her gaze narrows.

"I thought I was never going to see you again."

I fix her with a bored stare. We aren't getting into *that* tonight.

She'll have plenty of time to hate me later.

When she realizes she's not getting an answer out of me, she falls back into the seat with a huff.

"Just let me out."

"I can't do that, Mila."

Pulling out onto the street, I merge with what little traffic is out at this time of night and start toward the motel. She doesn't think to ask how I know where to go, and I'm glad.

Instead, she's chewing on her bottom lip, glancing around us nervously as if SWAT is going to pop out of the manhole cover beside us at the light.

"You're acting suspicious," I tell her when she checks behind us for the third time.

"Sorry," she rolls her eyes. "It's my first vehicular homicide."

"It's only vehicular homicide if he dies. He'll live. Painfully, for a while, but unfortunately, he'll live."

"You just said earlier you hope he died."

"Hope and fact are two different things, little devil."

"Don't—don't call me that."

"Too far?"

She glowers at me, cheeks burning a pretty pink.

"Fuck you, Christian."

"Good girl. The scared and helpless act was getting old."

"I don't want you here."

"You shouldn't be out alone."

"Right," she growls, and I love that I'm getting under her skin. It almost feels like old times. "I'm working on my teleportation skills. I'm sure I'll have it down in no time."

I cock a brow at her, and her cheeks burn when she turns away from me.

Little brat.

"People are dangerous, Mila. What do you think those men would have done to you if they would have gotten ahold of you?"

She rolls her eyes for the second time since she's gotten into my car, and I have half a mind to pull her into the back seat and make them roll for real.

"I'm well aware of what they would have done."

"Are you?"

"What do you want?" she snaps, angry tears pooling in her eyes. "Unlock the door."

I chuckle darkly. If only she fucking knew . . .

"No."

I barely register her slapping me until the sting bleeds across my cheek. I run my tongue over my teeth, and her eyes widen at the dark chuckle falling from my lips.

Fuck, I've never been so hard in my life. It's been too fucking long.

"I'm sorry," she breathes, backing up until her back rests against the door, her eyes brimming with tears. "Just let me go."

She'll learn not to apologize for defending herself, but for now, I relish in the soft purr of her voice, filled with fear for what I might do. There was a time when all I wanted to do was protect her. That need is still there, but it's also tinged with the desire to see her beg for me. Plead with me.

Need me.

"Let you go? We're just getting started, sweetheart."

She glowers, tears gathered in her long eyelashes. Like a kitten denied milk.

"What do you want?"

"You."

She shakes her head. "No, you don't. You're here for a reason, and we both know that isn't me."

"Does it matter?"

I know I'm being cruel, but I've had six months to fantasize about this exact moment. When the scent of her honey and vanilla is back in my space, clouding my judgment. When she's staring at me with those eyes like fucking moonlight, and I can finally reach out and touch her.

She'll never know what I did. She'll never know what it took to leave in the first place.

"Forget about me," she pleads, soft gray gaze desperate.

And then she pushes the door open and runs before I can even think about reaching for her. I lean back in my seat, watching her take off down a nearby alleyway.

I'll let her run and tire herself out even more. It'll ensure a smooth flight to where we're going.

Unfortunately for her, this chase is over. Not that it's not been fun, but I'm getting tired of seeing her starve herself. It's time to stop running and pay the piper.

She put a bullet in my chest. Now, she'll pay for it with her life.

I chuckle darkly to myself, shooting off a text before I pull away from the stop light. I'll let her think she got away. Let her pack in a frenzy. Maybe I'll even give her a head start.

Either willingly or by force, this ends tonight. Mila Carpenter will be mine whether she likes it or not.

I'm a Cross; when I want something, I make it happen.

"See you soon, little devil."

CHAPTER
Eleven

MILA

He found me.

He fucking *found* me.

My legs burn with each step I take, but I don't stop. I can't. I have to get the fuck out of here before he catches me for good. This time, I don't think I'll make it out alive. All this time, I've been worried about the ghost of my past, but it's been him.

God, how could I have been so stupid?

Barreling through my motel room door, I nearly fall on my ass as the water from the light rain outside causes me to slip on the tile. I catch myself on the bed, falling to the dirty carpet and drawing my knees up to my chest, my body frozen.

He's here.

He's actually fucking here.

What the hell am I going to do?

"Get up," I mutter, forcing my legs to move, even though they're shaky.

I don't know when the next bus will arrive, but I'll hike until

As a last resort, I can make my way through the woods. He won't find me out there.

I scurry around, shoving all my stuff in my bags without any order. I don't have time for order.

I don't know where he went after I ran, but if I know him, he already knows where I am.

Fuck, I have to run.

A knock sounds at the door and I hold my breath, that old familiar feeling of dread washing through me.

Fuck.

Of course, he's been following me.

One doesn't simply shoot Christian Cross and get away with it. There are always consequences.

"Casey, dear," June's voice filters through the busted wood, and instantly, I let out a sigh of relief. I'd forgotten I was supposed to meet her.

"Just a minute," I call, my voice shaking. I shove the remaining items in my bag before I zip it all up just as another knock sounds.

Sorry, June. A little busy trying not to get murdered here.

Rushing to the door, I open it, prepared to tell her I'm leaving with no questions asked.

Then I stop dead in my tracks when it's not the light brown pair of gentle eyes that belong to June on the other side of the door.

No . . . It's the deep blue eyes of the devil himself.

"Oh, fuck."

Christian leans against the doorframe, looking up at me through his lashes. Every single nerve ending in my body short circuits, and that's the only telltale sign that lets me know I'm—unfortunately—still breathing, and this is real.

He holds up a syringe, clear liquid sloshing around inside as if it's mocking me.

—Scratch that. This is *really* real.

I fall back a step. Christian steps into the doorway, blocking the only exit.

"No more running, Mila."

He's so fast, I barely register the sting in the side of my neck until the burn of whatever he'd injected me with slips through my veins.

I stumble the moment the room rushes around me, the edges of my vision instantly darkening. It feels like slowly slipping under the water, allowing it to rush over you and steal your senses one by one until there's nothing left.

Like drowning. Christian Cross feels like drowning.

"Chri-chri—"

I can't get the words out. My tongue feels heavy in my mouth. The world rushes around me, the ground tilting on its axis underneath me, and I sway, nearly crashing to the floor.

Christian catches me, arm around my waist, and walks me backward until the backs of my knees hit the bed behind me. I don't even realize I'm lying on my back until his eyes are over mine, consuming me.

The old, familiar scent of him washes over me.

Leather, whiskey and the forest mixed with that little bit of something mouthwatering that's completely him.

What used to mean safety now means sure death at the hands of the only man I've ever loved.

How egregiously poetic.

"Shhh . . ." he whispers, pressing a gentle kiss to the side of my face. I blink up at him through the tears in my eyes, his gaze consuming me. My voice gets caught in my throat, and I can feel myself sinking into the bed beneath me. "Let it all go, sweetheart."

He's here to make me pay for what I did to him.

Tears slip out of the corners of my eyes, and I fight the poison slipping through my veins with everything I've got, but it's no use. I can't move. All I can do is feel him as the darkness carries me away.

"I told you I would find you, Mila," he murmurs, brushing a

loose curl from my forehead. His eyes are darkly deranged. Maddeningly handsome but so chillingly calm it steals my breath away. Or maybe that's just the drugs he injected me with. "There's not a corner of this earth where you'll ever be able to hide from me."

Then everything fades to black.

———————

I'm dead.

That's the only explanation for the splitting migraine radiating through my temples.

My head feels like it was split right down the center, and when I open my eyes, it throbs even worse.

What the fuck happened?

The pain is the only thing that tells me I somehow managed to survive, and judging by the fact that I'm no longer staring at a stain on the ceiling that looks like Bob Marley, like the one at the motel, I'd say last night wasn't just some crazy-realistic dream.

Which . . . can only mean one thing.

I wiggle my hands and toes as the blood spreads through them. My legs and back are sore, like I haven't moved in days, and my mouth is dry like I've been sucking on sawdust.

My eyes water as I take in the rough timber ceiling, the soft, warm glow of a lamp on the nightstand, and the antique quilt covering me.

Was I kidnapped by Christian Cross, my former bodyguard and love of my life, or someone's sweet little grandma?

Somehow, I sit up, gazing around what can only be described as some kind of cabin straight out of a fantasy novel.

I'm in a bedroom I don't recognize, surrounded by the softest sheets I've ever felt before. Outside, the wind howls, and one glance at the window shows me it's pitch black with darkness.

Which brings me to my next problem.

He found me.

Not the one I was expecting, but *him*.

And now I'm fucked.

"I've got to get out of here," I whisper to myself, wincing in pain when I throw the covers off me and scoot to the edge of the bed. Either he spent the night using me as a punching bag after he injected me with whatever the hell was in that syringe, or I fell harder than I thought on the pavement.

My heart bottoms out in my chest when I stand, and the bed creaks under my weight. I listen for any sounds of footsteps, but none come. In front of me, a railing overlooks what has to be the first story of the cottage, and warmth radiates from below with the cackle of a fireplace.

I listen for any sign that he could be near, but I'm met with nothing but silence. My bag sits in the corner and I silently tiptoe over to it, lowering to grab my shoes off top. I slip them on my feet, gritting my teeth at the pain radiating through my shoulder. When I'm done, I sling the bag over my shoulder and start towards the stairs.

Only something stops me.

Shaky visions of the other night dance through my head. Opening the door to the one man I thought I'd never see again, standing outside my motel room.

Him injecting me with whatever he used to knock me out.

Waking up here, surrounded by his scent, but him being nowhere in sight.

It's a trap.

He wouldn't go through all the trouble of finding me just to let me run out in the dead of night after a nap.

Carefully, I drop my bag to the floor, backing away from the door. Kicking off my shoes, I sink back to the old mattress.

Will he kill me?

I shot him. I shot him and ran, and he swore he'd find me if it were the last thing he did.

"Welcome to the land of the living."

I jump, letting out a scream at the voice that sounds right behind me. I whirl so fast my hair slaps me in the face, a tangled mess of knots from sleeping on it for God only knows how long.

None other than Christian Cross sits in the chair beside the bed. Conveniently, the one area of the room I didn't glance at before I got up.

Seeing him now, in the flesh, is like seeing a ghost, and I can't describe the pain in my chest from the wicked gleam in his eyes.

Like he wants to hurt me.

"*You.*"

"Hello, little devil. Miss me?" He cocks his head, his gaze traveling over me with a dark glint in his deep blue eyes. It's been six months of running since I last saw him. Six months of wondering if he was alive and if the bullet I'd used to shoot him had killed him on that rooftop.

Tears sting in the backs of my eyes at the visions of that night on the hospital rooftop. Watching him lay there, helpless after I shot him and knowing there was nothing I could do to stop it.

He stands to his full height, a force to be reckoned with in the small cottage. Rippling muscles under a black T-shirt. Harsh jawline. Beautifully devastating eyes that shine in the glow of the bedside lamp. He's just as handsome as he's always been.

Only now, he's going to make me pay for what I did.

I stumble back, holding my hands out in front of me as a panic I've never experienced takes hold.

"Stay away from me," I warn, backing into the dresser and making it rattle from the impact. My voice is scratchy from how long I slept, and my mind is foggy like I'm just waking up from a year-long coma.

Hell, maybe I am, and I just don't know it. It would explain how sore my back is.

Christian chuckles, stepping towards me, and I back up, gripping the dresser for support because my legs threaten to give out on me.

"What's the matter, sweetheart?" He takes another step forward, and I realize I have nowhere left to run. "No gun to stop me this time?"

"Christian," I warn, pressing myself flat against the walls. Tears burn in my eyes, and in the dim lighting of the bedroom, he looks like a demon stalking towards me. "Please, just let me go."

He chuckles darkly, his eyes flashing with a caustic violence I'm not accustomed to. Not from him.

"I'm afraid I can't do that, Mila."

He rounds the bed, and I push off the wall, but he's faster, catching me around the waist and hauling me back into his front. I fight in his hold, a breathless cry leaving my lips, but he's too strong and has at least a foot or more of an advantage on me.

He tosses me on the bed and climbs over me, his body caging mine even as I fight him. He brings his hands up, and instinctively, I flinch, cowering from the blow I've subconsciously come to expect.

"Shhh . . ." he soothes gently, his hand instead brushing the hair back from my face. "I'm not going to hurt you."

Like a scared dog, shivers roll through me, and I bow my head to the side, shutting my eyes.

"I do-don't believe you," I manage to croak, fighting against the onslaught of voices battering at the inside of my head just from his body on mine, pinning me down.

Dirty little whore.

Look at all that blood.

Your tears are so beautiful, tinged in red.

I suck in a ragged breath, and his fingers slip over my face, down the scar on my jaw, then up to the one at my hairline.

"You left me on a rooftop to bleed out, Mila," he whispers, his face so close to mine, I can smell the mint and tobacco on his breath. "I told you I'd always find you."

"You don't understand," I whimper, but it's useless.

"I understand perfectly, little devil," he murmurs, dropping his lips to my ear. A shiver runs down my spine, and I'm more than a little embarrassed about the heat gathering in my stomach from the rough grain of his voice. "Now . . . you're going to tell me why."

"I can't," I breathe, shaking my head, but his fingers grip my chin, forcing my gaze to his. It's like staring into the center of a black hole. Humming silence and the promise of death loom in the depths of those eyes.

The same eyes I've laid awake at night thinking about. The same ones that used to look at me with a kind of adoration you only read about in romance novels and books like *Pride and Prejudice*.

Now, they hold nothing but bitter darkness.

"I never meant to hurt you," I whisper.

"Oh, but you did, baby." His voice has an edge to it I can't understand. This Christian isn't the one I fell in love with. This Christian is volatile. Deadly.

Not a care for anything in the world, let alone me. Probably not even himself.

"And now you're going to fix it."

"How?"

He cocks his head to the side, eyes glinting with dark amusement.

"Guess we'll see, won't we?"

I shake my head, tears slipping down my cheeks and onto the cotton sheets below, but he merely smirks.

"What do you want from me?"

"Hmm . . . What *do* I want from you?" he muses, his fingers slipping lower over my sternum where I know he can feel my racing heartbeat. "Tell me who you were running from, and I'll think about letting you go."

I stare at him, my pulse racing in my throat with uncertainty.

"Just tell me what you want, you freaking psychopath," I growl, fighting again against his hold, but it's no use. He's a foot taller than me and at least a hundred pounds of muscle heavier, especially after my lack of food in the last few months.

In a flash, his eyes darken to midnight, his gaze searing on my skin as he looms over me. His voice is low and soft, deadly calm, sending a shiver of fear through me.

Who is this man? This isn't the Christian Cross I left on the hospital roof all those months ago.

"Revenge."

My stomach turns, but even worse, my heart aches like it's being ripped out of my chest. I never wanted to hurt him. I never wanted to be the one to put that bullet in his chest.

"Is this about the rooftop?" I breathe, my voice catching in my throat. I knew that if he didn't die from what I did to him, he would hate me for it. I never expected him to find me, though. Not before *he* did.

"Is this about money?"

He brushes the hair back from my face, letting out a dark chuckle. "I've got enough money to buy anything in the world, Mila. What I want can't be bought."

In a fresh wave of anger . . . I fight against him, my hand connecting with his lip and my knuckles grazing along his teeth. It hurts, but I'm too busy processing what he said to give it any care.

"Fuck you!" I growl, bucking underneath him, but he's too big, and I'm out of breath. Am I that weak? "Get the hell off me!"

He simply takes my hands in his, pinning them above my head while I continue to give him everything I've got. His breathing is just as erratic as mine, but the bastard hasn't even broken a sweat.

"Don't mistake my kindness for weakness, Mila," he warns, brushing his nose along the side of my face, inhaling my scent like he's committing it to memory. "I don't tolerate temper tantrums."

"Get off *me*!" I spit, but he just laughs in my face.

"No."

"Are you insane?"

God, he has to be because the asshole laughs.

"What?" I challenge. His hand lets go, and he fists both my wrists in one of his hands. His free hand slips down, over the curves of my neck, then lower, to my stomach. "I shot you, and now you're just going to kidnap me and rape me? Use me to carry out whatever your sick little revenge plan is?"

His eyes light with dark amusement. "We both know if I wanted you, I wouldn't have to rape you, sweetheart. And unlike your stepdaddy, I prefer my women willing."

"Oh, how noble of you," I roll my eyes. His fingertips dance across the bare skin where my shirt has just barely ridden up above my jeans, and despite everything, heat settles in my core from the brush of his fingers. "I hate you."

"That's a shame," he murmurs, his hand sliding up my side and bringing goosebumps in their wake. "Because I *love* you," he taunts, throwing the exact words I'd said to him when I shot him back in my face.

"You're an *asshole*."

"So I've been told." His fingers graze my racing pulse in my throat before slipping up to tug my bottom lip from between my teeth. His gaze flicks from my eyes down to my lips before coming back.

"So, what? Why did you bring me here?"

He leans in, pressing his lips to my ear, and I hate that my body responds to his touch, heat gathering between my legs. "I told you, sweetheart. You're going to give me everything I've ever wanted."

"Christian, you can't be serious. You can't kidnap me."

"Oh, I think you'll come to understand exactly how serious I am." He pauses, looking down at me. I hate the amusement in his gaze. "You going to hit me again if I remove my hands?"

"Probably."

Shaking his head, he stands, towering over me. His dark stare bleeds into mine, stealing my breath.

"Welcome to hell, baby." His teeth glint wicked and sharp in a cruel smile. "I'll be your tour guide."

A ringing cuts through the throbbing pulse in my ears, and he smirks down at me, turning away to answer his phone. I listen to the sound of another man on the line, but I can't make out what he's saying.

Instead, I do the only thing I can think of and grab a dusty, hardcover bible resting on top of the nightstand.

And then I swing it at his head.

I catch him off guard, knocking him forward. He stumbles into the wall with a curse and drops his phone.

I don't stick around to see what he does next, though, taking off towards the stairs like a bat out of hell. I nearly pitch myself down the iron staircase in my flurry, and my ankle throbs with a dull pain, but I ignore it. I'll find somewhere once I'm out of here to lay low and lick my wounds later. For now, I have to run.

It takes a few moments before Christian's dark chuckle sounds from above and his footsteps sound on the floorboards near the stairs. He's not even running, but he manages to reach the bottom of the stairs just as I'm barreling towards what I hope to God is the front door and running into the night.

The cottage is small and in the wilderness, surrounded by trees at the edge of a large open field. From what I can see in the dark, there's not a single light in any direction and my only hope is that he didn't drag me out to some deserted island where I'll never be able to escape.

"Mila . . ." Christian's voice looms from the darkness, raising every hair on the back of my neck. "You're not going to get far."

My heart pounds in my chest, my mouth dry, but I don't stop.

I left my bag behind. My sweatshirt and my hat, my *fucking* shoes, but none of that matters if his only plan is to turn me over to God knows who when this is all over.

I'd rather freeze to death than ever see that man again.

"Little devil . . ." Christian calls, way too close for comfort when I push through the thick underbrush and into the trees. "Come back inside. You haven't eaten in days."

"Fuck off!" I yell back at him, my voice shrill with fear and the rushing wind around us. Why the hell is it so windy?

I push faster, forcing my legs to carry me through the heavy thicket when my foot catches on a rock, and I fall straight to the ground.

I groan the moment I land, my elbow erupting in pain. I lay there for a moment, sputtering as my body registers the sudden sound of his footsteps gaining on me.

He's going to catch me.

Hauling myself to my feet, I rush through the trees. Limbs scratch my face and snag my worn clothes, but I don't stop running.

Never stop running.

Unless, of course, you nearly run straight off a cliff overlooking jagged rocks below and the rough waves of what can only be the Pacific.

Oh my God.

He really did bring me to a deserted island.

Christian stops a few feet behind me, and when I turn, horror-struck to face him while the rush of adrenaline that was carrying me washes away like he'd doused me with a bucket of cold water.

"Told you, you wouldn't get far."

His voice is dark and full of malice. A deadly conviction that I am, without a doubt, completely and utterly fucked.

Christian steps into me, his hand coming up to wrap around my throat and tug me away from the edge of the cliff.

All five stages of grief slip through me before the only sensation

I can feel is sinking.

"We finally get that island vacation we always talked about," he sneers, and it's at that moment, nearly two days without food catches up with me, and everything goes black.

CHAPTER
Twelve
CHRISTIAN

She's silent while I carry her back to the cottage, her face pressed to my chest despite her blatant hatred towards me.

Not that I give a fuck.

She can hate me all she wants.

All that matters is that she's here, safe, and there's nowhere on this little island where she can run that I won't find her.

Being shot by the single most important person in your life has a way of helping you see the world through eyes of newfound clarity.

Instead of waiting for the world to be a better place, I should have locked her away and thrown away the key. I should have been there.

I won't make the same mistake twice.

The lighthouse and cottage loom up ahead of us through the trees. I step through the heavy thicket of underbrush, making my way across the clearing toward the glow of the front porch light.

Inside, I carry her straight into the bathroom. Her clothes are tattered and dirty, and her hair is matted from sleeping for nearly

She doesn't fight me when I sit her on the counter, crossing to the large copper clawfoot tub in the corner.

The cottage isn't much, but it has everything we need to survive. Heat, four walls, and modern plumbing. There's hardly any cell phone reception out here, and the only way to access the island is the service road, which, consequently, I would see before anyone ever made it across.

Not to mention the thick gate blocking out the outside world.

We're well and truly alone, and I can't say my cock doesn't harden at the knowledge that I get her all to myself for now.

I cut the water on, washing out the tub from years of dust and not being used. I should have had the cottage ready, but there was no guarantee I would find her when I did.

"What are you doing?"

"*You* are going to take a bath, and then you're going to eat like a normal fucking human being."

She glares at me, her cheeks red from the wind whipping at the cliff and the tears still on her face. I have half a mind to spank her ass for daring to go near it but concede to give her this one strike simply because she didn't know.

I stop up the tub and throw some soap under the water because we don't have bubbles on this island before returning to her.

"Take off your shirt."

"Excuse me?"

I fix her with a bored stare.

"Clothes off. Leave them in the sink. They're caked in mud."

She makes no move to remove anything and, instead, swallows over the lump in her throat.

"Mila, I need to check your ankle and the cut on your hip where you fell. That means either you remove your clothes, or I will."

"I'm fine," she argues, gripping the counter on either side of her.

I cock my head, stepping up in front of her. She quickly glances at the door before her tongue darts out to lick her lips, and she looks back at me. Like a rabbit caught in a trap while a wolf approaches, she searches for an escape, but as I told her on the cliff, there isn't one.

I reach for the hem of her shirt, and she jerks away from me.

"I can do it," she growls, pushing me away.

"Then do it."

Her cheeks flame, burning hot, while the water warms the small bathroom. It's not the cleanest because I haven't had time to clean it yet, but it's better than the mud coating the entire left side of her body.

When I brought her here, I only had time to change the sheets and split some firewood before she woke. I didn't want her waking up to an empty cottage alone and confused. Tomorrow, I'll fix the hole in the roof and the loose floorboard by the front door before she manages to hurt herself on something else.

"Can I have some space?" she asks, and I step back, leaning against the wall, and wait. She meets my gaze with a narrowed one. "Are you going to watch?"

I shrug. "I'm not going to look away if that's what you're asking."

Shaking her head, I watch the embarrassment course through her. She looks anywhere in the room but at me, hastily ripping the shirt over her head and dropping it to the floor.

It feels like a punch to the gut, seeing the pink scars marring the smooth skin of her stomach. The once clear skin, now littered with the carvings of a madman, wreaking havoc on her mind.

I grit my teeth to the point I fear they might break. My hands fists, lead shooting through my chest with the rage that slips over me like a mask.

I want to gut him. String him up by his useless cock until his weight rips it off of him.

Most of all, though, I don't want her to see my anger.

Brushing it off, I step forward and help her slip her leggings off until they land in a puddle on the floor.

I move to grab her ankle, and she tugs back out of my grasp, so I fix her with a look and reach for it again. It's swollen with a slight sprain, but she'll recover quickly.

I move onto the cut on her hip, where a dark purple bruise is forming. There was blood, but it's clotted over, and I doubt it'll bleed again. Reaching behind her, I open the medicine cabinet on the wall, finding a spider the size of my head instead of peroxide and a bandage, so I quickly shut it before Mila can see.

The last fucking thing I need right now is a spider meltdown.

Ignoring my dick pulsing in my jeans, I bend down between her legs to look in the cabinet below. Mila tries to pull back out of the way, her cheeks crimson, while I do my best not to stare at the thin piece of fabric shielding her from me.

If this is going to work, I need her salivating for me. Fucking aching with as much desire for me as I have for her. Until then, I have a feeling me and my fucking hand are going to become very well acquainted.

I find a first aid kit under the sink and grab it, avoiding what appears to be a dead mouse from the eighteenth century and straighten. I open up the kit and grab the peroxide. Mila winces when I pour it over the gash on her thigh, her hand instantly gripping mine.

We both pause, looking down at where her nails are digging into my skin. My cock strains against my jeans, begging me to step between her legs.

"It stings," she breathes, drawing her bottom lip between her teeth. In another life, I'd pull it free with my own and slip my tongue along hers to take her mind off what I'm doing to the cut along her leg.

"Stop hurting yourself," I murmur, cleaning the cut of any mud or debris she could have gotten in it when she fell.

"Are you . . . going to hurt me?" she asks, so quiet, I can barely hear her.

The pad of my thumb strokes over the smooth, bare flesh of her thigh, my other coming up to trace the rough edges of one of the words etched into her stomach.

"I've traveled three thousand miles to find you," I murmur, leaning in until my lips brush over her ear. She shivers, her body both straining away from me, but her nails dig deeper into my flesh to hold me there, hovering between her legs. "I'm going to fucking hurt you . . . but I'll make you beg for it."

I rip myself away from her before I can do something stupid. Like drop to my knees and show her exactly what I've been thinking about the last six months.

"Come here."

"I can do it."

She hops down from the sink, only to nearly collapse when her sprained ankle hits the floor.

Instinctively, I snatch her around the waist and turn her back to me. I grit my teeth when I see the heavy scar that spans the length of her spine.

My fucking girl . . .

"Let me, Mila," I murmur when she tries to prevent me from unhooking her bra. I keep my eyes down because I know she doesn't want to be seen by me right now and drop the bra to the pile on the floor before hooking my fingers in the material of her gray thong and dragging it down her legs.

There will be plenty of time to touch her later. When she wants it. For now, I'm content just having her in my space, even if she is being a little fucking headache.

When I'm done, I lift her into the tub, drop to my haunches beside her, and lather a washcloth with soap.

She shivers while I wash her, and neither of us mentions the tears that silently slip down her cheeks while I do.

And for the first time in nearly a year, things don't feel so fucking bleak.

"This place is disgusting," Mila grumbles, emerging from the bathroom as I'm setting out two bowls on the table.

I pause at the sight of her, the blood roaring in my veins when I see her in my sweats and baggy T-shirt. Wet hair cascading down her back in golden ringlets. Her cheeks are rosy from the warm water, and her soft gray eyes shining in the dim lighting overhead.

Fucking divine.

"As opposed to the five-star resorts you were hiding out in?"

"I was *not* hiding out."

"So, this whole fake identity, starving yourself act was for fun?"

She glares at me. I glare right the fuck back.

I take a seat, motioning for her to sit across from me. "Sit."

"I'm not a dog."

"No, but you are a b——"

"Don't you *dare* finish that sentence, Christian Cross," she growls, and I stifle a chuckle at her defensiveness.

"Brat."

Her stomach growls between us, and her cheeks blush a dark pink. I cock a brow at her, waiting for her to make up some other excuse as to why she can't just eat the food she clearly needs.

"I'm only sitting because I'm tired. Not because you told me to."

"Noted," I murmur, watching her sink into the chair across from me.

Honestly, it probably tastes like shit. I'm a shit cook. It's just beef stew, but it's the best I could do on short notice. Plus, I knew this place would be chilly after being abandoned for so long.

"Where are we?" Mila asks, swirling her spoon around her bowl. I feel like I'm babysitting a fully grown toddler.

"America."

"That's comforting."

"Somewhere in Washington. Shipwreck Island. The nearest town is ten miles away. Not that it matters."

She rolls her eyes, taking a bite of soup.

Fucking finally.

"That's comforting," she grumbles.

"Should be. You stirred up quite the mess back home."

"Home," she snorts. "What's home?"

"Your mother and siblings, for one," I point out, and she frowns down at her bowl. "Did you ever stop to consider them before you pulled your little disappearing act?"

"I did what I had to do," she says, pretty gray eyes meeting mine over the table. "Just because you don't understand doesn't mean it would have changed things."

"Try me."

"I'd rather not."

"You can play the victim all you want, Mila. Either way, you'll still be stuck on this island with me until I get what I want."

"And what is it you want?"

"Revenge."

She rolls her eyes, chuckling humorlessly at her stew.

"Of course. Revenge against who?"

I smirk, cocking my head to the side. "I'd rather not say."

She shakes her head, closing her eyes as if she can will herself off this island. Unfortunately, for her, there's about half a mile of rough current stretched between us and land. She's not getting away from me that easily.

"So, you brought me out here to some deserted island with a cottage that leaks, no supplies, and no way out?"

"Oh, there's a way out. Just not for you."

"Of course, there's not. Anything else I need to be aware of? Any bodies stashed away where I might happen upon them?"

"None that have seen the light of day in the last hundred years," I retort. "Though, you're welcome to make friends all you want with whatever ghosts linger around here."

She smiles sweetly, her tone dipped in venom.

"I might just do that. The company's a little lacking."

I let her little dig go and move on to the next order of business.

"Tomorrow, we will have visitors. Try anything, and their deaths are on you."

"How romantic of you," she muses, finishing her bowl and pushing it back from her. "How about we murder some puppies while we're at it?"

"Puppies are in short supply around here unless, of course, you've got them stashed away in that Mary Poppins bag of yours."

"Fresh out," she chimes, crossing her arms over her chest. "There are plenty of pigs around, though."

"Says the woman who just rolled around in the mud outside."

"I wouldn't have fallen in the mud if someone hadn't kidnapped me and dragged me to a deserted island for their little revenge plot."

Oh, sweetheart . . . you have no idea that things I have in store for you.

"I wouldn't have to kidnap you if you hadn't shot me and left me for dead on a rooftop so you could run off."

She looks like she wants to stab me, but there are no knives on her side of the table. I can't lie and say it's not intentional.

"Why not just kill me and get it over with?"

"As it turns out, I have other plans for you."

She rolls her eyes, chuckling humorlessly.

"Right, silly me . . . far be it from me to believe you actually cared."

She can think whatever she wants. In the morning, she'll still be waking up under my roof in my bed, whether she likes it or not.

"Good, now that that's out of the way, who were you running from? Besides the obvious."

"I wasn't running from *you*," she grits, crossing her arms over her chest and throwing herself back in the chair. I don't miss the wince she makes. "And it's not like it matters anymore, right? I'm on a deserted island in the middle of nowhere."

"I'll find out, Mila. And when I do, you better hope they're already dead."

She's scowling at me, but I don't miss how her eyes flick down to my lips quickly as if she thinks she can hide it. The way her chest heaves with each heavy breath.

The way her tongue darts out to lick her bottom lip . . .

Fucking hell.

I force myself to step back and carry our dishes to the sink. I'll wash them tomorrow. I'm tired. Mila's tired. Fuck, how long has it been since I've gotten more than a couple hours of sleep in the front seat of a car?

"I'll take the couch. You can have the bed."

She doesn't respond.

It's probably best that way.

"I'll help you upstairs."

"I can do it," she grumbles, rising from her chair on unsteady legs. I concede to let her limp her way upstairs. If she wants to be stubborn, she can be stubborn in all the extra time it takes to walk the short distance by herself. Maybe then she'll think twice about it.

I watch her go, my mind running rampant with all the questions I have yet to find answers to. The moment she's gone, I pull out my cell, but there's no service. I'll get a cell booster soon, but for now, I shove it back in my pocket, my mind working overtime.

I have her now, but it's only a matter of time before someone comes looking. Shipwreck Island may be one of the most reclusive locations in the States, but that doesn't mean it will stay this way.

Especially not with the hit out on her pretty little head.

Unfortunately, I can't change it tonight, so I make my way towards the bathroom, grabbing the trashcan as I go, and focus on the things I *can* change.

Guess I'll start with the gargantuan fucking spider in the medicine cabinet.

CHAPTER
Thirteen

MILA

I never pictured my prison being an island in the middle of the Pacific. I also didn't think it would smell like a mothball's asshole, either.

Christian is nowhere to be found when I wake, and I'm grateful. After last night, I woke up this morning thinking, surely, I must have dreamed it all.

One look around the dusty cottage told me that was, unfortunately, not the case.

I'm sore, my ankle hurts, and I feel like I could sleep for a week.

When the skies outside brighten, I force myself to climb out of bed, nearly tripping over Christian's Gerald the Giant sweatpants that *have* to be sixteen sizes too big for me in my attempt to make it downstairs.

Once I finally reach the bottom, I can hear the sound of the shower running in the bathroom, and my stomach dips to my toes at the thought.

Last night really happened.

Then, I find toast on a plate on the table with a jar of homemade strawberry jam beside it. The note beside the plate has one simple word, but it's enough to bring tears to my eyes.

Eat.

Looking at that stupid jar of strawberry jam, my throat tightens.

It's just a jar of jam, but it's also so much more. He remembered. One simple conversation years ago, but somehow he knew. He may have kidnapped me, he may be plotting to use me for revenge, but there's part of him that still cares, even if he won't say it.

That's not exactly a good thing.

I eat my toast in silence, surveying the small cottage interior. In another life, it would be cozy. The rough oak walls and the timbered floors. The stone fireplace with bits of sparkling rock glinting under years of soot.

Cobwebs hang from the corners, a fine layer of dust covering every surface. The décor is old and functional, but it holds a certain charm. Someone lived a life here. Maybe they built a life here.

I'm just finishing when a knock sounds at the door. My stomach drops, my hand paused with the last bite halfway to my mouth.

My first thought is that we're on a deserted island and that whoever's at the door must be a ghost coming to play a cruel joke on the strange new woman hiding out in its house.

My second thought is one of slight relief.

Christian said we would have visitors.

Maybe it's the devil, come to drag me away from this island. Surely, hell would seem like a tropical vacation compared to spending eternity in Christian's frosty presence.

I blow out a deep breath, rising from my chair, albeit shakily, because my ankle is still sore from biting it in the mud last night. A fact I refuse to tell Christian, no matter how painful it is, because fuck him.

Hobbling my way to the door, I pull it open, finding an older gentleman I don't recognize and June standing on the cobbled front steps.

So, I didn't dream it . . . June was helping Christian.

Traitor.

"Oh, hello," the man greets, an underlying Irish accent cloaking his voice. "You must be Mila."

I clear my throat, glancing nervously between them.

"Um . . . hello."

"Oh, Rudy, she's obviously terrified. Poor thing looks sickly."

Okay, now that was rude.

June steps up in front of Rudy, her smile gentle despite her crude assessment.

"Hi, dear. I know I said my name was June, but I'm Paulina. I'm happy to see you made it okay."

As if I had a choice.

"This is Rudy, the caretaker of this island and a good friend of mine."

"Pleased to meet you," Rudy says, holding out his hand. I don't take it. After a moment of uncomfortable silence, Paulina elbows him, and he drops it back to his side. It's then I notice the cloth sacks behind them filled with groceries and toiletries.

"It's okay," Paulina says. "You don't need to be afraid of us. We're here to help."

As the kidnappee in this situation, I've got to say, it's pretty hard to believe her.

"'Bout time someone fixed this old heap up," Rudy grumbles, looking up at the awning above him. "I've been waiting for the Pacific to wash this place away for years, but it refuses to die."

"Stop it, you'll scare her," Paulina scolds, reaching out to pat my hand. Instinctively, I jump back.

"Careful," a voice sounds behind me, and prickling awareness slips up the back of my neck. "That one bites."

Oh, great. His royal asshole has arrived.

"Christian," Paulina smiles.

I back up to move out of the way, unfortunately running right into the very naked, very *wet* chest of Christian.

I jump when I collide with him, my gaze latching onto the tattoo on his chest and the single water droplet that slips overtop the ink, all the way down to the towel wrapped dangerously low around his hips.

What do they call those lines in men's hips? The ones that make women go feral?

When my gaze rakes over the hard lines of his abs, slipping up his chest and finally meeting his piercing stare trained on mine, my mouth runs dry.

"Put some clothes on," Paulina orders, hauling her bags into the house and passing Christian like she sees well-defined six packs rippling with tattoos and water daily. "You'll catch a cold."

"It's fifty degrees out," Christian retorts, shutting the door behind Rudy when he enters and follows Paulina to the kitchen table. I keep my distance and try not to stare at his butt underneath the towel when he steps over to join them.

"All the more reason to get that roof fixed," Rudy grunts, removing things from the bags. At least the cottage is outfitted with a fridge, even if it does look like it stepped right out of the nineteenth century. "Winter will be here before you know it."

"The boy just got here, Rudy," Paulina says, handing off items to Rudy to put away. "And judging by the state of *that* one, he's been busy."

Standing in a pair of Christian's giant sweats and one of his T-shirts, cuts and bruises on my face, and a sprained ankle, I'm sure she's right. I blush at her measurement of me, wrapping my arms around my chest as if I can shield myself from her meticulous gaze.

—And maybe hide the fact that my nipples are hard as diamonds.

Clearly, it doesn't do much to help my case when all three

people in the room lock eyes with me in my newfound rooted spot in the corner by the door.

"Oh, sweet thing, I'm sorry." Paulina drops whatever she was holding and makes her way across the room, but I back up, stumbling into the wall on pure instinct. My heart ricochets in my chest, my throat threatening to close with her outstretched hands reaching for me.

I don't know these people. In the last week, I've been stalked secretly, stalked openly, chased by a group of dangerous men, watched someone get run over by a killer Challenger, drugged and kidnapped.

Oh, and I fell in the mud and probably sprained my ankle because my psychopathic ex-boyfriend was chasing me.

How willing would *you* be to let some random woman—*who*, by the way, sold you out—pull you in for a hug?

"Look, I picked something out especially for you," she says, reaching for a separate bag. She holds it out to me, but I can't bring myself to take it. Not because I'm not grateful but because a sickening heaviness slips through my stomach that threatens to bring my toast back up.

Paulina must sense my unease because she concedes and pulls it out of the bag for me.

"Christian said you like books, so I picked up a couple I found at the store."

Warmth pools behind my eyes at the cover of the book on top. The name scribbled in elegant writing at the bottom one I know all too well.

"I didn't mean to upset you," Paulina says softly, but I can't take my eyes off my sister's name on the front cover of a new book I hadn't even realized she'd written. We used to sit and talk about her writing for hours, coming up with stories together, naming characters.

"Mila's had a rough couple of days. Let's give her some space,"

Christian murmurs, his voice rising above the ones in my head telling me that I'm a worthless sister who missed the birth of her first nephew, book releases, my other sister's new store opening, and countless other milestones.

Milestones I'll never be able to get back.

"Thank you," I say, my voice sounding small even to my own ears. I hate it. I force myself to unwrap my arms from around myself and take the books, which puts a smile on Paulina's face. "I love reading," I add, just because she brought me a nice gift, and here I am crying all over it.

"Of course, dear," she says quietly, and there's a heaviness in the room now that I can feel everyone's eyes on me. "You just let me know when you're done with those, and I'll bring more."

I give her a gentle nod, trying to inconspicuously clear my throat of the lump that's formed there. Thankfully, Rudy saves me by launching into a list of things that need to be fixed around the island.

"And that boat. Get rid of it."

"Oh, what's he going to do with it, Rudy? It's not like he can haul it off the island," Paulina chimes, walking back over to the table.

"Sink the fucker."

"Language," she chides, and the two continue to remove items from their bags and place them on the table.

In the meantime, Christian meets my gaze, noticing me still attempting to become one with the oak paneling behind me.

He holds out his hand with a bottle of my favorite shampoo, and my stomach tightens.

Carefully and as silently as possible, as if I can avoid drawing attention to myself, I cross the small space between us, placing my books on the table and taking the shampoo.

I haven't had good shampoo in ages.

And cue another thing I'm crying about because this psychopathic Mila-napper remembers things about me that even I can't.

Christian and I stare at each other, and the air hums with electricity. Warmth settles deep in my stomach and makes my toes tingle.

Warmth that will undoubtedly only break my heart in the end.

Even so, it's one small truce on a long list of the many fucked up problems between us.

—But it's a start.

Christian retreats to the bedroom upstairs for a moment to put on some clothes while I hang back and put things in the fridge for Paulina when she hands them to me.

Thank God because my body was starting to get confused. For a moment, I was worried that I was actually *enjoying* the vision of Christian in nothing but a towel.

Then, he comes downstairs fully clothed in a pair of jeans that should be illegal on a butt as nice as his and a black T-shirt under a flannel, and I realize, with despair, that it wasn't the towel at all. It's just him.

Someone save me from myself.

"I'm having some things delivered within the next couple days," Christian says, completely oblivious to the little X-rated film my mind is conjuring against my will staring him. "I'll pick them up once we're settled here."

"Of course," Paulina winks at me. "Just gives us another excuse to come out here."

"One thing you don't need is excuses," Rudy grunts, but Paulina ignores him.

"It's no trouble."

"I'll come in and get it. I don't want you running back and forth for us. We're just trying to get set up here."

"Oh, nonsense," Paulina says. "Rudy just wants to come out here and muck about. You know how old men get."

"I'm not old. I'm age-challenged," Rudy smirks, wagging his brows at me where I stand behind Christian's shoulder. I don't know why. Right now, he's just the lesser of two evils.

Crazy person I *know* versus potentially crazy people I *don't*.

"Well, why don't *we* stay behind and help you get this place in order?"

"No, you've done enough," Christian says, shaking his head. "I'll clean the place up."

"I can help." My voice must be startling because everyone turns to stare at me at once. I hang back against the fridge, awareness slipping through me like an electric current.

Christian is the first to speak up, breaking the silence.

"Mila and I will clean up," he corrects, nodding to the dry goods laid out on the table in front of him. "You two have done enough."

On day one of my captivity, Christian and I barely speak, save for dinner when he pushes another bowl of beef stew in front of me and tells me to . . . "*eat*".

On day two, I spend the day limping around while he's off doing whatever it is he does when he's avoiding me and cleaning what I can with my ankle still sore.

By day three, I'm in full cleaning mode and halfway through Bailey's book, so I'm actually *glad* when he leaves.

The moments he's here are tense, filled with silences my brain tells me to fill with useless words that my mouth won't allow me to speak.

Neither of us has addressed the elephant in the room. The fact that he still hasn't told me why I'm here, and I still haven't told him why I shot him.

It's a conversation I would rather not have, even though a part of me always knew it was inevitable.

How do you explain to someone that you didn't want to hurt them? That doing so was the only way to save their life?

That watching the blood ooze out of the wound in his shoulder still haunts my nightmares?

That night weighs heavily on my mind while I scrub every nook and cranny of the cottage, down to the dead mouse under the bathroom sink and what I *think* was once a sac of potatoes that's evolved into a self-sustained bundle of rotted roots.

I clean the cabinets and the fridge. I even take apart all the drawers and wash every dish. I scrub the rough floors on my hands and knees, and I manage to finagle two broomsticks taped together with ancient duct tape I find in the closet off the kitchen to get the ceiling.

By the time I'm finished, the place sparkles, and I've finished Bailey's book.

Life would be great . . .

Except it's not.

I clean because I have nothing else to do, so when I run out of cleaning, I start walking. I'm a walking conundrum, a fact that's not lost on me in my stewing as I walk the entire island . . . twice.

Today is like any other day. Christian left early this morning, and he's been hammering away at the roof since, replacing busted tiles on not only the cottage but the old lighthouse that stands proudly overlooking the jagged rocks below.

I'll admit, a tiny sliver of me wishes him to fall, but then the instant guilt washing through me quickly dismisses the idea. As much as I want to, I can't hate him. At least, not all of him.

He may have left me. He may have promised me the world and then broke my heart the moment I gave it to him. He may have even kidnapped me with the intent to exact revenge on a man who tried to *buy* me like a prized breeder pig at an auction.

He's also the same man who remembered I would *only* eat toast with strawberry jam from a single conversation we'd had years ago and my favorite shampoo. The one who looked at my scars and didn't let me see how disgusted they made him. Who washed me with as much care as you would a baby and then force-fed me his godawful beef stew.

"It's not magic," Christian calls from his spot, leaning against the broken-down fence post in the front of the cottage. I see he must be taking a break from being *Bob the Builder*. "No matter how many times you walk it, shit never changes."

I throw him a finger over my shoulder, and even though my feet are tired, I start the trek again, just because he's pissed me off.

He shakes his head, chuckling under his breath and returns to his hammering while I make my way back towards the trees.

Shipwreck Island is fully equipped with everything you'd ever need. Well . . . except for a way out. A barn sits overtop the cliffs, the center taken up by a massive boat that I'm betting is the one Rudy spent twenty minutes talking about how to sink the other day. The lighthouse is fully operational, but it's no longer in commission. Why, I don't know.

There's another, smaller shop with every ancient tool you can think of and a cellar that looks like it stepped right out of *The Shining* off the house.

My favorite place, though, is the greenhouse.

It's made of stained glass, green and shining in the sun. A few panes are missing, but otherwise, it's in remarkably good shape for the rough weather of the island. Inside is filled with weeds, and though I've never been able to grow a single thing and have killed every plant I've ever come into contact with, I'd love to plant a garden of wildflowers inside and watch it grow.

I pass by it, though, because what's the point in cleaning it out? It's not like I'll be staying here. Not permanently, anyway. Whatever Christian has in store for me, I doubt it lies in the greenhouse.

So, I walk.

And then I walk some more.

By the time I reach the other side of the island, I'm ready for a break, so I drop my ass on the rocks, looking out over the sea. If you squint really hard and cock your head at a forty-five-degree angle, you can just make out land.

If I grew a mermaid tail and bulked up the muscles of an Olympic diver, I might just be able to cross a quarter of the straight.

Something tells me that's precisely why Christian picked this island. Close enough to get supplies out here.

Too far for me to be stupid enough to swim it.

Did I mention I hate him?

I blow out a breath, watching a leaf fall to the ground from above. It's September, which means the trees will be changing soon. Most of the trees on the island are Washington pines, but the few oaks dispersed in the forest are starting to lose their very first leaves to the chill in the air.

Something tells me, if I were a leaf, I'd be the first to go.

Listening to the wind rustle, the leaves kick up around me, drifting out over the ledge. It's the same ledge I almost tumbled over the other night, complete with jagged rocks and certain death below.

It takes me a solid few seconds to realize the leaves don't *stop* rustling when the wind does, though.

I pause, ice slipping down my spine, and my first thought is to scream. Something tells me Christian wouldn't let me get far enough away that he couldn't hear me if I were in danger—collateral and all—but the moment I open my mouth to try, the sound gets caught in my throat.

I stumble back, catching myself before I make a grave mistake and plunge to my—well, grave.

"You're not funny," I snap, looking all around me for the source of the sound.

Who am I kidding? Unless a rogue seal made it up here, it has to be Christian. There's no one else around.

But . . . seals are a lot louder than that, and whatever it is, it doesn't stop.

"You don't scare me, Christian."

Okay, he actually *is* scaring me right now, but I'll be damned if I let him know that.

"Damnit, asshole, get out here or leave me alone," I bark, annoyance flaring in my chest.

Imagine my surprise when Christian barks back.

I pause, feeling both relief and despair when a thin, injured wolf hops out of the brush, holding his paw up and surveying me for danger.

He's soaking wet, his wiry black fur matted and clumped with dead leaves. There's white around his face, making him look like a ghost. He hunkers down as if he's afraid I might hit him, his big brown eyes staring up at mine in fear.

"Oh my God," I breathe, sinking to the moss-covered ground. "It's okay. I'm sorry. I didn't mean to scare you."

He gives a subtle wag of his tail and backs up when I inch closer. I stay low, holding out my palm for him to sniff.

"It's okay. I won't hurt you."

His eyes tell me he doesn't believe me, and I understand. I wouldn't trust a random human, either.

"How did you get out here? Surely you didn't swim all this way?"

I close the short distance between us, my knees wet through the material of Christian's sweatpants, but I pay it no mind. Gently as I can, I reach out and stroke the top of his head, and though he jerks under my palm, he doesn't run.

"You must be starving," I whisper, petting his crusted fur. "And cold. "

I could take him back to the cabin, but there's no guarantee Christian will let me keep him. If he finds a wild wolf, he'll probably lay an egg. He'll shoot him if he tries to bite either one of us, no matter how scared or hurt the poor dog is.

Sometimes, fear makes us do irrational things. I'm a living

testament to that.

"Guess what Christian doesn't know won't hurt him . . ." I murmur, stroking the top of the dog's head. "At least, I think."

Standing, I dust off the front of the flannel coat Christian had made me wear before I left the house.

"Come on. I know somewhere you can be warm."

CHAPTER
Fourteen

CHRISTIAN

Mila Carpenter somehow always manages to find herself in danger. Or maybe danger finds her.

Either way, she's going to be the fucking death of me.

Following Rudy and Paulina's departure, we spend the next four days in near silence, avoiding each other as much as possible and fixing shit around the island.

Mila sticks to the indoors, cleaning up the years of dust and animal debris. When she's not, she's walking the island. I stay outside, tending to the holes in the roof, replacing broken lights and otherwise, finding anything I can fucking do so I don't have to spend any more time than is absolutely necessary in her intoxicating cloud of honey and vanilla and soft fucking smiles that makes think irrational shit.

I've jacked off more times than I can count in the last week, and while that would usually be enough, it just pisses me off and leaves me feeling like a fucking creep, dreaming of a girl who can't even stand to look at me half the time, let alone be in the same room with

she's not just as drawn to me as I am her, but she can't hide the pretty little blush on her cheeks when I catch her staring at me. How her gaze lingered on my abs when I stepped out of the shower in just a towel the other day.

She can't *hide* from *me*, and she hates it.

Whether she's in Los Angeles, Wichita, or at the bottom of the fucking ocean, she's mine. I'll fucking find her.

She's my obsession. My own personal brand of heroin, created to ruin me.

From the moment I laid eyes on her, I knew I was fucked. There's always been this deeply rooted part of me with the need to protect her, even if I didn't understand it at the time.

Now, that time has come, and even if she doesn't understand my need for revenge, she will someday. She'll hate me for it, but we don't all get happy endings.

Least of all, Mila and me.

"I'm going into town."

"When will you be back?" Mila asks quietly from her place on the old couch. I'm surprised she got it as clean as she did.

"A few hours. You have everything you need, and if there's an emergency, I left a cell phone on the table." I hold up my hand when her eyes light up. She didn't think I'd be stupid enough to leave her an actual phone, did she? "Don't get excited. It only contacts me."

She purses her lips, opening up her book again.

"I think I'd rather take my chances with whatever mongrel comes knocking."

Little brat.

"Suit yourself."

She doesn't respond, choosing to ignore me instead.

It's probably for the best.

I start towards the door, but her voice rings out behind me, causing me to stop.

"How are you getting there and back? A quick walk along the bottom of the ocean? I heard vampires don't need to breathe. You know, because they're not human."

"The gate works just as well."

Her eyes widen around the edges before they narrow to slits.

"Before you get any ideas, I also have the only key and it's ten feet tall."

Her lips purse and I grin.

Yeah, nothing to say to that.

"Need anything while I'm out?"

She returns to her book. I notice she's rereading Bailey's most recent release for the second time. I'm just glad Paulina was able to find it.

"A bullet."

"I'll see what I can do," I mutter dryly, stepping out and slamming the door shut behind me.

When my phone rings, I'm just pulling to a stop in front of the path that leads to the island. Looking down at the name that pops up on the screen, I debate on not answering, but I figure I've let her suffer enough.

"Hello?"

"So, *now* you answer," she scoffs, and I can almost *feel* her roll her eyes from here. "Why are you avoiding me?"

"I'm not avoiding you." *I'm avoiding everyone.*

"Bull. You know I've been trying to get ahold of you for weeks?"

I do know. In fact, I've pressed the ignore button on every single call. The last time I spoke to her, I was sitting outside one of Mila's little homes away from home, watching a man try to break into one of the cars parked out front. That was two months ago.

"Levi's avoiding me. You're avoiding me. Dad's *dying*. Did you all forget we have a business to run?"

Guilt washes through me, and I scrub a hand over my face. My sister's the middle child of the Cross siblings and, consequently, the one who got stuck running the lodge since our father fell ill. Not that she doesn't love it, but the lodge is huge, and Bella's always been one for dramatics.

Still . . . I should be there. At least for moral support. Especially with our dad lying in his suite, dying of the cancer that's infected his body.

Bella—not one to be silenced—continues to read me the riot act.

"Do you know how hard it is to run this lodge? People constantly asking question after *stupid* question. And guess what? I have to have *allll* the answers, because if I don't, then everyone's mad at me."

"You're right."

"It's like you're just figments of my imagination, and I'm losing my mind, and let me tell you, Christian Cross, no one likes a psycho in the hospitality world. . . wait . . . What?"

"You're right, Bella," I sigh, looking out at the lights of Shipwreck Island. "I'm sorry I haven't been there."

I can tell she's surprised because she actually falls silent.

"Oh . . . well . . . I know I am," she says with an air of aloofness in her tone. I stifle a chuckle. Sometimes, she reminds me so much of our mother; it's uncanny.

"What about the Founder's Day banquet? Are you at least coming to that?"

"I'm not a founder."

"Christian," she groans. "You can't make me go through that alone. You know I hate Founder's Day."

"You're in charge. Why not just skip it?"

"Because it brings in a *ton* of revenue, which, in case you forgot, we need. Or do you want to have to get a real job again?"

"I have a real job," I reply.

"Oh, really. And what is it? Another six years in LA doing God only knows what?"

"Yak grooming in Southern Montana," I reply without missing a beat, and she scoffs. I can almost hear her roll her eyes. "You should try it sometime."

"Yeah, I'll take your word for it."

"I'll take your word for it. You know, if I didn't know better, I'd say you guys are hitmen."

"Don't be ridiculous. You really think Levi could keep it a secret for this long?"

Our brother, the middle child, has a knack for running his mouth about anything he thinks will land him in a woman's bed. I have a feeling, being a hitman, would be one of those things.

"Fine," she grumbles, falling silent on the line.

"Bella?"

She lets out a shaky breath. I know she's lonely. I know she hates that we left her at home to handle the lodge on her own. I also know she's well taken care of and protected there.

"He's dying, Christian . . ." she says softly, and I can hear the tears in her voice.

"I know."

"You should see him. Before . . . his mind is completely gone."

I grit my teeth, my hand tightening on the phone. Seeing my father is the last thing I want. We've never gotten along, especially after my mother died.

He was always a dick. Harsh and demanding, even when Mom's death was fresh. He was hardest on Levi, but I think it's just because he knew he couldn't control me and that, eventually, I grew too big for him to hit. That's when he turned to my youngest brother, and I regret not killing him when I had the chance.

Now, he's a husk of who he once was and not even able to go to the bathroom by himself, let alone hit anyone. He's just a decrepit old man, dying alone in his overpriced bed in the lodge my mother's father built from the ground up while Bella runs things there. Getting his ass wiped by a nurse who hates him and couldn't care less if he died tomorrow.

Where Mom was a bright, shining light in our family, Dad was the darkness that snuffed that light out.

I guess my biggest fear in life, if I wanted to be truthful, is turning out just like him, so I do whatever I can to never have to face that version of myself.

I'm not sure I could live with it.

"I'll see what I can do," I murmur. "I've got a few things to finish up before I come home." *As soon as Mila's not waking up in a cold sweat every night.*

Bella is as far removed from both Levi's work and mine as humanly possible. Not that I've *been* working. I haven't worked a real job in an entire year because I've been too busy chasing after the little blonde brat who waits for me beyond the water.

I guess it does pay to be a billionaire's son, sometimes. Even if I don't want anything to do with the money or the lodge that reaped it.

"Christian . . ." Bella starts, concern in her voice. "I want us to be a family. A *real* family."

"We are a family," I reply, even if I know what she means. "I'll always have your back. Even if you don't see it."

"I want us to be a family that spends time together."

I look across the water, watching the steady flicker of the lights in the cottage window.

"We will be. Soon."

She starts to argue her point, but I cut her off.

"I've got to go. I'll talk to you soon."

I hang up before she can respond, gritting my teeth while I start the car back up. Lead fills my chest at the thought of another silent night, sitting in front of the fire until I can't keep my eyes open anymore. Watching . . . Waiting . . . while the little blonde upstairs cries in her sleep.

If she knew what I'd do for her, she'd be fucking terrified of me. Maybe I should tell her. End this dumbass idea in my head that I can ever give her what she fucking deserves.

Unfortunately . . . I'm not that selfless.

And I'm fucking obsessed.

CHAPTER
Fifteen

MILA

I never thought the simple sound of a door closing would send a shiver down my spine until this very moment.

I've been cooking—a real meal. I wanted to do something nice for Christian since he took care of me. I mean, not that he doesn't have to, he literally kidnapped me . . . I just know as far as captivity goes, this situation could be worse.

And . . . maybe I also wanted to find a bit of common ground between us.

"You've been busy," he murmurs from behind me, and a shiver of awareness slips up my spine.

My stomach twists uncomfortably.

"I . . . thought you might be hungry."

Turning around, I find him leaning against the door. His eyes sweep over my bare toes, up my legs covered in his sweats, and to another one of his T-shirts I'm wearing. Something dark flashes across his gaze before that look of indifference slides into place, but I saw it.

Maybe I mean something more to him than he's willing to let on. For some reason, the thought makes my heart flutter.

Idiot.

"Looks good," he says, stepping into the kitchen and going to the liquor cabinet on the wall. He gets out a decorated crystal lowball glass and a wine glass before filling both while I turn away to hide the blush on my cheeks. By the time I'm setting our plates on the table, he's returning with our drinks, and I'm actually grateful for the wine he offers me.

When we sit at the table on opposite sides, a silence falls over the room that's impossible to ignore.

"Did you . . . get everything you needed?" I ask, taking a bite of chicken even though I can't taste it over the nerves fluttering in my stomach.

"You could say that," he murmurs, taking a bite while I watch him. If it's awful, he doesn't show it.

We sit in silence for a moment, both of us too engrossed in our own thoughts to pay attention to each other. At least, I am.

"Spit it out, Mila."

I take a drink of the wine, and I'm not surprised that it's delicious. Seems like everything he gives me is laced with shit that makes me never want to leave.

Except for that awful beef stew.

"Are . . . are you going to kill me?"

He doesn't move, save for the one minuscule tick in his jaw.

"Jesus Christ," he murmurs under his breath, sitting back in his chair. He grabs his whiskey, downing the glass, and pours a second.

"It's just that . . . If you do, could you not tell my mother?"

"Mila," he mutters gruffly.

"No, this is important."

"No, the fuck it's not. I'm not going to kill you."

Tears well in my eyes, but they don't fall . . . for once.

That's not the answer I thought I was going to receive.

"So, what are you going to do to me, then?"

He stares at me long and hard, like he's contemplating throwing me off the cliff out behind the cottage. Maybe it would be for the best. Let me float to Timbuktu, where I can live out my days with all the other degenerate runaways.

"Why all the questions?"

"Why all the evasive non-answers?"

"Because regardless of what you think about it, you're stuck here."

"Yeah, making friends with the dust bunnies and the giant spiders," I grumble, rolling my eyes.

"Keep rolling your eyes at me," he warns, his voice gruff. "See what happens."

"Fine," I say, stabbing a potato a little too hard because I'm picturing his head instead. "We'll move on. What is your job?"

"I'm not answering any more of your useless questions."

I swear to God.

"Then, I'll starve myself until you do."

Just to get my point across, I shove my plate back from me.

He wants to be stubborn? He will soon find out I wrote the fucking *book* on stubbornness.

"Mila, eat the fucking food."

I just stare at him.

"You're acting like a child."

Cue more staring.

"Jesus Christ," he sighs, rubbing a hand over his face. I'm happy to know I'm getting under his skin. Serves the asshole right. "Fine. I worked for the FBI."

"FBI? So, you were undercover like Logan?" Last year, my new brother-in-law went undercover to bring my stepfather down. He also fell in love with my sister in the process, but in my opinion, he never stood a chance. I saw the way he looked at her. Like she was the only woman to ever walk the surface of this planet.

He was doomed from the start.

"I was," Christian says, his tone clipped.

"Why did it end?"

"Because I said it did."

"That's not an answer."

"And yet, it's the only one you're going to get."

I almost roll my eyes, then think better of it.

"So, you came to work for Marcus. Were you and Logan working together or something?"

"Something like that."

If I were a brave woman—which I'm not—I would kick him in the shin.

"How can you afford all this if you only worked for the FBI? Surely, they don't pay enough."

His jaw tightens, and he pushes his empty plate across the table. Something about his expression seems grim. "You aren't the only one who comes for a wealthy family, Mila."

"What does your family do?"

His shoulders tense. "They own a lodge."

"So, a former FBI agent with a rich family, troubled past, and mysterious island in the middle of nowhere. You sound like Batman."

I'm actually surprised by the slight hint of amusement in his eyes.

"Batman is a children's concept."

"Hardly. Have you seen half of those comics?"

"Has Batman ever killed another man?"

I freeze, the wine in my mouth slipping down my throat when I hold his stare.

I let out a deep breath. "I'm sure he has."

"And if I told you I'd killed people?"

"Did they deserve it?"

He shrugs. "Suppose they did."

I let out a breath through my teeth, reaching for my wine.

"Then, I'd say it makes you a good guy. You know, when you're not kidnapping people."

Christian's gaze darkens. "I'm not a good guy, Mila."

"Murder doesn't make you bad, Christian. Not when it's against those who have done far worse."

"And what would you say is worse than murder, little devil? Isn't it the ultimate sin?"

I swallow over the lump in my throat, *that* night of all things slipping through my mind.

"I don't believe in sin," I admit, studying the dark purple hue of the liquid in my glass so I don't have to look at him and feel the full weight of his stare. "Sin implies you can be forgiven. Some people don't deserve that."

"And the man who attacked you . . ." My spine stiffens. "What would you say he deserves?"

"For me?" I ask honestly and he waits for my answer. "I would say death. For someone else? Say a little girl kidnapped from her mother? I'd say death is too kind for him." Finally, I force myself to meet his gaze. "What would you do if he came across your path?"

He watches me, gaze unreadable, and for a moment, I don't think he's going to tell me. Why would he? It's a hypothetical situation, anyway, but he's already determined I'm not strong enough for his world.

"I'd start by taking his hands," he murmurs, shaking me from the fog. "I'd slice off each of his fingers. Then, each of his toes, one by one, so he could feel every second of it. Then, I'd pull his teeth. I'd make it hurt. It would be bloody." He pauses as if he's formulating the plan as he speaks. "I'd make sure he cried for his mother until the bitter end because it would be music to my ears while I removed his arms and legs until he was nothing but a torso and head. And once I was finished with him . . . I'd leave him alive, out in the middle of nowhere in the heat of the day, so the birds could eat him while he begged for mercy with every ounce of energy."

My heart flutters in my chest, sickness pooling in my stomach, but it's not for what he said.

It's because I don't feel a shred of remorse for that man.

That evil, awful man deserves all of that and more.

Christian raises his glass to his lips, finishing the rest of his whiskey in one drink. "So you tell me, little devil . . . does my punishment count as a sin?"

I shake my head. "No."

He stares at me for a second longer, like he's trying to determine if I'm lying, but I'm not.

"If I ask you something, will you answer it?"

"Haven't I answered all your questions thus far?"

Save for one . . .

"Yes."

"Then ask."

"Promise to be honest with me?"

I sound like a fool, asking a man who lied to tell me the truth, but at this point, I'm out of options. He stares at me for a moment as if he's going to say no, but finally, he nods.

"Yes."

"It's about . . . us."

My cheeks burn bright under his gaze as he sits there, unmoving, like someone jammed a rod down his spine.

His jaw feathers, eyes flicking over my face as if he's

gauging my reaction.

"What's your question?"

"Was it all a lie?"

"Not in the way you're thinking it was."

What the hell does that even mean?

I can't help but roll my eyes.

"Then, why did you leave?"

He doesn't seem to like that because his gaze narrows, but he doesn't say anything.

A heaviness settles in the air between us. The thick silence makes it hard to breathe.

After the beach, he took me home, laid down with me until I fell asleep like he always did, but this time was different. He was different.

I never thought that when I woke up in the morning, he'd be gone.

Now that I've asked the question, I'm not sure I even want to know the answer. Wouldn't it be easier to just ignore the past and accept that those two people who were "in love" are no longer here?

"Why did you shoot me?"

My stomach drops to my toes.

"You said I could ask a question."

"I never said I'd answer."

"I have a right to know." I grit my teeth, smacking my hand on the top of the table at the rush of anger that surges through me. I'm sick and tired of everyone hiding things from me. "I waited for you for three months and you never called. Never showed. You completely ghosted me."

I can stop the tears welling in my eyes any more than I can stop the pain that threatens to rip me in half.

"Fine," he murmurs, so dark a shiver runs down my spine. When I meet his gaze, it *burns*. "You want to know what happened?"

"Yeah," I stutter, forcing my chin up. "I do."

He chuckles darkly, scrubbing a hand over his face.

"Using you to get closer to Parker was the easiest route. You were starving for attention. You needed someone to make you feel safe. Wanted. I played the part because it got me closer to the target, and you got a little piece of yourself you felt was missing."

Something sickening slips through my veins. A bitter embarrassment that I ever thought he cared. Everything I've always silently thought to myself after he left. Every time I blamed myself for his departure . . . it's all true.

"Satisfied?" he asks, his chair dragging against the floor with a screech as he gets up, slamming the front door behind him without another look back.

———————

"Chris-tian."

"That's my girl," he purrs, the sound muffled by my thighs on either side of his head. His tongue slips through my folds, milking the orgasm that sent electric zaps down my spine. His hands hold my hips, his eyes darkly amused while he watches me try to catch my breath.

It's been three months of this . . . torture.

Every day, it's the same. He comes to my room, catches me in the pool house, when we're alone in the car together . . . He always makes me come. Whether it's from his tongue or his fingers, it always ends with me gasping out his name and a panting wet mess before he kisses me until my lips are sore.

Unfortunately, that doesn't mean he fucks me.

Christian's never let me touch him. Any time I try to wrap my hand around his cock and push him past the boundaries he's set for us, he breaks away, and the moment is over.

I can't help but feel like something is wrong with me because he never lets it go further than just my orgasm.

Still, as one-sided as this is, it never stops me from allowing him to do it again.

"Fuck, look how pretty you are," he groans, the deep rumble slipping through my body and going right to my core.

Slipping back up my body, his lips capture mine, kissing me deeply. I whimper into his mouth, wrapping my arms around him when he settles back into the pillows beside me.

"It's raining," I point out, still breathless. He looks to the open hatch in the back of the SUV, watching the steady fall of the raindrops outside.

"I like the rain," he murmurs, his arm under my head. He pulls me closer to him, my legs intertwined with his, and presses his lips to my forehead.

"What about thunder?"

He pulls back, deep blue gaze searching mine. He's turned the back of the SUV into a makeshift bed, complete with blankets and pillows.

The back is open, overlooking the valley below as March brings about warmer weather.

Honestly, looking up at him, I find I never want to leave. If I could freeze time and live in just this moment, I would.

"Storms are the earth's way of cleansing itself." He shrugs. "That's what my mother used to say." He pauses, studying my face. For what, I don't know. "What's on your mind, little devil?"

I suck in a deep breath, mulling the answer over in my head. "Just wondering when all this is going to end."

"Your stepfather?"

"Us."

He's quiet, and something slips across his gaze. Before I can read his expression, it's gone.

To say I've fallen in love with Christian Cross is an understatement.

I'm obsessed with him. The darkness in his gaze and the way it sends shivers down my spine. The way he kisses me, as if he's dying to taste me and he'll lose his mind if he doesn't. How he laughs and how his hand feels in mine. His rough callouses against my home manicure.

"You need to forget about me, little devil."

Forget? That's impossible. I know as well as he does that a part of me will always crave him. Need him with every fiber of my being.

Right person, wrong lifetime.

Oddly, the thought makes my chest ache.

Before he can see the tears burning in the backs of my eyes, I close the distance between us, kissing him. He lets me, his hand sliding up to the back of my head to pull me closer. I love his roughness, as if he's barely holding on by a thread. I love how much bigger he is than me when he covers my body with his, careful not to put all his weight on me. Like I'm breakable, but his to break.

"Christian," I breathe against his lips, a fire scorching through my veins. "I want you."

"Mila," he warns, his voice rough and his hands tightening in my hair. He's told me no a thousand times. What's one more?

"Please," I breathe, my hand slipping between our bodies. I watch his reaction when I fist his hard cock through his jeans. His eyes grow dark, his jaw feathering, and I swear I feel it growing in my hand.

His fingers tighten in my hair, roughly dragging my head back and his gaze searches mine.

"I'm not the man for you, Mila."

You're the only man for me.

"Please, Christian?" I try again, my voice so soft, it's barely legible over the rain pounding the roof over our heads. "I want it to be you."

"Fuck," he curses under his breath when I tease him, reaching for the button on his jeans. He places his hand over mine, but he doesn't stop me when I pop it through the loop.

I have no idea what I'm doing, but when I lower his zipper and reach inside his boxers, running my fingers over the smooth skin of his erection, he inhales sharply, his eyes as dark as night.

While I've got him compliant, I lean forward, despite the bites of pain in my scalp from his fingers, and press my lips to his. I don't even know if he knows how hard he's gripping the roots of my hair, but the pain stirs me on. I kiss him gently, and he doesn't kiss me back when I wrap my fist around him, stroking him slowly from root to tip.

I've never had a dick in my hands before, but judging by how much is left that my hand can't cover, Christian's size is impressive. My mouth waters when I press my lips back to his, my tongue darting out to lick the seam between his lips. Wetness leaks from the head of his cock, and I stroke him again, needing to know that he feels the same way I do. That I'm not going insane on my own.

"Fuck, Mila," he grits, his hand catching mine and stilling my fingers. He leans his forehead against mine, his breathing ragged, and I don't move, my hand still wrapped around his cock. "You don't know what you're asking for, little devil."

"I do." I nod against him, swallowing past the lump in my throat. For months, he's made me come over and over until my legs are shaking, and I'm passing out in his arms. For months, I've begged for him, needing to feel him without any barriers, and he's denied me. If he didn't keep showing up in my room every night, I'd think he just wasn't that into me, but he keeps coming back, and I keep allowing it.

"You're going to hate me when this is done."

Unfortunately, I don't think I could ever hate him.

"No."

"Why me, Mila?" he rasps, brushing his knuckles down my cheek. "I can't give you what you deserve."

I shake my head, letting out a shaky breath. I slip my hand out of his jeans and up the hard ridges of his abs under his shirt. I want to feel him. Soak in his warmth and never leave the back of this Suburban.

"Because it's always been you," I breathe. I don't want anyone else. It has to be him.

My fingers reach his chest, and his heart beats fast under my fingers.

I would smile, but I'm too enraptured with him to even move. The way he holds me like he can't bear to lose me. The way his eyes consume me, devouring me until I'm stripped bare of all my secrets.

I can see him at war with himself. Fighting with whatever demons he's been running from. I want to take them away. Make him feel what I feel.

Leaning into him, I press my lips against his again, testing the waters. His fingers tighten in my hair, and he tugs me harder against him until there's not an inch of space between our bodies. He kisses me like a man starved, a deep groan traveling up his throat.

"You're going to fucking kill me."

"Holy shit," I gasp, shooting up in bed. I clutch my hand to my chest, my heart racing underneath my fingers, and look around.

Christian's. I'm at the cottage.

That fucking explains it.

It's with some annoyance, I realize I'm incredibly hot . . . and turned on.

My nipples strain against my tank top, my core is throbbing, and my skin is coated in a light sheen of perspiration.

Just like it would be if he were here.

Am I that far gone that I'm having sex dreams of the man who kidnapped me now?

God, Mila. Give it a rest.

I glance at the clock. Three in the morning.

Figures I'd have a sex dream about Christian Cross during the witching hour.

"I need a glass of water," I grumble, angry at my body for having the female version of a hard-on for a man who not only kidnapped me but plans to use me in his little revenge plot. Which, might I add, he hasn't told me who or what he's getting revenge on.

I listen intently for any signs that he may be home, only hearing the soft drip of the kitchen faucet before I tug on one of his flannels, which is basically a robe.

Padding quietly down the stairs, I make my way toward the kitchen, passing through the living room on my way.

Only I stop short the moment I see him.

Christian must have fallen asleep when he came back inside. I don't know where he went, but I stayed awake until I couldn't keep my eyes open any longer before conceding defeat and going to bed.

Now, I'm regretting it because he's passed out on the couch, no shirt on and glorious abs on display for everyone to see.

Well, really, just me. The creepy night stalker watching him sleep.

I pause, watching the even rise and fall of his chest. I had thought seeing him sleeping would make him look less . . . devastating.

Now, I can see, I was wrong.

The hard muscles of his abs and chest move with each breath, making the tattoos on his skin look like they're alive. *CROSS* is written in big, bold letters across his chest. An intricate clock tower design over his abs, and right above it, the bullet I'd lodged in his shoulder.

It's the three letters—*MRC*—with the date of November eighth a year and a half ago, on his chest that cause my heart to fall to my stomach.

"It's rude to stare."

I let out a squeak, spilling water down the front of my *white* tank top when Christian's eyes open and zero in on the now see-through material.

Great job, Mila. You're a one-woman wet T-shirt contest.

"I wasn't staring." I totally was. I tug my flannel-turned

robe tighter around myself, but it's thin, so the material instantly gets wet, making it look like my nipples are leaking.

I hate it here.

"I had a nightmare, and I needed a drink."

Quickly regretting that decision.

"About what?"

I swallow hard past the lump in my throat.

"Nothing."

Before he can say anything else and my skin can melt off from the embarrassment because I can't stop picturing him between my legs, I make a mad dash to the bedroom, wet nipples and water in hand, and hide out under the covers.

My God . . . living under Christian Cross's roof is turning out to be more complicated than I thought.

I need to get out of here.

CHAPTER
Sixteen

MILA

"Phantom . . ." I call softly, slipping into the greenhouse. Today's been quiet. Unsubstantial. No new visitors have arrived, and Christian and I have barely spoken. I'm honestly glad. After dinner the other night, I'm not sure what we'd say to each other that wouldn't just leave me feeling pissed off and used all over again.

After force-feeding me eggs and toast for breakfast, Christian disappeared into the lighthouse as he has every day for the past week, leaving me alone in the cottage. By evening, I snuck out as I always do and made my way to take care of Phantom.

I named him Phantom for the white around his eyes, making him appear almost ghostlike.

—And because the markings in his fur remind me of the Phantom of the Opera.

Luckily, with Christian holed up in his little mancave, I've been able to sneak out of the cottage and come out to the greenhouse to care for him.

He never lets me get too close, growling at me from the moment

I enter, but he does let me feed him whatever I can scrounge up from inside.

Today, he's lying on his side when I enter, and though I can see he's breathing, the fact that he doesn't immediately raise his head and growl at me fills my stomach with dread.

"Hey, buddy . . ." Cautiously, I drop to my knees beside him. "You okay?"

He doesn't lift his head, his breathing shallow. He whimpers, and I hover over him, searching for what might have caused his distress.

"You were just growling at me yesterday. What's wrong?"

He doesn't answer, but I look him over, checking his ears without touching him, then glancing at the few teeth I can see.

Then, I see his paw and the dried blood caked to his pad.

"Okay, we can fix this. Let me see," I whisper, like Christian might be hiding behind the overgrown weeds in the corner rather than inside his lighthouse, doing whatever it is he does in there all day.

I reach for his paw, being as gentle as I can when I turn it over to inspect it. Embedded in between the pads, a piece of sharp glass is stuck in the skin, and the sight of the blood makes my head spin.

Pull it together, Mila. He can't take it out himself.

I blow out a breath between my teeth, shutting my eyes against the wooziness that threatens to drag me under.

"Alright, don't panic."

I think I'm the only one panicking here, but someone's got to say it.

Phantom cocks his head at me, attempting to pull his paw back, but without much force. I can't imagine how much pain he must be in.

"I'm going to pull it out," I tell him, crouching to get a better vantage point.

I know next to nothing about caring for the injured paw of a dog, but I'm not about to let him suffer, and without a vet anywhere in the next five miles, I'm his best bet.

"Okay, this will hurt a little."

I reach for the glass, steeling myself and gritting my teeth, just as Phantom tries to tug his paw away. The moment I touch the glass, my fingers connecting with the sharp edges, he yelps in pain and nips at me.

My first instinct is to jerk back at his vicious growl, but I keep hold of the glass, pulling it out in the process of falling over on my ass.

The moment it's gone, Phantom starts licking his battle wound, and I . . .

I look down at my hand to see blood oozing from several teeth marks on my wrist.

Well fuck.

That hurts.

My head spins at the blood, tears welling in my eyes despite myself because the adrenaline of the moment is wearing off.

Pain throbs in my wrist, and I clutch it to myself, afraid to look at the bite and see how bad it is. I know he didn't do it to hurt me. Animals aren't that different from humans. Pain makes us fight back against whatever caused it, and for Phantom, I was responsible for his momentary agony.

My head spins, the room rocking on its axis around me. I fall back to lay amongst the thicket of weeds growing through the rough stone floor, closing my eyes, and try to calm my breathing.

A wet nose touches my face, and I cautiously blink an eye open, finding the black wolf towering over me and watching me with a thoughtful expression.

"I don't like blood," I explain, forcing a breath through my mouth.

God, why is it so hot in here all of the sudden?

One . . . two . . . three . . .

He leans closer, sniffing my face, my hair, then moving down to my hand, still clutched tightly to my chest.

"It's okay," I breathe, reaching out with my other hand despite just being bitten moments before. Some part of me knows he didn't mean it and that he's sorry. "I know it was an accident. Is your paw better?"

He responds with a lick to my cheek. An unspoken apology and thanks for removing the broken shard of glass. I force myself to sit up, patting his head and leaning my cheek against his warm fur to let the nausea pass.

Nervousness stirs in my stomach, but I continue to stroke the top of his head, knowing that there's no way I'll be able to keep this from Christian.

He'll shoot him, and I can't let that happen.

A quiet tear slips down my cheek, contempt sliding up my throat.

Why does everything have to be so damned difficult?

"It's okay," I repeat, even though deep down, I know it won't be for much longer.

When I exit the greenhouse, the sun is starting to set, and with a heavy feeling of paranoia, I clutch my bloody wrist to my chest and hurry towards the cottage, praying with every step that Christian is still up in his mancave.

Blood seeps from the wound on my hand, and I keep it curled into my chest, wincing at the pain that throbs with each step. When I near the house, I pull my borrowed coat sleeve down to cover it, making my way towards the front door.

Only, it opens before I reach it.

Christian stands in the doorway, a volatile presence against the fading sun.

His stare stills the beat of my heart, clouding over like a storm washes across the sky when he notices the blood dripping from my fingers onto the rough stone beneath my feet.

"What happened?" I jump at the sound of his voice, my stomach plummeting at the calmness in his tone.

I've known him long enough to know a calm Christian is a dangerous Christian.

"It's nothing," I lie, holding my hand tighter. "I slipped. I'm fine."

He takes a step towards me, his front nearly pressed against mine, and looks down at the blood staining my coat. An icy sensation trails down my spine, sending a shiver through me at the violence in his gaze.

"There's a dog in the greenhouse, isn't there?"

I don't even have to answer him. One look at my face is all he needs before he's pushing past me and pulling the pistol from his waistband as he stalks across the yard.

My heart cracks and hand forgotten, I run after him.

"Wait!" I shout, but he doesn't stop. "It was an accident."

He racks the slide, not even bothering to look at me when I grab his arm and attempt to pull him back.

"It was an accident. He's hurt!"

"Mila, go in the house."

"*No*," I growl, jumping in front of him. I'll throw myself in front of the dog if I have to. I won't let him hurt him. "You can't *do that*." I shove him with everything I have, but like a brick wall, he doesn't even move.

"There's no place for biting mutts on this island," he replies cooly, stepping into me and forcing me to fall back a step. I grip his shirt, but he just keeps walking, moving past me despite my struggling. Tears burn on my cheeks, the wind whipping my hair in my face, when I throw myself in front of him and the greenhouse again.

But, like the force of the sea, he only stops because he wants to. Not because *I* made him.

"He was hurt, and I pulled a piece of glass from his foot. He didn't mean to. I won't let you hurt him."

His gaze fills me with ice, his stare lethal.

"Let me?" he mocks, stepping into me. "You seem to have forgotten, what you want, doesn't matter anymore."

I slap him so hard my hand vibrates with the sting. His head snaps to the side, the skin instantly reddening with both the blood on my hand and the force behind it. When his gaze slips back to mine, he's never looked more like the devil than he does right now.

At the same time, I spin to run back towards the greenhouse, he catches me around the waist, tugging my back into his front with one arm around my stomach, the gun in his other hand. The air wheezes out of me, and an icy fear settles in my stomach.

Not for me, but for Phantom, because if Christian won't listen to me, there's no doubt in my mind he won't think twice about shooting the dog who bit me.

"Let go of me!" I growl, but I may as well be fighting off a grizzly bear. He presses his lips to my ear, the warmth of his breath against my neck sending a shiver down my spine. Tears spill from my eyes, a sob wracking up my throat as sorrow threatens to suffocate me.

"You seem to have forgotten; temper tantrums don't work on me.

"Please, don't kill him—"

"You have no choices here, Mila. Right now, you are mine to feed, to protect, and to clothe. If I say you're going to wear something, I expect you to smile and say, *yes, sir,* in that pretty little voice of yours. If I tell you no dogs if they're going to bite, that's the way it's going to be. No arguing. No running off. And no fucking temper tantrums."

He lets me shove away from him, and I crash to the grass below his feet, nothing more than a piece of garbage beneath his feet, just like Phantom.

He meets my tear-filled stare with his icy one, and I realize there's not an ounce of emotion in his eyes. Not anymore.

"What happened to you?" I breathe because I can't help myself. My stomach is in my throat, and the perimeter of the island is threatening to close in on me.

Beyond the cliffs, the waves crash against the rocks, but it's nothing compared to the turmoil in my chest.

"Perhaps it's the bullet still lodged in my chest," he sneers, his lips curling up at the sides in a dangerous snarl. "You know, two inches to the left, and I would have died. Not that you care, right? You delivered that punishment on a silver platter. Didn't you, little devil?"

Something breaks inside me, and it's then I realize I really don't know Christian at all anymore.

I glare at him, fresh tears burning in my eyes, and for the first time since I woke up in this fresh hell, I can't turn them off.

God, what did I do to him?

"Sometimes, I wish I would have just used it on myself instead."

He stares at me, watching the descent of a tear as it runs down my cheek, dripping to my bloody coat below.

"Go inside."

And then he stalks past me, making his way toward the greenhouse to shoot the only thing worth saving on this godforsaken island.

CHAPTER
Seventeen

CHRISTIAN

I f someone had asked me five years ago where I saw myself in this very moment, it wouldn't have been stalking into a desolate greenhouse to shoot a dog that bit the girl who shot me.

It also wouldn't have included the burn in my chest from the tears in her eyes.

Who the fuck does she think she is? What happened to me? As if I'm some damaged replica of the man she used to know. The man *she* shot.

Like she's some fucked-up little Mother Theresa, running around and rescuing whatever she can. I don't need her rescuing. My soul was damned a long fucking time ago.

The man she knew is dead. She killed him when she fired that bullet in my chest.

It takes a monster to kill a monster, and that's exactly what I've become, regardless of what little Mila Carpenter has to say about it.

I shove past Mila, ignoring the lead filling my chest from a few simple tears, and make my way toward the old, broken greenhouse.

When I enter, I shut the door behind me, and a growl sounds from somewhere nearby.

"Fuck off, dog," I murmur under my breath, only to turn around and find the dog in question isn't even a dog. It's a wolf. Or a mix of one.

His fur is black, a strange white coloring around his eyes. There's no doubt he's hurt by his inability to move right when he stands.

"I swear that woman and her soft fucking heart," I growl under my breath when the dog attempts to take a step towards me, only to fall back to his stomach with a whimper.

I run my thumb over the grooves in the grip of my pistol, staring at him as he stares at me. Both of us probably thinking about the same fucking girl.

"Jesus fucking Christ," I grumble under my breath, scrubbing a hand over my face. Consequently, some of Mila's blood is still on my cheek.

It's obvious the dog needs help, and guilt washes through me, but I know part of that is just the girl I left crying in the center of the clearing. The need to go to her pulls at me like a magnet, and I hate the fucking feeling. She gets under my skin and makes me question myself and why I am the way I am. Makes me want to dry her tears, even if I'm the one that caused them.

"Let's get something straight," I murmur, dropping to my haunches in front of the mutt. He cocks his head to the side, his brown eyes boring into mine as if he understands what he did. "You bite my girl again; no amount of her tears will save you."

He lays his head down on the old quilt I'd stripped off the bed inside when we arrived, looking up at me through soft brown eyes.

I shake my head, standing.

"That was your only strike," I reiterate. And then I head to the door.

As expected, Mila's in the same place I left her when I exit the greenhouse.

What's not expected is the hot and unpleasant feeling that slides down my throat when I see her sitting there dejected, like she has nothing left in the world.

I don't like it.

No . . . scratch that.

I fucking hate it.

I wish I would have just used it on myself . . .

She doesn't look up at me when I approach, and I don't say a word, silently bending down, lifting her into my arms, and carrying her back toward the cottage.

"Did you do it?" she asks softly. Something dark settles in my chest, where she lays her head, her eyes closed against the tears clinging to her lashes.

"I didn't shoot him."

She lets out a shaky breath, drawing her bottom lip between her teeth despite the cut from her chewing on her lip.

Ever wanted to feel like the world's biggest douchebag?

Take a walk in my shoes when Mila Carpenter's around.

I carry her through the front door and straight to the kitchen table. She doesn't look up when I sit her down in a chair, tug her coat off her arms, and cross the room to get the first aid kit from the bathroom.

All but a week here, and I've had to use the fucking thing on her twice.

"It's just a scratch," Mila mumbles when I return to the table.

It's not, but I let her think that.

I grab a rag and wet it with cool water, crossing back to her at the table. I tug a chair up beside her and pull her between my legs, my knees on either side of hers.

I reach for her hand against her chest, but she refuses to give it to me.

"Let me see."

"I don't want to."

I swear to fucking God.

"Mila. Let me see," I try again, gentler this time, when I really just feel like breaking something.

She swallows past the lump in her throat and finally relents, slowly holding her hand out to me, dripping in blood. I take her delicate fingers in mine, turning her hand to the light and she shuts her eyes, looking away.

"You don't like blood, now."

It's not a question.

"Blood is blood," she replies cooly, a shiver moving through her. "It's how it gets to the surface that bothers me."

Something about that pisses me off.

"If we're going to coexist together on this island, I need you to be honest with me," I tell her, wiping the blood from her fingers. Her wrist isn't bleeding anymore, but she will need stitches on at least one of the gashes.

She's silent, staring at the table beside us instead of at her hand.

"I was . . . afraid you'd hurt him."

Fuck.

She looks away, her cheeks red and swollen from the tears still fresh on her face, and I'll admit, the sight of them makes me want to burn the world to the ground.

"I overreacted," I murmur, pouring peroxide over the cut. She winces and bites her bottom lip. The words taste like battery acid on the back of my tongue. Admitting you fucked up always does. "I'm sorry."

She pauses, her brow furrowing.

"Did you just apologize?"

Little brat.

I pull out the needle and thread from the kit, threading it through and aligning myself to place a couple stiches.

"This will hurt," I tell her, and she finally meets my gaze with her pretty gray one.

"Okay," she breathes.

I've given stitches to myself and others so many times I've lost count. The sight of blood has never bothered me. Especially not after seeing bullet wounds, people getting stabbed. Murders.

The sight of blood on Mila's soft skin, though, is something else entirely.

I push the needle through the torn flesh, and Mila lets out a soft breath through parted lips. I don't look up at her, keeping my hold steady and place the first stitch.

"I'm sorry, too . . ." Mila says after a beat, and the urge to tug her into my lap just to fucking hold her burns in my chest.

I can't, though. I fucking can't because that option was taken from us.

When I place the third and final stitch, neither of us moves for a moment, save for me cleaning the blood from her wounds.

"Where did you learn to give stitches?" Mila asks quietly, watching me clean the drying blood from her skin with the rag. The rest of the wounds aren't as deep and have already started healing.

"My mother," I reply, voice huskier than before. "She was a nurse."

"You've never spoken about your mother to me before."

I grit my teeth, wrapping her hand in a layer of gauze to keep the stitches from getting caught.

"You never asked."

She's silent for a moment, nibbling on her bottom lip. If I could touch her, I'd pull it away from her with my own and then wipe the worry off her face with a brush of my tongue.

Because I can't, though, I'm forced to watch her worry herself to death.

"She died," I murmur. I don't know why the fuck I'm telling her this. I don't speak about my mother with anyone. Something forces me to, though, and I'm betting it's the little voice in the back of my head that always says stupid shit when Mila's around.

"I'm sorry," she breathes, her hand brushing against mine where a scar runs through an ace of spades on my wrist. "I guess we're more alike than we thought."

Her father. He died before she was old enough to remember him, yet I know that's not why she's sad. She's sad for me. And I don't deserve it.

Gently as I can, I reach up, capturing a drying tear on her cheek with my thumb. Her eyes widen for a moment, but for the first time since I brought her here, she doesn't shrink away from me.

Instead, she leans closer, her breathing heavier, and her eyes soften to a look that both hits me right in the fucking chest and aches in my cock at the same time.

"What do you want, Mila?" I ask, my voice quiet. Barely audible over my own breathing mixed with hers.

"I want . . ." she pauses, her eyes half-lidded and hazy in the dim light overhead. My dick pulses in my jeans when her tongue darts out to lick her lips, my mind running through every possible scenario of how this could end, but knowing none of them end with her in my arms again.

That ship hasn't just sailed, it's fucking sunk.

But . . . with her pretty gray eyes filled with something warm and thick, our breathing heavy in the air between us, and her soft hand in mine, it's easy to forget.

Her fingers close around mine and her breath hitches when mine dance across her knee. She doesn't push me away, and for the first time since I brought her here, there's no panic in her gaze at the touch of another person.

"I want you to keep touching me," she whispers, almost like it's a question.

I tug her towards me until she's inches away, and her breath catches, her eyes widening with a split second of fear before it's replaced with something else.

We've been tiptoeing around each other on this island, and it's getting to my head.

Her lips hover over mine, and the scent of her honey and vanilla washes over me, stealing my breath and making my cock throb in my jeans.

It's that split second of fear, though, and the uncertainty in her gaze that prevents me from moving further.

Finally, I force myself to release her. Then, I force myself to ignore the dull ache in my chest and stand from my chair.

Fuck, I *force* myself not to think about the fact that while she may have blood on her hands, mine are too dirty to even touch her.

She doesn't belong in my world any more than I belong in hers, yet . . . I can't say the idea isn't fucking tempting, nor that the thought of her disappearing again doesn't make something dark and twisted growl in the back of my head.

"Go get cleaned up," I murmur, standing from the chair before I can do something stupid. I head towards the door, gritting my teeth at the bitterness burning through my veins. "I'll get the dog."

She doesn't respond, and I don't look back, walking out into the night to go get a fucking wolf and bring him inside just so I can see her smile.

Mila doesn't ask when I place him on a blanket near the fireplace, but I don't miss the soft smile on her face when she turns away.

And that's when I know I'd do anything to see it again.

Things go quiet online in the days that follow me stitching Mila's hand. There are no signs of anyone actively looking for her, which means they're hiding it, and I need to find out why.

Luckily, the weather keeps anyone from coming to the island for a few days, with the waves crashing over the path.

This also means that it's just me and her stuck in the cottage with a wolf who looks at me like he wants to bite my dick off any time I come near her.

Mila dotes on the dog, naming him Phantom for the marks on his face and because, in her words, Christine should have chosen the Phantom.

Whatever the fuck that means.

It's on our third day that tensions run high. I'm making lunch when Mila drops her hairbrush for the fourth time in the bathroom, letting out a string of expletives under her breath that would make even the most hardened criminals blush.

I can't help but chuckle, turning the burner off to the stove and crossing over to the bathroom.

"Let me try."

She glares at me in the mirror, tears shining in her eyes, but concedes, grabbing her hairbrush and handing it to me.

I step out into the living room, sinking into the couch and motioning for her to sit in front of me.

We haven't touched each other since the other night, so she's hesitant, wrapping her arms around her middle and stepping over in between my legs. I toss a pillow to the floor and motion for her to sit.

Carefully, she sinks down, pressing her back to the couch between my knees and drawing her legs up to her chest.

I brush her hair, smoothing the strands still wet from her shower while the wind howls outside the window, and begin to braid it.

"Did your mother teach you how to braid?" she asks softly, watching the fire crackle and pop in front of her.

"Learned for my sister," I murmur without even thinking.

She's quiet for a moment, processing what I'd said.

"How old is your sister?"

"Twenty-five," I reply dryly, smoothing the soft strands of her hair down with my fingers. "Paulina couldn't braid, and I knew someone had to learn to do it."

"Are you related to June—I mean, Paulina?"

"My aunt," I reply. "She moved in to help take care of us. Dad wasn't around. Always working."

"It's nice that she was there after your mother . . ."

"Died?"

Mila's silent.

"I was a handful," I murmur. "Pretty reckless."

She opens her mouth to speak. Probably to tell me that it wasn't my fault, but she doesn't.

"Did she ever have any children of her own?"

"No. As far as I know, she never wanted any and never married. She semi-adopted us to help our dad out, but I don't think she ever planned on taking care of her sister's kids."

"I can't believe everything she told me was a lie." She shakes her head.

"Not all of it."

She pauses, turning over her shoulder to face me.

"You were there?"

"Reading the paper in the back."

She gawks at me.

"How long were you planning on kidnapping me, then?"

I push her to face forward and resume braiding.

"Since the moment you left, though . . . I must admit, I didn't think it would take that long."

"Good," she huffs. "I can't believe I didn't notice you."

"No, but you never did, did you?" I smirk because I feel her stiffen in front of me. "You were never alone, Mila. I was always there."

She shakes her head, hugging her knees tighter.

"I'm sure my mother sent you. Did it ever occur to you that maybe I wanted to be alone?"

"Your mother had nothing to do with it, Mila."

She falls silent, watching the flames in front of her while I work on her hair.

"I always thought I'd adopt," she says quietly after a while.

It's the first time I'm hearing it.

"You never told me that," I murmur, repeating the words she'd said to me the other night, and she shrugs.

"You never asked."

We fall silent, me braiding and her watching the fire.

"Why should Christine have chosen the Phantom?"

"What?" she asks softly.

"You said Christine should have chosen the Phantom. Why?"

A shiver runs down her spine when I brush over the top of the scar that peaks out from under the collar of my T-shirt she's wearing.

Scars I haven't been able to get out of the back of my mind since that first night I bathed her.

"The Phantom was dedicated," she whispers as if saying such a thing is treason. "He was obsessed with her, yes, but he knew the parts of her soul that no one else did. The pain of losing her father. The loneliness of her childhood."

"He murdered a fair few people if I remember correctly," I point out.

"He did," she concedes softly. "He also loves the dark, ugly parts of her. Raoul loved the idea of her, based on an image he created in his head. Not the real her. The real Christine is much more complex than he can imagine."

I finish her braid, tying it off at the end and smoothing it down her back.

"So you're saying love transcends violence?" I ask when she stands, lightly running her hand over the braid.

"I'm saying even villains need to be loved," she whispers. She meets my eyes, her cheeks glowing red before she looks away. "And sometimes a dark soul doesn't mean a dark heart."

CHAPTER
Eighteen

MILA

S mile for the camera, little whore."

My head whips to the side as a fist connects with my cheek, and pain explodes behind my eyes.

"Fucking bitch," the man inside me growls, the rotten face of his clown mask looming over me in the dimly lit basement.

I can't speak around my gag, but my cries come out muffled and garbled from behind the piece of dirty cloth.

Not that anyone would hear me, anyway. He made sure of that.

Just let me slip away . . .

Let me close my eyes and not wake up again . . .

"So fucking tight," the man raping me grits between his teeth, his head kicked back towards the ceiling as he thrusts between my legs.

His knife digs deeper into my flesh, and my back arches as my body desperately fights to get away, but it's no use.

"You fucking love this, don't you? Want me to cut you again?"

Another slice comes, and this one feels like he's tearing me in half. The pain is excruciating, unlike anything I've ever felt, as he carves my body with his sins *the world to see. I scream, but no sound comes out, like I'm under the surface of the ocean, drowning as water fills my lungs.*

This is how they'll find me—carved and bound to a mattress in a dirty basement.

I'm going to die down here.

I shriek, my head thrashing back into the bed as tears slip uncontrollably down my cheeks. I can't move from the rope securing my wrists above my head. I lost feeling in my arms ages ago.

"Mila." The voice is sharp, tinged with the agony I feel as the man between my legs comes, covering my blood-soaked stomach with his vile seed.

"Oh, fuck . . ." he groans when he slips back inside me, his fingers tracing the open wounds on my stomach. "Fuck you're tight for a whore."

He wastes no time, stabbing into the flesh right beside the first letter, and my vision goes dark as the pain blinds me.

"Mila, baby. Wake up."

I crane my neck, trying to force my eyes to open at the voice, but I can't. I can't move. I can't fight. I can't even fucking breathe.

He's going to kill me.

Please, kill me.

"That's it, little whore," he chuckles, the large, overpainted lips of his mask curled into a sneering smile. "Let them know how much you're enjoying yourself."

"Mila," the voice growls in my ear, and I scream, fighting back at the hands that reach for me. I fly away from their touch, crashing to the floor from the bed in a painful tumble. A dark silhouette looms over me from the darkness of my bedroom, and I throw myself back into the side of the bed.

"No!" My voice is hoarse when they reach for me, clawing at the man in the darkness with everything I have.

Not again . . .

"Mila," a gruff voice sounds, and hands clasp around my wrists, holding them against a hard chest.

"Please," I beg silently, my heart feeling like it's going to burst through my ribcage as the agony drags through me like hot coals.

It's him. He's found me.

"It's me, little devil."

Reality washes over me like a cold bucket of ice water when I smell the familiar scent of leather, whiskey, and the forest.

He *found* me.

I want to push him away. I don't want him to see me like this, but I can't shove him away. Not when he's a shining beacon while I'm lost in the storm of a century.

"They're going to kill me," I croak, my eyes blurry from the tears clogging my vision. My chest seizes as the invisible hands wrap around my throat, bleeding the life from my body until I can't hold on anymore.

"Never." It's rough and violent. A dark promise that some twisted part of me knows he'd keep. "Come here."

I can't even fight it. Not when he falls to his knees in front of me and not even when he tugs me into his lap, his arms banding around me to crush me against his chest. My throat burns, my heart beats a mile a minute, and my vision swims with hot tears.

Christian sits back against the side of the bed, his hand on the back of my head when I bury my face in his neck. He doesn't move save for the soft strokes of his fingers down the ends of my hair and the movements of his chest beneath my cheek.

I cling to him, my arms around his neck and my body shaking with the force of the violent sobs that refuse to stop. My fingers fist the material of his T-shirt like he's a life raft out at sea, and I'm on the verge of drowning. He makes a rough noise with the sound of the hoarse cry that leaves my lips, and a tremor moves through him as he holds me tighter.

"Breathe, baby," he murmurs, his lips against my hair and I can't escape the way he says it. Like if I were to stop, I'd be unleashing the darkest depths of hell on the world.

As if his own life depends on it.

A clap of thunder sounds outside, but here in his arms, I don't even jump. Not when this is all a dream, and I'll wake up alone tomorrow morning.

I'm not the final girl. I'm not the girl who gets what she wants. This isn't a romance book where he comes in and confesses his undying love for me. This is a dream that my mind formed to save me from the nightmare my scars created.

So I soak him in, allowing myself to give into the fantasy that I could be his and he could be mine. The voices can't reach me here. The hands can't reach me in his embrace. It's just me and him, wrapped in each other's arms in the quiet solitude of a sleepy cottage while I shatter into a million pieces in his lap.

He may be harsh. He may hate me for the bullet still lodged in his chest. He may be the devil, himself outside of my dreams . . . None of that matters when he's the one thing that chases my demons away amid the warzone my mind has become.

He presses his lips against the scar on my forehead. "You're safe with me," he whispers, his voice vehement and dark beneath the pouring rain outside, and in this dream, I actually believe it.

A shiver moves through me, and I sink into him, soaking in his warmth as it bleeds into my soul. I don't know how long we stay there, but the tears fade. His hand running soothing circles over my back doesn't. It's not until he slowly stands, carrying me over to the bed, that I even realize I'd fallen asleep.

When he lays me back against the sheets, something sharp and agonizing aches in my chest.

"Please?" I whisper, my throat in danger of collapsing again. "Please don't leave me."

I know it's weak. I know it will only blur the lines in my head when I see him tomorrow. I also know I can't stop it. Real Christian would tell me I'm pathetic and to grow up. Stop being afraid of the dark like a child. Dream Christian climbs into the bed beside me, pulling me back into his chest before covering us with the comforter.

"Never, little devil."

And then he presses a rough kiss to my cheek with a quiet "Sleep" and holds me like it's his dying wish.

Like I'm his.

The unfortunate difference between actual Christian and dream Christian, though?

When I wake up, only one's real. And I'm in bed alone.

———

The morning after my Christian-infested nightmare, I'm in a foul mood by the time I make it down to eat breakfast.

To make matters worse, Christian has chosen today, of all days, to *not* retreat to his office the moment dawn crests on the horizon.

And he doesn't have a shirt on.

When I reach the bottom of the stairs, I freeze when he regards me indifferently over a pan of scrambled eggs and bacon.

We've come to a sort of truce in the last couple days, but with the rain dredging outside and his incessant need to be . . . *here*, I can feel the tendrils of my sanity starting to shred, one by one.

"You're here."

He cocks a brow, loading the two plates in front of him.

"I am."

Fuck.

"Why?"

"Because I live here."

Double fuck.

"Eat."

"I'm pleased to see you're as chipper as ever," I grumble, padding across the kitchen barefoot in just his gigantic T-shirt toward the coffee he'd brewed. He looks down at my toes as I walk, probably noting the red polish Paulina brought me before he shakes his head and takes his seat.

I fill my coffee mug, adding enough cream and sugar that there's barely any coffee in it before I begrudgingly sit across from him.

"Sleep well?" he asks, not even bothering to look up from his food.

"Like a baby," I lie, praying to God I didn't make any noise mid-nightmare. That's *not* a conversation I want to have.

"You're in a fine mood this morning."

I smile sweetly, hoping he can see the glimmer of hate in my eyes.

"Captivity has a way of dampening the soul," I reply, sipping my coffee loudly.

His eyes darken, and it looks like he can't decide if he'd rather spank me or kill me.

Please let it be the latter.

"Are you bored?" he mocks. "Need me to find some chores for you, sweetheart?"

"No thanks. My schedule's pretty packed between self-loathing and loathing *you*. I'm finding it difficult to manage as it is."

"Right, I wouldn't want you to stress yourself out between your hobbies of backstabbing and dirty motel hopping."

I smile sweetly, hoping my voice is laced with as much venom as what's coating my heart.

"As opposed to kidnapping and world domination."

He takes a bite of eggs, his eyes glinting wickedly.

"The only thing I plan to conquer is what's between your legs."

I can't fight the blush on my cheeks nor the dip in my stomach that makes it feel like I'm standing in an electrified pool. I also can't fight the stubborn streak my mother always hated.

"What's between my legs is none of your concern. I wouldn't fuck you if you were the last man on earth."

"That right?" Christian smirks, flashing that cocky grin at me that always got me before.

171

Unfortunately, it still works.

"I'd be willing to give you some pointers if you need help getting laid. You could start with your incessant need to kill innocent creatures."

"That what you want? Want me to bring a girl home and fuck her in the same bed you sleep in."

Bitter jealousy slips down my throat right along with my coffee. I know I brought it on myself, but thinking of him with another woman fills me with a sense of betrayal.

"Do whatever you want." I shrug, though warmth burns in the backs of my eyes. Stupid tear ducts. "I'm just a prisoner here, right?"

"Did I strike a nerve?"

I push my empty plate back from me, leaning back in my chair.

"You can say whatever you want to me. I'm past caring."

"Is that so?" he challenges, a hint of a wicked smile on his lips. "No fight for me this morning?"

"I'm done fighting. It's not like anything that happened between us meant anything, anyway. I was just the easy, idiotic whore who thought she could save you and ended up almost dead because of it."

And then I realize what I'd said.

Fucking way to go, Mila.

I've never seen someone's face get so red, so fast.

"Want to run that by me again, Mila?."

Fuck, fuck, fuck.

I grab my coffee and move to stand, but his boot hooks in the bottom of my chair, dragging it back to the table so fast that I almost fall out of it.

I can't help but glare at him, even if he is looking at me with a darkness that sends a shiver of fear down my spine.

God, I hope he didn't hear what I said.

"Repeat what the fuck you just said," he grits, his tone conveying my little slip-up, in fact, did *not* go over his head.

"Which part?"

"Don't play dumb with me, Mila."

"Or what?" I counter, forcing my chair back and standing. Heat rushes through my blood, my temper flaring. "You're going to kidnap me? Drug me? Use me? I don't care anymore, Christian. I stopped caring the moment you walked out in the middle of the night and didn't come back until you felt sorry for me."

He regards me with that same bored stare, but there's something else lingering beneath the surface. Something heavy and thick and dark that swallows all the air from my lungs and makes ignoring the fluttering in my stomach impossible to ignore.

"Felt sorry for you? Is that what you thought?"

"It's what I know," I growl.

"That the angle you want to play it?" He cocks a brow. "The unfeeling little brat and not the damsel in distress now?"

"No one asked you to step in and try to save me."

"No? Would have saved a lot of fucking headaches in the long run if I'd left you to wonder the streets."

My breath catches in my throat. Violence slips through me in waves. I suddenly want to hurt him as badly as he'd hurt me when he left without a word.

With a snap of my wrist, my coffee soaks his face.

There's a clock ticking somewhere nearby. I know this because it's the only sound while Christian and I stare at each other in the seconds that follow.

"Mila . . ." he starts, cracking his neck while beige-colored coffee runs down his cheek.

I don't like how calm he is. Somehow, he's never looked more terrifying than he does when his gaze locks with mine.

"Run."

I don't think, I just dart. Fear bubbles up in my chest when I hear his heavy footfalls on the floor behind me. I make it to the back door, only to nearly sink to my knees and beg for forgiveness when it rebounds off his boot, sending it smacking back into the wall with a harsh crack.

"Please—" I try, but it's lost on him. I'm well and truly fucked now. I try to skirt past him, but he catches me around the waist, hauling my back to his front and picking me up, carrying me straight inside towards the bathroom.

Is he going to drown me?

"What's the matter, little devil?" he sneers in my ear, his breathing just as heavy as mine when he drops me on my feet in the shower and climbs in behind me. He spins me around, pinning my hands above my head with one of his, and reaches for the faucet. "Afraid to get a little wet?"

I scream when the ice-cold water from the showerhead cascades over us, drenching us both down to the bone. He doesn't seem to care, too pissed off to worry about the frigid arctic waters spilling from the taps.

"Christian," I growl, surging against him, but he doesn't release me, pinning me with his entire front molded to mine. I can feel his cock digging into my stomach.

Oh my God . . . is he turned on?

He cocks his head to the side, his gaze darkening when my tongue darts out to capture a water droplet on my lip. A shiver moves through me, but despite my struggle, something warm settles in my core with the brush of his knee pressed between mine.

Oh my God . . . am I turned on?

"Let me go," I growl, despite the heaviness settling between my legs.

"Play with fire, sweetheart, you're going to get burnt," he rasps, water running down the side of his face and over his scar.

I surge forward, and for a split second, my hands are free before he pins them back to the tile. In the process, my leg wraps around his hip in an effort to try and throw him off, but it only opens me up to feeling the friction of his jeans brushing against the cotton-covered center of my thighs.

Please, God. Anyone but him.

He pauses when he sees my reaction, his gaze dark as sin.

In a millisecond of a moment, he readjusts, and my eyes flutter closed at the overwhelming sense of longing I haven't felt in nearly a year. My blood vibrates in my veins, the rush of adrenaline sliding down my spine and heading straight to where his thigh brushes against me.

All the fight leaves my body, replaced with a fire that laps at my skin. He repeats the motion, and my head falls forward to rest on his shoulder from the moment of shame that envelops me.

"No," he grits, so quiet, I can barely hear him. "You look at me."

He pushes me back, releasing my wrists, and the blood tingles as it rushes back through them.

I should push him away. I should call him every name under the sun for what he said in the kitchen.

In that moment, though, all I can think about is how good the friction of his thigh feels against my clit.

His hand goes to my hip, kneading the flesh, before he moves me over his leg. I bite back the desperate whimper that tries to claw its way free, holding his gaze as he does.

"Mila," he grits, his voice rough and uncontained when I grind against him. He repeats the motion with his hand on my hip, and this time, a shudder ripples through me as the burning hot lust ignites in my stomach. "What do you want?"

It just had *to be him.*

"I want you to shut up," I whisper. He presses his lips to the hollow where my shoulder meets my neck, and a shiver rolls through me. My nails dig into his shoulders, soaking wet from the icy water long forgotten overtop of us. His hand tightens to bruising strength on my hip, his other sliding up to fist the curled ends of my hair and drag my head to the side to grant him more access.

A soft whimper leaves my throat while we grind together

shamelessly, neither of us speaking past hushed groans that rumble through his chest and the soft sighs that slip from my lips.

My eyes flutter closed, my pulse racing in my throat, and I lean my forehead against his shoulder in an effort to survive whatever this is that's happening between us.

When a moan claws its way from my lips, he pushes me back against the wall, his body crowding over mine and his hand slipping down to my thigh. He lifts my leg, and my arms go around his shoulders, allowing him to roll his hips into me and draw out the pleasure burning through me.

His tongue slips up the side of my neck, a quiet groan leaving him while we rock together. He nips and sucks a path up the smooth column of my throat, along my jaw, to rim the shell of my ear. Goosebumps pebble on my flesh, and I arch my neck to give him more access, my teeth grazing his shoulder to silence his name, leaving my lips.

He's going to make me come, and we're still fully clothed.

My teeth sink into his shoulder, and he rocks against me harder, a growl on his tongue and my orgasm in the palm of his hands.

"That's it, Mila. Make yourself come."

"Please," I pant desperately against the side of his neck, unsure if I'm begging to come or for death at this point.

"Whose pussy is this, Mila?"

God, I hate him.

"Christian . . ." I growl, but his hands grip me tighter, aligning his hips to brush against my clit at the perfect angle. My eyes roll back, my mouth watering, and my nipples hardened peaks against his chest.

"Whose pussy is this?" he repeats. "Answer the question, Mila."

God have mercy on me.

"Yours." My eyes screw shut as the lightest waves of my orgasm start to trickle through me.

"You get off on my darkness, don't you, sweetheart?"

I can barely hear what he's saying over the rush of blood in my ears, but at this point, I'd be willing to call him daddy if it got me what I want.

"Yeah, you going to come on my cock?"

"Yes," I groan, my head kicking back and my eyes clenching shut. The breath is stolen from my lungs, and I fall into him, my teeth nipping at his neck while he growls above me. Everything in me tightens, shattering from the pleasure that courses through me, a white-hot light shooting behind my eyes.

"Fuck, that's a good girl," he grits, drawing out my orgasm with the brush of his thigh. He pulls back, moving to capture my lips, but at the last second, I evade his kiss. Kissing Christian will only further the depravity in which I want him.

An orgasm is bad enough. Kissing him would be a fall from grace.

The moment my orgasm fades, reality comes rushing back in the form of cold water and post-coital shame.

I just ground shamelessly against the man who broke my heart, used me for years, and kidnapped me for revenge against God knows who.

The same thoughts seem to hit Christian at equal time. He pauses, both of us watching each other in the chill from the shower above, and a shiver moves through me that's actually from the cold this time and not the heat of his body grinding against mine.

He doesn't say a word as he places me on my feet and reaches over to cut the shower to warm, and neither do I.

"Get dressed. Rudy and Paulina will be here soon," he murmurs like nothing happened. Like he wasn't the least bit affected by what we just did. He steps out of the shower while the warm water starts to heat me from the inside out, but it can't replace the heat left behind by his touch on my body.

He gives me one look that says everything. That can't happen again.

Then he walks away, quietly exiting my room and leaving me standing in the shower, shivering from the fire he'd just awoken in my blood.

CHAPTER
Nineteen

CHRISTIAN

I've never been an irrational man.

In my line of work, it's important to remain calm. Have a clear head in case shit goes south.

Right now?

I'm wishing there wasn't a pane of glass separating me from putting a bullet in Collin's head.

There's nothing wrong with Collin in particular. He's worked for my father for two years now, and I've never had an issue with him. He helped me handle my little Jerry problem back in Wichita, and he's always done right by my family.

Right now, though?

I've never hated the kid until I saw Mila smile at him.

Standing at the window of my lighthouse office, I can see him, Mila, and Phantom in the front yard. Collin tosses a stick, and Phantom bounces after it. Mila laughs.

This morning floods back like a fucking tsunami, and just like that, my cock's rock fucking hard in my jeans all over again.

I've jerked off twice in the three hours since then, and yet, it feels like I've done nothing but play some kind of painfully masochistic game of edging.

The way she ground against my cock, silently begging me to keep going. Her teeth in my neck. The fire in her eyes when she told me to shut up. The neediness in her voice when she growled my name.

My fucking name. Not any other goddamn man on this planet. Not *Collin's*. Mine.

She doesn't smile at you, though.

I shake my head, grabbing a pack of cigarettes from the front pocket of my flannel and lighting one up. I've been trying to cut back—you know, health and all—but after this morning, health can suck a dick.

The only thing that stopped me from canceling Rudy and Paulina's visit and dragging her up to the bed to make her come until she spilled every one of her secrets was the knowledge that she wasn't ready. The fear in her eyes when I found her last night in the midst of her nightmare and the trust this morning when she ground on my cock.

Like she knew I wouldn't push her past her limits. Like I was giving her back a piece of her soul that was stolen from her.

I raise the cigarette back to my lips, and I swear I can smell her honey and vanilla on my skin, clouding my judgment and spreading her fucking sunshine all over my island.

Collin tosses the ball, and Phantom takes off after it. Mila laughs, turning that megawatt smile on him.

Then she reaches out and touches his arm.

I may or may not be reaching for my gun when Paulina enters the room behind me.

Fuck the window. I'll buy a new one.

"None of that."

I drop my hand, clenching my fist in my pocket instead. "Why is she smiling at him like that?"

Paulina steps up to the window, looking past me to the scene below with a gentle smile.

"Seems she finds him funny."

"He's not fucking funny," I murmur under my breath.

"You cannot shoot your employee for making her laugh, I'm afraid."

On the contrary, I *could*. I just have to be willing to pay the consequences, and weighing out my options right now, it doesn't seem like it's all that bad of an idea.

"A word of advice, if I may?"

"That's never stopped you before."

She ignores my comment and nods past me to the window.

"If you want her to smile at *you*, I would suggest doing something with her besides kidnapping her and forcing food down her throat."

Touché.

"I'm keeping her alive."

"A life of fear is not a life worth living."

"What's she got to be afraid of?" I ask, even though I fucking know Paulina's right to some regard. I may not have actively hurt her physically, but I know there's a part of my girl that never forgave me for leaving, even if she doesn't know why I did it.

There's also the fact that she was running when I caught up to her. And then there's the drugging and kidnapping her . . .

"What am I supposed to do with her? Braid each other's hair and sing campfire songs?"

Paulina shrugs. "You could start with getting the girl some actual clothes. She can't live in your sweats and giant T-shirts for the remainder of her days."

Fuck. I like my clothes on her, though.

Paulina places her hand on my shoulder, and I grit my teeth, brushing a thumb over my lips.

"If you want her to *stay*, then you've got to give her a reason."

"Who says I want her to stay?"

She smirks, pursing her lips.

"No one had to."

My phone buzzes, and I pull it out of my pocket. A sick sense of joy passes through me at the number on the screen.

"If you'll excuse me. I have to take this."

Paulina smiles, heading toward the door.

"Think about what I said."

"Will do."

Once she's gone, I answer the phone, raising it to my ear. Mila smiles, and something in my chest burns hot and unpleasant in the bullet wound in my chest. I rub the spot, a plan weaving its way together in my mind.

"Hello?"

"It's done."

Click

I can't help but smile to myself, knowing what's coming. Seconds later, there's a ping on my laptop, and I click on the incoming email, reading over the information.

And then I laugh.

I fucking laugh because if I don't, I'll fucking shoot someone, and Collin's looking like the perfect target right now.

How could I have been so naïve? Letting her run the way she did. Letting her get out of my sight?

I was a fool to think she'd actually do it. That she hadn't been forced by some unknown hand.

Mila Carpenter is made with sunshine, whiskey, and that little bit of heroin that keeps you coming back for more.

She'd never hurt a fly . . .

Unless, of course, she thought she was saving its life in the end.

Pictures of that night flashed through my mind. The scars on her skin when I bathed her. How completely fucking demented the carvings are. Like the tattered and charred edges of humanity clinging to someone's soul.

If I let myself think about it, *really* fucking think about it, I can't contain the emotions swirling in my chest.

I can't explain the feeling in the pit of my stomach. Rage. Bleeding, simmering, all-consuming rage that makes my hands shake, and my teeth clench to the point I worry they might shatter in my mouth.

I should have fucking been there, and then this wouldn't have happened.

I've always known it was my fault. Now I have the fucking proof.

I have to make it right.

Knocking on the window, I shoot Collin a look while the smile on Mila's face fades.

Mila glowers up at me, all pretty yellow hair and smokey gray eyes, and the *hate* that seems especially reserved for me.

Collin, on the other hand, gets the idea, running off to help Rudy fuck around with the old boat in the barn, his shoulders stiff.

I chuckle under my breath, raising my cigarette back to my lips.

"Not so fucking smiley now, are you, dickhead?"

Mila's finishing the dishes from dinner while I carry in more firewood when she spots the book I'd left for her on the table. I'd had Paulina find me a copy to bring out to the island.

Rudy, Paulina, and Collin stayed for dinner, and it was the most normal this cottage has felt since the moment we arrived. Mila even laughed at something I said, which surprised the hell out of me.

Since, we've been operating under a fragile truce, neither of us bringing up what happened this morning.

I can't lie and say it's not at the forefront of my mind, though.

"What's this?" she asks, holding it up for me to see.

I shrug. "Thought we could read it."

"We?" she asks, puzzled. Her delicate brows knit together, her soft eyes shining in the warm glow of the cottage lighting.

"Yeah, we," I murmur, dropping the fresh logs by the hearth. I actually wanted it for her, but the idea popped into my head after my conversation with Paulina today.

"How do we read a book together?"

"You read . . . and I listen."

"We could take turns," she offers, falling into a spot on the couch and tucking a blanket around her. Phantom jumps up beside her, laying his head in her lap, and bitterness slips through me.

Jealous of a fucking dog now.

I throw another log on the fire because the wind is howling outside tonight, and she's always cold.

Clearing my throat, I don't answer her, but I can feel her gaze on my back when I slip my flannel off.

When I pour myself a glass of whiskey and sit down beside her, Mila's still watching me with those eyes that see right fucking through me.

"You don't like to read."

"I like to read, just fine," I murmur, taking a drink. The whiskey coats the back of my throat, the burn chasing away the memory of her teeth sinking into my neck.

Fucking hell.

"It takes me a minute," I admit through clenched teeth, my gaze trained on the fire in front of me. "Words and shit on the page get jumbled, and I have to reread it. Just easier to let you read it out loud."

I don't know why I'm telling her this. I've never told a fucking soul.

"You're dyslexic?" Mila asks softly.

"Something like that."

Gently, like I'm made of sharp thorns and poisonous leaves, Mila places her hand on my chest and pushes me back into the couch.

I let her because this is the first time she's touched me on her own.

The moment I'm resting back against the cushions, she drops her hand. Picking up the book and looking over the cover.

"I've never read this one," she says, her gaze flicking up to mine. "I might butcher some of the language."

"Says the girl whose mother made sure she read Aristotle and Shakespeare."

She blushes, rolling her eyes, but the ghost of a smile pulls on her lips.

And it's because of me.

Eat a dick, Collin.

"You handle the asshole killing, and I'll read the classics after dinner for us? Deal?"

I smirk, falling back into the cushions and getting comfortable. "Deal."

CHAPTER *Twenty*

MILA

As it turns out, I can't sleep.

Christian dozed off while I was reading to him, and though my eyes felt heavy, I found that once I got to bed, sleep was nearly impossible.

I can't get him out of my head.

The touch of his hands on my body. The taste of his skin under my tongue.

I also can't stop thinking about how I want to feel those same hands doing *other* things to me.

I've laid awake for what feels like hours, listening to the sound of the waves crashing against the jagged rocks below the cliff and attempting to ignore the dull ache in my core.

It's Christian. The man who broke my heart.

The man *I* shot.

I shouldn't be feeling anything for him other than fear because he kidnapped me.

Just when I think I've got him figured out, he surprises me. Just when I think he's the biggest asshole in the world, like with his little caveman show for Collin—who, might I add, was just being nice—he goes and does something like finds *The Phantom of the Opera* novel, just so I'll read it to him.

Which brings me to my next dilemma. The way my heart ached for him when he explained how hard reading is for him. I had thought when I started reading, he would have checked out, but he stayed silent, listening to me read for almost two hours before he finally fell asleep.

I know he's not resting well enough. It's a fact I've felt guilty about since he brought me here. I'm sleeping in the big, giant bed by myself while he's roughing it on the couch every night, despite my pleas for him to take the room.

He's just . . . a contradiction. How a man can be selfish enough to kidnap me, but also one of the most selfless people I know, is confusing to me. My brain doesn't know how to label him because he's never been inherently good or bad. He's just . . . Christian. One foot in the dark and the other teetering on the edge.

Somehow, I know the longer I stay here with him, the further I'll be forced to step over that edge, too.

I watch the moon in the sky outside the window, wishing it was raining. I've found the rain on the metal roof helps me sleep and keeps the nightmares away. At least most of the time.

I'm struggling to decide if my dream after my nightmare last night was just that. A dream? Or if Christian had really held me in the dark when I thought surely I was going to suffocate from the invisible hands that had wrapped around my throat.

He'd seemed so . . . cold at breakfast, and then when he dragged me into the shower, he was like an inferno, swallowing me whole.

The way his fingers glided along my wet skin. The way he held me, letting me control what happened . . .

"Goddamnit," I grumble to myself when my core pulses, remembering how he'd made me tell him my . . . body belonged to him.

I could just do it myself. What's the shame in that? I'm in bed alone. Well . . . Phantom's beside me, but I could always politely ask him to move to the floor.

Somehow, though, I know it would only piss me off because my hands aren't *his* and I'd be left unsatisfied.

I have to try, though.

Slipping my hand under the covers, I brush them along the planes of my stomach, slipping under the waistband of my panties. My core is soaked and burning hot, and the moment I touch myself, my cheeks burn with shame.

I haven't done this in nearly a year. Not that I exactly had the desire to before Christian came along and fucked with my libido.

Now, it's all I can think about.

And that's going to be a problem.

I withdraw my hand, falling back and staring at the ceiling.

If I go out there right now and ask him to . . . help me, there's a chance he could deny me, and that would make breakfast tomorrow *really* awkward.

There's also a chance he could laugh in my face. I know my body is damaged. I know my scars make people uncomfortable. I can barely look at them myself.

But to see that look in Christian's eyes?

I'm not sure I would survive that kind of humiliation.

Closing my eyes, I lay in bed and count backward from one hundred.

When I open them, I'm still wide awake and burning up, so I kick the covers off and let out a deep sigh.

"This is ridiculous."

Clambering from the bed, I roll my shoulders and pad towards the stairs. If Christian Cross doesn't find me attractive anymore because of the scars that litter my body that I have no control over, then he doesn't have a right to say what I do with it.

Making my way down the stairs, the fire has died down, but the embers glow enough to light Christian still asleep, where I'd left him on the couch. He's got a throw over him from when I went to bed, but right now, with him asleep, it's almost easy to picture him as the scared teen who had just lost his mother.

I know he wasn't a bad kid. No kids are born bad. It's the world that makes them behave the way they do when they lash out. When my father died, I was too young to remember him. My mother and my stepfather were the only real parents I ever knew and look how that turned out.

I can't imagine having to do it alone. Having to find your place in a world that is designed to hate you because your family is dead.

With my stomach in my toes and a fire coursing through my veins that can only be described as Christian Fever, I sink down to the couch on my knees beside him, my fingers reaching out to brush over the ink on his arm.

Only the moment I touch him, I'm thrown onto my back, a very big, very *angry* Christian looming over me.

It's the cold steel of a gun pressed to my temple, though, that sends a shiver through me.

"Jesus fucking Christ, Mila," he growls, dropping the gun to the floor. I don't miss the tremor that moves through his hands the moment he releases me. "I almost fucking shot you."

He sinks back to the couch and lets out a deep breath.

"I'm sorry," I breathe, rising and pressing my back to the couch cushions. I won't lie and say my heart's not racing from having a gun pointed at my head, but I can say I'm not afraid because I know he didn't do it on purpose. "I didn't mean to startle you."

"Fucking hell," he grumbles, scrubbing a hand over his face. "What's wrong? Are you okay?"

I draw my bottom lip between my teeth, my cheeks burning hot when his eyes finally slide over me. He takes in my lack of pants, the thin strip of lace covering the center of my thighs, then the T-shirt that rests just on my hips from where it's bunched up, and his eyes darken.

The silence hums in the air between us.

"Mila?" His voice is noticeably huskier now, his gaze penetrating through the darkness.

"I . . ." Can't speak, apparently.

Guilt washes through me. I woke him up and I can't even say why.

"I couldn't sleep," I whisper finally, like the Pope is hiding around the corner to condemn me for speaking about it out loud.

Christian's jaw feathers, his eyes never leaving mine, despite my inability to meet his gaze head-on for more than a few moments.

"How can I help?",

I chew on my bottom lip, my stomach fluttering with butterflies.

My gaze flicks to his.

"Are you horny, little devil?"

God, I should have never come down here.

"Mila."

"I'm sorry," I breathe. This was a mistake. I move to stand. "I shouldn't have bothered you."

He snatches my hand, halting me. He's quiet for a moment, studying me, while I study the design in the armchair behind him like my life depends on it.

"Don't be sorry for needing me."

My gaze shoots to his. Neither of us move, my heartbeat stalling in my chest under those eyes.

"Do you want me to touch you?"

I swallow past the thick lump of embarrassment in my throat. I shift uncomfortably on the couch, the action creating enough friction between my legs to turn the low, smoldering fire into a dull roar.

I nod, biting my lip hard enough to taste blood.

"Use your words, Mila."

Fuck.

Why do I have to use words when he can already see what I want?

"Yes," I breathe. And then, because I feel like it needs to be said. "I'm not ready for . . . *that* . . . but we could try something else?"

Christian's jaw ticks. His shoulders tight.

Time stands still, and I'm not sure either of us breathes. This changes things. Big things.

"Sit back."

I don't move for a long moment, but when Christian locks eyes with me, the glimmer of the fire in his eyes, it almost feels like a dare. Like he doesn't believe I'll actually do it.

Falling back on my ass. I sit back against the arm of the couch. Christian's face is a mask of indifference when he slips from the couch and moves to the coffee table in front of us instead.

"You're sure?"

Yes.

No.

"I think so."

"I need you to be sure, Mila."

Fuck.

What's the worst that can happen?

Actually, scratch that. We all know that never ends well.

"I'm sure," I nod slowly.

"Sit in front of me. Put your legs up on either side of the coffee table."

I blow out a shaky breath but comply, my bare feet on either side of his hips and my knees locked together in front of him. Christian slips his fingers up my calves, over the goosebumps pebbling my flesh, and for a brief, shining moment, I thank Paulina for thinking of bringing me razors.

"Spread your legs, Mila."

I hadn't realized I had been clenching my knees together like there was a piece of paper being held between them. I release them, letting them fall on either side.

Christian rubs a hand over his mouth, his gaze locked on the center of my thighs.

"Tell me you want me to touch you."

I already did that.

"Please, touch me . . ." I breathe again.

Holding my gaze, he slips from the coffee table, falling to his knees between mine. Reaching behind him, he tugs his shirt over his head, and it's really not fair. He may as well be chiseled marble. I'm sure there are thousands of women who would pay money to see what I'm seeing right now. Christian Cross on his knees in front of me.

He tosses his shirt aside before his hands find my legs again. I have to spread my legs almost painfully wide to keep my feet on the coffee table, but when his hands slide up my bare thighs, I realize that's the least of my worries.

My stomach tightens when he reaches my hips, his fingers kneading the flesh. He tugs me to the edge of the couch, his hands sliding around to brush along my inner thighs.

"Relax, Mila."

My gaze locks with his. I hadn't even realized I'd been holding my breath this entire time.

"What are you going to do?" I ask, voice shaky.

"What I've been thinking about since the moment I brought you home."

Oh, God.

"Eyes on me," he murmurs, leaning down and pressing a kiss to the inside of my thigh, right above my knee. I've never been kissed there, and with the warmth that slips through me, I fear he just created a new fetish.

As if he's testing the water, he moves just a little bit higher, dragging his lips along my skin. My gaze stays locked on his, and when I don't push him away, his tongue darts out, licking my skin up to my inner thigh.

I let out a breath through my teeth, a shiver slipping through me, and Christian chuckles sinisterly.

"Can you focus on my tongue? Focus on how it feels on your skin."

"Y-yes."

"Good girl. Give me a word."

"What?"

"A word to let me know if you get overwhelmed. Or if something doesn't feel right. You say that word, and I'll stop immediately."

I suck in a deep breath, but he waits patiently, eyes on mine.

"Shipwreck," I exhale, finally.

Christian smirks, pressing a kiss to my inner thigh, much, much higher than the other.

"Shipwreck," he repeats.

My throat threatens to close when his fingers hook in the waistband of my thong, his thumbs dragging the material down my legs. He leans back, pulling them off completely until I'm exposed to him, and tosses them behind him.

His gaze centers on my open thighs and heats to a scorching burn.

"Fuck," he murmurs under his breath, bringing his lips back to my skin. He continues to press kisses and swipe his tongue over my inner thighs, avoiding my pussy completely. When I arch my back in an effort to move him closer, he nips the tender flesh of my thigh.

"Patience, little devil," he warns, and my cheeks burn with the heat of a thousand suns. "Can you do that for me?"

God, why does he have to be so hot when he speaks like that?

"Yes." I'm only a little embarrassed about the breathlessness of my voice.

"Good girl," he says again, and it's at that moment I realize I'd do anything to hear him call me his good girl.

Holding my gaze, he slips his hand between us, his thumb swirling through my arousal and coating his finger when he dips it inside me. He continues to kiss up my thigh, getting higher and higher, and just when I think I'm going to lose my mind, he delivers the first swipe of his tongue, licking me from where his fingers enter me to my clit in one fluid motion.

My head sinks back into the couch, my eyes fluttering at the sensation.

He lets out a satisfied groan that rumbles straight through me to my core.

"Fucking perfect," he breathes against my pussy, swiping his tongue through my folds and spearing it inside me.

Those old familiar feelings start to rush in through the cracks. The voices telling me to fight him off. To rake my nails across his face and fight with everything I have. My hands tighten to fists in the throw and the couch below, my mind running rampant now that he's touching me.

"Focus on me, Mila," Christian murmurs from between my thighs. He pulls back, slipping one long, thick finger inside me instead. "Feel *me*. Not them. They can't get to you."

I nod, sucking in a breath through my rapidly closing throat.

"They'll never get to you again," he continues, pushing his finger in and out of me, letting me adjust to the size. "Just feel what *we're* doing. What *we* want."

Smile for the camera, little whore.

"Please," I whimper, but even as I beg for him to stop, I know I don't want him to. I knew what I was asking for when I came down here. I knew the struggle it would be.

I also knew that the moment he made me come this morning, I didn't want to live in the shadows of what they'd done to me anymore.

Christian shakes his head, his eyes boring into mine.

"You know how to make it stop, Mila."

I nod, drawing my lip between my teeth. I know if I said the word, he would stop, no questions asked.

Keeping his fingers inside me, he reaches for the book still on the coffee table, placing it in my hand.

"Read."

"What?"

Has he lost his mind? I can barely form a coherent sentence.

"Read it aloud while I make you come."

"Christian . . ." My voice is husky with both want and devastation. The hair on the back of my neck stands up like those demons are hiding just beyond the reach of the light from the fireplace.

"Do you trust me?"

Do I trust him?

I may not trust him with my heart, but with my demons, there's not another soul on this planet that could chase them away quite like him.

"Yes."

"Then be a good girl and read that book while I enjoy *my* pussy."

Did he just . . .

"You're insane," I whisper, and his eyes light with wicked amusement.

"Oh, sweetheart, you have no fucking idea."

He nods toward the book, and with a shaky voice, I start reading where we left off. He lowers back down, his gaze locked on mine, and draws his tongue along my clit. I gasp, gripping the book tightly in one hand, the other diving into his hair while he sucks me into his mouth.

He groans, using his free hand to push my knee up beside my breast, the other slipping out of me to spread me open for him.

Warmth rushes through me when his tongue finds my clit again, my head lulling back against the cushions and a moan escaping my lips.

Then, he pulls back.

Fuck, I forgot to read.

I resume from a new paragraph, not even sure where I'd left off and Christian circles my clit with his tongue.

"*Fuck, Mila. Like fucking candy, sweetheart,*" he growls against my skin. The roughness of his voice shoves any of my reservations away, replacing them with a heat that threatens to scorch me alive.

My nails dig into his scalp, my fingers fisting the roots of his hair to drag him closer. His slide under my ass, raising me up to meet his tongue, and my head falls back on a moan.

"Christian," I whimper, eyes clenched shut and skin flushed.

"No, you look at me when you moan my name," he growls, and my eyes spring open to meet his. "That's it," he purrs, his voice sending a shiver down my spine. "You aren't reading."

A tremble moves through me, my legs shaking. He lifts one, positioning it over his shoulder and opening me wide before he flattens his tongue and runs it along my pussy.

My head falls back, the book all but forgotten beside me when my hand falls, my back bowing off the couch.

"Oh, God . . ." His teeth graze my clit, before he sucks it into his mouth, fluttering his tongue over the sensitive bud.

"That's it, Mila," he murmurs. "Pray for me, sweetheart. Show me how it feels to be your god."

My eyes roll back, my spine arching to get him closer. Fire spreads through my veins, making my toes curl as the pressure expands and expands, drawing up until I know I'm either going to explode or have the strongest orgasm I've ever had before.

"Christian, please," I whimper, and he must know exactly what I need because he latches around my clit, sliding two fingers inside me and curling them up to brush over a spot I didn't even know existed.

Stars burn in my eyes, the sound of his rough growl, his tongue fluttering over my clit—it's all too much. My core pulses around his fingers, and the final moment that drives me over the edge is when his teeth lightly graze my clit, before he swirls his tongue through my slickness and sends me over the edge.

"*Christian* . . ." My head falls back to the couch. A moan rips free from my throat, and the pressure expands, forcing the orgasm to rip through me.

This orgasm is different, sliding through me in wave after wave of mind-numbing release. I don't think. I *can't* think about anything but him as my hips move against his tongue, and he growls against me, continuing his torture until I'm nearly shaking and pushing him away.

The moment his tongue leaves me, and he climbs up my body, a heavy sense of relief washes over me.

I'm not broken.

I'm. Not. Broken.

"Good fucking girl," he praises, kissing a path up the side of my neck, rimming the shell of my ear, and then finally, nipping over the pulse point in my throat.

All the while, shivers roll through me, and I collapse back on the couch.

When he pulls back, he's watching me with a darkness in his eyes I've never seen before. This look is different. Tinged in possession and something softer. Something that makes my heart beat wildly in my chest, and my toes tingle.

"I'm sorry for waking you," I whisper because now that I've come, the guilt is starting to wash through me. The shame that I could enjoy something like that, despite the marks on my body saying that's exactly what I am.

"Come here."

I stare at him blankly when he rises, sitting on the couch beside me.

Watching me carefully, he leans back, holding out a hand.

A shiver ghosts through me, and slowly, I place my hand in his, letting him pull me into him. His arms come around me, his chin on top of my head while mine is against his bare chest, listening to the rapid beat of his heart.

"What . . . about you?" I ask quietly, the prospect of touching him almost as terrifying as not touching him. As not allowing myself to give into the experience and stop being afraid of what might happen afterward.

I've been on this island for nearly a month and already, I feel like I'm a completely different person than I was when I ran. Revenge or not, I know it's because of him.

He presses his lips to my forehead, his voice rough and raspy. "Sleep."

CHAPTER
Twenty-One

CHRISTIAN

The first thing I notice when I wake up is how fucking hot I am.

The second is Mila grinding against my rock-hard cock.

"*Fuck*," I breathe, blinking up at the ceiling while Mila shifts over me, trying to adjust in her sleep. Looking down at her, the bright sunlight streams through the windows in the front, highlighting her hair in a million different shades of golden wheat. Her lashes sit heavily on her cheeks, her soft lips pouty and so fucking kissable, I reach up, brushing my thumb over them to tug her bottom lip from her teeth.

She moves again, and the friction would bring me to my knees if I weren't lying down, her laying on top of me, our legs tangled together, and her arm wrapped over me.

When she stirs, letting out a soft little moan in her sleep, I can't help myself, gripping her hips to still her.

Mila's eyes blink open when I press my lips to her forehead.

"If you don't stop grinding on my cock, little devil, it's going to

A shiver slips through her and she lifts her head, her cheeks darkening when her eyes find mine.

Fuck . . . those eyes. I could get lost in those fucking eyes.

My hand slides down her back, resting just above the curve of her ass, the soft skin tempting and warm.

"Good morning," she breathes, uncertainty in her gaze. We haven't ever slept together. Not even before. It's a big step. Probably not one either of us is ready for, but I haven't slept that well in years.

I reach up, brushing the hair back from her face and ending with my knuckles slipping over the blush down her cheek.

"Good morning," I murmur, my voice rough with sleep and the need to go take care of the problem pressed between us.

I've stroked myself off every day since I brought her home. It's just her. Having her in my fucking space. Especially when she fought me. I've always loved her fucking fire, but now, after being denied it for nearly a year, I've become an addict.

"I need you to get off me, Mila."

She swallows over the lump in her throat, her hand resting on my chest. I hope to God she can't hear how fast my heart's beating.

"I'm sorry," she whispers, "I shouldn't have fallen asleep."

Fucking hell.

I still her before she can climb off me, guilt washing through me. I wanted her here. I'm not sure I would have given her up, even if she had tried to get up.

"You did nothing wrong."

"Oh . . . then . . . what's wrong with you?"

She shifts again, and I grip her hips hard, holding her in place.

"My cock's rock fucking hard, and I'm trying to do the right thing with you, for once."

Normally, I wouldn't be so forward about it, but with her looking at me with soft puppy-dog eyes, I need her to understand it's not because I don't want her.

Fuck, she's all I've fucking thought about for the last six months.

Probably longer.

She draws her lip back between her teeth.

"What if I don't want you to do the right thing?"

How the fuck am I supposed to navigate this?

"Mila," I grit, my hands tightening on her hips when she shifts against me again, deliberately grinding her bare pussy on the ridge in my jeans.

"Shhh . . ." she whispers, slipping a little further down the couch. "You didn't . . ."

"Didn't what, Mila?" I'm taunting her, trying to force her to say it with her words rather than implied reasoning.

"You didn't come."

Fuck.

Neither of us move for a moment, the sound of her breathing heavy and mixing with mine.

"This wasn't about me."

Something flashes in her gaze, almost like a challenge, and I'm not sure I'm fucking prepared for the patience it's going to take to deny her. My self-control is barely holding on as it is.

With her gaze on mine, Mila reaches between us, her palm finding me through the jeans I fell asleep in last night and her fingers wrapping around me as best she can.

I grit my teeth to stifle the groan that rumbles up my chest, the friction on my cock enough to drive me fucking insane.

I can see the thoughts racing through her head. How unsure of herself she is. I know this is too fast for her. I also know Mila, and we won't ever get anywhere if she thinks she's cheating me.

"Fuck," I grit, pulling away from her. I stand from the couch, and Mila falls back to her ass, her gaze on the rug I'm pacing on top of.

"I'm sorry," she rushes, her voice soft, higher pitched than usual.

It feels like I've been kicked in the dick, despite how utterly fucking hard I am.

"I don't want you doing something because you think it's what I want, Mila," I murmur, voice gruff even if I try to smooth it over.

She doesn't respond and when I look back at her, a tear slips down her cheek.

Fucking hell.

"Hey," I try, forcing a gentleness into my voice I'm not accustomed to.

This shit is new for both of us. After everything that happened, I wasn't sure if she'd ever want to be touched again.

I cross the space between us, sinking down to my haunches in front of her. She doesn't look at me, so I take her chin in my thumb and forefinger and force her gaze to mine.

"Damn near all I can think about is you," I murmur, deciding a little bit of the truth might not fucking hurt for once. "I jerk off in the shower every fucking morning like a goddamned teenager because I can't get your soft little moans out of my head."

She finally chances a look at me, those soft eyes glinting with tears in the morning light. So fucking unsure of the hold she has over me.

"But I also don't want you pushing yourself too hard."

"Can we . . . try something?"

Lead fills my chest, my cock pressing hard against the zipper of my jeans. Fuck, what I wouldn't give to try something. I'd fucking try anything if it gave me even a moment of goddamned peace.

Standing from her, I drop my hand and step back.

A look of defeat crosses her pretty features before I push the coffee table back across the room and grab the armchair from the corner.

"What are you doing?" she asks softly when I place it right in front of her, sinking down into the worn leather and spreading my knees on either side of hers.

"Compromising."

She stares at me curiously when I scoot in front of her, nodding to her legs.

"Place your feet on either of the armrests."

Her cheeks instantly darken, her eyes widening. That lip goes back between her teeth, and she hesitates.

"You going to make me do it for you?"

I wouldn't force her, but the challenge is enough to push her into motion.

Eyeing me with defiance, she places one foot on either armrest beside me, swallowing over the thick lump in her throat.

Not that I'm much better. The sight of her pretty pink folds glistening in front of me has my teeth grinding, a tremor moving through my hands when I unbutton my jeans.

Mila's breathing grows shallow, and she watches as I pull my cock out. I'm so hard I could shatter fucking diamonds across my dick.

I lean back in the chair, getting comfortable, and Mila's eyes follow my hand when I stroke my cock once, biting back a hiss through my teeth at the friction.

"Show me how you make yourself come, Mila."

She looks up at me, striking gray eyes wide underneath thick lashes and her breathing shallow. Fuck, she's so pretty. My mouth waters to taste her again. Touch her. Make her let out those pretty sounds that keep me awake at night.

I'm not blind. I can see the way I get under her skin. How even though she can't stand the touch of a man, the touch of the devil, she craves.

She lets out a shaky breath, her eyes flicking from my cock to my gaze, growing half-lidded and hazy. A shiver moves through her, and her cheeks flame, but her hand slides down her stomach, over the material of my T-shirt she's wearing, to slip along her folds.

"*Fuck*," I breathe, stroking myself slowly in time with her circling her clit. She watches me, her eyes rotating between mine and my hand on my cock. "Tell me how you feel, little devil."

A tremble moves through her, her tongue darting out to lick her lips.

Fuck me.

This is a big step. Getting her to trust me again. Making her need me as bad as I fucking need her.

Showing her that the words carved into her stomach mean nothing between us. She's mine, and I'm hers, and the man who defiled her isn't worthy of licking the ground she walks on.

"Good," she says, voice breathy and soft, filled with lust that goes straight to my cock.

"Are you here with me, Mila?"

She nods her head, her fingers dipping inside herself to gather her wetness on her fingers. When she removes them, they're glistening with her come and visions of last night flash in my mind. Her on her back underneath me. Her thighs clenched around my head when she came.

Her moaning my name and grinding herself against my tongue.

"Feel how wet you are, sweetheart?" I rasp, stroking my cock harder, my chest rising and falling with my rapid heartbeat. She swirls her fingers up to her clit, her back arching off the couch and her eyes locking with mine. "See how fucking hard you get me?"

"Christian," she mewls, her eyelashes fluttering on her cheeks and a flush working up her neck.

"Forget about everything and just be here with me, Mila. Feel me."

Her eyes tighten, her fingers working her clit faster. I speed up my pace, a groan passing my lips as heat lances up my spine.

"Feel good?"

"Yes," she whimpers, her breaths panting between each stroke of her fingers on her pussy.

"That's *my* pussy, Mila. And when I fuck you, you're going to feel me for days. You won't be able to come without me inside you. That what you want? To be at my mercy."

"Christian," her head kicks back, and I can see she's so close to coming, she can fucking taste it. Good thing, too, because I'm not sure how much longer I can hold out.

"You want my cock? Fucking you until you can't think of anything but how good it feels inside you?"

She clenches her eyes shut, and all I can do is grin savagely as her perfect little body tightens in front of me. Writhing with the need to come.

"Fuck, I can't wait to watch you take me," I growl, and she moans, the sound damn near sending me over the edge. I lean forward, my eyes transfixed on her as she makes herself come. "You going to be a good girl and come for me?"

"Yes, please, Christian . . ." she moans, even though she's the one controlling this. She needs me to push her there.

"Come for me, Mila. Let me see you let go," I grind out between my teeth.

She moans, her head falling back against the cushions, her fingers moving faster, harder until her body tightens, the orgasm ripping through her.

Finally, I let go, coming so hard I see stars behind my eyes and squirting into my palm with a feral groan. When both of us float back down to reality, her eyes lock with mine.

Then she fucking giggles.

I cock my head to the side, the sound doing something to my chest. "Are you laughing at me, little devil?"

She grins, and I realize this is the first time she's smiled at me in a year. A real fucking smile.

She smiles at *me*.

Eat shit, *Collin*.

"I just realized Phantom got the whole bed to himself while we slept out here on this tiny couch."

I chuckle under my breath, tucking myself back in my jeans and rising from the chair.

"Fucking dog's got it better than most humans."

I'll admit, I didn't like the little fucker at first. But . . . like everything on this damned island, he's growing on me.

I head to the bathroom and clean up, cutting the water on for Mila to take a shower before I head back out to the living room. When I return, she's curled up on the couch, in danger of nodding off again.

Stooping down, she lets me lift her up into my arms, carrying her to the bathroom, a breathless laugh leaving her lips.

Somewhere along the way, the lines between us became blurred. Instead of thinking about how I'm going to get her safe and back to her family, I'm suddenly thinking about ways to keep her here.

It's dangerous. Stupid fantasies that will never come to light.

When I sit her on her feet, though, and there's a moment where both of us are breathing the same air, my dick telling me to kiss her despite her pushing me away before, and my head telling me it's for the best if I don't . . . those lines might as well be nonexistent.

"Take a shower. I'll start breakfast."

Levi: We need to talk.

I ignore my brother's text as I have every day for the last three weeks and watch Mila clean out the greenhouse below.

Not that anything will grow inside with the cold coming soon, but I'm happy to see her find something to do with her time while I'm in the office.

I was finally able to get ahold of the footage from that night at the hospital. The car that dropped her off was a blacked-out Volvo SUV.

They pulled up to the curb by the road and barely stopped before they pushed her out onto the sidewalk, leaving her there to bleed out.

If it weren't for the homeless man sitting against the side of the building who alerted the hospital, who knows how long she would have laid there, waiting for help while she bled out?

It pissed me off. Seeing her like that, broken and bloody and all fucking alone. I want to skin the men who did this to her alive and leave them in a field to rot on wooden spikes in the hot sun.

Sometimes, I sit and think about all the things I'm going to do to them when I find them. How I'm going to make them bleed. Cry for their mothers and beg for mercy.

It won't come, though. I'll let them choke on their own blood, slowly downing themselves until they aren't alive to hurt anyone ever again.

Especially not her.

I'm standing at the window, watching Mila cart out a bucket of old vines and leaves, when my phone buzzes in my pocket.

I pull it out, gritting my teeth when I see the name, but I answer it anyway.

"I told you I would call."

There's silence on the other end of the line, and I cross the room to my chair, my eyes going to the photograph I'd pulled out of my wallet still laid out on the desk.

Absentmindedly, I rub the ache in my chest. Fucking bullet.

"You've found her."

"I did."

"And? Does she know?"

"No."

"Fuck," the man on the other end of the line sighs. "I'm coming up there."

"You have a wife to think about. Your mother needs you."

"*She* needs me too," he growls. "It's my job to protect her."

"Not anymore."

He chuckles darkly. He knows what I did. Shortly after he married his wife, I changed the course of both our lives. I don't regret it. He may not like it, but I'd do it all again in a heartbeat.

"You don't get to make that choice," he grits.

"I already did."

"You remember what I said if you hurt her?"

His voice is menacing, and if it were anyone else in the world, I'd probably laugh. Mason Carpenter isn't one to fuck with, though.

"Because I have to say it," he says, holding his wife's hand as she lays in her hospital bed, passed out from being shot only hours before. "I'll fucking kill you if you hurt her."

"I'm doing this for her."

"Kill me, and there's no guarantee she gets out of this alive."

"Fuck," he grits, letting out a deep breath. He's silent for a moment, and I almost think he hung up when he speaks again. "Hannah's pregnant."

"Congratulations." I mean it. Mason's gone through some shit, but he's a good man. Loyal. Big as a fucking linebacker, but he deserves this. So does Hannah.

"Thanks," he says dryly.

"Honeymoon faze over, already?"

"Fuck no," he murmurs.

At one point, Mason and I were close. Like brothers. He's the reason I started working for Parker in the first place.

We all wanted the same thing: Parker dead.

"So what's the problem?"

"You've met me," he murmurs. "I'll find a way to fuck that kid up."

Mason doesn't talk about his feelings. Most men don't, but he may as well be a fucking closed door, chained shut. I can relate.

Feelings aren't something I fuck with, either.

"Kids don't know it's your first time being a dad," I say, remembering something my mother once said. "They just want you to be there and to try. You're going to be a good father, Carpenter. Hannah's going to be a good mom."

He's silent for a moment. "She'll be the best."

"I'll call you when I need you," I tell him, standing from my desk. "If you show up here unannounced, I'll shoot. I even see the whites of your eyes."

"Christian," he says before I hang up and I pause. "Bring my sister back."

CHAPTER
Twenty-Two

MILA

"Mila, get the fuck down from there!"

I shiver as the wind whips my hair into my face, looking down over the edge of the hospital building.

My mother swore she wouldn't bring me back here. She swore and then she did it anyway.

Now they're here.

It would be so easy to jump. So easy to let this all end so no one else has to get hurt.

Why doesn't he understand that? That my presence is only causing more pain?

I hate him. I hate him for making me love him. I hate him for lying to me about who he was. I hate that after everything he's done, his leaving, his aiding the enemy, there's still a massive hole in my heart where he should be.

Most of all . . . I hate that I still love him despite all of that.

"Why can't you leave me alone?" Guilt washes through me, this feeling of loneliness gnawing at my insides until I feel like I'll bleed to death from the inside out.

head spins, the edge fading in and out of existence, and I take a step to the side to steady myself.

It would be so easy . . .

"Mila," Christian grits, his voice filled with anger. I turn around, and his eyes look to the ledge, then they meet mine, and there's nothing but hatred in that gaze that used to look at me like I was the only girl in the world.

"Let me go . . . please?"

"Mila, you jump off that roof, you're killing us both. Remember that."

He doesn't understand. They're coming back, and when they do, it won't be me they'll hurt.

I almost laugh. Why does it always have to be death?

Chaos swallows us both the moment the wind batters against my side, and I stumble, my sneaker slipping on the damp metal. Christian lunges forward, catching me around the waist, and we both topple to the ground below the ledge, a grunt forcing its way out of him and my breath being crushed from my lungs when he catches me on the concrete of the rooftop.

No, I have to do this.

I struggle in his arms, fighting with everything I have, but he's so much bigger than me. So strong, where I'm weak after weeks of toeing the line between life and death. I thrash against him, and he struggles to gain control, pinning me against his chest.

"Let me go!"

"Goddamnit, stop it!"

It's when a deafening pop sounds through the air that both of us freeze.

"What the—"

I look down to where a dark spot is appearing in the front of his gray T-shirt, my entire body filling with ice.

No.

No, no, no, no.

"You shot me?"

I shake my head, the words getting stuck in my throat as the pain erupts in my chest. I look down at the pistol in my hand.

Did I shoot him?

Horror washes over me, my eyes filling with tears.

How did I do that? How could I do that? I shot him. I shot Christian.

"*I'm sorry,*" *I whisper, the gun falling to the rooftop in a pool of his blood leaking from the wound. My head spins, my stomach filled with dread.*

How could I shoot him?

"*I'm so sorry.*"

"*Mila—*"

"*Shh . . .*" *I breathe, my hands roaming over him as a shiver wracks through him.*

How could I shoot him?

How did I do that?

Ripping the jacket off my shoulders, I grab his hand. They'll be coming soon, and I can't let them find me. He won't let me go, and my being here only brings more pain.

I place the jacket over his wound and force his hand to hold it there; the pain, unlike anything I've ever felt when a tremor moves through him. A sob wracks through me, my tears mixing with the light rain falling from above.

His phone hasn't stopped ringing since he followed me up here and finally, I reach over and pull it out of his pocket, my brother's name lighting up the screen. I answer it, placing it to my ear.

"*He's on the roof.*"

Christian's face is pale. His skin slick with perspiration.

Panic swells in my chest with the knowledge that this may be the last time I ever see him.

"*I'm so sorry,*" *I whisper, and he stares up at me, his eyes fluttering over thick lashes. Steeling myself, I bend down, pressing one soft kiss to his lips. "I love you.*"

He opens his mouth, but no sound comes out. Just the decrepit gargle of death as his eyes glass over.

I killed him.

I killed him

"*NO!*"

I batter at his chest with my hands, desperation clinging to every one of my senses.

This is a mistake. I couldn't have killed him. He can't be dead.

"What are you crying for?"

I shake my head at the evil, awful voice.

It's not real.

"You did this. Look at me."

I keep my eyes clenched tightly. Refusing to open them.

I didn't do this.

"Look. At. Me."

Sitting straight up on the couch, a scream of fear rips its way from my throat. I fight at the hold of the hands reaching for me, panic slipping through my veins like venom.

"Mila."

Strong arms hold me against a warm chest, a hand coming up under my chin to force my eyes to look up into two deep blue ones.

"You're here."

Leather, whiskey, and the forest fill my senses, a sense of calm washing over me like a bucket of ice water.

He's not dead.

My hands shake as they roam over him, but there's no blood.

A dream. It was another fucking dream.

Angrily, I shove away from Christian, rising from the couch. It's the middle of the day and I'm stuck in my own brain. The nightmare still clings to the edges of my mind, burrowing it's way in deeper until I can't escape.

"I need a drink," I grumble, storming towards the stairs.

"Mila."

Christian's footsteps are heavy on the staircase behind me, but I don't stop. I'm in no mood to explain what that dream was about, nor do I want to think about it.

Crossing the living room, I head straight to the liquor cabinet hanging on the wall and pull out his precious bottle of whiskey, popping the cork off and putting the bottle to my lips for a drink.

Only it's ripped away before I ever get the chance.

"Stop," I grit, whirling on Christian only to find him shoving the cork back in the bottle and placing it back in the cabinet.

"What we're not going to do is drink."

"Why? Men do it all the time."

"Drinking won't solve your problems."

"In case you hadn't noticed, I can do bad, all on my own. I don't need you to feel sorry for me."

"Good. I don't."

"That's nice, Christian. You know, maybe you should go into counseling. You have a stellar approach," I mutter dryly, tears welling in my eyes as I stomp towards the bathroom.

"Where are you going?"

"I don't want to do this right now."

"Mila, get the fuck back here."

"Or what?" I challenge, spinning back to him so fast, my hair whips me in the face.

"This is what you want to do? Relive the same fucking night over and over, or do you want to move past it?"

"Stop!"

"No," he argues back, his voice raising over mine. "You want to wallow in your self-pity, or are you going to do something about it?"

"I don't want to do any of it anymore!"

My chest heaves with the force behind my words. My ears ring in the silence, my throat sore and tight.

"I am so *sick* and fucking tired of everyone thinking I'm *wallowing* in self-pity." I scrub a hand over my face, refusing to look at him. If I look at him, I know I'll break.

A chuckle tears from my throat, but it lacks any real emotion.

"Do you know what it's like to wake up alone in a hospital bed covered in your own blood?" He's silent, and I can feel his eyes burning my skin. "To not know if you're having your period or *instead* . . . thinking you'd never really made it out and everything you'd gone through the past few weeks was all just some bullshit dream meant to fuck you up before you die? Have you ever known what it's like to lose something so precious and have to live with the guilt?"

I meet his gaze, and there's not an ounce of emotion in it. Nothing but silence. I can tell by the look in his eyes he didn't know.

Fuck, no one knew.

"To hear your own mother *crying* when she thinks you're asleep to her boyfriend because you can't even stand to be in the same room as her, let alone give her a hug. To have to look at your body in the mirror and *hate* yourself because all you can see is the reminder of what happened carved into your skin and know it's *your fault* ?"

The silence is so loud it buzzes in the air around us.

"Because I do," I breathe. A tear slips down my cheek, and I swipe it away. I won't cry. I've spent weeks of my life crying.

"Not that it makes a difference to you," I utter under my breath. Why am I telling him any of this? He's already said he doesn't care. The Christian in my dreams and the Christian right in front of me are two very different people. "I was just the easy one, right?"

Christian doesn't say anything, his gaze trained on the wall behind my head. I keep waiting for whatever words of wisdom he thinks he has because that's what everyone does. They say some bullshit line about how it'll get better. How it'll hurt a little less as time wears on, but none of them really know. They're just trying to make themselves feel better by offering me a stick disguised as an olive branch.

"Get dressed," he says after a long moment, and I just blink at him. I guess I was so lost in my own thoughts I'd almost forgotten he was there. He turns to me, and his gaze holds a look I can't place. Something dark and teeming with anger but broken and savage at the same time. Before I can place it, it's gone.

"What?"

"Get dressed. We're going somewhere."

"Where?" I ask, a sense of longing filling my chest at getting off the island.

"You'll see."

"What is this place?"

Christian pauses on the stairs when I don't move from my place on the sidewalk. To be honest, the old brick building on the outskirts of Seattle looks abandoned from the outside, but he takes my hand in his, pulling me up the stairs anyway.

We haven't spoken since we left the island an hour ago, and to be honest, being out in the open is terrifying, even if the neighborhood around us is calm and quiet.

"I have something to show you."

"You sure you're not leading me in here to murder me?" I taunt, but it lacks its usual enthusiasm after that hell storm that was my latest nightmare. I want to tell him about it, but . . . I also don't. I want to move on and forget any of it ever happened, but I can't.

Christian punches in another code to a big metal door and pulls it open, letting me slip inside.

Contrary to the outside, the inside is alive and bustling with activity. People mill about the long hallway of what looks like an old school, and chatter can be heard from the rooms on either side.

"What is this place?" I ask quietly as he leads me through the crowds. People stop to stare, mostly at him, in awe. It's as if he's a god, come down to grant wishes to the peasants.

"This, little devil," he murmurs, pulling me closer to his side, his hand tightening around mine, "Was my work."

My skin warms when he touches me. This feels . . . intimate. *Too* intimate, but I don't pull away.

"Your work?" I cock a brow at him, confused, and he nods, stopping by a woman surrounded by people. She's older, and you can tell she runs things by how everyone is crowded around her, asking her questions.

"Well, tomorrow, you've got the bathroom on the second floor," she tells a young woman who groans. "Don't think I won't check."

"Fine," the woman huffs, then her eyes land on Christian.

I know that look.

. . . I don't like that look.

She looks at him like he's her hero, and I feel guilty for the bitter jealousy that creeps up on me.

"I didn't think you'd show up here," the woman says, pushing her hair back from her face.

She's beautiful. Striking red hair and pretty freckles on her nose. Her brown eyes are soft and warm as if she knows him.

"Kelly . . . If that's what you're still going by," Christian greets, giving her a nod. He doesn't release my hand, even when I try to slip back. "This is my wife, Mila."

What a *liar*.

I hold my hand out, but she doesn't take it, so I let it fall awkwardly to my side.

"Nice to meet you, Mila," she says, and I feel another pang of guilt for the disappointment in her voice. "And it's Lindsay, actually," she corrects Christian.

"Nice to see you're sticking to your real name," Christian says just as the busy woman finally turns to us.

"Haven't seen you in a while." Then, her gaze turns to me. "Special case?"

"My wife," Christian lies. "Mila."

I roll my eyes at his use of *my wife* and hold out my hand again. This woman shakes it, and I think it finally clicks for me what this place is.

"Finally. It's about time," she chuckles, offering me a soft smile. "She's beautiful," she tells Christian, who smirks. "Names Pat," she explains. "This is my house, and these are my girls."

"Pat runs the rehabilitation center," Christian explains quietly in my ear. "Girls come here after they're removed from whatever situation they were in, and she helps them get back on their feet."

"This is your job?"

"Was," Christian corrects. "Pat's been here as long as I can remember."

"She'll just make you clean toilets," Lindsay complains quietly.

"Speaking of," Pat says, turning back to her. "Are your chores done?"

"No," Lindsay grumbles, her cheeks darkening.

"Off you go."

Lindsay disappears, muttering under her breath, while Pat shakes her head.

"First step to rejoining society is teaching them a strong work ethic. Can't have them going out there and ending up right back where they started."

"So, this is a place for people . . ." I start, but the words trail off.

"People who went through hell."

I swallow past the lump in my throat, looking around. They're all so . . . normal.

"Each of our girls was a victim of ST," Pat explains. "We don't like to say the word around here. It can be triggering for some."

"Miss Pat," a young voice says, and my heart flutters when I see the little girl who can't be more than eight years old when she tugs on Pat's hand.

"Why, yes, Miss Lily? What can I do for you?"

"Can you braid my hair?"

"I can't braid," Pat says. "I'm sorry. Never learned."

"I know how," I say, surprising even myself. There's a brief moment of silence, and I know Pat's going to shut it down, but before she can, Lily speaks up.

"Can *you* braid my hair, then?"

"What do we say?" Pat corrects her. "This is Mrs. C."

"Please?"

I look back at Christian, who gives a subtle nod.

"I would love to."

Lily squeals in delight, grabbing my hand and tugging me down the hall and into one of the classrooms. Christian hangs back, but I only have a brief glimpse of him watching me before she pulls me around the corner.

The classroom turned bedroom is what you'd expect out of a dormitory. Bunk beds line each of the walls, with the center of the room open with a table littered with crayons and coloring books. A couple girls sit, chatting while they draw, but Lily pays them no mind.

"This is my bed," she says proudly, pulling me to the pink-covered bottom cot, the wall littered with pictures she's drawn.

"It's a very nice bed," I concede when she pushes me to sit down on it. It's not. It's worn and used. There's a spring sticking out of the mattress on the side, but it's all she has, and that makes my throat swell.

She rifles through a little plastic trunk underneath before producing an old hairbrush that appears to be older than I am.

"Here. And you'll need this." She hands me a string of silk ribbon that matches her bedding. My heart stutters in my chest when I realize it's a piece that tore.

I'm thankful when she turns around and grabs one of the little chairs at the center table, pulling it between my legs and plopping down in it.

She can't see the tears in my eyes that way.

I have a feeling they've seen enough heartache and pain to last a lifetime here. They don't need mine, too.

"How long have you been here, Lily?" I ask while I brush her hair. The couple of girls who were coloring have left, so now it's just her and me in the bedroom. It's calm. Peaceful despite what this place is. I imagine it's become a sanctuary for people like Lily. I don't know her story, but to end up here, of all places when she should be enjoying her childhood, it can't be good.

"Ummm . . . Two years. I think." She shrugs. "I don't know. I've lost count."

I clear my throat, combing through a particularly bad knot in the back of her head while trying not to hurt her.

"Do you like it?"

"Yeah. Miss Pat lets me help with the cooking and the dishes. She's teaching me how to read right now. I read a whole book the other day without her help."

"Wow," my voice croaks. "That's impressive."

"Yeah, but the other girls can already read, so maybe not."

"Miss Pat seems like a very nice lady."

"She is. Way better than my last mother. She yelled a lot."

"Moms do that, sometimes," I murmur, thinking of my own mother, whom I haven't spoken to since the wedding.

"My first mom was the best, though. She used to bake cookies. That's all I remember."

"I love cookies."

"Me, too. I like oatmeal raisin."

I crinkle my nose, chuckling.

"Yuck. You like wrinkly grapes?"

"They're good," she admonishes, turning around to face me. Her soft blue eyes twinkle with mischief. "What's your favorite?"

"Sugar. Sugar cookies are the king in the cookie world."

"Bo-*ring*," she laughs, then her eyes catch on my hair. "You have pretty hair. What happened to your head?"

I swallow past the rock growing in my throat. My scar.

"Uh, well . . ." I stammer, my cheeks flaming red. "I was in a sort of accident."

She stands, then, lifting up her shirt to showcase a deep scar on her stomach, surrounded by small white marks.

Marks of a knife. Marks that match mine.

My stomach clenches, my mouth filling with saliva from the nausea roiling in my stomach.

She's so young and . . . little.

"Me too." She pauses, suddenly shy. "Is that why Mr. C loves you so much?"

I nearly choke on air at her observation.

It's because he called you his wife, the voice in the back of my head chimes.

"Mr. C is a good man," I say softly, patting the chair in front of me, and she sits back down. She's quiet for a long moment while I braid her hair.

"You don't have to be afraid anymore. At least, that's what Miss Pat says. I still get scared, sometimes."

Me too, I want to say, but she's a child. From the looks of things, she's come a long way from wherever she was when she first arrived.

"We all have nightmares," I say finally, twisting her blonde locks down her back. "We just have to teach ourselves that they are just that, now. Nightmares and not real life."

"Just got to put one foot in front of the other," she chimes happily, kicking her feet in the chair.

"Did Miss Pat teach you that?" I chuckle.

"No. Mr. C."

My heart flutters in my chest, the familiar burn on my skin at his proximity alerting me of his presence before I even see him. Peering back over my shoulder, I see him leaning in the doorway, watching me with a strange look in his eye. Pride? Possessiveness?

Something that definitely shouldn't be there. Not between Christian and me.

"All done," I say after a moment, and Lily squeals, rushing over to a mirror with a crack in the center to inspect my braid job. I'll be honest—I'm not the best, but she doesn't seem to care, beaming ear to ear and touching the small pink bow lightly.

"How do I look, Mr. C?"

"Like a princess," Christian murmurs, winking at me when she twirls. "Miss Pat's waiting for you," he says. "Said you always help her with dinner."

"Oh, yes. I'm *very* busy." She huffs like she's got a full itinerary of tasks that need to be completed for the day. "I have to make the pudding, and then I need to roll out the dough for our bread."

She starts to hurry out the door but pauses, spinning and rushing back to me when I stand from her bed. The force behind her little body colliding with mine nearly sends me falling back on my ass when she hugs me.

"Thank you, Mrs. C."

I force myself to swallow and not let the tears that gather in my eyes fall down my cheeks.

"Anytime, Lily."

CHAPTER
Twenty-Three

CHRISTIAN

"You shouldn't lie to them."

"I was wondering how long it would take you."

She narrows her gaze on me across the car and I don't have to look at her to know her cheeks are bright red.

"Well, I am *not* Mrs. C," she huffs, leaning back in the seat.

Not yet.

"Some of the girls get a little . . . attached."

"So, you used me," she points out, and I make no move to deny it.

"Shall we even the playing field, little devil? I can think of plenty of ways you can use me in return."

"You're impossible," she groans, brushing a hand over her face to hide her smirk.

"You're beautiful."

She shakes her head, turning back forward, and I chuckle under my breath.

So easy to rile up.

"So, some of the girls get attached . . ." she says, and I can tell she's nervous to ask. One glance at her, and I see her shifting in her seat. "Lindsay, or whatever her name is. She seemed . . ."

"Attached?"

She nods, biting her lip between her teeth.

I cock a brow at her, and she avoids my grin.

"This new side of you is turning out to be my favorite."

"What, curious?"

"Jealous."

She gawks at me, her mouth falling open, and my mind goes to all the dirty, filthy things I want to do to her.

Between our argument earlier and watching her come out of her shell at Home of Hope, to just having her in my fucking space, filling the car with honey and vanilla, I'm starting to think this hard-on is perpetual. I'm not sure it'll ever fucking go away.

"I am *not* jealous," she argues, though her tone of voice suggests the exact opposite. "I'm observant." She brushes her hair off her face. "They totally saw through your lie, by the way. I don't even have a ring."

"That can be arranged," I murmur dryly, running a thumb over my bottom lip.

"I'm serious, Christian."

Funnily enough, so am I.

"Lindsay was a case I took while I was away. It was simple. In and out."

"Last year?"

"Last year," I nod.

"Is that why you left?"

I grit my teeth, mulling it over. For once, I decide to tell the truth.

"No, it had nothing to do with why I left."

"You're her savior," she says after a moment when I don't answer. She shrugs. "It makes sense."

It doesn't. I'm not their savior.

"I'm no one's savior, Mila."

She's quiet for a moment, and I know what she wants to say. I'm happy when she doesn't. The last thing I need is her thinking this is anything but what it is. My bringing her back to her family and putting an end to a problem I created. Nothing more.

I've known she would hate me since I walked back into her life. She will, too, soon enough.

"It's better she gets the idea out of her head now rather than later."

"Do you . . . you don't think it'll hurt her, thinking we're married?"

To tell the truth, I don't really care. Not in the way Mila does. She's worried about her feelings. I'm just worried about the effect it'll have on her treatment. Lindsay, like a lot of women at the home, doesn't know what real love looks like. Fuck, I don't either, but I know it's not me.

"No," I answer, hands gripping the steering wheel tightly. "I think it's best she learns to focus on herself now and worry about shit like that later."

"Easier said than done," Mila says dryly, sinking back into the seat and resting her head on the headrest. I side-eye her, and her expression's grim. I don't fucking like it. "What about Lily?"

My spine stiffens. "What about her?"

"What's her story?"

I grit my teeth, pulling down the path that will lead to our island. "It's dark, Mila."

"Everyone's story is dark in the wrong light, Christian."

I shake my head. Lily's story is one that keeps me up at night when I can't sleep. I've watched her grow up from a five-year-old crying little girl to an eight-year-old that doesn't take shit from anyone.

Oddly enough, she reminds me of Mila.

"She was sold by her grandfather to pay off an underground brothel in New York."

She's silent and I feel her stiffen beside me.

"How old was she?"

"Five."

"And her mother?" Mila asks quietly. "She spoke about her."

"She was murdered. Shortly before Lily was sold."

She lets out a deep breath, trying—and failing—to discretely wipe a tear from slipping down her cheek. My chest feels tight. Heavy with each breath. I think I surprise even myself when I reach across the center console and place my hand over hers in her lap. She jumps but doesn't push me off.

It shouldn't mean anything, but a new kind of darkness stirs inside me.

The dangerous kind.

Carefully, like I might bite her, she twists her hand over and entwines our fingers. Both of us are silent.

Why does holding her hand feel like the most intimate thing we've ever done?

"I would like to help her," Mila says softly.

"What would you like to do?"

She blinks at me like she's surprised I'm open to the idea.

"New bedding, for a start. Their blankets are tattered. All of them."

I nod, my fingers tightening around hers when she attempts to disentangle them.

Fuck her, she's not getting it back.

"She's been there a long time. Three years in a month or two."

"And she has no family?"

"None that wouldn't put her through a worse hell than what she's already suffered."

She's quiet, staring out the window ahead. I wish I could step inside her mind and see what's really going through that pretty little head of hers. Especially after I found her screaming and in a full panic.

"Mila."

She peeks over at me, finding me watching her.

"Do you think I'm being harsh with my own mother? Disappearing the way I did."

It's the first time she's spoken about her mother out loud.

"I think you were dealing with a lot of shit happening all at once."

"I don't know," she breathes, a tear slipping down her cheek and falling on top of my head. "I can't help but feel like maybe if I had spoken to her . . ."

"This trip wasn't about guilting yourself, Mila. You're allowed to have demons, just like everyone else. It's what you do now that matters."

"I feel guilty for the way I left. In the middle of the night. She didn't deserve that. She . . ." Mila turns away, wiping her hand across her eyes.

"It's not about who deserves what."

Part of me wants to tie her to my bed until she tells me who was after her. The other half is prepared to burn the world down and rid it of anyone who could even have the chance.

"Thank you. For today. I know it's outside our rules."

"Don't thank me, Mila."

I pull to a stop at the dock, and neither of us moves, staring out over the water at the dim lights of our island.

"Why do they call it Shipwreck Island?"

"Because there's a ship sunk just off the north side."

A shiver rolls through her at the thought, and she falls silent for a moment.

"You know, when you're not stroking your own ego, kidnapping someone, or being a flaming dickhead, you aren't so bad," she smiles.

"Thought I was an egotistical asshole?" I muse, throwing her earlier words back at her.

"You are," she admits quietly. "But you're also a good man."

We both fall silent, and the air between us hums with unspoken shit I'd rather not think about.

Like the way my chest tightens when I look at her.

Or how my heart quickens when she smiles.

Definitely not the picture I've kept in my wallet for three years that's worn and tattered from being taken out and held too many times.

Fuck.

Something sickening slips through my veins. A bitter resentment that I can't tell her about our past. That I didn't leave because I didn't care.

I did care. Just way too fucking much.

"I'm not a good man, Mila."

"I . . . think you're afraid of anyone finding out you are."

I grit my teeth, my hand tightening on the steering wheel.

"I've hurt a lot of people. Killed a lot of people."

"Would you hurt me?"

I'd chop my fucking dick off first.

"If I had to."

She's silent for a moment, and I wait for her to exit the car. The part of me that wants to take her in the cottage and spend the next five days reminding her exactly who the fuck I am wants me to grab her and drag her inside.

Slowly, she raises up on the seat and moves towards me as if she's approaching a wild animal. Right now, with the scent of her enveloping me, she's not fucking wrong.

"*Mila,*" I grit, my voice rough when she slips into my lap.

I push the seat all the way back as she hovers over me, her legs straddling me on either side and her cunt pressed against my dick.

Fuck. Me.

Her eyes are heavy, her lashes fluttering over her cheeks when she looks down at me in the darkness of the car. It's nearly pitch black, save for the dash and what little light streams through the tinted windows, but she's never looked sexier than right now, taking what she wants.

Fuck, I want to give that to her.

My hand slips up the back of her smooth calve to the pulse point just behind her knee, my fingers digging in.

She leans forward, her lips hovering over mine, and my cock presses painfully against my zipper at the taste of her. "You have until the clock strikes two to do whatever you want to me," she breathes, her pulse fluttering.

My gaze flicks to the clock.

Three minutes.

I'll make it fucking count.

Most men would reach for her pussy, slip their fingers inside her until she caved and stayed longer than her allotted time. This isn't about getting her off, though. It's about making her desperate for me. It's about getting her addicted to me.

So, when her lips meet mine, my hands start to roam. I go for all the places I know will have her wanting more.

I kiss her rough, my tongue tangling with hers and drawing a whimper from her throat that has me gripping the backs of her thighs until I'm sure there will be bruises from my fingertips tomorrow.

Good. I want her to have a reminder that I was there.

She kisses me while I explore her body, memorizing the way it feels in my palms after so much lost time. My hands slide over her ass, then under her dress, toying with the edges of her panties. Then they slip down to her front, stroking over her inner thighs. Goosebumps rise on her flesh under my hands, and I bite back a smile against her lips when her breath hitches.

Her hands come up to my shoulders, the blunt ends of her nails scraping across the back of my neck, and a tremor rolls through me.

The kiss grows stronger when I grip her hips and roll her over my cock, just once, to let her feel me against her center. She's so fucking warm, I can feel her through my jeans and boxers, and it takes everything in me not to fuck her right here.

"Christian," she breathes, and I groan when she breaks the kiss, my fist tightening in her hair while I nip a line from her jaw down to her throat when she meets the next thrust of my cock.

Fucking perfection.

She lets out a desperate whimper, and her head falls back to the ceiling with a shuddering breath.

Then, as quickly as it started, it's over.

"Times up," she breathes, shakily climbing off my lap and practically hurling herself out the door.

I want to go after her and drag her back. I want to pin her to the bed and make her come until she tells me her secrets. I *want* her screaming my name until it raises the dead on that miserable, sunken ship just past our island.

Unfortunately, none of those things will happen tonight.

"Fuck," I rasp under my breath, my cock aching in my jeans. I scrub a hand over my face, my gaze finding her standing at the front door, waiting for me.

I can't keep her, but the thought is enough to have me picturing just how pretty she'd look in my bed. Coming home to her happy and smiling every night. Fucking her into the early hours of the morning and crashing with her wrapped in my arms, only to do it all over again the next day. Sounds like fucking heaven.

And also as unrealistic as a world with no crime.

Getting out of the car, I slam the door behind me, unlocking the front door while Mila heads inside without a word.

The air between us has shifted. Something tense and volatile lying just beneath the surface.

The thought of giving her up puts me in a dark mood. Like I either need to fuck her or kill someone.

There is no in-between.

I have a plan.

Is it a good one? Fuck no. In fact, it has a high probability of getting me shot.

Am I going to do it anyway?

Watching her take one last glance out over the water towards where the ship lies underneath the glistening black surface, I already know the answer.

CHAPTER
Twenty-Four

MILA

You can do this, Mila.

It's Christian.

One foot in front of the other.

I let out a shaky breath, my hand hovering over the doorknob to the lighthouse.

Get in there, champ!

Okay, my inner pep talk is getting a little out of control.

Steeling myself, I push the door open and step inside. It's a warm day today, and the sun is shining outside, so the first floor of the lighthouse glows.

Distracting myself, I picture what kind of furniture you could put in the circular room. Another living room? A reading nook?

Shut up, Mila.

"Fuck," I breathe. I take the stairs up to the second floor, pausing outside Christian's office.

The worst he can do is kick me out.

I think I'd probably pitch myself off the cliffs, but my inner monologue isn't wrong.

Tentatively, I knock, worrying it was too soft before I hear his voice like warm dark chocolate drift through the door.

"Come in."

A shiver rolls through me, and I twist the knob, stepping inside.

Christian sits behind his desk, closing his laptop that was open in front of him. His brow tips up, and he smirks, the look in his eyes going straight to my core.

Why does he have to look so . . . devastating?

"Miss me, little devil?"

I wipe my sweaty hands on my jeans, drawing my bottom lip between my teeth. I stay back against the door while he watches with dark amusement in his gaze. I expected him to yell at me for coming up to his office when he was working, but judging by the look in his eyes, he'd been thinking about me, too.

I can't believe I'm doing this.

Christian leans back in his chair when I slip the jacket off and drop it in the chair in front of his desk. He turns to face me when I approach, and somehow, this is far more terrifying than anything that's happened in the last year.

His eyes drop to my worn sneakers, slipping up my jean-clad legs over his T-shirt, covering my breasts, before finally meeting mine. It should make me want to back out, the degradation in his gaze, but it only makes the fire burn hotter.

I clear my throat, unable to push the words out.

"You want my fingers?" He raises a brow, and delicious heat slips down my spine. I shake my head, my cheeks flaming under his heavy gaze. "My tongue?"

I shake my head again.

Why is this so hard?

"Use your words, Mila. You want me to drop everything and fuck you? That can be arranged."

"Not . . . yet," I say, breathless. "We're uneven."

He pauses for a moment, studying me. After a moment, his gaze goes dark as night.

In this moment, I realize I'm fucked. I've never cared as much about pleasing someone as I do when I watch him run a tongue across his teeth, his abs flexing under his T-shirt.

He's taken my body to places I never knew existed—places I never thought I would reach just because of my past. He forces me out of my head and lets me experience true pleasure and pain in a way I didn't know I would crave.

"You want my cock in your mouth?" The way he says it, so dirty and full of promise, sends a shiver through me. Slowly, I nod, my tongue darting out to lick my lip.

Christian's jaw ticks, and he studies me for a moment. Finally, he leans further back in his chair, his leg kicking out in front of him. His arm rests on the armrest, his other coming up to run a thumb across his lips.

"Crawl to me."

I still, my heart bottoming out in my chest.

"What?" My voice sounds small, even to my ears. Fragile.

I refuse to be fragile anymore.

He holds my gaze, raising a brow as if he's daring me.

"Get on your knees, put that pretty little ass in the air, and crawl to me."

He can't be serious.

I've never even given a blowjob before, and he wants me to crawl like a pornstar across the hardwood floor?

But . . . looking in his eyes, I see a promise. He is. And if I want it, I'm going to have to work for it.

Goddamn him.

"Fuck you," I snap, tears burning in the backs of my eyes. I make my way to the door when his harsh laughter sounds behind me.

"Too proud, little devil?"

I grit my teeth, spinning back to him. Of course not. I just . . . I don't want to give him the satisfaction.

Goddamnit.

I lick my lips, and his eyes follow the movement. Something hungry passes through them before it's replaced by a look of indifference.

He wants me as bad as I want him. He's just afraid to show it.

"You want my cock?" he taunts, cocking his head. "Crawl to me. Unless you'd rather spend the rest of the day thinking of how my cock would have felt sliding between your pretty lips."

I hate him.

I hate him, and I crave him. I've never been so at war with my own emotions.

It's not as if I'm not scared. I'm fucking terrified, but with him in control, I feel comfortable giving myself over to him because I know he'll never let me crash.

Gritting my teeth, I step back towards the desk. My thighs are slick with need, my pussy throbbing with the beat of my heart. It's the middle of the day, and here I am, sinking to my knees in the office of the psychopath who kidnapped me, about to crawl to him so he *lets* me suck his cock.

What has the world come to?

Holding his gaze, I slowly, sink to the carpeted floor.

Deciding to see how far I can push him, I make sure to arch my back, holding his gaze as my hair falls around my face. My hips move sensually, and his eyes follow their sway as I come to rest at his knees. Sitting up on my legs, I smile angrily.

"Better, *sir*?"

He smirks.

"It's a start."

His cock is hard. I can see the outline through his dark jeans. My mouth waters despite the nerves swirling in my stomach.

"Scared?" he asks, leaning forward enough to run his thumb over my bottom lip.

Yes.

"No."

His fingers slide back into my hair, roughly jerking my face up to meet his gaze. A slight tremor moves through his hand, and a sense of power I never knew fills me.

"So fucking beautiful," he rasps, and my heart flutters for an entirely new reason.

He watches me, his gaze running over my face as if he's studying a priceless artifact.

"You want my cock in your mouth?"

God, his words are so dirty, but something in my core tightens, and I nod my head, licking my lips. This is what I've been craving. The high he gives me when he's growling my name. At *my* mercy.

"Ask me nicely."

A rush of resentment washes through me at his bossiness. This was supposed to be a test to prove myself.

Then, I realize the way my core pulses and tightens at his words. How much I like that he's in control, showing me that he's got me.

This is exactly what I need to fight off the voices in my head. Total surrender.

A shaky breath leaves me. "Please?" I ask, and his eyes grow half-lidded and hazy with dark lust. "Please, can I suck your cock?"

"Undo my belt," he says, his voice rougher than usual, and birds swarm in my stomach.

—We're way past butterflies at this point.

I swallow self-consciously when he lets go of my hair. Gripping his belt, I undo it when he sits back. The clang of the buckle sounds too loud in the quiet office.

My hand shakes, my mouth impossibly dry—a real problem at a time like this—when I slip my hand into his boxers and pull his cock out.

God, I don't know if I'll ever get used to his size.

My gaze flicks back to Christian's, and he eyes me with a slight amusement in his heated gaze that makes me angry. I refuse to let him win.

"I thought you weren't scared?"

I glare up at him, stroking him from root to tip, and his nostrils flare. The tip of his cock glistens with precum, the thick veins dark and angry where it stands straight up.

"Mila."

My stomach dips at the demanding tone of his voice. Like a man on the brink of losing control.

I lean forward, pressing kisses along the head of his cock, delighting in the way his abs draw up tight at the contact.

I slip my lips lower, over the veins and to his balls, my tongue darting out to lick his heavy sac before moving higher.

I don't have any idea what I'm doing, but he doesn't seem to mind if the way he's tensing under my hands is anything to go by.

I tease him, staring up at him from beneath my lashes while I slide my tongue along his length. His hand slips back into my hair, fisting the strands, and he jerks my head back, forcing my gaze to meet his nearly black one.

God, he looks like he could murder someone. My stomach tightens in anticipation.

"Mila. Suck my cock."

Heat travels through me, pulsing in my core. Swallowing my fear, I tug at his hand in my hair, raising his cock to my lips before slipping him down as far as I can into my mouth. It's awkward and messy, but he lets out a curse as his head falls back to blink at the ceiling.

"*Fuck*, that's a good girl."

I pull back, swirling my tongue around the head, before I push him further into my mouth, only able to swallow half his length before I'm choking and sputtering.

"That's the sound I've been waiting to hear," he grits roughly. His hand slaps my cheek. Not hard enough to sting, but enough to have my pussy tightening with need. "Open your mouth and stick out your tongue."

I oblige, and he does the most savage thing I've ever experienced and spits on my tongue.

God, forgive me.

"Suck."

I let out a small moan, slipping his cock back between my lips and taking him deeper. My tongue slides along the underside, and my fist wraps around the bottom half, feeding him between my lips. I don't think I've ever been this turned on in my life.

"That's it." His thumb captures a tear on my cheek. His gentleness is a stark contrast to the burn of his hand in my hair. "Suck my cock like a good girl, little devil."

My pussy clenches, and I set up a steady pace, rocking on my knees while I bob my head on his cock.

"Fuck, you're so much sweeter when your mouth's full," he murmurs, and I glare up at him, letting him feel a brush of my teeth. His fingers tighten painfully in my hair, and I'm sure some of the strands rip free, but I don't stop sucking. "I fucking dare you, Mila. Try to bite me. See how well it ends for you."

My clit throbs at his dark words, and as much as I hate to admit it, my body responds. The wetness coating my inner thighs is enough to drive me insane, as is the incessant throb in my clit.

I suck him harder, my eyes rolling to the back of my head as he grits his teeth.

That power could get addicting. Mark my words.

His hand in my hair guides me over his cock as moans spill past my lips. I shift on my knees, rubbing my thighs together to relieve some of the pressure. "You want me to fuck your face?"

I blink up at him in acquiescence, and he growls, the rumble traveling through his body and straight down to my core.

"Fuck," he grits, brushing the hair back from my face. "Tap my thigh if you want me to stop."

Holding my head in a firm grip, he pushes up into my mouth, his cock slipping into my throat until tears spill past my lashes. I force a breath through my nose to stave off a gag as he hits deeper than I was able to.

"So obedient. You going to swallow my come like a good little slut?"

I moan, sending vibrations through his cock, my thighs rubbing together to try to lessen the ache. His hand locks under my jaw as he pushes past the confines of my throat, forcing me to take more of him than air. Tears stream from the corners of my eyes, but I refuse to tap out.

"Relax your throat and let me in, sweetheart," he grunts, pushing further. "Fuck, let me see how much you want me."

My chest flutters at his words, and I force myself to suck a breath through my nose, letting him fuck my mouth until drool slips down my chin. His fingers dig into my skin, and the sting slips down to my pussy.

"Stick your tongue out," he hisses between his teeth, pulling his cock out of my mouth and linking his fingers over mine, stroking his length. Watching him stroke himself with my hand is probably the hottest thing I've ever seen, but I don't tell him that. Sticking my tongue out, he holds me there, his eyes boring into mine when he grunts, coming with a deep, soul-snatching growl. "*Fuck, Mila . . .*"

His come hits my tongue, my cheek, and my lips. The taste of him blooms in my mouth and I swallow it down greedily. I hold still, mostly because his hand is forcing me to, but also because watching him come for me is madly unsettling, and I wonder if this is how he feels when he does it to me.

I want to see it again. I would pay money to see it again.

A shudder moves through him that he covers up by scrubbing a hand over his face before he looks down at me. I caught it, though, and something warm and unwelcome ignites in my chest. Something that definitely shouldn't be there for a man who kidnapped me and is holding me hostage on a deserted island.

"Open," he orders, his thumb swiping through the come on my cheek. I open my mouth, and he wipes it on my tongue, pushing his fingers to the back of my throat and making me gag. My core tightens at the savage look in his eyes. "Swallow." I do, and he chuckles darkly, not an ounce of amusement in those dark eyes. "That's my good girl."

He reaches for my hand, tugging me to my feet, and I stand on wobbly legs, my pussy crying out at the friction from my panties.

"Bend over."

"That wasn't for me," I gasp, and he just swats my ass, pushing me to stand between his legs. He shoves me towards the desk, standing behind me. He places a hand on the center of my spine, bending me down to rest my shoulders and cheeks against the flat surface.

"This isn't either."

He swats my ass before slipping my jeans down my legs. I shiver in the cool air of the room, despite how hot I am, when the phone rings from beside me on the desk.

"What?" he snaps, sinking down in the chair behind me with the phone pressed to his ear. My cheeks flame that someone is calling him while I'm standing in front of him, ass on display and his come on my face. "I'm in the middle of something."

There's a pause as the person says something else on the phone, and he runs his fingers over the soaking-wet seam of my panties. I grit my teeth, biting down on my arm to keep quiet when he slips them to the side and slides a finger inside me.

"I have something time-sensitive on my desk, and you're keeping me from it."

There's another pause while he pumps his fingers in and out of me, slowly drawing out the torture, before he hangs up with a rough breath.

"Christian—" I start, but it ends with a moan when he runs his tongue through my folds.

My eyes roll back in my head, and my front bows off the desk. Holy shit.

"You enjoyed sucking my cock, little devil." It's not a question. More of an accusation.

"Yes," I breathe, my fingers gripping the other side of the desk while he dives back between my folds with a deep groan of satisfaction. He swirls his tongue up to the tight ring of muscles at my ass, and I jerk forward on the desk before his hands lock my hips in place.

"Breathe," he instructs, his voice rough, and something presses against the hole, stealing my breath away. I shudder when his thumb enters me, his tongue immediately going back to my pussy as he fills my ass.

"Christian," I moan, my eyes screwed shut from the pleasure barreling through me. My legs shake with the effort to hold me up, and I'm so close to coming I can taste it. "Please."

His thumb moves in and out of me slowly while he licks my clit in lazy strokes. He closes his lips around the nub, fluttering his tongue, and my legs threaten to give out.

"I'm going to fuck you here soon," he breathes against my skin, slipping deeper inside me, and my pussy clenches in response. "You want that? You want my cock in your ass?"

"Yes," I breathe, actively working to breathe as he continues his assault on my body.

"Fuck, I've been dreaming of you," he grits, and I don't even know if he realizes what he's saying before he closes his mouth around my clit and sucks me into his mouth until I'm gasping underneath him.

I can't stop the orgasm from shattering me into a million pieces. I cry out, my voice hoarse and my hips bucking wildly while he milks the pleasure from my body. I collapse to the surface of the desk, shaking, and he has to hold my legs up to keep me from falling to my knees again.

I shiver when he pulls me back from the desk, placing me in his seat before crossing the room to grab a box of unopened tissues from a drawer in the corner.

Of course, they're unopened. I doubt Christian Cross would ever get sick.

When he returns, my heart is racing, and my skin is damp with perspiration. It all happened so quick, but now that it's done, I'm waiting for him to kick me out.

Instead, he surprises me when he gently takes my hand, pulls me to the edge of the seat, and kneels down in front of me.

"Let me see," he murmurs, a strange tenderness in his voice that I've never heard from him before. I tilt my head to him, and he wipes the drying come from my face and the makeup that ran from under my eyes. Keeping my gaze, he then gently cleans between my legs, and it's enough to make my cheeks burn brightly.

"Okay?" he asks, his eyes betraying his carefully concealed concern. I wait for the fear to slip through me, my throat closing over painful breaths, but . . . nothing comes.

There are the usual thoughts. *Whore. Broken. Damaged.*

But when he tucks a curl behind my ear, searching my gaze with a fine-tooth comb, I realize, no matter what his reasoning is for bringing me here, he's the only person I would choose to heal with.

Christian is all man. Rough and hard. The darkness in the light.

He's also seen every one of my horrors, my nightmares, my inability to be touched when I first walked into the cottage, and he's never made me feel like I was anything other than me.

"I'm good," I whisper, and a smile tugs at the corners of my lips.

Christian runs the back of his knuckles down my face, a smile pulling on his lips, and for once, this feels normal.

We feel normal for the first time ever.

"I've got a phone call to make, and then I'll be down for dinner, okay?"

"Who called?" I ask when he pulls back and helps me stand. My legs are wobbly when he stoops down to slip my jeans back up my legs.

"Rudy," he murmurs, and something about the way he says it and the fact that he won't look me in the eyes tells me it's a lie.

Why would he lie about who's calling him?

"What would Rudy want?"

"Probably to talk about that damned boat," he grunts.

"Are you—"

He silences me by tugging my hand, forcing my body to his. He presses a kiss to the corner of my lips, and the silence stretches between us as we breathe each other's air for a moment too long.

I want to kiss him.

God, do I want to kiss him?

I can't, though. Kissing Christian would open up the door for those feelings I'm desperately trying to keep at bay. Kissing is a lover's game, and he's already made it clear we will never be that again.

Eventually, he's going to use me for his revenge. Whatever that revenge may be, what's happening between us is transient.

Until then, I'll use him to get myself back.

I step back, my head spinning from lack of breathing.

"I'll go start dinner."

"You . . . don't have to sleep out here."

Christian pauses as he sets up the couch for the night, his eyes flicking to where I stand at the foot of the stairs.

God, why do his eyes feel like stepping naked into the center of a crowded football stadium?

"I just meant . . ." Fuck, what did I mean? "You can sleep in the bed if you'd be more comfortable."

Inviting Christian to sleep with me—actual sleep—sounds like a worse idea than reusable toilet paper, but I hate sleeping in the big bed by myself, knowing he's out here cramped on the couch.

He stares at me for a beat, and the air hums in the silence stretching between us.

Okay, maybe this was a bad idea.

"I'm closer to the door," he murmurs finally, and embarrassment floods through me like hot tar.

Way to go, Mila.

"Right," I nod, forcing a smile on my ever-burning cheeks. "I'll see you tomorrow, then."

I hurry upstairs before he can see the bitterness coursing through me and practically swaddle myself in the blankets as if they can hide me from the weight of my actions.

Why would he want to sleep with me? Why would I even ask such a question?

It's not like it makes a difference where he sleeps. *He* kidnapped *me*, remember? I should get the bed on the principles of hospitality.

So why do I still feel like I ate a bag of sour candy?

My heart collapses when I hear the creak of the stairs, and I quickly rearrange as if I were getting ready for bed and not contemplating leaping from the back cliff to sink amongst the broken ship to hide from the embarrassment of being rejected.

When he stops at the top of the stairs, I force myself to meet him with an indifferent gaze.

Something tells me he can see right through it, though, judging by the way his eyes light with dark amusement.

"I get the side closest to the stairs."

Alarms sound in my head when he steps over to the bed, leaving me frozen in place right in the center.

They get infinitely louder when he reaches over his head and tugs his shirt off.

My eyes travel over the thick, hard ridges of his abs, the tattoos, the sculpted V leading down beneath the jeans he's wearing. Then . . . he shoves his jeans down his legs, standing before me in nothing but a pair of boxers with the best butt I've ever seen.

"My eyes are up here."

Fuck.

I quickly look away, fluffing my pillow aggressively, and he chuckles under his breath, sliding into the bed beside me.

Okay, now that he's in it, this bed feels small. Like baby mattress small. I'd forgotten how it feels to fall asleep next to him.

Not to mention hot. He's like sleeping next to a space heater. In LA, it was a minor inconvenience. Here in the cold Washington fall, it's far too tempting to curl into him.

He settles on his back, and so do I. A silence falls over the room, and neither of us speaks. Nor moves.

Hell, I don't even breathe.

"Are you warm enough?" I ask after a moment, just to break up the silence.

I know, me personally? I'm on fucking fire.

"I'm good."

I swallow over the thick lump in my throat.

This is just like those damn romances where there's only one bed.

"I can scoot over—"

"Mila."

Fuck.

"Stop."

My voice squeaks when I respond. "Stop what?"

"Overthinking."

May as well ask me to stop breathing.

"I'm not."

"Little liar."

"What's your family's lodge like?"

He's quiet for a moment, thinking.

"Big. In the mountains. It was passed down from my grandfather to my mother."

"And now, it's your legacy?"

"Something like that," he murmurs.

"Tell me about something," I offer, rolling onto my side facing him. It's a mistake because he's even more devastating in the dark.

"About what?"

I shrug, tucking my hands under my head.

"Anything."

He cocks a brow, side-eyeing me.

"You want me to tell you a bedtime story?"

"No," I grumble, rolling my eyes. "Just anything. Something that you've never told anyone."

He's silent for a long time. I wait patiently, watching him look up at the slats in the ceiling above.

Just when I think he's either fallen asleep or he's going to deny me, he speaks.

"When I was a kid, I had this dog named Pepper. She was just some little mutt, but she was a good dog. She fucking loved pancakes. Mom would make pancakes every Saturday, and the damned dog always got the first one."

"Your mother had her priorities straight," I chuckle softly.

"She fucking loved that dog," he murmurs, shaking his head. "Sometimes I wondered if she loved the dog more than us kids."

"You have siblings?"

His jaw ticks, and his eyes finally find mine.

"I had three. Two—now. A brother and a sister. I'm the oldest."

Figures. He has big brother energy.

"Can . . . I ask what happened to the other?"

He stares at me for a beat before facing back toward the ceiling.

"Gone. Died in a fire the night Mom did. Up at the old cabin, Dad used to own."

"I'm sorry," I breathe, warmth pooling behind my eyes. Why am I always crying when he tells me about his past?

"Don't be. Shit happens."

"You have such an absolute view of it," I murmur. "Most people would struggle with losing their family that way."

"No use being sad over shit you can't change," he mutters gruffly. "Mom was a good person. A good mom," he adds after a moment. "Just prefer to think of that rather than what happened to her."

"What were they like?"

He smirks, chuckling under his breath.

"You and Mom would have gotten along. She would have loved you."

"Why do you say that?"

"Because Mom had a knack for finding the sickest creature she could to try and nurse it back to health."

"She sounds lovely," I quip, and he smiles softly.

"She was. Too fucking nice for her own good. Dad didn't deserve her. She may not have realized it, but I did."

"Why do you say that?"

He's silent, turning to look at me. His eyes search mine, sliding from my lips up to my hair. A tingling sense of awareness slips over me, but I force myself not to hide.

"A lot of men don't deserve the women who love them, Mila."

I can't decide if he's talking about us or in general, so I chose not to allow myself to think about it. Thinking about it will only get me more questions that I'm not prepared for the answer to.

"Or maybe a lot of men are too hard on themselves." He doesn't respond.

"Not my father."

"You don't get along."

"We never have," he murmurs. "He was always a dick. Mom was everything Dad could never be, and he hated her for it."

"What was your mother's name?"

"Mom was Elizabeth. My brother was Sebastian."

My eyes are growing heavy, but there are so many questions I want to ask him that he would never answer before.

"I'm sorry you lost them," I whisper. He opens his mouth, but whatever he was going to say is lost when I reach for his hand, wrapping my fingers around his.

It's hard to believe the mountain of a man beside me would be the same person as the kid who must have been terrified. Part of me wishes I could go back in time and stop those things from happening, but I also know everything happens for a reason, and no matter how painful it was, it shaped who he is today.

How many girls would he not have saved had he not been through so much bad himself? Would he have left Washington and come to LA, or would he still live here, living a completely different life, right now? Maybe married with a couple of kids. A dog they rescued from the pound and a house with a white picket fence.

I can't stop myself from picturing what his wife would look like. Beautiful with a gentle smile and soft hands. A kind heart, just like his mother. Maybe she'd make pancakes every Saturday for him and the kids, or maybe they'd spend the morning lazing around in bed together.

Whoever she is, she's beautiful. Perfect for him in every sense of the word.

I hate her. I hate her, and she's not even real.

"You were sent to us by the FBI to bring down my stepfather, weren't you?"

"I was."

"So . . . that's why you and Bailey . . ."

"I never wanted your sister, Mila."

"Oh."

"I was meant to gather intel. The easiest way to do that was through the people closest to Parker. Bailey thought I wanted her, so I played into the role. Nothing more than a few off-hand comments."

"Makes sense," I grumble, because that doesn't mean I don't hate it.

"Bailey's a good girl, but . . ." he reaches up, brushing his knuckles down my cheek. "Unfortunately, I couldn't get this little blonde brat out of my head . . . still can't."

My chest clenches with the butterflies taking flight in my stomach.

"You shouldn't say things like that to me."

"And why's that?"

My heart feels like it's going to fly out of my chest.

"Because it makes me think thinks I shouldn't."

He opens his mouth to speak, but I cut him off.

"You said you *were* in the FBI. Why did you stop?"

He blows out a breath through his teeth, his chest heaving. He's quiet, and I almost give up when he speaks.

"I didn't quit. I was fired."

"Why did they fire you?"

"Because a year ago they wanted me on another job. I refused."

"Why would you refuse?"

He looks at me, studying me.

"You know why, Mila?"

Tears sting in the backs of my eyes and I look away. So much has happened that led us here, and yet, I'm learning more and more about him every day.

His fingers intertwine with mine, and we hold each other's hands for a long time, neither of us speaking. After a while, he releases me, only to hold out his arm instead.

"Come here," he murmurs gruffly, rolling onto his side to face me.

I stay where I'm at, eyeing him apprehensively.

"It's not like you're not going to end up here, anyway. Just so we can sleep," he explains, holding his arm open for me to slide into.

I go, nestling into his warmth, and a cold chill sweeps over me when he wraps his arms around me, holding me against his chest.

Just like old times . . .

"What you said last week . . ." he starts, his voice barely legible over the crashing of waves against the rocks outside. "You lost something precious . . ."

"*We* lost something," I whisper softly, a silent tear slipping down my cheek. "I don't know when it happened. Probably when you . . .visited me."

Thinking about that day, the moment I found out? It *hurts*. Like running a knife over the same wound, letting it heal, and then repeating the process over and over again.

"I wasn't far along." I clear my throat past the lump lodged there. "I didn't even know."

Absentmindedly, his fingers stroke over the scars on my stomach, but he doesn't speak.

"I'm sorry I didn't tell you sooner," I whisper, blinking back the tears that cling to my lashes and willing the familiar numbness to take over. "It . . . just hurts knowing . . ."

His arms tighten around me and he presses his lips to the side of my neck where my hair's fallen away. It's gentle and sweet. Protective and possessive. Everything I've always wanted from him and everything I know I never should.

"The Universe put those men on this planet, Mila," he murmurs roughly against my ear. A shiver ghosts up my spine despite the warmth of him at my back. "And when I find them, I'm going to take them out."

He leans down, pressing a kiss to the top of my head before leaning back against the pillows.

"Sleep."

CHAPTER
Twenty-Five

MILA

I don't think I've ever been this excited in my life.

"What are the rules?" Christian asks, buttoning up my coat like he's my dad sending me off to my first day of school. It's not even cold out, but because he's taking me off the island, I don't argue.

"You've asked me that three times."

Cocking his head, he tugs me closer by the pockets of my coat. My heart lurches in my chest, my nipples brushing against the lace of my bra.

What has he turned me into?

"And now I'm asking you again."

My tongue darts out to lick my lips, my mouth impossibly dry simply because of his presence. It's been three days since I gave my first blow job, and I've found myself wanting to do it every day since, just because I like the way I can make him fall apart.

He pinches my chin between his thumb and forefinger, tilting my gaze up to his, and every nerve ending in my body short circuits.

."

My stomach sinks. I *need* off this island. Just for a few hours, so I can feel like a person and not just a very sexually satisfied captive.

"Like what?"

"Like you're thinking about my tongue between your legs."

I wasn't thinking about that.

I definitely am now.

"That what you want?" he taunts, voice low and dark as sin. He steps even closer until I'm forced to fall back to the table, my ass resting on the edge. "You want to cancel our trip and let me spread you out on the bed? Make you come on my tongue until you can't remember why you wanted to leave in the first place?"

A shiver ghosts up my spine when his thumb brushes over my racing pulse.

The asshole's trying to con me into giving up my day of almost freedom.

"You fight dirty," I grumble, and he chuckles darkly.

"Play dirty, too," he smirks. "What are the rules?"

I let out a huff. "No running off by myself. If I see something suspicious, tell you. If I see anyone I recognize, tell you. If anyone asks, you're Christian Smith, and I'm Mila Smith, your devoted wife of two years." Had to roll my eyes at that one. "Don't tell anyone I've been kidnapped in an attempt to one-up you . . ."

"And?"

"And no smiling. No breathing. No blinking. No chewing gum . . . Did I miss anything?"

"Yeah." He takes my jaw in his hand, forcing my gaze to his when I attempt to climb down from the table. "The moment you feel overwhelmed, tell me. We'll come home."

Home . . .

That's actually kind of sweet.

I swallow past the lump forming in my throat, the heavy silence between us weighted with everything neither of us has been willing to discuss. How I shot him. How he left me.

We've both made mistakes. I actively make them every day when I don't tell him the truth about that night and why I did what I did on the hospital roof.

I want to tell him. I want to share that with him, but . . . it's hard. Pain is hard. It's ugly and disgusting. It *hurts*, and we've both been hurt enough for a lifetime already.

Telling him now just rehashes old wounds that are finally starting to scab over. I'm not sure I'd survive ripping them open again.

"Talk to me, little devil. What's on your mind?" he asks quietly, studying my eyes as if they're a window to my thoughts.

God, I hope not. I'd hate for him to see how fucked-up my mind *actually* is.

"Do you . . . you don't think anyone will recognize us . . . right?"

It's been weighing on my mind since I woke up this morning, and he told me we were going into town over the French toast I'd made us for breakfast. The possibility of someone recognizing us.

I don't know anything about the area, but Christian says the town is small. Filled with happy people who are none the wiser that we're hiding out here instead of just keeping up with the lighthouse. I also haven't been out since that single time he took me to Home of Hope, and that was just a there-and-back trip. I barely got to see the outdoors.

Christian reaches up, brushing a curl from the scar on my forehead, and my toes curl at the touch of his fingers against my skin. Then, like it always does, my anxiety rears its ugly head, and I can't help but picture the day this will all come crashing down around me.

The day he sends me back to LA or wherever he plans to get rid of me.

"I've been checking around. I wouldn't take you out if I thought there was even a possibility of someone finding us."

I let out a shaky breath, nodding.

I can do this. It's just a trip to town, right? Just a little trip to town with Christian, who may as well be four secret service men in one. Nothing bad will happen . . . right?

"*Mila.*"

I hadn't even realized I was spacing out, imagining the bus stop in Arizona all over again.

"Sorry," I breathe, wiping my clammy palms on my jeans.

"You're safe."

"Easy to say when you aren't the one kidnapped."

"Don't think of it as kidnapped. Think of it as spontaneous relocation."

I can't help but roll my eyes, a chuckle sliding through my teeth.

"Don't think of us as fake husband and wife, then. Think of us as mutually hostile sexual partners."

He cocks a brow, stepping back from me and holding out a hand to help me hop down from the table.

"So . . . husband and wife."

"You're impossible," I say to the back of his head when he leads me toward the door.

"You're beautiful."

It's just a store.

Just a store with people who sell store things.

"Mila."

"What are we doing?"

Christian looks down at his giant T-shirt I'm wearing and my worn and tattered jeans.

"You need clothes, little devil."

"I like wearing your clothes," I murmur, and when something

sinful passes through his gaze, I realize what I just said and have to explain. "You know . . . because they're baggy and comfortable."

He can see right through me, but he doesn't argue it.

"We'll just get some stuff so you can feel like you again."

"I already feel like me." It's a lie. I don't even know who *me* is anymore.

Christian calls my bluff on this one, shooting me a look that says as much.

"What are you worried about?" His tone softens, and when I look away, the asshole grips my chin and forces my gaze back to his.

"Nothing."

Another lie.

Why can't I stop lying?

"You're safe, Mila," he says, his tone conveying he'll make sure of it. "I've checked this place out already."

I saw my bottom lip between my teeth, looking back to the front of the store.

I haven't been in a clothing store since before the attack.

"I have to try on clothes," I admit finally on a breath, and it feels like a crater opens up in the center of my chest, stealing all the oxygen in my lungs.

"You will."

He doesn't get it. Tears sting in the backs of my eyes, and I shake my head, still looking at the front of the store. A few women walk in while I'm watching, and my throat threatens to close.

They look so . . . happy.

"Your scars are your biggest strength, little devil." I turn to look at Christian just as he reaches up, catching the lone tear that trails down my cheek. Of course, he would know this is about the scars. Why wouldn't he? He knows everything. "Use them."

I stare at him for a beat, staring into his deep blue ocean eyes. Eyes I could look at for hours.

"I don't know how," I whisper, and it feels like dropping a

weight off my chest to finally say that out loud.

"Would it make you feel better if I waited in the car? Let you go in alone."

I would rather chew off each of my toenails individually.

"No-please—"

He silences me by pressing a finger to my lips.

"Then, I'll be right there with you."

Leaning across the center console, his hand slips around the back of my head, and he presses his lips to my forehead. It's the most gentle he's ever been, and the crack in my heart that was already bleeding for him widens to a fissure.

"Come on. We've got a whole day planned."

Christian leads me out of the car and into the store, taking my hand in his when we enter. It's loud and bright, full of colors and women laughing as they sort through clothes. Looking over at the mountain of a man beside me, the scar on his face, and the dangerous look in his eyes, I almost laugh. I would if I weren't so damned nervous.

Christian does *not* belong here.

"How can we help you?" a young woman asks Christian, completely ignoring me.

That's fine. I'm too busy having an existential crisis over looking at pants.

"We're fine. Just looking."

"Well, if you need anything, my name's Callie, and I'd *love* to assist you."

Okay, that's too far. I mean, I'm right here. I literally had his dick in my mouth three days ago.

Callie, who just has to be one of the most beautiful brunettes I've ever seen, senses my displeasure and backs off, heading to the counter to do whatever homewreckers do.

Christian, on the other hand, just chuckles, shaking his head and tugging me along to the first aisle.

"I must say, I like this new side of you, little devil," Christian says, stopping at the T-shirts.

"She was totally hitting on you. I'm supposed to be your wife," I whisper, sticking close behind him while he looks at shirts.

Christian only smirks.

"Luckily for you, I prefer little blonde brats."

My next retort is lost on the tip of my tongue. That's not what I expected him to say.

Eat a bag of dicks, Callie.

He chuckles, motioning to the wall of clothing in front of me.

"Pick your poison. What do you like?"

"We established that I like your clothes."

He shoots me another look. I'm getting a lot of those lately.

"We'll start with shirts. Then jeans. And then whatever else you want."

"You don't need to buy me clothes, Christian." It feels weird because I know there is no way in hell I'll be paying for any of it. I had six dollars and a Chuckee Cheese token to my name when he "spontaneously relocated" me in the middle of the night.

"As I've said before, you are my responsibility to clothe, to feed—"

"And to protect," I grumble, crossing my arms over my chest. "I know."

Cocking a brow, he steps towards me. Then he does it again until I'm backed into the racks of shirts.

Leaning down, he lowers his lips right to my ear. "Don't make me take you to the dressing room and spank your ass, little devil. I'm fully committed to finding you something you'll feel comfortable in while we're here." Leaning back, he tucks my hair behind my ear, his gaze hot on my already burning cheeks. "I want you to see yourself the way I do."

"What? Damaged goods?"

Anger flashes across his gaze before it's quickly masked by a look of indifference.

Uh-oh. I shouldn't have said that.

"I want ten of everything. Ten pairs of jeans. Ten T-shirts. Ten frilly shirts. Some shoes. Dresses. Whatever the fuck you need, I want ten of it."

And then he steps back to peruse the aisle.

I leave Christian to quietly sulk in the T-shirt aisle and head off to find the "frilly shirts", as he likes to call them. I managed to find a few and then a few pairs of jeans in my size. I pick out a new pair of sneakers, adding it all to the shopping basket I find along the way before I make my way back over to where he stands in the back of the store, a few T-shirts in his hand that he must have picked out for me.

"I don't need a dress," I tell him, hoping he's not still pissed off at me for what I said.

When he doesn't respond, I know he is.

Fuck.

"I'm . . . sorry. For being rude," I murmur. His shoulders stiffen, but he doesn't turn around. I hate that I drove that wedge between us. Sometimes, when it all gets to be too much, I just . . . lash out. "I appreciate everything you've done for me, and I just—"

"Pick out a dress."

My throat tightens, and I continue to stand there and stare at him.

Finally, he turns over his shoulder, cocking a brow at me.

"Why?"

"Because you need one."

"For what?"

His gaze narrows.

"You'll see."

I don't know if I like the sound of that.

"What kind of dress?"

He shrugs, looking back at the wall. Then, something catches his eye, and he pulls it from the rack. It's a butter yellow sundress with little blue and white flowers on it.

"This."

It's beautiful. But . . . I haven't worn a dress in over a year.

"Are you sure?"

He nods to the dressing rooms. "Go try it on."

He takes the basket from my hands and hands me the dress, which he somehow managed to pick out in the perfect size.

It's odd . . . being public with Christian. We've been living together up at the cottage for nearly a month now. Basically, husband and wife who almost hate each other with a really shitty sex life. But being in public almost seems *too* domestic. Like at any second, I'll turn around, and it will all be gone.

Quietly, I make my way into a dressing room, closing the curtain tight behind me. Christian waits outside, and my cheeks flame, just knowing that he knows I'm changing in here.

See, I told you. Too domestic.

Slipping my clothes off, they feel tattered and trashy compared to all the new clothes we'll be buying today. Not that I don't love them. My old clothes have seen shit. They've lived a life on the run. Sleeping in busted motel rooms and dirty bus stations.

These new clothes could never compare.

"Everything okay?" Christian asks after five minutes.

No. Everything is not okay.

I'm stuck staring at my reflection in the mirror. This is the first time I'm really seeing myself in months. I've gotten thinner. My hair isn't as shiny as it used to be. My curls are flat, and my skin is pale.

I look like death's little sister with an affinity for brightly colored clothes.

Tears pool in my eyes, and it only takes a second before my entire emotional barrier crumbles around me.

Sinking to the carpeted floor, I pull my knees up to my chest and bury my face in my hands.

This sucks. It all sucks.

"Mila, I'm coming in."

"Don—"

Too late. He pulls back the curtain and sees me crying on the floor like a child who didn't get her way, and his shoulders stiffen. He closes the curtain behind us and drops to his haunches in front of me while I hastily try to turn the tears off like a broken faucet.

"Hey, look at me."

He tugs my face to him, and I close my eyes, hating that he can see me at my most vulnerable. Hating that even though he's the man who kidnapped me, he's also the one who calms the storm ravaging my mind.

"What's going on?" he asks quietly, his voice gentle. "Don't like the dress?"

"The dress is beautiful," I whisper.

"Then, what is it? You want to go home?"

I shake my head. As overwhelming as it may be, I'm not ready to go back to the island. There's still so much to see.

"Then what?"

"Nothing," I whisper, scrubbing a hand over my eyes.

"Something."

I chance a glance at him and find him studying me.

I wish he couldn't see me. Especially now that I know what he's seeing. The scared, translucent, damaged girl with lifeless eyes.

"You can tell me. I won't be angry."

Fuck. Why can't I just cry in peace?

Oh, right. Because I'm a captive hiding out in a dressing room, crying because I feel ugly.

"I think I should put the dress back," I breathe, and something flashes across his eyes, too quick for me to place.

"Why?"

I look away from him, rising to unsteady legs.

"I . . ." God, I can't believe I'm telling him this. "It doesn't look good on me."

He fixes me with a hard stare, his jaw clenching and unclenching in the silence that follows.

"Come here."

The dressing room is only a few feet wide as it is long, but I close the minuscule distance between us hesitantly.

In a rush, he takes me by the arms, forcing me to turn around and face the mirror. Face myself head-on.

"Please stop," I whisper, wishing with everything I have that the mirror in front of me would disappear.

"Stand there."

Christian steps behind me, his fingers slipping down the goosebumps on my arms while he watches me over my head.

"What are we doing?" I ask when he zips the dress up in the back.

"Look in the mirror, Mila."

I swallow over the lump in my throat, meeting my own gaze. I want to look away as fresh tears burn behind my eyes, but when I try, he reaches around and takes my chin, forcing my eyes forward.

Lowering his voice, he drops his lips to my ear, pulling my back into his front.

"I'm going to show you what I see."

I shiver from the warmth of his breath against the side of my neck when he lingers, his stubble against my skin bringing goosebumps to the surface. His lips skate down the side of my neck, over my racing pulse point, to my shoulder.

His hands slip along my stomach as he works his way down. My eyes flutter when he reaches the hem, his thumbs dragging over the material of my panties.

My heartbeat quickens, my head falling back to rest against his shoulder when one hand comes up to grip my throat while the other dips inside the waistband of my panties.

"We're in public," I breathe, biting back a moan when his

fingers dip inside me.

He presses his lips to the side of my face, eyes glinting savagely in the mirror when they meet mine.

"Does that scare you, little devil?" he rasps, voice low and quiet. He draws his finger through my folds, then moves higher, circling my clit.

I bite my lip, a gasp threatening to tear free and grab hold of his wrist.

"Does it haunt you what you do to me? Knowing my cock's hard against your ass, begging to slip inside you? That I stroke myself in the shower every morning because all I can think about is how pretty you'd look riding my cock?"

"Christian," I breathe, unable to look away with what he's doing to me.

He steps closer to the mirror until we're nearly face to face with our reflections, his other arm wrapping around the front of my shoulders to band my arms to my chest.

"Look at yourself, Mila. See what I see, yet?"

"What?" I pant, my thighs quivering on either side of his hand. Heat slips into my bloodstream, and my hips move on their own volition, rocking against his hand.

"See the blush in your cheeks? The brightness in those pretty fucking eyes? How bad you want to come from my fingers. *Feel* what you fucking do to me," he rasps, nipping the shell of my ear. "The prettiest fucking girl I've ever seen."

Rocking his hips into me in slow, even rolls, I feel his erection digging into the small of my back.

"Do you know how fucking hard it is to be the good guy? To not fuck you when you ask me to? Take this slow with you?" He changes the angles of our hips, bending me forward slightly until I'm forced to catch myself with my hands on the mirror.

This new angle forces me to meet my own gaze. There are sparks hidden in the gray depths of my irises. My cheeks are pink and flushed, my hair falling around me in small ringlets. My chest heaves with each breath, my body drawn tight as he continues to swirl his fingers around my clit.

"I'm going to come," I whisper, hoping to God no one out in the store can hear us over the chatter and the loud music.

"Are you?" he drawls, his cock hitting the curve of my ass when he rolls against me. I nod my head, desperate for release, and he takes me right to the edge.

Then, he removes his fingers.

I gawk at him in the mirror, and he places a kiss to my cheek, his lips lingering.

"Feel what it feels like to be me, sweetheart? To want something so fucking badly but know you have to wait?"

"You're-you're—" I sputter, the orgasm fading second by second, leaving behind an achiness that I know only he can relieve.

Stepping back, he releases me, tugging my dress down over my hips and pressing a kiss to the top of my head. His eyes meet mine in the mirror, alive with wicked amusement.

"So fucking pretty," he murmurs, and my cheeks flame. "You'll get what you want, sweetheart. Just not here."

Stepping away from me completely, he opens the curtain and grabs the basket.

"And the dress stays on. I like it."

I watch him walk off, gawking.

It takes a minute before I turn to follow him before I pause, looking at myself in the mirror.

A girl stares back at me. Broken, damaged, and pale . . .

But also a woman with bright, shining eyes. With soft ringlet curls. A healthy blush on her cheeks.

You're the prettiest fucking girl I've ever seen.

I just hope someday, I can agree with him.

CHAPTER
Twenty-Six

CHRISTIAN

This plan is either fucking genius—

—Or really fucking stupid.

"This place is amazing," Mila beams, looking back at me with the biggest fucking smile on her face. She's got her hair down and that dress on. I took one look at it and knew she would look fucking phenomenal in it.

I rub the spot in my chest absentmindedly, a grin tugging at the corners of my lips.

Goddamn, she's fucking pretty . . .

Paulina was right. Seeing her out of my sweats and off the island was exactly what we needed.

Mila's the type of girl who deserves wide open spaces. Space to grow. Space to be herself. Putting her in a cage dims her light, and I'd rather take another hundred bullets to the chest than snuff it out for good.

"What is this place?" she asks, falling into step beside me. I tug her close, intertwining our fingers together.

"The fair," I glance around, a sense of unease stirring in my chest. As much as I want her to enjoy her day of freedom, it doesn't mean I fucking like it.

The only thing that helps is knowing I've got men stationed around the park, keeping an eye on shit so I can show my girl a good time.

"Are you sure this is okay?" she asks quietly, her fingers soft in mine. I'm realizing now that holding her hand was, in fact, a bad fucking idea. Now, I don't want to give it up.

"There's nothing to worry about."

And if there is, I've got a gun in my waistband. One on my ankle, and another in my pocket, with a full mag of hollow points in all three.

No one's fucking touching her.

Today is about having fun, and I hate the fucking look of fear hidden in her eyes. I'm not sure what I was thinking, bringing her here, but I just . . . needed to give her something that didn't involve the island or the men hunting us down. Time for just the two of us where there wasn't an elephant in the room. The fair seemed like the best place to do that.

"When was the last time you came to a fair?" I ask, and she looks at me like I've lost my mind. I stare at her in disbelief. You've got to be fucking kidding me. "Really? Never?"

She shrugs. "It just wasn't something I think any of us considered. You know my mother."

"Yeah," I nod, and she chuckles. She's not wrong. Monica Parker would have lost her shit if any of the girls had so much as thought about going to a carnival.

But . . . That means she's never had cotton candy. Never had a corn dog from the fair. Never ridden on a Ferris wheel or a roller coaster and almost vomited.

Fuck that.

"Come on."

"Hey!" She stumbles along behind me when my fist tightens around hers, and I pull her through the crowd. We've got a lot to do, and now that I know she's never experienced any of it, I need her to experience *all* of it.

. . . With me.

"Where are we going?" she asks, managing to fall in step with me. I slow down so she can keep up.

"We're going to have fun," I murmur, my voice tight. I don't like having her in a crowd, but I know as well as anyone else that keeping a wild animal caged will only drive it toward the desire for freedom faster.

Besides . . . I have a feeling it'll be a very, very long time before she wants to have fun with me again when she finds out my secret.

"You know, when you growl it at me, it doesn't sound like it's going to be much fun."

I pull her to a stop at the first item on the list. Cotton candy. I've never cared for it, but it's on the list, so it has to be done. I pay the man and hand her the cone, which she eyes like it's made of kryptonite.

"I thought this was a myth," she chuckles, and I grit my teeth, leading her away from the vendor.

"Try it."

"How?"

I pull her to a stop in the line for the Ferris wheel, rip a piece of the sugary fluff off, and hold it in front of her mouth.

"Open."

She eyes me, and I fully expect her to deny me, but to my surprise, she opens her mouth, sticking her tongue out and allowing me to place the ball of baby pink fluff on her tongue. My fingers graze the warmth of her mouth, and my cock pulses against my zipper when she closes her lips around my fingers, sucking off the sugary sweetness as it dissolves on her tongue.

"Mmm . . ." she moans, her lips vibrating around my fingers

when I slowly slip them from her lips.

Christ, she's going to be the fucking death of me. Death by permanent fucking hard-on.

I grab another bundle, raising my fingers back to her lips, and, this time, there's no hesitation in her gaze when she opens for me. My gaze darkens at the flicker of lust in those pretty gray eyes, and I let out a quiet groan under my breath.

"Suck," I murmur, my voice little more than a growl.

She hollows out her cheeks, another soft little moan slipping from her lips when I press my fingers deeper into her mouth, needing to know how it would feel if it were my cock she was sucking like a popsicle.

"Good fucking girl," I praise quietly, my other hand holding her cheek. Fuck, I want to taste her. Slip my tongue through the sweetness in her mouth from both the cotton candy and her.

I press into her, my front against hers, and every soft curve of her molds against my hard ridges. Her eyes widen and I think she might actually let me.

Fuck, I'm so hard right now.

"Excuse me?"

You ever hear a noise and just fucking *know*, if you had to listen to it all day, every day, you'd pitch yourself off the highest fucking building you could find?

A woman a few feet away glares, her arms crossed over her chest, and her hip jutted out in attitude. I half expect her to tap her foot as she glares at me.

Oh, goody.

I cock a brow at her but don't step back from Mila even when she places her hand on my stomach, her palm dangerously close to my cock.

"There are kids here."

She's right. There are plenty of kids here. There's also no law that states I can't kiss my woman in public.

"Plenty of—"

"Christian," Mila cuts me off, placing her hands on my chest. I release her and step back with a smirk at the woman over her head. "We're very sorry," Mila says, her cheeks flaming red before she turns over her shoulder and shoots me a look when Supermom walks away in a huff. "That was bad."

I press my lips to her ear, breathing in her sweet scent. Fuck, I have no control when I'm with her. "That was nothing, sweetheart."

I turn her around and pull her back against my front. I lean into her like we're any other loving couple when in reality, I'm enjoying seeing how far I can push her until she breaks for me. Until she's a shaking, needy mess begging me to fuck her.

The dressing room comes to mind. Her grinding her hips against my hand desperately. Practically begging me to fuck her right there.

Fuck, pressing against her as right now, I want to rock my hips against her ass, but I don't. This is still new to her, and as much as I love pushing her past her limits, I want her to be comfortable while I do.

So, I decided to tease her instead.

"Maybe I should invite her back home with us when I fuck you for the first time."

"Christian," Mila admonishes, but an unmistakable shudder moves through her. We move forward in line, almost to the front now, and all I can think about is what I'm going to do to her when I get her alone.

Well . . . Mostly alone.

There won't be any supermoms to save her in the air, and judging by the shiver that moves through her where my lips are pressed against her racing pulse in the side of her throat, she knows it too.

"Would you like that, little devil? Showing her that I belong to you and only you while my cock's buried deep inside you? That my cock is yours to take whenever and wherever you want?"

Her tongue slides out to lick her lips, and the movement goes straight to my cock.

Of course, I'd never let anyone see her or the things I do to her, but watching the way her cheeks darken and her breathing goes shallow is addicting.

I release her the moment the car opens for us to slip inside. It's a private car, so the sides have taller walls than most, and that's fucking perfect for what I want.

The next item on the list?

Watching her come at the top of the Ferris wheel like we're teenagers again.

I help her step inside, and she scrambles to get away from me when I crowd behind her, shutting the door behind us with a snap. Then, we're moving, and I'm tugging her back into my side. My hand on her bare thigh and my cock pressing painfully against the zipper of my jeans.

I bring my lips down, gliding them across her skin the moment we're out of eyesight of the people below.

"Mr. Cross," she breathes, though her eyelashes flutter, her lids closing at the brush of my tongue on her skin. Fucking divine. "If you brought me up here because you think I'm going to sleep with you, it's not happening."

"Not yet," I correct, kissing my way up her jaw. Fuck, she smells like heaven. "And when I fuck you, little devil, it's not going to be just a few minutes."

"Then, what are you doing?" Her voice is shaky, breathier than usual, and so fucking sexy.

"Reminding you whose pussy this is," I murmur against her cheek, and anything she was about to say is lost when I lean down and suck the flesh below her ear, eliciting a sharp intake of breath. "Fuck, I'm burning this dress when we get home."

"Don't. I like it," she breathes, her hand coming to rest on my thigh. It's the most she's touched me on her own since she had my cock in her throat, and the knowledge that she's getting more comfortable with me sends a shot of electricity through my veins.

Slipping my hand up her side, I push her hair off her neck and lay it back over her shoulder while she stares up at me from underneath thick lashes. Under my fingertips, I feel her heart rate rise to dangerous levels, and I bite back a smile.

My other hand slips over the smooth skin of her leg, toying with the hem of her dress. She lets out a deep breath when I stroke her inner thigh, her hand resting over mine.

"Christian," she gasps when I hike the dress up, letting it pool in her lap. She clenches her thighs shut, trying to cover herself and searches around as if a bird's going to broadcast her bare pussy for the entire park to see. Gently, I push her hand away, forcing her legs back apart.

Taking her chin in my hand, I bring her to face me. "Do you trust me?"

Her gaze travels from my eyes down to my lips, then back up again, and I watch her swallow heavily.

"Yes," she breathes, so quiet, I barely hear her.

"Then trust me to take care of you." I kiss the side of her face, feeling her skin warm under my lips. Fuck, I need to kiss her. To taste her.

"Spread your legs."

I tap her inner thigh, and she obliges, spreading her legs, though I can feel the tension radiating through her. As if I'd ever let anyone see her come undone for me.

I meant what I said when I found out about Phantom. Right now, she's mine to feed and care for. She's also mine to please and to play with until this is over.

If anyone thinks they're taking her away from me, they better bring a fucking body bag—and it won't be for me.

My hand slides up to grip her dainty throat, the other slipping back under her dress.

"Look at me," I murmur when she screws her eyes shut, her tongue darting out to lick her lip. Her fingernails dig into my skin. The last time, I had marks for days. This time, I'll get them tattooed there.

"Christian," she begs, though I'm not sure even she knows what she's begging for. I grin, nodding to the door.

"Don't you want to come, sweetheart?" I purr, slipping my tongue along her jaw and nipping the smooth skin. Her breath hitches, coming in short, shallow pants. "Aren't you ready for me to please my pussy?"

She lets out a soft whimper when I nip her ear lobe, my tongue soothing the sting.

"Yes."

"Put your leg up on the door and look out the window, Mila."

My fingers gently brush her soft inner, thigh over the curve of her mound, then lower until I'm just barely cupping her through the lace of her panties.

"Don't make me tell you again," I warn, my voice deeper and hoarse with the need to feel her.

Whimpering softly, she kicks her leg out, placing it on the edge of the door, spreading herself wide for me. We both glance down to where I slip her panties out of the way, my finger slipping between her folds.

"Fuck," I curse under my breath just as we crest the top of the Ferris wheel. Three rotations is all I'll get to make her come. The cart stops, and we sway in the air for a moment, but I don't think either of us is really paying attention to the scenery right now.

"What if someone sees?" she exhales under her breath when I rim the shell of her ear. I slip lower, my tongue tracing the smooth column of her neck before I suck on the flesh over her racing pulse.

"Does that make your pussy wet, sweetheart?" I taunt, slipping a finger inside her and gathering her arousal before moving higher to swirl it around her clit. She bites her lip, looking down at what I'm doing to her. "Knowing someone could see you with my fingers buried inside this sweet little cunt?"

She feels so fucking tight, it's a wonder my cock ever fit the first time. My mouth waters to taste her, and I raise my fingers from her pussy, slipping them in my mouth. I groan, leaning forward and spitting on her clit, and her eyes flutter, heavy and delirious on mine.

Slipping my saliva around the swollen bundle of nerves between her legs, I draw a soft moan from between her lips.

Fuck me. That shit can get addicting.

"Yes," she admits, her head falling back against the seat behind us when I pinch her clit between my fingers, her lips parting on a silent breath. I slide a finger back inside her, aligning my palm to connect with her clit while I push them in and out of her.

"It turns you on for them to know this pussy belongs to me? That soon, I'm going to spread you out in my bed, and you're going to be coming all over my cock?"

"Christian . . ." she breathes just as we near the bottom of the wheel.

"Put your leg down."

Quickly, I still my hand, my thumb giving her gentle, minuscule strokes over her clit when we reach the bottom.

The moment we pass, I push her leg back up and sink inside her again.

"*Fuck*," I curse under my breath, feeling her walls tighten around me. She's tighter than I remember. I press against her walls, pushing up to that spot that has her eyes rolling back and her head hitting the seat behind her. "Such a pretty little pussy, sweetheart. Look at me."

She shivers, her eyes opening to meet mine, a haze covering the pretty gaze. I continue to move inside her, pushing her to accept me while I work a second finger in.

"How's that feel, Mila?" My voice is rough with the need to fuck her until I've had my fill of her. Maybe then, I could get her out of my fucking head long enough to breathe.

"G-good," she trembles, drawing her bottom lip between her teeth.

Fuck, I'd love nothing more than to kiss her. To swallow her desperate little whimpers on my tongue, but she's not ready. Somehow, kissing is more intimate than my fingers in her pussy, even to me. Kissing implies there's love or the possibility of it. Kissing is a selfless act. A connection neither of us prepared for.

So, instead, I do the next best thing. Leaning down, I tug the top of her dress down, exposing her tit to me, and suck the hardened nub into my mouth, lacy bra and all.

"Oh my God," she breathes, her hand tightening around mine between her legs as I continue to pump in and out of her.

Fuck, it's not enough, but it's all I'm willing to give either of us right now. I can't be . . . whatever she needs me to be. I'm not gentle. I'm not soft. I'm not good at wiping tears away. I can fuck her, but I can't let her lose herself in the process.

She went through hell. Pure fucking hell. I can't be another monster in her nightmares.

So, for now, I'll make her come in any way I can think of until she's ready to take me.

"So fucking sweet," I murmur against her nipple, my tongue drawing even circles around the bud. I lean back up, pressing my face to the side of hers. The cart starts to come down for the second pass, and just in time, I lean back, tugging her dress back up to cover her and stilling my movements in her cunt. She buries her face in the side of my neck, her skin damp against mine. "Bite me if you think you can't stay quiet."

Just as we pass the people still waiting in line, I add a third finger, stretching her, and her teeth dig into my skin. I bite back a groan, keeping my fingers locked inside her and my face blank while I push in, pressed all the way to the hilt.

As soon as we're cruising past the people still waiting in line, I tug her knees apart and place her foot on the seat between my legs, opening her up to me. Her head falls back against the seat, her skin flushed, and her breathing heavy.

"Fuck, look at you," I grin, moving slowly. Letting her get adjusted. "How's that feel?"

"Good," she whimpers softly, eyes on mine.

"You want to use your safeword?"

"No," she attempts to shake her head, but I've got her throat firmly pinned to the seat.

"You've got three of my fingers buried in this tight little cunt, sweetheart."

"Christian," she whimpers desperately against my neck, her hips moving to meet my thrusts.

"I know, sweetheart. You've got three minutes to come, Mila. Think you can do it?"

She screws her eyes shut, and my free hand reaches up to cup her cheek, turning her face back to mine. I hold her there, my stare eating up hers while I finger her pussy at a ruthless pace.

"Answer the question, Mila."

Her teeth chatter at the onslaught of pleasure, her nails digging into my wrist to the point of pain. The pain keeps me grounded. Keeps me from stripping her bare and fucking her right here and giving Supermom something to really throw a fit over.

"I don't know," she breathes, and I can see in her eyes she's actually not sure. She wants to. Fuck, she wants to, but her mind's holding her back. I want to steal those memories away from her in that very moment. Keep them locked away inside me so she never has to feel those things again. Until she's free to live the life she deserves and not whatever was handed to her.

"This is my pussy," I murmur, pressing a kiss to the corner of her lips. It's not kissing her if I don't completely press my lips to hers, right? "And I say it can."

I continue my movements, adding my thumb to circle her clit in rapid strokes while I do.

"Eyes on me, little devil," I instruct, holding her gaze. Her pulse flutters against my hand, and her eyes grow half-lidded and hazy when her pussy starts to tighten around me. "Let me see you fall apart."

We pause at the top of the Ferris wheel, and the view of the Olympic Forest is nice, but nothing looks as good as the pleading in her eyes.

"Christian," she breathes, her teeth digging into her bottom lip so hard, I worry she'll break skin again.

"You going to come for me like a good girl?"

She nods, her eyes fluttering closed when I tighten my hand around her throat.

"Let me have it, Mila," I press my lips to the side of her face. Those moonlight eyes lock with mine, hazy and soft with desire, and it's at that moment I know I've signed my own fucking death warrant.

She can take whatever she needs from me. The world can have whatever's left.

"I need to feel you come."

She shivers, trembles moving through her, and just when I change my angle, curling my fingers up to stroke that sensitive spot inside her, she moans, her cries ringing out between us when her pussy clamps down on my fingers.

"Fucking Christ, little devil," I grit, pumping inside her as best I can while she comes undone for me, her come seeping out around my fingers. "So fucking beautiful."

I press my lips to her neck, nipping the flesh between my teeth. It's not nearly as hard as she bit me, but it gets my point across. She's mine to please. Mine to protect.

She shivers when she comes down, pretty eyes meeting mine. She glowers at me, opening her mouth to snap at me, but I silence it with a press of my lips to her forehead, my hands on either side of her face. It's softer than I've been with her in a long time, and I know it's fucking with her head.

Hell, it's fucking with mine.

"Come," I say the moment the wheel reaches the bottom. I take her hand in mine and lead her towards the exit. "We've got a whole lot more ground to cover before we get home."

CHAPTER
Twenty-Seven

CHRISTIAN

"Did you have fun today?"

Mila peers at me over her shoulder as we climb the path up to the cottage, me carrying the bags of clothes we got her today. She's got her shoes in her hand, her bare toes on display, and the moonlight dancing across her golden hair. The moon is high in the sky, thunder rumbling off the coast. It won't be long until it starts to pour, which means we'll spend the night inside. Me listening and her reading.

"I . . . did. I had the most fun I've had in a long time," she smiles, and it does some shit to my chest. I'm starting to think she's got a fucking telekinetic bond with the bullet still there. "Thank you for taking me off the island. And for getting me clothes. And for showing me the proper way to win that ring toss game."

"What was your favorite part?"

Her cheeks flame and I know what she's thinking. Can't say I disagree with her.

"The cheese on a stick."

Fucking gross.

"That it?"

"And . . . I think I have a new appreciation for the Ferris Wheel. Even though that was my first time on one." She looks out over the water behind me. "Washington is beautiful."

"It grows on you," I murmur, shifting all the bags to one hand and slipping my fingers around hers. She lets me, and for once, she doesn't shrink away from my touch.

"I'm sure it does," she says softly, her bare toes padding along the cobbled stone path.

Something twists inside me. "Not sure?"

"I like it just fine, but . . . I mean, I haven't exactly gotten to see much of it. Besides the island, of course."

Guilt washes through me, but I push it back. I'm doing this to keep her safe. It's not permanent.

"You said your brother texted you earlier. Is everything okay?"

Fuck.

"We've got some shit to work out," I murmur, scrubbing a hand over the back of my neck.

"Sounds like most families."

"Most days, I want to kill the fucker," I grumble. "I know the feeling's mutual."

"Oh," she says softly, falling silent as we near the front door.

"But . . ." I concede, tugging her hand until she comes to a stop on the steps. "My brother and sister are two of the three people in the world that mean the most to me."

Her eyes widen, her lips parting on a silent breath when she stares up at me through thick lashes.

"And who's the other?"

Reaching up, I brush my knuckles down the side of her face. "I'm not sure they exist anymore, but I'll never stop searching for them."

She's silent, soft gray gaze searching mine, and in the dark, the words come easily. It's easy to face the past when she can't feel how hard my heart's beating. When she can't see the tightness of my jaw or know of the bitter acid burning the back of my throat when I think about that summer we spent wrapped in each other.

"How long are you going to hate me for leaving?" I ask quietly because I know there's a part of both of us that can't move past it. She probably feels that if I hadn't left, she never would have been attacked.

Oddly enough, I can't get the same thoughts out of my head.

"I . . ." she starts, only for the words to fall and her lips to clamp shut.

I told her once she can't hide from me. I meant it more than she'll ever understand.

"I think the real problem was I couldn't hate you, even when you were breaking my heart," she whispers, and everything falls silent. Fuck, even the waves quiet down. The air around us hums, and a volatile energy cackles between us.

"You were never meant to be mine, Mila. I took you. The world took back."

Something passes through her gaze. A bitter resentment for my choosing to leave. She doesn't know why I did it. She probably never will, but in her eyes, I didn't fight for her. I abandoned her at a time when she probably needed me most.

Even if I never left her side.

"It's not like it matters anymore, right," she says, turning to step inside, but at the last second, something like panic rushes through my veins, and I drop the bags, wrapping an arm around her waist and tugging her back.

I step into her, pressing her back against the door and looming over her. Her hands rest on my abs, sending heat straight to my cock.

"Go on," I murmur, my nose sliding up the smooth column of her neck. "Tell me you hate me, Mila."

I know she wants to. She wants to tell me she wishes I would have stayed gone. How much she despises me for leaving.

She can't, though. It would just be another lie between us.

"Tell me I'm worthless and that you never want to see me again."

Her breath hitches, her fingers fist in the material of my shirt, and my abs flex underneath her hands.

"Tell me not to kiss you," I breathe, heart fucking pounding in my throat.

My lips hover over hers, the air between us humming with electricity. Every nerve ending begs for me to kiss her. I never thought I could get so fucking wrapped up in the way another person's lips feel against mine until I'd been denied kissing Mila Carpenter.

"Touch me," she whispers in the darkness surrounding us. "Please."

A groan rumbles through my chest, vibrating against her fingers, and she sucks in a shaky breath when I bend down, gently pressing my lips to the side of her throat instead of her mouth. I suck the flesh, nipping the racing of her pulse like I can punish her for denying me her lips. She rolls her hips into mine, grinding into my hard cock nestled against her stomach. "Tell me what you need," I rasp, against her throat, nipping and sucking a line down to her collarbone.

"You," she breathes, and I smile wickedly while my thumb toys with one of the buttons on her dress. My fingers brush over the skin below her ass, and there's a brief and shining moment where I have her in the palm of my hand.

"Do you need me here?" I ask, my hand slipping over her stomach and up to toy with her nipples through her dress and bra. Her eyes clench shut, a shaky breath leaving her lips at the friction.

She shakes her head.

"How about here?" I taunt, moving lower until my fingers brush over her inner thigh, and she shakes her head again. "Going to have to use your words, little devil."

"Please don't make me say it . . ." she whispers, her cheeks flaming, and I can't help but smirk.

"You won't get what you want unless you tell me, sweetheart."

She closes her eyes, pushing out a soft breath between her lips. When she finally opens them again and turns those pretty eyes on me in the moonlight . . . fuck.

"Will you fuck me?"

It's unconfident, full of nerves and self-consciousness, but there's a determination in her gaze.

It's the hottest fucking thing I've ever seen.

And then a throat clears behind us.

I'm reaching for my gun when Mila jumps, letting out a soft squeak. Only the moment I turn, ready to shoot whoever the fuck thought they could come out to *our* fucking island, I'm met with a gaze that mirrors my own.

Levi Cross smirks, his gaze pinned on mine despite the gun I have aimed at his head.

I can't lie and say I'm not still thinking about using it.

Fucker interrupted me.

His lips pull into a grin, his gaze flicking from mine to Mila and back.

"Hello, brother."

"Mila, go inside."

She doesn't move, frozen between me and the side of the cottage.

"Hello, *Mila,*" Levi smirks, holding out his hand. I have half a mind to shoot it off. "I'm Levi Cross. Christian's charming, slightly more handsome younger brother."

"*Mila,*" I repeat through gritted teeth, my eyes never leaving my brother. "Go inside."

Slowly, I can feel her pull away from me, releasing my shirt where her hand was twisted in the material, holding onto me. I listen to the sounds of her footsteps, then the door shut behind me. Then, I lower my gun.

"What the fuck are you doing here?"

Levi shoves his hands in the pockets of his jeans, smirking.

"Thought I'd find you here."

"Doesn't explain why the fuck *you're* here."

"You weren't returning my calls."

"There's a reason for that."

I nod towards the lighthouse and he chuckles under his breath, stalking towards the door. I unlock it, pushing it open and let him inside before I shut it behind us.

"Upstairs."

"Love what you've done with the place," he taunts. "I heard the whole coastal vibe is making a comeback."

"Fuck off," I grunt, crossing to my desk the moment we enter. I pull out the bottle of whiskey I keep in there, downing a gulp of the amber liquid.

It doesn't do anything for me, but I'm not only pissed off, I'm shaking with rage.

"I almost fucking shot you."

Levi takes the bottle from my hand, taking a drink before eyeing the label.

"Expensive."

"What the fuck do you want? How the fuck did you find me."

He lets out a breath, sinking into the chair on the opposite side of my desk.

I'm too agitated to sit, so I lean against the side of the desk, facing him.

"We're brothers. I know you better than you think."

"Clearly not or you'd know I wouldn't want visitors."

"You bought the island under an alias, but you used Mom's maiden name. What did you expect?" he grumbles, taking another drink.

Because I can and because I'm older, *and* because this is my goddamned island, I take it back from him.

"Not all of us have the DEA pushing every little thing we do under the rug."

"Yes, well. Not that you didn't have the option."

"Too much paperwork."

"You mean not enough fun?" I don't like the way he wags his brows. As if I'm a fucking nutcase, murdering people for the fucking hell of it.

"I do what needs to be done. Not what the United States government lets me."

"You've just got to know how to handle your problems, brother," Levi chuckles, looking around my office. "I must say, I was surprised this is where you were choosing to hide out at."

"We aren't hiding."

"So it's okay if I let Mila's mother know where's she's staying?"

"Fuck off, Levi. Don't make me fucking shoot you," I growl, and he falls back in his chair.

"So testy, tonight. Would that have anything to do with your little br—"

"Don't fucking finish that sentence."

For once, Levi has the good sense not to push the matter. Maybe he's finally growing up.

"You've got five seconds to tell me why you're here or I'm throwing you off the cliff."

His smirk falls and he reaches into his pocket, tossing a flashdrive on the desk beside me.

"What's that? Your homework?"

"Plug it in."

I huff out a breath and reach for the drive, firing on my laptop, and plugging it in.

There's only one file—a video—and when I click on it, ice fills my chest.

I can't make it more than thirty seconds in before I'm shutting it down.

"Thought that might interest you."

"Where the fuck did you get this?"

"Picked it up off a guy in Oregon last week. Not the one I was tracking, but a customer."

I grip the edge of the desk so hard, the wood threatens to crack under my hands.

"Where the fuck did he get this?"

"I have information that he's in New York."

Immediately, I'm shaking my head.

"I'm not leaving Mila alone."

"If he's still out there, she'll never be safe."

"She's safe with me."

"That the card you want to play it? Why do you care, anyway? The bitch shot you."

I pull my gun on him so fast, he doesn't even have time to breathe.

"That's my *wife*."

He shakes his head, his face growing red with anger.

Good, because that makes two of us. I was seconds away from finally having my girl back.

"All the more reason to go," he says finally, the weight of that one single word settling in the air between us.

I let the gun drop, tossing it back on the desk and grabbing the whiskey bottle.

"And she didn't shoot me."

"Bullshit."

I eye him for a moment, before crossing to the front and pulling out the file I keep in the top drawer. Tossing it on the desk in front of him, I wait while he opens it to stare down at the first picture inside.

I notice he's quiet, faced with the proof we've been searching for, for the last fourteen years.

He freezes, silence falling over the room so thick, you can hear the waves crashing against the rocks outside.

Then, he chuckles. The sound low and dark, sinister.

"Fucking finally."

He tosses the folder back to the desk and leans back in the chair.

After a long moment, he finally speaks.

"You know this is never going to end, so long as he's alive, right?"

I grit my teeth. Of course, I fucking know.

"So long as she's alive, I'll never stop hunting."

Levi chuckles under his breath, shaking his head in disbelief.

"I'll be damned," he breathes and I hate the fucking grin that pulls on his lips. "You fucking love her . . . don't you?"

Love her? Fuck, I don't know.

Does it even matter?

I can never love her because loving her means giving her a death sentence that she won't walk away from a second time.

I can never love her. Even if there's a part of me that knows I always have.

"Of course, not," I scoff. "I'm fucking obsessed."

I can see by the look in his eyes that Levi doesn't believe me, but that's fine. He can think whatever he wants.

My world may revolve around Mila Carpenter and that pretty fucking smile, but hers has never revolved around mine. I've made sure of it.

When this is over, she'll go back to living her life and I'll go back to wasting mine, dreaming of her.

Pretty fucking ironic, isn't it?

"You're setting her up to hang if we don't take care of this. You know that, right?" he asks quietly and I can see for the first time since he showed up, what he's really worried about.

He's worried about what I'll do if they find her.

Crossing to the window, I look out over our island. Lightning strikes somewhere far off over the ocean.

"If we do this . . ." I turn back to face him. "There's no going back. I need to know you're on the same page."

For once, my brother looks serious.

"You made her a Cross," he shrugs. "We don't give up on each other."

I nod once, turning back to face him.

"We leave tomorrow. First thing."

"Guess we've got a change of plans, then."

"The plans changed," I murmur darkly. "The outcome will still be the same."

He scrubs a hand over his face, leaning back against the wall opposite me.

"So, where do we start?"

"LA."

"And when we do find him?"

I shrug. "Then, we kill him. Before he gets his hands on her again."

"Easier said than done," Levi grunts. "I've been trying for years."

"As have I. I thought he was dead when the trail went cold while I was in LA those last two years. Then . . . Mila happened."

"You think it was a threat?"

"I think it was an appetizer," I murmur darkly, visions of *that* night dancing in my head. The hospital. The bandages.

My little devil's scars that she feels the need to hide from the world.

Fuck, I have to do this.

"Not a word to Mila."

"She know . . . about the two of you?"

I grit my teeth. I knew my decision back then would bite me in the ass, but I also knew the ramifications of what would happen if I *didn't* make her mine.

"Not yet."

"You planning on telling her?"

"Soon. When she's ready."

A silence falls over the room. You could hear a fly drop dead in the back of the room. Both Levi and I lost in our own thoughts about how this will all come to a head.

I've got so much shit to get in order before I leave tomorrow, if I want Mila to be safe. Starting with speaking to Paulina. It's not the best plan, but it's all I've got, and if we're going to put an end to this, it needs to happen immediately.

"You can crash on the couch if you need. Storm's coming."

"No thanks. A little water never hurt anyone. I've got a room at the North Star Comfort Inn and Suites back on the mainland and a date with Debbie the waitress and a stack of pancakes tomorrow morning at eight a.m. sharp. I can't miss it."

Jesus Christ. Some shit never changes.

"Then, I'll walk you to your car."

"Eager to get rid of me, I see? After so much time apart?"

"When my wife's waiting for me in bed? Fuck, yeah, I am."

He follows me toward the door, chuckling, only before I open it, he places his hand on my shoulder to stop me.

"We're going to put an end to this, Christian."

We've been saying that for years.

"Guess we'll see."

Just as we step outside, into the night, thunder rumbles overhead and like God himself is pissing on us, an all-out torrential downpour starts.

I can't help but chuckle.

Fuck, Levi.

"Goddamnit," he growls under his breath.

"What's the matter?" I smirk, clapping him on the shoulder. "A little water never hurt anyone."

He just shakes his head, trudging out into the night.

"Fuck you."

CHAPTER
Twenty-Eight

MILA

I'm pacing the living room when I hear a thud from upstairs in the lighthouse.

I pause, listening for any sounds from the lighthouse, but none come.

This is bad.

This *feels* really bad.

Phantom whimpers, licking my hand.

"I know, buddy." He's grown just as attached to our little piece of solitude as I have.

While I wait for Christian to return, I busy myself with putting my clothes away alongside his in the dresser drawers upstairs. I also try not to pay attention to how . . . domestic we've become over the course of the last month.

Today was the most fun I've had in years. From the fair to the clothes, to the mind-numbing orgasm that left me walking around on shaky legs for the next half hour, I've never felt so . . . normal.

No one knew who I was. No one asked about my stepfather or

the rest of my family. No one knew of the things I'd seen.

Things with Christian are turning out to be comfortable—even if he *is* still planning on using me for revenge.

I find myself wondering if his brother has anything to do with it. Why else would Christian hold a gun to his head?

"Oh my God, what if he murdered him and tossed his body in the ocean?" I whisper to Phantom, who cocks his head to the side, staring up at me with his big brown eyes. "You're right," I concede, continuing my pacing. "I doubt anyone's throwing Christian anywhere."

What if he's hurt? What if his brother brought more people, and we just didn't see them? What if they're here to kill us both, and I'm sitting down here warm in the cottage like a sitting duck while Christian's bleeding out, in need of my help, upstairs?

"Fuck," I curse under my breath, running my hands through my hair. "What do I do, Phantom?"

He just cocks his head, staring at me intently.

"You're no help."

A thud sounds from upstairs, and my heart seizes in my chest.

"Fine. I'll go check on him. If he's okay, I'll come back here, and we can cuddle."

No response.

Carefully, I slip out the door, covering my head as the rain pelts down from overhead. I rush to the lighthouse, almost slipping in my sneakers in the wet grass.

A shiver rolls through me, and I rush inside, shutting the door behind me and letting out a deep breath.

I've only been in the lighthouse a handful of times, and every one of those times was with Christian. It's dark, save for the few dim lights along the staircase, and I make my way up, over the beaten cobblestone toward the second floor.

My heart pounds in my chest, echoing through my brain, until I finally reach the top, finding the door cracked.

"Christian?" I ask, tentatively knocking on the old wood, but no sound comes from inside.

Pushing the door open, I peer around. There's a bottle of whiskey sitting on the desk, the lid off. One of Christian's guns is sitting beside it. The one he had just pointed at his brother's head not even an hour ago.

I step inside, the scent of leather, whiskey, and the forest washing over me, bringing about a strange sense of comfort.

Maybe they took a walk. Why they would take a walk in a storm like this is beyond me.

My next thought is maybe they went back to the mainland, though I know Christian would have said something to me before he left.

There's a folder open on the desk, and I'm about to pass by it on my way back to the door when something catches my eye.

My heart stalls in my chest, and my stomach drops to my toes.

It's a marriage certificate signed by Christian Alexander. Cross.

The only problem is that the other signature . . . is mine.

I drop the paper like it's on fire, backing up rapidly. The walls are closing in on me, my throat constricting with each painful breath. My head spins when the room sways on its axis.

This isn't *real.*

I suck a deep breath in through my nose, trying to force it out, but it never comes.

No . . . It's impossible to breathe at all with the heavy presence I feel behind me.

"Mila."

Awareness slips through my veins, a violent shiver wracking through me.

"You . . . tricked me . . ." I breathe, my voice hoarse. I can't look at him. I can't see his face—the same one I've fallen in love with all over again—and know that he's been lying to me for months.

He tricked me.

Horror washes through me at the realization that all this time, I've been married to the only man I've ever loved, and I didn't even know it. Horror that he hadn't even planned on telling me.

I close my eyes, pushing out a ragged breath through my teeth, counting like I learned in the bullshit group therapy sessions my mother made me attend after the attack.

One . . . two . . . three . . .

One . . . two . . . three . . .

Finally, I force myself to turn around and face him. I find Christian standing in the doorway to the office, his expression guarded and dark, shrouded in shadows.

Like a demon watching me from the dark corner of a room.

Despite everything, my heart swells when I see him, only to burst with agony and fear at his secret.

"How long?"

Silence.

"How long, Christian?"

His jaw ticks. "Two years in November."

"How could you hide this from me?" I breathe, a tear slipping down my cheek. I'm powerless to stop it.

He watches its descent, staring at it with a darkness in his gaze that sends a shiver down my spine.

"You *lied!*" I screech, the rush of emotion overpowering and painful.

How could he do this to me?

Adrenaline bursts through me and paired with the venomous rage slipping through my veins, I lash out, shoving at his chest. He lets me, but he barely moves, though I gave it everything I had.

He attempts to catch my hands, but I back out of his grasp, the anger in my blood more potent and volatile than anything I've ever felt before.

"You left!"

"I kept you alive," he growls, voice rough and caustic. He

reaches for me, but I rip away from his grasp, stumbling back into the desk and sending the folder flying to the ground. The evidence of our tattered and broken love story covering the floor at my feet. "Your stepfather wanted to sell you," he sneers, his eyes glinting almost black. "Two million for your hand in marriage. I made sure that marriage was impossible."

"You tricked me into *marrying* you? Are you fucking crazy?"

"I did what I had to do to keep you safe," he argues back, his cheeks reddening and his eyes murderous. I've never seen him look so deadly. "Who do you think he was going to sell you to? Someone worthy? Because as far as I know, if you have to buy a wife, you probably don't fucking need one."

"You're lying—"

"I did what I had to do," he replies frostily.

And then it clicks.

"The day you took me to the lawyer's office . . . was any of that for my inheritance?"

He doesn't say anything, but his gaze hardens, his eyes burning with an intensity I've never seen before.

"Oh my god." I collapse back into the desk, my head reeling.

Everything makes sense now.

"You saw what your mother's life was like. Your sister. That the kind of life you want to live?" he challenges darkly, taking a single step into the room. My skin bristles, the hair rising on the back of my neck when he gets closer.

"I think you're a lying psychopath," I growl, scrubbing the tears off my cheeks. "I think you were scared after you tricked me into marrying you, and you ran off. Then, you came back because you felt sorry for me," I scoff, shaking my head. "I didn't need your pity, Christian. I needed *you*."

"And you fucking had me," he bites back. "Even when you couldn't see me, I was right fucking there, watching over you."

"You're a monster," I breathe, shivering at the coldness in his eyes. The eyes of my *husband*.

He scoffs, pushing away from me. "You've got to become a monster to kill a monster, baby." He paces the room in front of me, his lips curling back in a sneer when he finally meets my eyes. "You think I brought you here for fucking fun? To see how long it would take for you to crack and tell me why you shot me? I know you didn't fucking shoot me. I've had concrete evidence for weeks."

My breath catches in my throat, and the floor feels like it's falling out from under me.

I . . . didn't shoot him?

"So why am I here, then?" I whisper, so quiet, it's barely audible over the rain pouring outside. "If you took care of it, then why kidnap me and force me to hide out on your little island?"

This can't be happening. Today was such a good day, and now it's ruined.

He takes another step towards me, and I back up, my back hitting the desk behind me. My hand bumps into something on the surface of the desk, and instinctively, my fingers wrap around it.

The pistol.

Oh, fuck . . .

"I thought this was about revenge?"

"You and I both know this was never about revenge."

I shake my head, my mind spiraling out of control. "This is insane."

His jaw tightens, his eyes boring into mine. He doesn't see the gun in my hand when I lower it off the desk and hold it behind my back.

Please tell me it wasn't all a lie . . .

Imagine my surprise at the next words that leave Christian's lips.

"Whoever hurt you murdered my mother fourteen years ago. I won't lose you, too."

"How could you do this to me?" I whisper, and his cold, hard stare is unblinking. "Why couldn't you just let me go."

"Because the man who hurt you isn't dead."

"Who, then?"

He's never looked deadlier than when the next sentence leaves his mouth.

"My brother. Sebastian Cross."

I've got to get out of here.

"Mila, get the fuck back here!"

I can just make out the roar of Christian's voice over the wind rushing overhead. I don't stop, running until my legs feel like they're going to give out in the mud that's collected under the grass.

It was all a lie. All of it . . .

"Leave me alone!"

How do I tell him I hate him for how he looks at me? How all I can think about is that dark look in his eyes when he sees me. Darker than anything imaginable, as if he wants to cherish me and degrade me at the same time.

As if I'm something important to him.

I come to a screeching stop right at the edge of the cliff, the jagged rocks below beckoning at me. The pistol in my hand feels impossibly heavy and slippery with the water sluicing down my body.

Tears swim in my vision, hot against the cold of the rain, and I finally turn around to see him standing a few feet back, his eyes flashing with the steady pulse of the lightning in the sky behind me.

"*Mila, don't take another fucking step,*" he growls.

I laugh bitterly, the rain soaking through my clothes and freezing against my skin. "It was all a lie, wasn't it?"

A shot of adrenaline races through me at the look in his eyes. Unhinged, pure animal instinct.

He's so handsome, it hurts to look at him.

That's how the devil gets you.

"Mila, what the *fuck* are you doing?"

I suck in a deep breath—

God, this is going to hurt.

—Then I raise the pistol, pointing it at his chest.

His eyes darken past recognition, a demon taking over his features. Devastatingly handsome. Deathly sinister.

He chuckles wickedly, the sound dripping with malice, and for a single second, I almost back out.

I blink back the tears in my eyes, forcing myself to meet his dark gaze head-on.

"Who are you?" I whisper, voice barely audible over the racing of my own heart pounding in my ears and the thunder rumbling over the ocean.

"Mila, you *know* who I am." It's quiet. Resolute.

Why do I believe him, even when everything up to this point has been a lie between us?

"Do I?"

Christian doesn't say anything for a moment, and my heart bottoms out, cracking open like a fissure in the earth. Broken and desolate.

"Did you help him?" A traitorous tear slips down my cheek. He watches its descent, his gaze burning before it slips back to mine.

The air between us seems to cackle with electricity as that look in his eyes morphs into something inhuman. Demonic.

"Pull the trigger, Mila."

I let out a shaky breath, a quiet sob breaking from my throat as my body trembles. A rush of emotions swirls through me like a tornado touching down in the middle of the city, wreaking havoc in its wake.

One, though, burns brighter than all the others.

I can't fucking do it.

"You think I could watch someone rape you?" His voice is cruel, tinged with disappointment and disgust. "Slice you open and watch you bleed? Hear your pain and not want to fucking put a bullet in my head?" His eyes flash with venom, his lips pulling back in a snarl.

I close my eyes, desperately trying to push those voices out of my head, but it's no use. His hands are on me, grabbing me. His knife is in my skin. His smiling, plastic face burned into the backs of my eyelids, taunting me.

Born from the same blood as the man in front of me. My savior.

"Pull the fucking trigger," Christian grits, his voice deeper and darker than anything I've ever heard.

"You forced me to marry you."

"Yeah, I fucking did," he concedes, a wicked gleam in his eyes as he stares down the barrel of his own gun. "You know why?"

I shake my head, closing my eyes against the sound of his voice. The same voice that brings safety and comfort. The one who makes me feel like a real human being and not a defective replica.

Like a man fully disturbed, he takes a step towards me. I back away from him, but he doesn't stop. He steps into me until the barrel of the gun presses right to the center of his forehead, and my heart shatters at the sight of it glinting against the skin.

"I'm so fucking sick of pretending like you're not mine," he grits like it's ripping him open just as much as it is me. "You can hate me all you want, but he's still out there, and I promise you, he's a whole lot more fucked up than you or I could ever imagine. I'll be fucking damned if I let him get to you again. If that makes me the villain in your story, then put a goddamned bullet in my brain right here, little devil. Make sure I'm fucking dead this time."

I open my mouth, but nothing comes out but a quiet whimper. Tears cloud my vision, and though I hate them, I'm powerless to stop their descent.

"It's fucked up. It's toxic. I don't give a fuck. If craving you so fucking violently that I can't live in a world without you in it makes me the bad guy, shoot me."

I hate *him*. I hate him for who he is. How he can be the monster in the dark that comforts me. I hate myself for still being so in love with him, it aches in my chest. I hate that I can't outrun my past.

"I trusted you," I breathe.

"You can't do it, can you?" he rasps, pressing harder against the end of the barrel until I stumble backward, my sneakers slipping in the wet grass.

Christian doesn't care. He's too far gone.

"You can lie to everyone else, Mila. You can even lie to yourself . . . deep down, there's a part of you that fucking *knows* I'd chop off my own dick before I'd ever hurt you. I can't fucking do it."

"That's not true." I shake my head, but he cuts me off with a quiet chuckle.

"You think I left you because I had a choice? Because I wanted to?"

A shiver rolls through me at the air of a threat in his tone. Or maybe it's the way his eyes lock onto mine, and they don't leave. He could take the gun from me, and I'd be dead in the blink of an eye. Still, he'd rather I make the choice.

"I hate you . . ." I whisper, blinking back the tears in my eyes. I shouldn't have. It only makes it easier to see the ruin in his eyes, and my heart aches uncomfortably.

"Then pull the trigger. End it. You think I had something to do with that? I'm better off dead, anyways."

Something in me breaks, and I screw my eyes shut at the onslaught of the voices, overpowering every one of my senses.

How's it feel to be used like the worthless slut you are?

Smile for the camera, little whore. Show everyone how much you fucking love this.

Everything goes silent when I turn the gun on myself.

The cold steel against the side of my head should terrify me, but right now, it's like holding a Hail Mary in the palm of my hand. A last chance to get out of this nightmare once and for all.

Christian's eyes follow the movement of my finger.

"I don't want to remember anymore." The sob that rips from my throat is painful, stealing my breath and making me tremble.

"Mila . . ." Christian's voice is tight with blackness. So cold it would freeze hell over. "Look at me."

I keep my eyes screwed shut, clenching my teeth as the tears spill from the corners of my eyes.

"Look at me, Mila," Christian orders, and I blink my eyes, forcing myself to meet his gaze through my tear-stricken one. His presence is overbearing, forcing me out of my own darkness to meet *his*. "Is he here right now? Is he in control of you?"

I shake my head, a sob breaking from my lips. "It's not that simple."

"It is, Mila. You're the bravest fucking woman I know—"

"I'm not—"

"*You are*," he grits.

I don't want to listen to him. I don't want to hear him tell me I'm strong. A fighter. That's what everyone says, and it's never been true before. It's not now.

"You want to hate me, go ahead, but don't be a fucking coward."

I grit my teeth, my mind screaming at me to do it. Pull the trigger, and the voices will stop. Shut them up for good.

"Please?"

It's silent. So silent, I barely hear it, but when my eyes open again, Christian's mask has slipped, and it's not just the anger I see in his gaze.

It's desperation. Helplessness.

The gun slips from my fingers, falling to the grass with a deafening thud.

I can't do it.

Maybe because deep down, I know what he's saying is true.

Christian would rather die than hurt me . . . and I would rather live with the pain than let it all go.

The moment our worlds collided, there was a part of me that knew I would follow Christian Cross to hell if it meant I could spend eternity in his darkness.

Now, I'm finding his darkness is my light.

I stumble back with the weight of the gun out of my hand, slipping on the side of the bank.

In a flash, Christian grabs me, one hand on my waist to haul me back towards safety, the other around my throat, his fingers tightening over my racing pulse. A shiver of fear rolls through me, and even though I know he won't hurt me, the look in his eyes is fucking terrifying.

Cold, dark clarity. Like a man who's just realized his favorite toy is broken and now he has to throw it away.

"Why am I here, Christian?" My voice breaks when his fingers constrict, stealing what little air I have left.

"I let you go once, little devil," he murmurs, his voice dripping in venom. His other hand comes up, brushing the wet curl off my forehead, covering my scar. His eyes burst with something akin to annihilation. Like I've awoken a sleeping demon, and now it's come to collect my soul. "I won't make the same mistake twice."

His dark gaze burns into mine. My breath catches in my throat when he leans forward, pressing his forehead into mine, his breathing as ragged as my own from the adrenaline coursing through us.

"I hate you," I whisper because even if I don't actually hate him. I want to.

I want to hate him for making me . . . feel like this. This desperation. The desire to lose myself in a man like him. This need.

"And I've been fucking dreaming of you," he grits, his fingers gripping my hip with bruising strength.

And then, the barricades holding back months of anger collapse.

Tears sting in my eyes, and I shake my head. As if fighting them will make them stop. I almost laugh bitterly. I've cried so much over Christian Cross that it's a wonder I can cry at all.

I should be numb to it, but even now, hearing him say those words, my heart flutters painfully in my chest.

"You left. No word on where you'd gone. You just . . . vanished. And now you show up here expecting the same girl you knew before."

"You're *still* that girl."

I shake my head, a bitter laugh slipping past my lips.

"I'm sorry to burst whatever perfect bubble you're living in, but that girl is clearly gone." Even saying it, I want to break down. Tears clog my voice, the rush of adrenaline making my head spin. "Same with any feelings I had left for you."

"Bullshit."

"Excuse me?"

How *dare* he.

"Bullshit," he repeats, eyes flashing menacingly. "You can't fucking hide from me, Mila. I *know* you." He reaches up, brushing his knuckles down the side of my face, and a quiet whimper slips from my lips. I close my eyes as a tear breaks free, slipping down my cheek.

In a surge of anger, I hit him in the chest with everything I have. I may as well be beating up a brick wall. He doesn't even try to stop me.

Still . . . it feels so damned good, I do it again. And then, again. He takes my anger like it's nothing more than a lover's caress.

"I hate you!" I screech at him, and my legs wobble beneath me, threatening to give out as the sobs rip from my throat.

I hate this place. I hate him. I hate myself.

—I think I hate myself the most.

I hate my mind for what it can't tell me. For the secrets, it's hiding. I hate my body for reveling in his touch when I know he's not who he says he is. I hate the scars that cover every inch of my skin, even if some of them aren't visible to the naked eye.

I hate that even though I shouldn't, every fiber of my being craves his.

Christian catches my wrist before I can make contact again, and he tugs me against his chest, holding my arms down.

Every ounce of moral clarity I had before shatters.

When he tries to twist my arm back behind me, my lips crash against his. His kiss is ruthless, a deep feral groan rumbling in his chest against mine when he pulls me against him. We're teeth and nails and anger, swirling to create a vortex that I'm sure will either kill me or make me come without him even touching me.

Christian kisses me with a ferocity I've never felt before. With searing desire, demanding I give him every piece of me, even if those pieces are scattered and broken.

Deadly heat travels down to my core when his hand slips down my back, gripping the curve of my ass, and he lifts me. My legs lock around his hips, and neither of us breaks the kiss as he stumbles toward the cottage.

He drops me at the front door, pushing me back against the wall under the awning, and I've never seen him look so depraved.

"What do you want, Mila?" he grits between his teeth, and a shiver rolls through me.

"You," I breathe. And before he can even tell me to use my words, I fill the silence for him. "Fuck me."

"I can't be gentle with you right now, Mila. You've pissed me off." His hands vibrate against me, the vein in his forehead bulging with his heartbeat. I try to push his shirt up over his abs, but his hands catch mine.

"Right now, you need me soft. You need me to be patient. I can't fucking go there with you, Mila. The thought of you being afraid of me fucking terrifies me." Despite the rough growl in his voice, a tenderness blooms in my chest.

In an act of defiance, I reach between us, fisting him through the wet denim of his jeans and his jaw clenches. His hand comes up, dragging my head back at an almost uncomfortable angle to force my gaze to his.

My tongue darts out to lick the water off my lips. He watches the movement with dark clarity.

"Your darkness has never scared me, Christian," I whisper, still stroking him despite the bloom of pain in my scalp. It only eggs me on, stoking the fire of the infernal burning need swirling in my stomach. "Only your absence."

His tongue slides along his teeth, his eyes boring into mine like he can melt me where I stand.

"You remember your safe word?"

My stomach clenches, and I reach for the button on his jeans.

"Yes," I breathe.

He catches my hand, stopping me. "If you need it, use it." He nods towards the door. "Get inside."

CHAPTER
Twenty-Nine

MILA

I spin when he releases me hurrying through the door, but I only make it as far as the kitchen table before his arms are wrapping around me and he's pushing me back against it.

In a flash, he lifts me, depositing me on the table and kicking chairs out of the way. One topples to the floor but neither of us pays it any mind. His lips are back on mine and he feasts on me, his hands gripping my knees to spread me wide and allowing him to step between them.

The moment his hand finds me, I gasp, surging against his hand.

"Who's pussy is this, Mila?"

"Yours," I whimper and he growls. His other hand slides back into my hair, fisting the roots to force my gaze to his.

"Let's get one thing straight, Mila." With a snap and a sting on my skin, he tugs my panties until they rip off, falling down my leg. "I would rip the gates of heaven if God himself thought he could keep you from me, and I would raise hell just to drag you down there and fuck you on the throne."

My heart flutters at his words, my eyes brimming with fresh tears. I don't want to allow myself to believe him, but the desperation in his gaze, the tremor that rolls through him, can't be ignored.

I whimper, my eyelashes fluttering on my cheeks when he slips a finger through my folds, gathering the wetness there and swirling it around. He slides that finger inside me, hissing out a breath through his teeth.

He spreads my legs wider, and I reach for the button on his jeans, ripping them open and fisting his cock. It's impossibly hard and hot in my hand, and he pushes me off when I stroke him from root to tip.

Withdrawing his fingers, he grips my hip in one and his cock in the other, stroking it through my folds. My eyes flutter when he brushes against my clit, and when he notches himself at my entrance, a tingle of awareness slips through me.

I'm doing it. I'm really fucking doing it.

"Lighthouse," he reminds me—and then he's filling me in one push. He bottoms out halfway, and I cry out at the intrusion, the size of his cock burning with friction as he slips back out, only to drive back inside with a grunt.

"*Fuck . . .*" he rasps, his hands on my thighs, keeping me spread wide for him with bruising strength.

My back bows off the table, my pussy sucking him in greedily despite the sting of taking him so quickly. He pushes past all my barriers.

The thoughts cling to the corners of my mind, fighting with me to push him off. To rake my nails across his face and fight with everything I have. My hand tightens to a fist where he's pinning it to the bed, my mind running rampant now that I can't move.

I shake my head, gasping for breath through my rapidly closing throat.

"You're okay, Mila. Just relax and let me in." He pushes further and heat floods my core, and I bite my lip. A shiver rolls through me, a single tear slipping down my cheek to my hairline. It burns, but it's a good burn, feeling him stretch me as he rocks inside me. "You feel so fucking good," he rasps, pressing his lips to my racing heartbeat in my throat. "You're going to come like such a good little whore on my cock."

Smile for the camera, little whore.

He shakes his head, his eyes boring into mine from above.

"You want me to stop, just say the word."

"Please don't stop."

"Look at me, Mila." My eyes spring open, meeting his. "Your pussy, your ass, your fucking *heart?* It belongs to me. And the piece of shit that hurt you? He better hope to fucking God he's dead by the time I get to him."

He drags my hips up, aligning us so his cock brushes over that most sensitive part of me. He hooks one of my legs over his shoulder, the table rocking back and forth with how hard he's fucking me.

"Christian . . . *oh my God*," I gasp when his thumb finds my clit, circling the sensitive nub until my eyes roll back into my head. The chill mixed with the pleasure rippling through me sends a shiver down my spine, and my teeth chatter from the euphoria.

One of my hands grips the edge of the table, the rough wood digging into my skin, while the other grips his, holding my thigh. His fingers wrap around mine tightly, holding me while he fucks me ruthlessly.

"*Fuck*, you're fucking perfect," he rasps under his breath, his head kicking back with a groan. Beneath his shirt, his muscles ripple with the force of his thrusts, like a savage dark God who's hellbent on sucking the soul from my body with a single orgasm.

I claw at the table, desperate to grab *something* and hold on, but there's nothing. Nothing but him and what he's doing to me and the spot he's hitting inside me so deep, I didn't even know it existed.

So I fall, succumbing to the pleasure as it rips me to shreds, and a feral cry tears past my lips to rival the storm outside.

The orgasm is strong and intense, stealing my vision, my breath, my fucking soul until I collapse on the hood beneath him.

"There's my good little wife," Christian murmurs in my ear, crowding over me, his cock still buried inside my pussy.

I groan when he slips out of me, lifting me up into his arms and carrying me toward the couch. My legs lock around his hips, and I say a silent thank you to whoever invented hip slits in dresses. His hands cup my bare ass, his fingers dangerously close to my center, driving me mad.

Unable to stop myself, I lean into him, pressing soft kisses against the scratches I'd left on the side of his neck. My lips trace the column of his throat, and his grip tightens to near bruising strength when I nip the pulse point just beneath his ear.

A small tremor moves through him, his breath hissing out through his teeth, and a small smile of triumph pulls on my lips that I can do *that* to *him*.

He deposits me on his lap, falling to the couch, and my legs straddle either of his. I try to adjust, and his hands come to my hips, holding me steadfast above him. I shiver in his arms from my wet dress and the little electric aftershocks of my orgasm still rippling through me.

"Don't run, little devil," he rasps, eyes glinting in the moonlight overhead as he pushes my soaking wet dress up around my hips. "I've barely gotten started with you."

A water droplet slips between my breasts, and he leans forward, capturing it with his lips, a heavy groan rumbling through him when I jerk against his cock.

His arm bands around my back, his other under my ass, and he tugs me forward, pealing the top of my dress down with his teeth before sealing his lips around my nipple.

My head falls back, the wet tendrils of my hair curling over the curve of my ass, and I whimper at the graze of his teeth. I slip my hand between us, stroking feather-light touches over his cock before moving to the buttons of his shirt.

His lips slide up my neck, and he nips and sucks a line from my jaw to my chin before finally, his lips seal over mine, swallowing the sound of the desperate plea ripping from my throat.

I push his shirt back and run my hands over the hard ridges of his abs, reveling in the feeling of the tight muscles ripping under my fingertips.

I rock against his length, stroking his cock through my folds, and he growls, his hand tightening on my ass. His other grips my hair, tugging my head back at an awkward angle before he drives his teeth into the side of my neck.

"Chris-tian . . ." I gasp, heat radiating from the spot where his teeth mark me straight down to my pussy that jerks against him.

"You make me so fucking crazy, you know that?" He pushes me against him, and I shiver, the vibrations against my clit making me moan. "Sit on my cock, Mila. Show me how bad you want me."

I bite my lip, my hips continuing to roll against his, and my eyes screwed up to the ceiling.

When a moan slips past my lips, his hand in my hair tightens, dragging my gaze to his. I've never seen him look so murderous. He presses his lips against my cheek and snarls, his lips curling at the feel of my heat enveloping his length and his eyes nearly black.

"You have three seconds."

I whimper, and he releases me, leaning back against the seat and placing both arms over the back of the headrests on either side of him. Like the devil on his throne, waiting for me to kneel for him.

I grip him in my hand, holding his gaze as I rub the tip of his cock through my wetness, making his jaw clench. His eyes bore into mine as I slowly sink down, my mouth falling open as he stretches me.

I don't think I'll ever get used to his size.

"That's my girl," he rasps, his eyes locked where my body swallows him, sucking him in greedily despite two orgasms. "I'm all yours, little devil. Ride me."

My stomach clenches at his words, my core clamping down on him as I slip him further inside me, sinking down on his length. My eyes screw shut, my teeth grinding together as he fills me deeper than he ever has before.

My stomach clenches at his words, my core clamping down on him as I slip him further inside me, sinking down on his length. My eyes screw shut, my teeth grinding together as he fills me deeper than he ever has before.

My nails dig into his shoulders, and my knees shake on either side of his, but I don't stop rocking against him. With the way he's seated inside me, his cock brushes that sensitive spot that makes my teeth chatter and my morals completely disintegrate.

Christian's arm bands around my waist, and he tugs me against him, his body flush with mine. He captures my nipple between his teeth, sucking the hardened peak into his mouth and circling it with his tongue while I struggle to hold onto the last pieces of my soul that he doesn't completely own.

A cry rips from my throat, and my hips shake as my core tightens unbearably. "That's it, sweetheart," he croons against my skin, his gaze coming up to meet mine. "Let me hear you."

"Christian . . ." I breathe, my legs threatening to give out as the pleasure reaches a blinding fever pitch. "Please?"

I don't even know what I'm asking for, but he does. He grips my hips in his hand, curling his arm around my back and holding me against him while he bounces me on his cock. The couch shakes around us, the sounds of our bodies meeting filling the air as he fucks me until I feel like I'm coming apart at the seams.

God, I hope this boat's steady . . .

My fingers tangle in his hair, his digging into my skin as he grunts with each thrust, his cock brushing past my limits until I know, I'll feel him for the next week.

Lightning paints the sky bright blue, but it's nothing compared to the white light shooting behind my eyes as a strangled cry wrenches from my throat.

"Let go, Mila," he grits in my ear. "Give it all to me. Give me all your pain. All your pleasure."

And I do.

The anger, the fear, the pain, the pleasure . . . it all meets in the center of my core to form a nuclear meltdown that leaves me screaming so loudly that my voice grows hoarse. My pussy clamps down on his cock, and he grunts, the veins in his neck bulging as his cock thickens inside me.

He thrusts up into me, snarling as his own orgasm rips through him, his cock pulsing inside me with each thrust of his hips.

"*Fuck, Mila . . .*" he roars, pulling me tightly against him while my body spasms over his, the aftershocks of my orgasm rocketing through me as I slowly, slowly regain consciousness in my surroundings.

"Fuck," he grits, a tremor moving through his hands on my hips. "Fucking hell, Mila."

I shiver, collapsing above him when he pulls out. I'm shaking uncontrollably, my body vibrating with endorphins and my limbs aching and sore. I feel like I just ran a marathon and barely lived to tell the tale.

His breathing is as ragged as mine, and he combs my hair back from my face, tugging my head up to press a rough kiss to my lips.

"I live and breathe for you, Mila," he rasps, his gaze boring into mine. "I'll fucking die for you . . . but if you ever point my fucking gun at your head again, I'll tie you to the bed and spank your ass until it's black and blue. Understood?"

My breath catches in my throat, and my heart beats wildly. My tongue darts out to lick my lips, my mouth dry like he'd sucked all the moisture out of the air with that single statement.

The worst part is I know, without a doubt, he would.

"Understood?" He tightens his grip on my head and I give a

soft nod.

I let you go once, little devil. I won't make the same mistake twice.

"I understand . . ." I suck in a deep breath, my gaze locked with his.

Part of me is satisfied and exhausted. The other part of me—the part that won't shut the *hell up*—screams at me that I just became exactly what the scars on my stomach say I am.

A whore.

He deposits me on the couch and stands, disappearing into the bathroom. Tears build in my eyes as the humiliation sets in and I angrily brush them away.

This is what I wanted. What I asked for. At any time during that I could have said the safeword and I know without a doubt he would have released me.

So why do I feel so . . . dirty? Is it because I enjoyed it?

He was right. I wasn't ready. Part of me wonders if I'll *ever* be ready.

He comes back to the living room and I close my eyes, trying to shut the tears off, but, of course, it doesn't work. One slips down my cheek and I hate myself for it.

Great, here it comes. The whole *I told you so* speech.

I look away, slowly rising from the couch on shaky legs and hoping I don't look as stupid as I feel.

I go to step past him when he pauses, reaching out and grabbing me around the waist. He's not rough. Just firm, holding me in place when all I really want to do is run to the bathroom and barricade myself behind the door.

I don't want to look at him right now.

Not after he just ripped what was left of my soul to shreds and put it back together again with his touch.

"*Mila.*"

I force myself to meet his gaze, hating the single traitorous tear that slips down my cheek.

I open my mouth to speak, but he cuts me off, pushing me back down to the couch and pressing my legs apart. I'm surprised by the gentleness of his hands when he cleans me. The warm rag burns against my clit, a reminder that he was there and he had me coming on command like a dog in heat.

God, I was so stupid to think this could work.

"Come here," he instructs, tossing the rag in a hamper in the corner.

"I'm fine," I argue, but his fixes me with a stern gaze.

He doesn't say anything, but it's what he does that brings fresh tears to the surface.

Sliding his arms underneath me, he lifts me into his arms, carrying me towards the stairs. When we reach the bedroom, he slips my dress over my head and removes my wet bra. Stooping down, he helps me slide my sneakers off before he tugs me toward the bed.

I expect him to leave, but when I climb under the covers, he slides in behind me. His arm covers over my side, tugging me back into his chest, his body warm despite the cold that radiates through me. I shiver and when a silent sob slips through me, my shoulders trembling, he pulls back.

"Come here," he orders softly, pulling me around towards his chest and tucking me into his arms. He presses his lips to the top of my head, stroking my hair, while I bury my face in his chest, the tears refusing to subside.

"*Shh* . . ." he soothes, his lips at my forehead. "I'm here."

CHAPTER
Thirty

CHRISTIAN

The scent of vanilla and ocean water in the air is what wakes me early in the morning.

Blinking open my eyes, I find the sun is shining outside the cottage window, the rain having left everything clear and damp. The air is warm, and seagulls chirp overhead.

Looking down, my wife is lying on my chest in our bed.

Fuck . . . my fucking wife.

A deep sound rumbles in my chest, my cock hardening when I remember the way she squeezed the fucking life out of me last night. The fire in her eyes when she held my own fucking gun to my head.

The destruction I felt when she turned it on herself instead.

Reaching down, I brush the hair back from her soft face.

I didn't know something could scare me that fucking bad until my heart started walking around outside my chest.

A tremor moves through my hand, and I pull her closer, my fingers stroking through the curled ends of her hair.

If I could stay right fucking here and never have to give her up,

I'd sell my soul if that's what it took.

"Rise and shine, *lovebirds*."

Goddamnit.

Mila jumps, letting out a squeak. She raises her head from my chest, sleepy eyes meeting mine and stealing my breath away.

I open my mouth to ask her how she's feeling, Levi's voice sounds from downstairs and Mila launches off the bed, scrambling for her dress.

With a groan, I stand and wrap the sheet around my waist and head to the railing.

"Last call," Levi chuckles, grinning up at me like the idiot he is, and I swear to fucking God, I'd love nothing more than to toss his ass over the side of the cliff. "You know, if you weren't going to sleep in the cabin, you could have let me have it. Saw a spider the size of my dick in there."

I shoot him a glare, and he just stares back blankly.

"What?"

Jesus fucking Christ.

Without a word, shake my head and grab a pair of jeans from my drawer, just as he reaches the top of the stairs.

I reach for Mila, but she looks between Levi and me, then back to Levi, before she pulls back away from my grasp, her gaze dropping to her toes.

Fuck.

"Rise and shine, scrappy," Levi greets cheerfully.

Without a word, she pushes past him and heads downstairs, taking the ladder at the back of the boat and climbing down. Both Levi and I stare after her, Levi's brows drawing together in confusion.

"What did I say?"

I just shake my head, sitting forward and scrubbing a hand over my face.

"You didn't say anything. You're a fucking idiot, scaring her, yes. But this isn't about you."

"Oh . . ." he murmurs, and then as if he suddenly grew a brain in that fucking head and realized the gravity of the situation. "Oh, fuck."

I fall back to the bed with a sigh.

"Yeah."

"I take it she heard what we were talking about?"

"She *saw* what I left out on the table," I correct.

"All of it."

"Fucking all of it."

Downstairs, the bathroom door closes, and I grit my teeth when the sound of the lock clicks.

"You're sure you got the right information?"

Levi's gaze goes stern, and he looks out over the clearing.

"I've been tracking him for months. This is our only chance."

Fuck.

"I take it she didn't find your whole marrying her behind her back gesture romantic?"

"Fuck off," I grumble, turning towards the door. "We'll leave once I get Mila situated. I'm taking her into town."

"Probably for the best. Think I'll wait in the car. Things are bit . . . stuffy in here."

I listen to the sounds of Levi retreat back down the stairs while I pack my bag. When I'm done and dressed, I head down the stairs towards the bathroom, my chest tight.

Phantom pads over to me from his spot outside the bathroom door.

"She okay, bud?" He just stares at me like I'm an idiot.

Fuck, I've resorted to asking a fucking dog about my wife.

I step past him, patting his head, and raise my hand to knock on the door. Before I can, though, Mila tugs it open, a towel wrapped around herself and her hair damp from the shower.

Fucking hell.

I can't stop my gaze from raking over her, my cock pulsing at the water droplet that slips between her breasts.

She jumps back when she sees me, her eyes wide and guarded.

I fucking hate that I put that look there with every goddamned fiber of my being.

She sucks in a shallow breath, looking down at the floor.

"You're leaving," she says softly, and my chest tightens.

"Only for a few days."

She nods, but I can tell by the look in her eyes she doesn't believe me. It's my fucking fault. I left her when she needed me most. I lost her trust, no matter the reason. Now, after last night, I'm not sure she'll ever trust me again.

Somehow, even after everything we've been through, she's never felt further away than she does right now.

"I'm going to take you to the lodge, with Paulina. You'll want to pack some clothes."

She shakes her head, drawing that lip between her teeth. I notice it's bleeding from her worrying while she was in the shower.

"I want to stay here."

Out of habit, I reach for her, attempting to brush the hair back from her face, but she lurches from my grasp as if I might hurt her.

As if I fucking could.

My hand falls to my side, a bitterness sliding down the back of my throat.

"I can't risk you being by yourself out here. Phantom will go, too."

If something were to happen and the waves were too rough, no one would be able to get to her. Not to mention, with Paulina around, I'll have the peace of mind that she's eating and taking care of herself. Leaving her out here alone to sit with nothing but her thoughts and the nightmares that plague her dreams, I'm not sure if I'd come back to my wife . . . or what's left of her.

Tears well in her eyes, but they don't fall.

It still feels like I swallowed glass, though.

"Okay?" I ask, the hole in my chest aching more prominently today.

She nods, pulling her towel tighter around herself.

"I'll get dressed."

An hour later, we pull down the drive of the Oak Ridge Lodge and Resort. An overwhelming sense of foreboding hangs in the air as the oversized inn comes into view, nestled against the Mount Baker National Forest. With over a hundred acres, the forest stretches wide beyond our field of view.

I didn't want to bring her here—not until she was ready—but right now, it's the safest place for Mila with me out of the state.

I expect her to ask when she sees the old stone fortress, but she doesn't, remaining silent.

Fuck, she's been silent since we left the island two hours ago. I don't know why I expect any different.

I pull past towards the back lane that leads to the mansion I grew up in before parking and exiting the car. Mila follows, but Levi hangs back, leaning against the side of the car. He hates this house as much as I do. Phantom, on the other hand, couldn't be happier to piss all over everything in sight. Oddly enough, a sense of pride washes through me because I hate this place.

"There are my babies," Paulina gushes, rushing out the door and beelining straight for Mila. Surprisingly, Mila goes into her arms, letting her hug her.

Must be fucking nice, I think dryly, well aware that I have no one to blame but myself for the fact that my wife won't let me touch her.

"Rought night?" Collin chuckles, sensing my dark mood when I grab Mila's bag and head inside.

I swear to fucking God . . .

"You have no fucking idea."

He follows me when I bypass the front lobby and head straight upstairs to the live-in quarters. It's where Paulina and Bella live, so I know she won't be alone while I'm gone.

"You're sure about this?" Collin asks, stopping in the doorway to the suite I use if I'm ever here, his icy blue stare cocky while he watches me sit Mila's bag down on the large, Alaskan king bed.

"No."

"You know, you don't have to go."

I grit my teeth. As if it were that fucking easy.

"I do."

He steps into the room, his hands in his pockets. I can tell he wants to say something, but right now, I'm really not in the fucking mood.

I should be back on the island with Mila, talking this shit over. Not running off to find the man who raped her in the hopes that *maybe* when I'm done, I'll be able to piece some sort of life together with her.

"She's a strong girl," Collin starts, looking at the bag on the bed. "Full of light. Beautiful . . ."

Did I bring my gun in with me?

"Someday, someone's going to snuff that light out," he says quietly, his gaze meeting mine, saying everything I know both of us are thinking. "Think about that while you're gone."

He leaves me standing in the room, cement in my veins. Tugging the box out of my pocket, I place it on the pillow, my fingers brushing over the velvet.

I'm only sorry I didn't give it to her sooner. Maybe if I had, I—

Fuck it. There's no use in worrying about the past.

The only thing that ever did was get people shot.

When I make my way down the stairs, Mila is standing in the foyer, Paulina's arm around her shoulders, and their voices hushed.

"What the hell is going on?"

Mila jumps at the sound of the voice and Paulina says something else in her ear when my sister emerges from the direction of the kitchen, her eyes wide when she looks around at all of us.

"Bella—"

"Who is this?" Bella asks, her gaze lingering on Mila. "Are you here for the benefit?"

"Bella, this is my wife. I'm going out of town for a few days. Mila's going to stay here."

Bella freezes, her eyes widening. She opens her mouth with a barrage of questions, but I hold up a hand to stop her. Not that I didn't expect it, but right now is not the time.

"I'll explain more later, but right now, I have business to tend to, and Mila will be staying here while I'm gone. Paulina and Collin understand."

"You can't just show up here after *months* and leave some random woman," she side-eyes Mila, who looks like she's ready to throw up. Honestly, if I had a better plan, I wouldn't have brought her here, but Bella will come around. "In case you forgot, we have a business to run."

"And you're doing a great job at it."

"Bella," Collin says, placing his hand on her shoulder, but she shrugs him off.

Bella looks back and forth between Paulina and me, horrified.

"You're *okay* with this?" she asks Paulina and Paulina nods.

"Let's discuss this upstairs," she says quietly. "Away from the guests."

Bella opens her mouth to argue, but I shoot her a look that has her mouth clamping shut.

"I will explain everything later. Now, if you'll excuse me, I'd like to say goodbye to my wife before I go."

Bella glares at me and scoffs. "I swear you two get weirder and weirder."

Turning on her heel, she storms off, heading towards the stairs.

I shake my head, and Paulina gives me a soft smile, releasing Mila and walking over to me. She pulls me into a hug, keeping her voice low. "She'll come around, sweetie. We'll take care of Mila."

"I know," I grunt.

She leans back to look at me, pressing her palm to the scar on my cheek. I don't need to ask to know what the look in her eyes means.

"You come back to us. You hear me?"

"I hear you," I murmur, attempting to pull back from her. I don't do hugs. The most hugging I have ever done is Mila.

"I mean it, Christian Cross," she warns, finally freeing me with a stern gaze.

"Keep Collin away from my wife," I mutter quietly, and she shoves at my chest, giving me a demur smile.

"We're going to miss our flight," Levi calls from the doorway, and I shoot him a look, stepping away from Paulina and moving toward Mila. I make sure I keep my distance, even if all I want to do is pull her into me.

We've got a lot of shit to discuss but no time to do it in, and I fucking hate leaving her when she's looking at me like that. That haunted look in her eyes.

"I know this is fast, but I have to go."

She nods once, hugging her arms around herself.

"When will you be back."

"As soon as I can," I murmur, voice rough.

Fuck, I've never been good at goodbyes.

"When I get back, we'll talk. About everything," I murmur, giving her a look. She's still got secrets she's keeping from me about that night, and it's time we got it all out in the open.

I can see by the look in her eyes that I'm losing her.

My mind starts to race, coming up with pisspoor ways I can undo the damage I caused when she found those papers, but I know it would only drive her away for good.

I'll let her take the time while I'm away to think about it. Figure out her feelings.

And when I come home, I'll be better for her. I'll be what she deserves if it fucking kills me.

"Be safe," she whispers, so quiet, I almost think I imagined it.

But then those moonlight eyes lock with mine, and something warm and new and so fucking severe it steals my breath away and slides through my veins.

I love this fucking girl.

I think I always have.

Slowly, I step up in front of her, keeping my hands to myself, and press a single kiss to her forehead, committing her scent to memory.

I know she's crying because a shiver rolls through her, followed by a soft sniffle. I can't look at her, though. If I do, I won't take care of what I need to.

"I'll see you when I get home."

It's not until Levi and I are in the car that he lights the end of a cigarette and hands me another.

"Don't look back," he murmurs around the cigarette, putting the car in drive, and I don't because, for once, my little brother's right.

"Just fucking drive," I grit under my breath.

And then he drives us away from the only home I've ever known, resting in the heart of the girl with the moonlight eyes . . . with no knowledge of if we'll ever return.

CHAPTER
Thirty-One

MILA

"**W**here are we going?"

Christian looks across the car at me, a smirk lighting his handsome face.

"Wherever you want, but first, we have to make a pit stop."

"For what?"

"You have to meet with your mother's lawyer to get the paperwork narrowed out for your inheritance."

I groan under my breath, leaning back in the seat.

"From Marcus? I don't want it. It's blood money."

"This is from your father."

"So dead parent money," I shake my head. I didn't know my father. At least, not that I can remember. He passed in an accident when I was young.

Christian pulls to a stop in front of the old brick building downtown, looking at me before he gets out of the car.

"Think of it as money you didn't know you had. Parker was holding it in an offshore account. It's not a lot, but five thousand dollars is still five thousand dollars."

"Why would Marcus be hiding my father's money? And why does he have it in the first place?"

Christian cocks a brow at me.

"Does Parker do anything legally?"

"Touché."

He chuckles, climbing out of the car, and I begrudgingly follow him. He stops at the door, holding it open for me, but when we step inside, his hand goes to the small of my back.

I can't lie and say it doesn't shoot tingles up my spine. We haven't touched each other since our kiss at the club two weeks ago, but I've thought about it every. Single. Moment since.

Cheeks flaming and my mind in a puddle, we step up to the front counter, where he drops his hand. I let out a deep breath, the spot on my back where he'd touched me burning like he'd held a match to my skin.

"We have a meeting with Pierce at three," Christian tells the front desk worker as calm as ever, while I'm having an existential crisis because he touched me., who blushes and bats her pretty long lashes at him despite his hand still clasped around mine.

"Of course. Mr. Pierce will be right with you," she purrs, batting her pretty long eyelashes at him like she might take flight and land right in his bed.

I hate her.

Before we even turn away from the counter, a door to our left opens and an older man steps out.

"Ah, Ms. Carpenter. I'm so glad you could make it in," he says, though the look he gives me says the opposite. "Right this way."

We follow him down a corridor to an office in the back. He shuts the door behind us and motions for us to sit, and I do, while Christian stands behind me, leaning against the wall.

Mr. Pierce looks uncomfortable, dotting his brow with handkerchief from the front pocket of his suit.

"Just a few last-minute cleaning things to take care of," Mr. Pierce says, falling into the chair behind the desk. "Were you and your father close?"

I shrug. "He died when I was four, so about as close as a four-year-old can

323

get with anyone, I guess."

Mr. Pierce doesn't know how to respond to that, so he doesn't.

"Just a few papers to sign. Nothing too crazy," he says, even though the stack he drops in front of me may as well be a new iteration of the Bible.

"I have to sign all *this?"*

"Yes, well, your father had a lot of documentation we had to sort through before we could release the funds into your account."

"For five thousand dollars?"

Mr. Pierce chuckles under his breath, wiping his brow.

He's awfully sweaty.

I look back at Christian, who nods to me, and I let out a sigh.

"Let me help," Mr. Pierce says, his gaze flicking back and forth between Christian and me. "Here."

He takes the papers, folding them over one by one for me to sign. He glances at Christian a few times, and I realize he's scared of him.

Or he really has to use the bathroom.

Either way, he's nervous about something, though I can't tell what.

"Is there a problem?"

"Nope," he says cheerfully. "None at all. Lots to do today."

I continue singing my name until I feel like my hand is going to fall off, and just when I'm about to tell him I don't want to sign anymore, the stack ends, and he tugs it away from me like it's on fire.

"All finished. I've got everything I need."

"That was easy," I murmur. "I guess."

"You should be free to go."

When we're done, Christian leads me out to the Bentley, that damned hand coming resting on the small of my back, only this time, I feel his thumb slip along my spine and a shiver ghosts through me.

He's doing that on purpose. No one's that sexually attractive without trying to be.

"I can't believe all the paperwork he made me fill out," I complain when Christian falls into the driver's seat beside me. "And then he rushed us out like the building was on fire. And why was he so sweaty?"

"Mila?"

"What?" I snap, turning my gaze on Christian.

Instead of a response, he just takes my face in his hands, kissing me so intensely, I feel like the world tilts on its axis.

Every thought I'd had flies right out the window, along with any dignity I had left. His lips linger against mine, and when he pulls away, his stare is so dark, it sucks the air right out of the Bentley.

This man is dangerous with a kiss like that.

"Just shut the hell up."

When Christian said his family owned a lodge, I didn't know it would be the size of Manhattan. The main lodge itself sits atop a cliff, overlooking the forest-covered valley below like a silent stone protector.

The Oak Ridge Lodge is a fortress nestled amongst the tall Washington Pines of the Mount Baker National Forest. With three hundred and something rooms—I zoned out when Collin was telling me exactly how many— and multiple buildings, it's easy to understand that I got lost on my first day, post-Christian's departure.

—And my second.

—And maybe my third.

Fortunately, Paulina found me, gently escorting me towards the kitchen in the mansion, though it would be better described as a mini-palace, complete with its own hot tub and chef named Javier who makes the best scrambled eggs I've ever tasted.

"You're going to make me gain weight," I grumble to Paulina when she sets a mounded plate of bacon and eggs in front of me on the first day.

"Men like a little meat on the bones," she explains with a coy wink. "Makes things softer."

I close my eyes, willing that mental picture away because, honestly, I'm not sure I'm mentally strong enough to handle it right now.

"I'm going to pretend I didn't hear that."

On the second day, Paulina put me to work, sorting through an obscene amount of new clothes that Christian had apparently had delivered for me.

Asshole. As if I could be bought.

Still, I didn't mind because it gave me something to do besides stare into the abyss and wonder if I was a widow or just the reluctant wife who'd been pushed aside.

"Why do I need all these clothes?"

Paulina smirks while I reach for my fourth bag. Peaking inside, I quickly shut it again when I spot the lace and silk from some designer store I've never shopped at.

"You can't live in Mr. Cross's shirt for the rest of your life."

I look down at the worn, baggy T-shirt I've taken to sleeping in since he left.

It's not because it smells like him and his scent brings me comfort. It's just comfortable, and he's clearly not using it. Why let it go to waste?

"Watch me," I grumble shoving the lingerie, bag and all, in the top of the dresser drawer.

He's insane if he thinks I'm ever putting it on for him after what he did.

When I'm not being coerced into eating my weight in whatever delectable dishes Javier cooks up, I find myself either wandering the grounds with Phantom or sitting by the bay window in Christian's room that overlooks the forest beyond.

The property is sprawling at over a hundred acres and filled with wealthy tourists from around the world who came out for some fresh mountain air.

It feels like stepping right back into LA, and I can see now why Christian didn't bring me here after he found me. I do my best to avoid them. In fact, I avoid everyone. Especially Bella, who seems to have taken the same approach.

I can't say I blame her. How would you feel if your brother showed up after months and dropped off some random woman while you were trying to run a huge business?\

I'd probably be a little pissed off, too.

Paulina does her best to involve me, but I can see it's hard for her, not knowing when Christian will be back. Not knowing what to do with me.

As if I'm a problem that needs to be solved.

After spending so much time on the island, it's hard to believe I would miss it at all.

. . . but I do.

It's breathtaking and serene, watching fall roll in with a change in the leaves.

Still, I miss the island and the freedom it holds. I know Phantom does, too.

I guess, in some twisted way that makes absolutely no sense, I miss Christian too, though I'm trying to decide if it's the man I miss or just the idea of who I thought he was.

I can't fight the sinking feeling in my stomach. Like, what if this really is the end, and I never see him again? Or what if he does come back and decides he's tired of all the baggage that seems to follow me like a dark cloud?

My thoughts race through my mind day in and day out, and I can't shake the feeling that something's wrong.

I'm trying to be positive. I really am. Every day, I wake up with the best of intentions, but by nightfall, when no word comes on if he's okay, I find myself alone in his bed, holding that damned ring and staring at a wedding band I'm not even sure he ever put on.

I shouldn't care. He tricked me into marrying him. I mean, who does that? He stole my choice in the matter, even if it was with the best intentions.

I still do, though, and it freaking sucks.

I still can't believe everything that was going on behind my back. If I think about it too much, I get sick. I shouldn't be surprised. My stepfather was literally arrested for selling other humans. He sold my sister's body against her will. Why should I expect to be any different?

I can't escape the thoughts of what my life would have been like had Christian not done what he did. In a way, I'm grateful. In others . . . I wish I'd never met Christian Cross.

It just goes to show how twisted the world really is. How no matter what you *think* you know about your life, there's so much more happening behind the scenes that we're blind to.

Like . . . Sebastian. When I close my eyes, I can feel his hands on me. His knife in my skin. His breath harsh against the confines of that deranged mask that haunts my nightmares.

I never saw the attack coming, and I know it's my fault for being blind to the world around me. While I was nursing a broken heart, someone else was watching from the shadows, planning to shatter it completely.

Maybe if I'd been paying attention, I would have stayed home that night.

—I actually scoff out loud.

Who am I kidding? The moment I thought Christian was in trouble, nothing would have stopped me.

There are so many things I wish I could ask him. Like why he left? Why he couldn't just tell me the truth about my stepfather? Why he's never shared these little pieces of his life before?

I know I won't get answers, though.

I don't even know if he's alive.

—And cue another tidal wave of grief.

The sound of footsteps causes me to jump in my place at the kitchen table where I had been stewing over a barely touched grapefruit.

I hate grapefruit, but Paulina insists it's good for the heart.

The housekeeper steps into the room, a basket of towels under her arm. She's singing along to the earbuds in her ears and doesn't notice me until the last second.

The moment she sees me, she lets out a squeak, and the towels hit the ground at her feet.

God, do I look that bad?

"I apologize, Mrs. Cross," she winces, ducking her head. "I'll take these back and wash them again."

"Nonsense." I slide from my grapefruit prison stool and stoop to help her pick up the towels. Grabbing an armful, I drop the still-warm linens on the table.

She freezes like I'm going to bite her or something.

I'm not that feral, though, I guess I probably look it in Christian's baggy T-shirt.

The housekeeper is beautiful. Pretty light brown hair. Striking green eyes that appear almost catlike. What she's doing working here and not for some high fashion modeling agency, I have no idea.

She stares at me.

I stare back.

I'm *stellar* at making friends.

"Well, aren't we going to fold them?"

"That's my job."

"Would . . . you like me to *not* fold them?" I ask, dropping the towel in my hand back to the table.

"Sorry," she winces. "Sometimes, I don't think before I speak."

I can't help but chuckle. That makes two of us.

"I'm the last person in this ginormous house you need to worry about."

"No, Mr. Cross was very specific—"

"I don't see Mr. Cross here, do you?"

She blushes, tucking a strand of hair behind her ear and glancing around nervously.

God, what did he tell her? That my fingers aren't allowed to touch anything but expensive Egyptian cotton sheets?

"My name's Mila, by the way. You don't need to call me Mrs. Cross."

"Ava," she says, shaking my hand when I offer it to her. "How long have you and Mr. Cross been married."

I grit my teeth, aggressively folding a washcloth.

"Two years, I think. Maybe less. Who knows?" I grumble. "Not me."

She stares at me, confused.

Whoops.

"Sorry. It's complicated."

That's the polite way to put it.

"Isn't it always?" she chuckles, resuming her folding. "How long have you worked here?"

"No long," she shrugs. "About six months."

"Do you like it?"

"I can't complain. It beats . . . other things I could be doing."

"What made you want to work for *Mr. Cross.*" The bitter mockery in my tone helps me feel better when I say his name.

Ava chuckles. "Money, actually. I'm just working to save, and the Cross's pay well. My grandmother's sick, so this helps."

A pang of grief hits me in the chest.

"I'm sorry to hear that."

She shrugs, expertly folding the towels in front of her while mine look like a toddler snuck in and helped.

"My grandma raised me. It only seems right, I take care of her now."

With the towels finished, she loads them back into the basket. "Thank you for helping me. You really didn't need to."

I shrug.

"Got me out of eating that awful grapefruit," I say, and she laughs. "We should do this again. It was nice to speak to someone who either isn't appalled by my presence or dancing on eggshells."

She smiles. "I'd like that. Same time tomorrow?"

"It's a date."

CHAPTER
Thirty-Two

MILA

By the time the first week is up, I've managed to make friends with Ava. We take walks through the grounds together, sneaking off when she's supposed to be folding towels or dusting.

I won't lie and say I'm sorry. It feels nice to have a friend who I can actually speak to. All my life, all my friends were either connections through my stepfather and mother or my siblings. Speaking to Ava, though, I feel like a fully fledged person for the first time in months.

She tells me about her childhood and her family. Her mother's drug habits and her abusive stepfather. I tell her about the attack in very loose details. We play fetch with Phantom and enjoy eavesdropping on the conversations of the rich.

I feel like a teenager again, and it's then I realize while Christian may have been pivotal in healing something broken in my soul, Ava was crucial to healing my childhood and I, hers.

At night, though, everything comes crashing down.

the window, staring out at the trees and wondering where Christian is and why he hasn't called.

Did he leave me here with no intentions of ever coming back?

Surely not. His family is here. His home is here.

It doesn't make it any easier, though, as a few days bleeds into a week, and a week bleeds into a week and a half.

I can't escape the pit opening wider and wider in my stomach with each passing day.

So, I sit in his window, holding his ring and staring out over his property and wonder what the outcome of all this will be.

Paulina and Collin aren't telling me anything, but I know he's gone looking for his brother. Thinking about Christian in the same world as the man who raped me feels like fire ants are crawling over my skin, let alone the same room.

Thinking back to our last night together . . . how he'd held me, it's impossible to escape the gut-wrenching possibility that he may not come back.

Could I live with that? A world without Christian Cross, the only man I've ever loved?

Something tells me, judging by the heavy weight settling in my chest, it would be impossible.

On day eight, post-Christian's departure, I'm showering when I hear a thud from the room outside and pause in the middle of shampooing my hair.

"Phantom?"

"Get off the bed!"

I jump at the sound of the voice and Phantom's low growl from just outside the bathroom door. Naked as possible and dripping in water, I rip my robe from the rung on the wall and throw the door open, covering myself as I lock eyes with the most beautiful woman I've ever seen.

Her sleek and shining dark hair hangs down to her waist in big waves, perfect like glass. Her pale blue eyes regard me with confusion and outrage, assessing me wrapped in nothing but a robe and still dripping wet.

"Phantom," I snap when he growls again, positioning himself between her and me.

"That mutt was on the bed."

"He's a wolf, actually." Phantom lays down on the floor between the woman, and I press myself back against the wall in an effort to hide at least some of my naked body.

"Who are you?"

I pause. Did she really just come in here while I was showering and have the audacity to ask what *I'm* doing?

"Who are you?" I fire back.

"Talia Taylor," she says as if it should be obvious.

"Can I help you, Talia?" I reply icily. I only feel a little guilty about my attitude. I mean, she barged in on me, after all.

"Why are you in my room?"

"You're room?" I pause, a sickening sensation sliding down my room.

"Yes, *my room*," she snaps back, her gaze drifting over me where I'm still cowered against the wall with my robe covering me. "Don't tell me they let the housekeepers shower in here? This is supposed to be family only."

"Mila is family," Bella says, stepping into the room, clearly pissed off at having been woken up in the middle of the night. "What are you doing here, Talia?"

"Is that any way to greet an old friend?" Talia muses, poking the end of her nose with a long, stiletto nail. "I came for the Founder's Day banquet, obviously—you know I never miss it. This is my suite."

"This is *Christian's* suite," Bella corrects. "You'll be staying at the lodge this year."

"The lodge?" Talia scoffs. "But I've always stayed here."

"Mila's staying here. As I said, we have a room booked for you in the lodge."

"Mila can stay in the lodge."

Bella shakes her head. "She's Christian's wife."

And there it is. The look in her eyes . . .

She's in love with Christian.

God, could life get any more difficult?

Scratch that. I don't want to know the answer.

"Wife?" Talia beams, her smile in danger of cracking. "I wasn't aware Christian had married."

Me either, I think dryly.

"It was a surprise to all of us," Bella says.

"I'm sorry, Mila. You'll have to forgive me," Talia says, taking a step back. She makes a quick assessment of me as if she's suddenly regarding me in a different light. It's not a good one. "I just would have expected him to say something if there was a new woman in his life. He never mentioned you."

"Yeah, he didn't mention you, either," I grumble, but she ignores me.

"We've been friends for a long time," Talia explains, nothing fake or malicious in her gaze, but I can't escape the jealousy slipping through me like venom.

"More than friends," Bella interjects pointedly.

"Yes, I suppose that's true. Though, there's really no need to rehash first loves, is there? After all, we weren't married. Just engaged."

I feel the blood drain from my face, my gaze shifting to where Bella is watching me nervously.

It's true.

My stomach twists with resentment. I had always assumed that before me, he'd never really had any serious relationships. It's my fault for being presumptuous, but now that the leggy brunette standing in front of me is here, I realize there's no way in hell I ever stood a damn chance.

If Christian could walk away from Talia—a woman who exudes confidence and sophistication—how on earth could I ever expect to keep him?

"I'm sure Mila would like to get to bed, Talia. Let's leave her, and I'll take you to the lodge for a room."

"No, I'm sure there's been a misunderstanding," Talia says as if my standing in front of her with nothing but a robe covering my front is an everyday occurrence. Hastily, she tugs out her phone, pressing buttons on it faster than I can even comprehend. "I'll just call Christian and fix this."

"He won't answer," Bella says, crossing her arms over her chest with a bored look. "He's busy."

"Nonsense, we talk every day."

I think it would hurt less if she had waltzed right in here and slapped me in the face.

He won't answer . . .

Unfortunately, the pain blooming in my chest grows a thousand times worse when I hear his voice come through the speaker on her phone.

"Hello?"

"Christian," Talia whines. "I just got to the lodge, and I'm so exhausted, but I just came up to our suite, and there's a naked woman standing naked in here. What is going on?"

I don't even hear his reply over the ringing in my ears.

He answered . . . for her.

I don't realize my legs are carrying me into the bathroom until I'm standing in front of the mirror and listening to Talia's soft, fluttery voice from the bedroom.

I shouldn't care. It's not like he got down on one knee and proposed because he loves me. He forced me because he thought he could keep me safe. And he did . . . just not from the person that really wanted to hurt me.

I shouldn't care.

. . . But I do.

His ring burns my skin where it still sits on the chain around my neck. Suddenly, I feel stupid for wearing it.

Everything falls into place. All that time spent in the lighthouse. The trips to town without me.

God, I was such an idiot.

A tear slips down my cheek, and I only notice it when it catches in the vanity lights. Hastily, I scrub it away.

A tentative knock sounds at the door while I'm gripping the edges of the sink to quell the nausea, filling my mouth with saliva.

"Just a minute!" I call out, voice choked with the overwhelming anguish in my chest.

"Mila, it's Bella. I'm going to take Talia to the lodge. I just wanted to let you know it's taken care of."

He . . . sent her to the lodge?

I shake my head.

Stop making excuses for him, Mila.

"O-okay . . . thank you," I say softly. There's no way I can open the door and face her. Not when the tears in my eyes won't stop.

I listen to the sound of her footsteps and then the door close without moving. I stare at my reflection, my mind a mix of confusion and betrayal.

Maybe there's a rational explanation for all of this. Maybe there's not.

Either way, I'm finding it harder and harder to breathe when the world feels like it's caving in on me.

When I exit the bathroom, I cross straight to the door, locking it, before I climb into bed. I don't bother with clothes, wrapping the blankets around me against the chill in my bones.

Everything comes raining down on me all at once. From my missing "husband" to his ex-fiancé showing up to the Sebastian Cross still after me, I feel like I'm going to either lose my mind or wake up from a fever dream at any moment.

Phantom jumps up beside me, laying his head on my stomach, big brown eyes staring into my soul.

"What are we going to do, Phantom?" I whisper, but he doesn't have an answer for me.

And for the first night in a week, I dream of a leggy brunette in my husband's bed instead of the man who wants to kill me.

I've been lying awake, staring at the canopy above the bed for hours. Phantom lies beside me, fast asleep and I pet his head absentmindedly while I think about all the last year of my life.

The attack, leaving my family behind in LA. Losing Christian. Losing that little piece of both of us we will never get back. Fucking, Talia.

I think about Talia and her perfectly perfect shiny hair.

Is it wrong to hope it falls out in her sleep?

Instead of Talia, I try to focus on the good that's come from my little "spontaneous relocation" with Christian. My issues with touch are getting better. My nightmares aren't as frequent. I've started using good shampoo again.

But that makes me think about . . . *other* things.

Like the way he retrained my body to need him. How hot it is laying under the covers even without any clothes on because all I can think about is the feeling of his lips sliding along my skin . . . the way he shudders when he's inside me.

Great. Now I'm sad and *horny*.

"Fine," I grumble. After two hours of laying in the bed with sleep evading me, I give up.

I sit up, my eyes locking on the chair across the room. My mind runs wild with visions of how hot Christian would look sitting there, like a king on a throne. Shaking my head, I push the thoughts aside.

Bad idea, Mila.

Then another thought strikes me, this one turning the burning heat slowly slipping through my veins into pure ice.

Did Talia used to sleep here in his giant bed with *him*? Take showers in the same bathroom? Ride him in the fancy corner chair.

Bitter jealousy swirls in my stomach, making my chest ache. Not only is he not here for me to confront him, but his ex *is*, and she's staying for the Founder's Day party, which means I'm on my own in dealing with her for the foreseeable future.

How could he bring me here, knowing she would also be staying here and that I'd learn the truth?

I should have asked more questions. How long were they engaged? Why did they get *un*-engaged? Who proposed, and if she was his good girl, too?

No. Scratch that. I don't want to ruin one of the few things that bring me joy right now.

And he speaks to her every day on the phone? I've come to the conclusion he must have been doing it when he's hiding out in his office all day in the lighthouse. Maybe when he left the island, he wasn't really picking up packages at all, but instead, meeting her.

Oh my God. What if they fucked?

What if he met her, and they screwed in the back of his fancy car, and then he came back home to the little damaged girl he just *had* to take pity on and marry to save her from her evil stepfather's plans?

"This is too much," I grumble, slipping from the bed.

Deciding to get a drink and maybe food if Paulina isn't around with her grapefruits, I slip from the suite and make my way downstairs towards the kitchen.

I'm just about to step through the dark living room when a figure in front of the fire startles me.

Bella sits on the rug in front of the fireplace, watching the dancing flames. She only glances at me before she looks away and wipes her eyes.

"I'm sorry." I slowly back up towards the exit. "I didn't mean to intrude."

"Please . . ." she stalls, her voice quiet. "Stay."

Okay . . .

When I don't move, she turns over her shoulder, fixing me with a look.

"I'm not going to bite."

Funnily enough, her brother said the same thing, and we all know *that* was a lie.

Carefully, I pad across the room, sinking down to the faux bear skin rug in front of the fire beside her.

She takes a swig from the bottle of wine beside her before she hands it over to me. I've never been that into drinking, but right now, I think I'd drink pond water if it took my mind off her stupid, hot brother for even a moment.

I take a drink of the berry wine, wincing as it slides down my throat. Quietness fills the room as both of us watch the flames flickering in the fireplace in front of us. I don't think either of us is really in the mood to explain our inner battles, so we sit in uncomfortable silence.

Well . . . uncomfortable for me, at least. Just last night, we were avoiding each other like the plague, and now we're sitting criss-cross apple sauce on the floor while she cries silently beside me.

"What do you think the witches of Salem felt when they were being burnt alive at the stake?"

I'm so surprised by her question I have to take another drink to process it.

When her eyes meet mine, I can see she's not joking and genuinely wants me to answer. I was really hoping she wouldn't.

"I think it feels a lot like being sliced open." The scars on my body burn as if reminding me they're there. "Death by a thousand cuts."

She looks back towards the fire as if she's mulling over what I said.

"You were sliced open. Do the scars on your skin hurt worse than the scars on your soul?" When I don't respond out of confusion, she continues. "I saw them when I walked in on you earlier."

Well, shit.

"Looked like it hurt. Whoever they were, they were fucked-up."

"You have no idea," I grumble, a shiver ghosting through me at the mention of Sebastian, a brother she thinks is dead.

I take another drink of wine because it's easier than speaking about that night.

"Scars on the skin heal," I say after a long moment of silence. I hand her back the bottle of wine when she reaches for it. "The ones inside like to stick around."

"How many were there?"

"Men?" I ask. "One. One deranged, sadistic asshole." *Who just so happens to be related to you.*

She shakes her head, a tear beading on her lashes, but it doesn't fall.

"I was so confused when Christian brought you here, saying you were married," she admits. "But now I can see it."

"I'm sorry?"

She smiles softly.

"I've never seen my brother in love before."

My chest aches at the mention of *that* stupid little four letter word. That word has haunted me since I met him.

"I wouldn't say it's love."

"I would."

"Wouldn't you say he was also in love with Talia if he proposed to her?"

I hate saying her name. I hate it so much it burns on my tongue the moment it leaves my mouth.

She shakes her head, her gaze lingering on the fire.

"No. He's different with you. Softer." She gulps down some of the wine. "If he's got a weakness, then you're it."

My stomach bottoms out hearing that. I've never considered Christian to have any weaknesses, least of all me.

"I apologize if I made things uncomfortable earlier. With your . . . Talia . . ."

She shrugs. "She deserved it. Honestly, I was hoping you'd punch her." She side-eyes me. "Thanks for letting me down."

I chuckle when she grins, placing the bottle in my hand.

"I've always hated her," she says, drawing her knees up to her chest. Seeing her now, in nothing but cotton shorts and a tank top, it's easy to see how young she is. "I want to apologize for the way I treated you when you arrived. And for Talia. Not my finest moment."

To be twenty-five and have to worry about not only your dying father, but this lodge, all its guests and employees, and now me, hanging over her head . . . I can't imagine.

"I'm sorry for intruding. The marriage was fast," I tell her, hoping to build some sort of bridge between us where we can at least speak to each other. "It didn't help matters that Christian and Levi took off right after."

"You aren't intruding. It's nice to have another woman here my age. Don't tell Paulina." She shakes her head with a soft chuckle. "We all used to be so close. Don't get me wrong, they make sure everything's taken care of, but it's just me, Paulina, and Dad here, and well . . . Dad's not great company." She grimaces. "He wasn't good company before he got sick, though, so I don't know why I expected anything different."

"He and Christian don't seem to be close."

"They were never close," she grumbles. "Dad was always too hard on both of them. Sebastian, too. And I mean hard in the sense that left bruises and busted lips."

My skin bristles at the mention of his name.

Should have been harder on Sebastian, from the sounds of things.

"He was abusive?"

"He was." She looks down at her hands. "I suppose that's why Sebastian did what he did."

My blood runs cold, but I remain silent. I'm not sure how much she knows, and it's not my place to tell her.

"What did he do?"

She furrows her brow, looking over at me.

"He set the fire that killed my mother." She winces, swiping at the tear slipping from her blue eyes. Blue eyes so much like Christian's; it hurts to look at them. "At least, that's what they think. It wouldn't surprise me if it were true. He liked to play with matches, and he set the drapes on fire in one of the rooms at the lodge once. Dad almost beat him half to death."

"That's horrible," I breathe.

"I remember that night in my nightmares. Watching the house burning when we arrived. Mom and Seb had gone down early to get everything set up at the lake house for the weekend. It was supposed to be a family vacation. I was supposed to be with them, but I begged Dad to let me ride with him and Christian instead. When they found the bodies, Christian took Seb's death harder than anyone, I think. He told you they were twins?"

"No. *In fact, he didn't mention it at all.* "He didn't."

"Well, I guess probably because it's still hard on him. Sebastian was always the weird one. He was a loner. Never really had any friends besides Christian. They were nearly inseparable for a long time. They were about as close as Seb would allow. Christian always tried to get him to open up, but he never did." She shrugs. "When he died, it almost didn't change anything," she whispers as if speaking it aloud is a sin. "He was already a ghost . . . is it bad to say such a thing?"

Listening to her, I tighten my hands to fists in my lap to conceal the anger vibrating through me. He killed their mother. His *own* mother.

I hate him. I've never hated someone so much in my entire life, but I know if he were in front of me right now, I'd do everything in my power to kill him. For what he did to me, but also . . . for what he stole from the Cross siblings.

From Christian.

"No," I shake my head. "My father died when I was four. I never knew him the way my siblings did. It's almost like he never existed at all in my world."

"Wow," she breathes, chuckling. She wipes a hand across her eyes, brushing back tears. "Well, we can agree on one thing, then."

"Two." I hold up my fingers. "Talia's a dick."

She laughs, drying her face.

"And that." She glances at the clock above the mantel. "I need to get to bed. I'm going to be hungover if I keep drinking this wine."

She stands, and I follow when she faces me.

"I'd like to formally introduce myself."

"Okay."

"Hi, I'm Bella Cross. I'm twenty-five, graduated from Columbia with a degree in business that I hate, and I'm currently the acting general manager of the Oak Ridge Lodge, which is going to give me premature gray hair. What's your name?"

I chuckle, shaking her hand.

"I'm Mila . . . Cross. I'm twenty-four. Married to your brother, and I would love to help out in any way I can. There's only so many walks you can take along the same path."

She smiles. "We're going to get along just fine, Mila."

After Bella went up to bed, I made my way back to Christian's bedroom, my eyes heavy, but my mind too wound up to sleep. I step inside and close the door behind me, shrugging my sweater over my head and heading towards the bed. Phantom lays in the center, stretched out on his back and looking completely at ease.

"Listen, you can't sleep in the middle," I tell him, gently pushing him to Christian's side. "This is where I sleep, too."

He huffs out a breath, readjusting and getting comfortable, while I pull back the covers with a snicker.

I'm about to climb under the sheets when something heavy falls from the bed to the floor.

I freeze, looking around my feet for whatever it could have been, but it's impossible to see in the dark. Leaning down, I run my hands over the hardwood floor, my fingers bumping into something under the edge of the bed.

Grabbing it, I pull it out and hold it up to the moonlight shining through the window.

Oh, shit.

It's a phone. Nothing fancy, but a phone nonetheless. A note is wrapped around the outside of a rubber band. I take it, opening it up to read the jagged handwriting.

And then my heart goes cold.

Your family misses you.

CHAPTER
Thirty-Three

CHRISTIAN
LA, NOVEMBER, 9 MONTHS AGO

S ir, you can't go in there."

I don't stop, pushing through the double doors to the emergency room and shoving right past the nurse that tries to stop me.

She's chasing after me when I round the corner and see Mason Carpenter at the end of the hall, looking grim where he sits in a chair.

"I'm going to have to call security—"

"Call them," I snap over my shoulder and whatever she sees in my eyes must scare her, because she falls back.

"He's with us," Mason says, though he looks like he'd much prefer they throw my ass out, instead.

"You're sure?" the nurse asks and Mason just nods. She turns back to me, eyeing me reproachfully. "If you cause a disturbance, I'll have to have you removed."

"Good luck," I murmur and she saunters away.

Immediately, I move to step past Mason, but he puts a hand out to stop me.

"Mason, if you don't let me in through that door, I'll rip it off the fucking

the rage coursing through my veins, I know I could take him.

I also don't want to hurt him, but if he doesn't give me a choice, I'll do what I have to do.

"Mom told me what you did," he grits, his eyes narrowed and the vein in the center of his forehead bulging. "You know how fucking illegal that is?"

"She also tell you, she's the one who asked me to?"

He falls silent, staring at me.

"Why the fuck would she do that?"

I shrug. "Ask her yourself. Let me by."

Again, he stops me, a hand on my chest.

I have half a mind to break his fingers.

"She's not in good shape, Cross," Mason grunts, and I can see how tired he is. Fuck, we all are. As soon as I got the news, I left and flew straight to LA. I haven't slept in God only knows how long.

Not that I slept much before.

Lead fills my chest. The uncertainty of what I'm going to find when I walk through the door has been playing Russian Roulette with my mind all fucking day. "What happened?"

"They don't know who did it," he murmurs, shaking his head. "Fuck," he grits, scrubbing a hand over his face. "She's in a medically induced coma. They thought it would help because she's got broken ribs and a collar bone. A head injury."

I take a step toward the door and his voice rings out, stopping me in my tracks.

"There's something else."

I pause, not liking the tone of his voice.

Prickling, icy fear slips over me. I know the worst. Surely, there can't be more.

"She was pregnant," he says finally, his eyes darkening past recognition. "Eight weeks."

I'm thankful for the numbness that slips over me when he says those words.

I'm afraid if it hadn't, I would have destroyed this entire fucking hospital.

He shakes his head, his lip curling up in a sneer.

"You couldn't just let her go, could you? It was over."

"It wasn't over for me."

His eyes flash dangerously, and he steps in front of the door.

"When she wakes, she can decide if she wants to see you."

"Get out of the way, Carpenter."

"Fuck off, Cross. You left her. You said you'd keep her safe." He shoves at my chest, and I take a step back, anger bubbling just underneath the surface. "That's my little fucking sister."

"And she's my fucking wife.*" I shove him back, and he stumbles back into the wall. I'm too pissed off to care. The rage rushing through me all consuming.*

Silence falls over the halls and both of us stand on opposite sides, glaring at each other.

I step toward the door and this time, he doesn't stop me.

"She's going to hate you," he murmurs from behind me and I pause, hand on the doorknob.

"She already does."

"She won't eat."

I nod once, staring at the bedroom door down the hall that may as well lead to a tomb.

The whole fucking house is a tomb. The curtains are drawn and the lights dimmed. The only time that fucking door opens is when Monica steps inside to bring in a new plate of food and to remove the old, untouched one.

I fucking hate it. This . . . barrier separating me from her. I want to rip the door to shreds. At least then, I'd be able to see her. Know she's alive and not just another ghost haunting these walls.

The last time I saw her, she was in a coma and I haven't been allowed around her since. That was three. Fucking. Weeks ago, and I'm losing my goddamned mind.

"I'm not sure if I should take her back to the hospital. She'll hate me, but I fear I won't have a choice. It's been four *days since she's eaten anything. I can't even get her to drink."*

"Let me talk to her."

Monica shakes her head.

"It's not a good idea, Christian. She's already been through so much where you're concerned."

"Maybe that's exactly why he should *see her," Bob, Monica's therapist boyfriend chimes.*

Don't get me wrong. Bob's great. He's the nicest guy I've ever met.

He's just way too fucking chipper for my dark moods these days.

Everyone's been on edge the last few weeks. Since Mila came home, Monica expects everyone to walk on eggshells. As if her daughter is seconds away from a nuclear meltdown.

I wouldn't know. Again, *I haven't been allowed to see her.*

"Bob," Monica warns, and Bob holds up his hands to placate her.

"I'm just saying, it might give her something else to focus on other than what happened."

I scrub a hand over my face, pushing back at the tiredness that threatens to take over. I barely sleep now. Not because I don't have time—I'm just waiting around to see her—but because I can't get it out of my head. The way she looked in that fucking hospital bed. Beaten and bruised black and blue. How fucking small she looked covered in all those fucking bandages.

"Let me see her," I murmur, my voice rough with the need for sleep I won't be getting. Not anytime soon. Every time I close my eyes, all I see is her, and I'm filled with fucking rage all over again.

I want to gut him. I want to skin him alive and hang him out in a field for birds to pick at until he's nothing more than decay fertilizing the earth. Until there's not a single ounce of him left on this godforsaken plant anymore.

Monica eyes me, her gaze worrisome.

I know what she's thinking, and I get it. I also don't care.

A door won't stop me from seeing her.

A fucking nuke won't stop me from seeing her.

"Fine," Monica agrees softly, wiping a stray tear that slips down her cheek. Bob rubs her back. "But don't do anything to upset her. No lights. No asking how she's feeling. None of that."

The weight on my chest suddenly feels a thousand pounds heavier. I don't stick around, instead, striding straight for that fucking door.

I hate that fucking door.

I knock once, receiving no answer, and slip inside.

It's exactly as I thought it would be.

A fucking tomb.

The curtains are drawn tight, blocking out most of the LA sun outside. The room smells of old food and dirty sheets, and the silence is thick.

I step inside, shut the door behind me, and take in the small form nestled amongst the thick blankets in the center of the bed.

Mila doesn't move when I enter, her back to me and her gaze trained on the wall in front of her. Monica said this is all she does, since she came home. Sleep or lay here.

I don't bother with small talk; instead, I cross the room to where Monica just brought up the cup of broth, steaming on the nightstand, untouched.

I grab it, pulling up a chair in front of her, and finally, her soft grey eyes focus on me.

Fuck.

I've fucking missed her.

"You're dying."

She doesn't say anything at first, simply blinking up at me as if she's trying to decide if I'm real or fake and if she really cares about the answer.

"Good," she whispers, closing her eyes.

She's weak. Four days without food or water will do that to you.

"Is that it, then?"

Her eyes spring open, and she glowers at me.

"Leave me alone, Christian."

"I asked you a question, Mila."

"Why are you here? I don't want you here."

Because there's nowhere else I'd rather be than by your side.

"Answer the question. Do you want to die?"

I know I'm being harsh with her, but I know Mila. Maybe better than she knows herself. Monica tip-toeing around the elephant in the room isn't helping. Mila needs someone to challenge her. She always has.

"And if I do?" she snaps, her voice scratchy from a lack of water.

Sitting forward, I slip my hand into the holster at my back, holding the pistol out to her. She stares at it for a moment, then at me, her gaze ping-ponging back and forth like she can't fucking believe I'd actually give her a loaded gun.

I didn't, of course. But this gives her the illusion of choice, even if it's a false one.

"I don't want that," she whispers, a single tear slipping down her cheek and onto the pillow below.

"Then eat."

She tries to glare at me, but it's weak just like the rest of her.

"Your mother is this close to taking you back to the hospital."

She doesn't want to. I can see it in her eyes.

But . . . there's also a desperation there. A desperation to stay as far away from the hospital as possible after nearly three weeks there.

I hold both the broth and the gun out to her.

She takes the broth.

I don't help her sit up in bed, even though every one of my instincts is telling me to. She doesn't want to be touched, and I can understand it. So, when she manages to rest against the headboard, breathing deeply through her nose as the room spins around her, I hand her the mug without even so much as a brush of my fingers.

"When was the last time you took a shower?"

"You're welcome to leave if you think I smell," she grumbles, swallowing some of the broth. I can't explain the strange sense of relief that washes over me.

"I don't really give a shit if you smell," I murmur, shrugging my shoulders.

She says nothing, but her hands shake, holding the mug.

"It's pretty dark in here," I murmur. "There's a world outside these walls, you know."

"The world's a fucked-up place. I'm a testament to that."

"World's not fucked up. There's just fucked up people in it."

She stares at me, studying my face for a long moment.

"Did my mother send you in here to con me into leaving my room?"

"No."

"Then why are you here?"

"Would you prefer I leave you to wallow in your self-pity?"

Her jaw ticks, her eyes narrowing to slits.

All the while, I can't help but wonder how hot that broth is and how bad it's going to sting if she throws it in my face.

"I'm not wallowing. I'm working through it."

"By wallowing."

She huffs, shaking her head.

"You don't understand."

"I understand what happened perfectly. I also know you're stronger than it. Letting it defeat you proves nothing."

"It's . . . not . . ." her voice trails off, and she shakes her head because she knows it's a lie. "I just . . . every time I close my eyes, he's there."

Fuck, I wish I could take her pain. I'd do it in a fucking heartbeat if it meant the light in her eyes was still there.

"And he'll continue to be there for the rest of your life. Some part of you is always going to know what happened. You're going to have moments where you feel it like it was just yesterday and moments where it couldn't be further from your mind. He didn't kill you three weeks ago. Don't let him do it now."

She stares at me a beat, tears burning in her gaze, but they don't fall. They don't slip past the threshold, glistening in the glow around the edges of the curtains.

"I . . . finished it."

She sits the mug back on the nightstand, and I'm glad to see some color in her cheeks, even if it's only a small step. She may look alive. She may be breathing.

—She's still a ghost.

I nod, rising from the seat by the bed and taking the mug.

"I'm not going to tell you it's going to be okay," I murmur. I can't look at her because if I do, I'll reach for her, and that's the last fucking thing she needs right now. My touch. A man's touch. "That depends on you. I can tell you, your mother's worried about you. Your siblings . . . I'm worried about you."

Finally, I glance in her direction and the tears finally give way. I have to clench my fist to keep myself from wiping them from her cheeks.

"The rest is up to you."

Forcing myself to leave the room, I find Monica and Bob hovering in the hall. Monica's so elated that she'd eaten something that she starts to cry. Of course, she cries all the time, these days.

It's not until that night when I'm lying awake in my room across the hall that I hear the shower kick on. Getting up, I go and change her sheets. I don't know why. It's just something that I need to do.

I failed her as a man. As a husband.

I won't make that same mistake twice.

CHAPTER
Thirty-Four

CHRISTIAN

"**P**lace is a fucking shithole," Levi grunts as we walk up the broken sidewalk of the little bungalow in Santa Ana, California.

We've been in California for a week, tracking down traces of whatever happened that night. The house was easy to find. There are only a handful of houses that have basements in this state, and from Mila's recollection, it was pretty easy to narrow down the few that could be.

A happy birthday banner still hangs over the front door from whoever vacated this place a long fucking time ago. In the front drive, a broken-down car sits on cinder blocks, forgotten just like everything else on this block.

Most of the houses are empty; some burned so badly they should be torn down. The one we're at has boarded-up windows, but it hasn't stopped anyone from getting in through the wide-open front door.

Pushing the door open, my gun drawn, I nod to Levi, who keeps

of broken glass, animal feces, and used needles covering the floors.

The walls are busted with holes and graffiti. The carpet is gone, and old sleeping bags line the floor.

"Looks like it was a drug hide-out," Levi grumbles, stepping in behind me.

"Makes sense," I murmur, keeping my gun aimed as I push through to the bedroom at the back of the house.

We search the house, finding nothing but a few stray cockroaches that skitter off the moment they see us. The place fucking reeks, the LA sun doing nothing but making it worse.

"Clear," Levi calls from the other bedroom.

"Basement," I nod towards a door off the kitchen.

He pushes the door open, and I head down, careful not to slip on the mountains of trash covering the steps.

What I find at the bottom has my dick falling to my toes.

"Jesus fucking Christ," Levi breathes, his gaze raking over the room.

"Someone's been living here."

"Could be homeless."

Stepping over to the bed, I rip the tattered comforter off.

"I'd say this is our place," Levi grits, but I'm too busy staring at the large dark brown blood stain in the center of the mattress.

I'm going to fucking kill him.

"Fuck," Levi blows out a breath, scrubbing a hand over his face. "Now what?"

I cock a brow.

"Burn it down."

An hour later, we're parked up at the top of the hill that overlooks the valley below. Thick plumes of black smoke grace the evening sky as firefighters do their best but fail at putting the fire out.

I lift the cigarette to my lips, numb on the inside.

"You alright?" Levi asks, hands in his pockets where he leans back against the front of the car.

Yes. No.

"I will be."

Once I get my hands wrapped around the neck of the man who ever dared to touch my wife and watch the life bleed from his eyes, I'll be the happiest man in the world.

Until then, I'll burn down everything else in my path to get there.

"Help!"

"Has anyone ever told you how fucking annoying you are?" I snap, but Screamin' Pete doesn't even acknowledge me over his incessant shrieking.

"Help me!"

I'm this fucking close to reaching for my gun.

I pinch the bridge of my nose between my thumb and forefinger. Listening to this asshole for the last two days is giving me a migraine.

"Got a set of fucking pipes on him, doesn't he?" Levi asks, stepping down into the bunker. "Fucker could break the sound barrier. Guess they don't call him Screamin' Pete for nothing."

I shoot Levi a look and let out a breath through my teeth.

One . . . Two . . . Three . . .

"Help!"

Alright, I've had enough.

My fist connecting with "Screamin' Pete's" jaw is what finally shuts him up.

Thank fucking God.

"Jesus H Christ," Levi admonishes, stepping forward to check Pete's pulse. "You fucking knocked him out."

I shrug, cracking my bruised knuckles.

"He was giving me a headache."

Levi chuckles, scrubbing a hand over his dark hair. "And what about this one? He looks like he's about to piss himself." Levi stops, sniffing the air. "Nevermind. It's shit."

"He's crying," I murmur, stepping up to the table at the back of the room. There are a number of instruments lining the top, and I search for the one I want. When I grab it and turn around, Dave, Screaming Pete's pal, breaks down in sobs. "Funny enough, you were laughing the last time you saw this."

Dave's eyes clench shut, as if I'm the boogeyman, and I'll disappear if I close my eyes.

Unfortunately, I've met the *real* boogeyman.

He's kind of a dick.

"What the fuck is that?" Levi asks when I step up to the man with the collar in my hand.

"Heretic's fork," I reply, casually wrapping the leather strap around my finger. There's a set of prongs on each side, sharpened to small daggers that dig into the flesh under the chin and on the sternum if the wearer moves.

Pretty medieval to me, but hey, Dave likes to use it on teenage boys, so.

"You are one fucked up bastard, you know that Dave?" Levi asks, smacking him on the back, and I chuckle. I guess, sometimes, my brother is pretty funny, even if I want to shoot him most of the time.

"Alright, Dave," I start, nodding to Levi to remove the gag in his mouth. "Your turn. What do you know about this?" I hold the flashdrive up in front of him, but the single fucking second Levi removes the gag, Dave screams bloody murder.

"Help!" he bellows, his face beat red and his eyes filled with tears. "Somebody, please!"

"Jesus Christ," I let out a sigh. "Do any of you know how to speak?" I gesture back to Pete. "You want what he's having?"

"Help me!"

My patience is wearing thin.

And that's fucking saying something.

In a flash, my hand comes out, wrapping around Dave's throat and squeezing until he shuts the fuck up.

Finally. Silence.

"Are you done?"

Dave trembles under my hand, his skin slick with sweat.

"Levi's right. You do smell like shit."

"Told you."

"Now," I breathe, allowing Dave just enough room to breathe that he's not going to die before I get what I want. "When I remove my hand, you're going to tell me everything you know about the video on this flashdrive. You aren't going to scream. If you do, I'm going to hang you from the rafters by the balls. Understand?"

Dave has the good sense to nod. At least as much as he can.

"Good."

I release my hand, and Dave sucks in a breath, his shoulders shaking with blubbering sobs.

"Please," he begs. "I have a wife. Kids."

"Yeah," I nod. "I saw what you did to your son. Real fucked up. How do you think he'd feel about this?"

"You don't understand," Dave cries. "It was one time. It was a mistake."

"How do you think the women in your videos feels about that? Do you think she feels it was a mistake?

I'm actually lying. I couldn't watch the video all the way through. Made me fucking sick, knowing he'd done that to another person.

"You had this video in your possession. How did you get it?" I ask, my voice calm despite how irritated I'm getting. "I don't have all night." I shrug. "Neither do you."

"I don't know . . ." Dave urges when I move to slip the collar around his neck. I wait for him to elaborate because I've heard all this shit before.

You don't deal with assholes like Dave for years in the FBI and not get fed the same bullshit line a few times.

"I just sell the product. I don't know how it's made. I can give you the names of everyone who bought one. It's all back at my office," he rushes like I don't already have all that information. Unfortunately, Dave's customer base is getting a whole lot smaller as we speak. "You seem like a reasonable guy. You wouldn't want sick freaks like that walking the streets, would you?"

Fucking idiot.

"You know what, Dave, you're right." I step back, nodding to Levi like Dave here, really changed my mind about all the ways I'm going to torture him for the things I found when we searched his office on the upper side. "I *am* a reasonable guy."

"Right," Dave breathes, a ghost of a relieved smile on his lips.

"Which is why I'm going to give you one more opportunity to tell me the truth."

Dave's cheerful relief breaks and he's back to sobbing. It's getting old, honestly.

"Who the *fuck* gave you this video?" I ask, leaning forward until I'm right in his face and holding up the flash drive that contains Dave's little film. "Final Jeopardy, Dave."

But . . . he doesn't answer. He either really doesn't know, or he's dumb enough to try and protect the people he was working for.

"I had hope for you, Dave," Levi says with disappointment.

See. Sometimes, he's funny.

"Wait!" Dave screeches when I reach for the knife instead.

"Dave, if you're not going to talk, I have no use for you. I'm not running a bed and breakfast."

"I'll talk!" he squeals like a little mouse caught in a trap. "Franco

March."

"Now, who the fuck is that?" Levi asks, his eyes flashing to mine. Usually, in these types of circles, we hear the same names over and over again. Franco March is surprisingly not one of them.

"He's the middleman. He's who paid me."

"And where did you meet this Franco March?"

"Down by the docks. An old, abandoned carwash off Pine Street. He said he got it from a woman, but I he wouldn't tell me who."

My phone buzzes on the table behind me, alerting me that time is up.

"Seems like I've run out of time, Dave."

Dave shakes his head, his eyes filling with terror.

"No," he pleads. "I gave you what you asked for."

"Not really," Levi says. "You gave us a name. We want to know who's behind it at the top of the totem pole. Not really the same thing, now is it, Dave?"

"I say we leave him here for a night to think about it."

Levi shrugs. "Could be fun. Not like I've got any plans."

I nod, holding up the leather strap.

"You get to live, Dave," I cheer, nodding to Levi to lift Dave's chin. Dave blubbers, flinching when I wrap the leather around his throat. "For now."

"Please—"

I silence him by pressing the forks into his chest until pinpricks of blood rise to the surface. Then Levi lets go of his chin, and then forks dig in there, too.

Now, he can't talk.

I made it tighter than normal. If he moves his neck, the forks will only dig deeper into his skin. It won't kill him, but it'll hurt like a bitch. A small price to pay for all the fucked-up shit he's done, in my opinion.

"You know, Dave," I say quietly, right in his face, while tears leak out of the corners of his eyes. I'm sure he'll be hurting much more when I return. "The only thing I'm sorry about right now is the fact that you and the woman you hurt will have matching scars." My eyes flick down to the blood on his chest. "At least on the outside."

I straighten, head to the table, and silence my phone. My eyes catch on the screen. Some stupid little picture I snapped the week before we left of Mila curled up against my side, Phantom with his head on her hip.

It was just a normal day. It was raining like fucking crazy, and both of us were tired, so we laid down for a nap. It was the most domestic normalcy we've been able to find in this new life, and I didn't sleep a fucking wink because I couldn't stop thinking about where we go from here.

Fuck, I still can't stop thinking about it.

It's been a week and a half and, fuck, I miss my wife.

My *wife*. Who the fuck would have thought a man like me would marry a girl like Mila?

Definitely not me. Then, again. She didn't really get any choices in that.

Does it make me the bad guy if I'm not sorry? If I know I'd do it a hundred times over because it means she's safer than she was on her own?

Drugging her. Kidnapping her. Holding her on some long-forgotten island. All of it's led up to this point of no return and now that she knows the truth, I can't escape the feeling that I'll get the call that she's up and vanished.

—Again.

"She'll forgive you, you know?"

I grit my teeth, shutting my phone screen off. I'm not in the mood to talk about this shit with Levi. Seems he has other ideas, though, when he leans back against the table beside me.

"Not so sure with Talia fucking shit up, now."

I must admit, the arrival of my ex couldn't have come at a worse time. When I got her call the other night, I almost called New York off and went straight the fuck home.

I'm here for a reason, though, and that reason is my wife, even if she doesn't understand.

"She's a good girl," he shrugs. "She'll understand."

"Thought you hated her because she shot me?" I challenge, cocking a brow at him, and he grins.

"Never said I hated her for it. Just said she did and that you still decided you wanted to marry her."

"What can I say?" I grunt, lighting up the end of a cigarette. "I'm a glutton for punishment."

Or a fucking masochist.

Levi just shakes his head, chuckling. He opens his mouth, but before he can say whatever idiotic thing he was thinking, his face falls, and he groans.

"Not again." I look back to where he stalks over to Screaming Pete, who's consequently pissed himself all over again. "Should have put diapers on you two."

Grabbing my phone, I head up the stairs to our borrowed bunker, nestled into the woods of New York, and breathe in the crisp—clean—night air.

Breathing in deep, I let it out, watching the steam from my breath dissipate.

I'm getting closer.

I grab a chain around my neck and tug the little band out, holding it in the night. The jagged stone in the center glistens in my palm. Running my thumb over the smooth platinum keeps me grounded.

It also reminds me why I'm doing this in the first place.

She may not know why I married her, but I do.

Mila Rae Carpenter is mine, and I'll write it in the blood of any man who tries to take her from me to prove my point.

Jessi Hart

CHAPTER
Thirty-Five

MILA

"Going to catch a cold out here in the evening air."

I look up from where I'm sitting on the back terrace behind the mansion. It's become my secret place to come and hide when inside gets too loud and when my head feels like it'll explode if I don't get away.

The only difference is tonight, Paulina found me.

It's not like it's not safe. There are guards stationed all over Oak Ridge Lodge. Not to mention, wherever I am, Phantom is usually only a step or two behind me. Tonight, he's lying at my feet.

I promise you've never felt safety like having a giant wolf protecting you twenty-four-seven.

"I'll be okay."

The truth is, I've been cold since Christian left three weeks ago. Like permafrost has settled into my bones.

I can't escape the feeling that something bad is going to happen. Or maybe it already has, and I'm just too blind to accept it.

I've spent the last two weeks helping Bella with all her last-

banquet plans. I met Robert, the man she's been seeing, and had dinner with him and the rest of the family. I've spent countless hours staring at the canopy hanging over the bed, and I've even taken so many walks with Ava that I've memorized the walk through the trees.

I'm finally finding a place in Christian's world, and I must admit, it feels good to finally have some sense of purpose.

—Even with Talia looming like Satan's little helper wrapped in Gucci.

She was moved to the lodge, but that doesn't stop her from making her presence known. She has an entire entourage of people that follow her around, laughing at her stupid jokes and otherwise, fluffing her ego.

She shows up for dinner every night and I sit in uncomfortable silence while she recounts old stories of she and Christian's childhood together to Paulina who appears to barely pay attention.

Fortunately, with Bella in attendance last night, she quickly shut it down, and Talia sulked for the rest of dinner.

Life has moved on without Christian Cross here.

Unfortunately, I haven't.

"You know, staring at that ring isn't going to make it go away."

Paulina steps up on the porch, taking the seat beside me. I hadn't even realized I was holding Christian's ring until she said something. Looking down at it, my stomach bottoms out, and tears sting in the backs of my eyes.

I shove it back under my shirt. "Have you heard anything?" I know the answer, by now I ask every day. I can't help myself, though. I just need to know for sure.

Paulina grimaces, looking out over the forest beyond.

"Didn't think so."

"This is how this life is," she says gently. "You have to understand that there are things they will miss. Birthdays, anniversaries. There will be nights where you don't hear from them."

Or weeks . . .

"Except I didn't get a choice on if I wanted this life or not."

"Do any of us?"

"Did anyone ever trick you into marrying them?" I counter.

"Touché."

"They'll be missing Founder's Day."

"And I'm telling you, whatever they're doing has to be extremely important for them to miss that."

I shake my head, and a rogue tear slips down my cheek. Angrily, I scrub it away.

"Is it bad that I miss him?" I whisper like he may be hiding in the shadows, waiting to strike.

Truthfully, I'm angry. I'm angry with him for leaving me here. I'm angry at Talia for merely existing. Most of all, I'm angry with myself for missing him.

God, do I miss him.

The rippling energy when we're in the room together. The brush of his fingers on my lower back when we're cooking dinner together. The scent of his skin clinging to me after he touches me.

I love him, and I hate him. What kind of sense does that make?

Paulina's silent for a moment, thinking. "No. It's okay to love them and be angry with them for their actions. We are human, after all."

I draw my legs up to my chest, leaning my chin on my knee.

"Who tricks someone into marrying then? That's insane."

"I don't disagree. Look at the alternative, though. Being held to a contract to marry someone who would hurt you. Rape you."

"Don't make excuses for him."

"I'm not. I'm just giving you a different view of the situation. Tell me this, though," she pauses, chocolate eyes meeting mine. "If he'd asked, got down on his knee, and done it the right way . . . would it have changed the outcome?"

Fuck.

Silence hums in the air, and my voice gets caught in my throat.

"I don't know what you mean," I stammer, my cheeks hot despite the chill in the air.

I know *exactly* what she means, but I don't want to acknowledge it.

She chuckles, shaking her head.

"I've never met two people who were so hell-bent on convincing themselves they aren't in love."

I glare at her, and she smiles, reaching out to pat my hand.

As she does, my little secret vibrates in my pocket, and I clear my throat to cover up the sound. Luckily, Paulina doesn't seem to notice, standing and throwing her arms up with a yawn.

"Well, I, for one, am tired," she says, pointing a finger at me. "You should get to bed, too. We've got a big day tomorrow."

I smile, breathing out a sigh of relief when my pocket goes silent. At least there's some good to go around, even if the prospect of going to an event without Christian is terrifying.

"Can't wait."

I watch her climb to her feet. Leaning down, she presses a kiss to my temple, before disappearing into the house, leaving me alone in the night. Slipping the hidden phone from my pocket, it starts to ring again.

"You almost got me caught."

"Sorry," Savannah's voice filters through the phone. "You weren't calling, and I got worried."

"They found my hiding spot," I grumble, and she laughs.

"Who's they?"

"Christian's . . . mom of sorts."

"Ah. The mother-in-law."

"What are you talking about? Your mother-in-law is an angel."

"Yeah," I can hear her smile through the phone. "She is. At least you aren't Mom."

"If I had a mother-in-law like Mrs. Parker, I think I'd pitch myself in front of a train."

I've told Savannah everything. I just had to. I needed someone who I didn't have to lie to, and my sister's always been that person.

Like me, she doesn't remember our father much, either. She was only six when he died. For most of our life, we were just Marcus Parker's stepdaughters, and for five years of hers, she was subjected to his torment in the form of illegal sex parties where he'd sell her to his Hollywood friends.

If anyone would understand not only my side but also keep an open mind about Christian's, she would.

"How are things in LA?" I've spoken to her every night this week on my contraband phone about everything from Mom and our siblings to the weather.

I can't lie; it feels good to hear her voice.

"You ask me that every day," she chuckles.

"I know."

"They're good, though. I saw Mom tonight."

"And?"

"And she's getting by day by day. I think it helped that Hannah had a baby appointment today, and she got to see an ultrasound."

My chest aches. I miss my family. My brother's having a baby, and I'm a thousand miles away. I miss my mother most of all. I thought about calling her, but I know her. She'd have Savannah's FBI husband tracking me down by the time I got off the phone.

"I miss you guys."

"We've missed you," she breathes. "Things haven't been the same." Then, after a pause, "How are *you* holding up?"

"I'm alive."

"Mila."

"Savannah," I counter.

"You know what I mean."

I let out a deep breath.

"I'm managing."

"He's going to come home, Mila." I almost laugh that she knows me well enough to know that's what's on my mind.

"Trust me. Everyone from here to Nebraska has told me."

"I still can't believe you're married."

"Me either."

Absentmindedly, I reach into my shirt for his ring, pulling it out and holding it in the palm of my hand.

"Savannah . . . can I ask you a question?"

"You know you can. Whatever you need."

"How . . . how did you know Logan was the one?"

She blows out a breath into the receiver.

"Well, I think it would have to be when he learned what was happening to me, and he just held me tighter. People like that are hard to find."

My stomach cramps, and tears warm in my eyes.

"Love isn't hard, Mila. It's the people around you that *make* it hard. If you're questioning if you're in love with him, I promise you already are."

"Why do you say that?" I hate how small my voice sounds.

She chuckles softly. "Because if you're questioning it, that means you already know the answer."

I'm just drifting off to sleep when the sound of a creaky floorboard jolts me awake.

Someone is moving in the shadows.

The moon shining through the window provides little light, but I can sense him even before I can see him.

Relief floods through me when I catch that familiar scent hanging in the air.

Christian.

My heart lurches in my chest, and I sit up in the bed. His dark eyes rake over me like he was studying me, only to be caught in the act. My breath catches in my throat when his gaze flares, taking in his T-shirt I accidentally—on purpose—wore to bed because even if I can't admit it to myself, I missed him.

"You're back."

He doesn't respond, and I catch sight of the bruise on his cheek.

"Christian, what happened?"

About a million questions circle through my foggy brain, but I know he won't answer any of them. I look up at his eyes, noticing the dark circles. How tired he is. The stubble on his jaw only makes him look more savage, paired with the scar on his cheek. He looks like he hasn't slept in days.

Something about that makes my chest ache.

I move to slip from the bed, but he stops me with a shake of his head.

"Go to sleep, Mila." His voice is cold, but there's something there under the surface. Desire? Possessiveness? "I just came to check on you."

He starts to head towards the hall, but a surge of panic wells in my chest. This strange desire to not see him so . . . un-Christian like. So human.

"Wait," I breathe, slipping the blankets off my legs.

He pauses, his gaze slipping down to my bare thighs.

"Mila, I'm exhausted." His shoulders are stiff underneath his shirt; his body is wrung tight.

"Lay with me." I can't believe it leaves my mouth, but I can't deny the longing swirling through me to feel his skin against mine. To . . . comfort him. I know I'll wake up not knowing how I feel about him in the morning, but in this light, his shadows have never called to me more.

Christian looks as surprised by my request as I am, and for a moment, he doesn't move like he's considering it.

Then, his jaw feathers with tension, and he looks away from me. "Not tonight."

I try to brush his rejection off. Something happened, and even if he won't tell me about it, I can see it playing tug of war with him.

"Are you hurt?" I ask quietly.

He chuckles, and though it lacks its usual wickedness, it still sends a shiver up my spine. He steps across the room, stopping at the edge of the bed. His touch is soft when he brushes his knuckles down the side of my face and pauses when he reaches my chin. His thumb strokes over my skin, and he tilts my face up to look at him. In the moonlight outside, it's easy to forget everything that's happened to us. The bullet wound in his shoulder. The figurative one in my heart from where he left. His brother . . . It's easy to forget we aren't who we are instead of two people falling in love all over again.

Unfortunately, we are Christian and Mila. And this isn't a love story.

"I'm fine, little devil," he murmurs quietly, dropping his hand back to his side. "Get some sleep."

He heads into the hallway, disappearing into the darkness and leaving nothing but his scent behind when he goes. I stare after him, listening to the sounds of his footsteps as he makes his way down the hall.

This Christian is different. Almost . . . broken. Exhausted. Filthy.

The battle of wills rages inside my head, rendering me frozen in place, still staring after him. Slowly, I sink back into the pillows, staring at the canopy above me and listening to the faucet drip in the bathroom, but I can't ignore the ache in my chest.

On one hand, he asked me to leave him alone. On the other . . . he looked like he wanted to lay with me. He seemed so . . . desolate. Like a country field on the cold, foggy morning after the last battle of a war has been fought.

I glance back at the clock on my nightstand.

A little after three in the morning.

I look back at the canopy, my eyes running over the soft cream material.

I count each of Phantom's breaths from where he fell asleep beside me.

"Fine."

Carefully slipping from the bed, I pad over to the door and follow him out into the small living room off our room.

Christian may be the strongest man I've ever met, but I also know he's not one who likes to share his weaknesses or his failures. He stews on them until they eat at him, and regardless of whether it was consensual or not, he's still my husband in the most basic form of the word.

Something new and strange and tender blooms in my chest when I see him. He's never looked so . . . human.

He lays on the chaise lounge, his boots dangling off the end. His shirt is gone, and his arms are tucked under his head. The hard ridges of his abs rise and fall with each breath like he hasn't slept a single minute in the last three weeks.

Resigning myself, I step over to him and stoop down, gently removing his boots and setting them on the floor before I grab a throw from the back of the couch to throw over him. It will have to do.

I'm just draping it over him when his hand catches mine, startling me.

"*Mila.*"

Something about the way he says it makes my heart melt. Even mostly asleep, he knows it's me.

"Shh . . ." I breathe, brushing the hair off his forehead. He doesn't release my hand, his fingers locking mine in a death grip, so I pull the blanket up and slip onto the lounge beside him, curling up against his chest.

"I'm filthy, baby," he murmurs groggily, his eyes still closed and his voice barely audible. Like he can't fight sleep, but he also can't fight his need for me.

I can't keep my heart from beating awkwardly and the soft smile from tugging at the corners of my lips at the old nickname, even though I know I shouldn't read too much into it.

"I know."

It's strange . . . holding him the way he used to hold me until I fell asleep. He's always been this immovable force. The one thing in this world that I could count on to not crumble when I can barely hold it together at the seams.

Now, I'm realizing that even the strongest have their weaknesses, and Bella was right. I think I'm his. God knows he's always been mine.

"Come here," I whisper, tugging at his shoulder. He lets out a deep groan that rumbles through his chest, reaching for me. When he wraps his arms around my waist, burying his head in my chest and inhaling deeply, like he's missed me as much as I've missed him, I realize nothing could make me leave this bed right now. The world could burn down around us, and I'd happily watch it go up in flames.

I curl into him, our legs entwining and my fingers rubbing down the hard ridges of his back until his breathing evens out again. I force myself to focus on that because if I let myself wander, I'll realize how completely and utterly in love with him I am, and nothing good could ever come from that.

Not with his secrets. Mine. The danger that seems to be lurking around every corner. His undeniable need to push me away while simultaneously holding onto me with an iron grip.

His murderous, psychopathic brother.

Tomorrow, things will go back to normal. We'll be at each other's throats, and he'll see that I'm not worth all this trouble.

For now, I just hold him, letting him sleep after whatever hell he went through, and try not to let my heart get too wrapped up in the way he clings to me like I'm the angel coming to drag him out of it.

CHAPTER
Thirty-Six

CHRISTIAN

My heavy eyes open, and I blink at the bright light streaming through the window.

"Fuck," I grunt, clenching them shut again and reaching for the space around me, finding it empty.

I sit up, my head spinning with panic.

"Mila!"

"I'm here," she says softly, and my eyes lock on her in the chair.

Jesus fucking Christ.

I blow out a breath, scrubbing a hand over my face.

"Are you okay?" she asks softly, hanging back.

"Come here."

She doesn't move.

"Mila, I don't give a fuck about any of it right now. Come here."

I expect her to argue, but instead, she carefully pads over to me, hesitating when she reaches my side.

I reach for her, taking her hand and leaning back into the lounge, pulling her into my lap. She comes, her legs on either side of

I just hold her.

Just fucking hold her because I've spent so long wishing I could.

We're silent for a while, and neither of us move.

"What did you do while I was away? Was Bella nice to you?"

"Bella was good. I like Ava, too. I've been helping Bella with Founder's Day preparations."

"Good," I murmur gruffly. I've yet to see Bella, but I know that's another bridge I'll have to mend. "Anything else happen while I was gone?"

She grimaces, her cheeks burning.

"I met your ex."

Fuck.

She must feel me stiffen because she sits back.

"Why didn't you tell me you were engaged before?"

Because I prefer to forget.

"Because it doesn't matter. You're my wife."

"She doesn't seem to agree," she says, moving to get off me, but I tighten my hold on her hips, keeping her grounded on my lap. My cock sits heavily between us, hard as fucking diamonds after three weeks without her.

"I don't give a shit what she agrees with. You're my wife."

"Why is she here?" she grumbles, twisting her hands in her lap, and I let out a sigh.

Fucking hell.

"Her family and mine were always close, so she comes every year. I didn't care if she stayed in my room because I don't use it. I forgot about her. I'm sorry."

"You said I'm sorry," she teases.

Little brat.

"You answered her call . . ." she says, her eyes on her hands. "Why didn't you call me?"

"Because if I did, I would have come home."

She pauses, her eyes flicking up to mine and something soft and warm passes across her face.

"Where do we go from here?" Mila asks, and I reach up, brushing the hair back from her face.

My eyes coast over her. "To the shower," I reply, my hands tightening on the curves of her ass. "You're filthy, Mrs. Cross."

"Wonder why?" she muses, her cheeks flaming. "And don't call me that. I haven't changed my name."

"No?"

She stares at me for a beat before her eyes widen.

"You didn't."

"And if I did?"

She shakes her head, but there's a ghost of a smile tugging at the corners of her lips.

"I can't even be mad. I should have known."

"Go start the shower," I swat her ass. "I'll be in in a minute."

She climbs off my lap, and I watch her go, stretching my arms out over my head. I'm stiff after ten hours of sleep, but it was worth it just to hold my wife.

My wife. My fucking wife.

Rising from the lounge, I move to unbutton my jeans, but before I can, a sound catches me off guard.

What the fuck was that?

I listen intently to the dull hum of something electronic going off in the bedroom, my heart coming to a slow, screeching stop. Stepping into the bedroom, the sound of the shower filters through the open bathroom door when I enter. I pause as the vibrations continue.

What the fuck?

Going over to the bed, I move the pillows and the sheets. Nothing.

The vibration dies.

Then, almost immediately, it starts up again.

Grabbing the corner of the mattress, I lift it up, and there, indented into the bottom, is a goddamned phone.

Picking it up, I let the mattress fall with a deafening thud.

A number I recognize flashes on the screen, and I silence it, unlocking the cheap little burner phone and scrolling through the call logs. No messages have been sent, but about a dozen calls have been made in the last week to one single number in none other than Los Angeles, California.

You've got to be fucking kidding me.

"I can explain."

It feels like someone stuck a branding iron in my chest. My hand closes around the shitty little flip phone, red clouding my vision.

She's been fucking calling Savannah.

She's been *calling* Savannah.

I can feel Mila's presence in the doorway behind me. I can't turn around, though, because if I do, I know I'll fucking scare her because all I want to do is bend her over the side of the bed and spank her ass.

"Do you have any idea what you've done?"

She's silent, and her fear is palpable.

"I just wanted to speak to her . . ." she breathes. "It's been so long—"

"Do you know how easy it is to track a cell phone?" I reply, my tone calm despite the war waging inside me.

"I-I didn't—"

My self-control snaps, and with a growl, I throw the phone as hard as I can at the ground, shattering it into a million pieces.

Mila lets out a yelp, and when I turn back to her, she's pressed into the wall like she can slip through it and disappear.

I should stop. The fear in her eyes is like a branding iron on my skin. I fucking can't, though. I'm too pissed off.

"I'm sorry," she breathes, voice high-pitched with terror.

"What the fuck were you thinking?"

She's silent for a moment, and I watch all five stages of grief cross her delicate features before she finally speaks.

"I was alone—"

"You had me," I growl.

She narrows her gaze on me, her eyes shining with unshed tears.

"Did I, Christian? Because it's looking a lot like I spent the last three weeks wondering if you were alive or dead."

"Back to feeling sorry for ourselves, are we?"

"Feeling *sorry* for myself?" she snaps, her gaze shining with unshed tears. "I just found out the person I trusted more than anyone else in the world *tricked* me into marrying him. *Then*, he disappears for three weeks with no word of where he's gone. My stepfather was trying to sell, and you knew about it the whole time. Oh, and let's not forget, your brother the psycho murderer raped and beat me half to death. And you think I'm feeling *sorry* for myself?"

"I came back," I grit, but she shakes her head, a tear slipping down her cheek.

That single tear may as well be a fucking nuke with the rage that burns in my veins.

I did this. I fucked up again.

"That's not always enough, Christian," she growls. "The first time you left for three months. This time, it was three weeks. What's it going to be next time? Three days? Three years?"

After almost a month of fucking missing her. Of thinking of all the ways, I'd apologize if I could. Of being beaten and battered dreaming of her, my temper finally snaps at arguably the worst moment it could.

"What do you want, then, Mila?" I bark, my voice louder than it's ever been with her. She falls back a step, her eyes going wide through the tears swimming in her gaze. "You want an annulment? Want a divorce?"

She looks at me like I've slapped her. Like she finally sees the monster, I am underneath it all.

My brain registers that I should stop. My heart figures this out, too.

My mouth says burn it all to the fucking ground.

"What?" she asks softly, hurt in those fucking eyes that stay burned into my brain. "You want . . ."

All I want to do is throw her over my shoulder and haul her to bed, spend a few days showing her exactly how much I fucking missed her, but I know I can't. Not here and not when she could barely look at me when I left.

We have so much shit to work out between us; it feels like we're running in place. Collin's words replay over and over in my head, reminding me that I'm just one more fuck-up away from possibly losing her forever.

How the fuck am I supposed to keep her and not steal her light? That light that drew me to her in the first place. Her soft, gentle heart and her childlike wonder of the world around her.

I'm too fucking damaged, too dark, and there's no doubt in my mind she was handcrafted to ruin me.

I shrug, chuckling dryly. "If you're so fucking miserable, you can't go a few more months without speaking to your family. Without putting fucking *everyone* in danger, including yourself, then go." I nod to the door, knowing that even as I say it, I'm destroying what little common ground we managed to find last night. "Go, Mila."

"Stop," she whispers, closing her eyes. Tears slip down her cheeks, and I know I should stop. I'm only killing us both, but deep down, I fucking know Collin's right.

I'm going to ruin her.

"If you can't feel my heart and know that you are the only fucking thing that kept me alive the last three weeks, then you're free to leave." My chest heaves with each breath, my hands shaking. "This time . . . I won't chase you."

She lets out a quiet sob, but I can't stay and watch her break down because of me. I'm a fucking coward because knowing she's in pain, all I want to do is pull her into me and beg her to let me try again, but I know it will only make it worse.

So now that her soft heart's effectively shattered at my feet, I turn around and leave.

That seems to be the only thing I'm fucking good at anymore.

What do you think God does to men who capture angels and clip their wings? Steal the light from the heavens and corrupt it?

The gun drowns out any of the voices in my head with the sharp ping of a steel hitting steel.

Unfortunately . . . it can't drown out my sister.

"Hey! Asshole! I'm trying to talk to you."

And I'm trying to ignore you.

"I'm not in the mood, Bella."

In fact, the only thing keeping me from marching back upstairs and tying Mila to the bed is the knowledge that even if I'm pissed off, I know it would terrify her and my irrational fear of her being afraid of me.

Not that it matters. I gave her freedom. I opened the door for her to leave and after everything that's happened between us, I know there's no reason she'd stay.

Bitterness slides down my throat, sour and violent.

"What the hell are you doing?"

I grit my teeth, lowering the assault rifle back to the table in front of me. The private shooting range at the back of the property is in the trees, shielded from the lodge. It's one of the only places on the property you can be alone and a place I used to frequent often.

"Practicing."

Bella's eyes widen before her brow furrows.

"For what?"

My temper flares and I jam a new mag in.

"Do you want something, or did you just come out here to be a pain in the ass?"

Bella cocks her head, her hands on her hip. Somedays, she reminds me so much of our mother, it's haunting.

"Why did you invite Talia to the banquet?"

I cock a brow at her, unease swirling in my chest.

"I didn't."

"Bull. She says you did," she snaps, crossing her arms over her chest. "She also says you speak to her every day."

Fucking women.

Reaching into my pocket, I pull my phone out and toss it on the table in front of her.

"You want to verify, go right ahead. I haven't spoken to Talia in a year."

Conveniently, since the last time I was home.

"Well, she's here for the banquet, and she's causing problems. Do you know how rude she was to Mila?"

I grip the gun tighter, my knuckles cracking under the force.

"Mila's not my problem anymore."

Bella stares me down.

Yep, definitely our mother's twin.

"You can't be serious. You love her."

"Does it matter?" I fire back, and she falls silent, her eyes glossing over with tears. "Mila is leaving."

"She can't," she says through the tears in her eyes. "What happened between you two?"

"She lied to me."

"Oh, give me a break," she growls. "You lied to her when you married her in secret." She watches for my reaction, a vindictive little smile crossing her face. "Yeah, I know things. Just like I know you're in love with her."

I'm not in the mood for this conversation.

"My love life is none of your concern. I suggest you worry about yourself."

"Christian . . . you can't let her leave. You're different with her. She belongs here."

She belongs here. I can't help but scoff. I've been forcing her hand every step of the way.

That ends today.

A tremor rolls through me when I think about coming home to her last night. The way she wrapped herself around me. Like she'd missed me as much as I missed her.

Of course, it was all fucking bullshit.

She's never been in this as deep as I have, but it's for the best.

Every single person I've ever cared about has either turned up dead or damaged.

I can't do that to her again. No matter what the possessive little voice in the back of my head says.

Her eyes filling with tears may as well be permanently burned into my brain. The hurt in her gaze when I told her to leave, even as she begged me to stop.

She still cares about me, even after everything I've put her through.

I fucking hate myself for it.

"Leave it alone, Bella."

The words taste like battery acid on my tongue.

Bella's eyes narrow, and a tear slips down her cheek. I shouldn't be speaking to her about this. She's got enough on her plate with the party tonight, and even if I can't have what I want, there's no reason for her to suffer the consequences.

Unfortunately, Bella's not done, so being the asshole I am, I raise the gun back up and start shooting again. This time, the bullets drown out the sound of her voice.

"You're such an asshole!" she shouts over the gun before turning and storming off.

Unfortunately, she has no idea how right she is about that statement.

I am an asshole.

Someday, Mila will figure it out, too.

I need to be alone, anyway.

CHAPTER
Thirty-Seven

MILA

I *won't chase you . . .*

My husband is magnetic.

Women want him. Men want to be like him.

He keeps his distance from the women who approach him, but when each one comes up prettier than the last, all I can think about are his harsh words.

I won't chase you . . .

His ring still sits heavily over my heart, as if reminding me that, for all intents and purposes, he told me he was done with me. With my dramatics and venom. My rough edges and thorns.

We may still be married, but marriage is just a word to pretty up what it really is. A contract. Judging by the fact that he hasn't even glanced my way once tonight, that contract is about to be null and void.

I'm angry with him. Angry with myself. I'm Sick with jealousy when woman after woman comes up to him, speaking to him. Laughing with him because *I* can't.

I'm in love with him, and I know he loves me, but sometimes, that's not enough, is it?

Like the idiotic fool I am, I fell in love with the secret language that only he and I seem to understand. The way he holds me when the world feels like it's closing in on me. The way his body shudders when he presses himself inside me.

The way he clung to me like he'd been starved for me after being gone for three weeks.

I want to hate him, but in the end, I can't.

I can't hate him for saving me. I can't hate him for marrying me, even if it was all a trick. I can't hate him for leaving because I know the real Christian, and I also know he wouldn't leave unless he had to.

Most of all, I can't hate him because no matter how toxic it may be, I've fallen in love with every dark, deadly part of him.

A laugh sounds across the room, and a shiver runs up my spine. Talia.

She's as beautiful as ever—her long raven hair sleek and cascading down to the curve in her back. She looks elegant and poised in a black cocktail dress, the back completely open to showcase her thin waist. She leans in close to Christian, her hand resting on his arm.

From this distance, they look like lovers. The way she looks at him. He delicately removes her hand from his arm, but the fact that she's touched him pisses me off. Especially after he answered her call and couldn't find the time to call me.

They're the picture of a power couple. A tux looks good on him, and my heart aches to be near him, even though I know I have no right.

Was I wrong? Probably. Am I sorry? No. I miss my family. I've been away from them for too long.

"Trollop," Bella murmurs, stepping up beside me.

Talia laughs at something Christian says, and I've never wanted to bite someone more than I do at this very moment.

I hate her.

Turning away from the scene, I down the rest of my drink.

"Whoa, killer, slow down."

"What's it matter?" I grumble, chewing loudly on a piece of ice since using my teeth for other purposes would probably land me in jail. It's not like my husband would bail me out. He'd probably pay them to keep me. "We're done."

"You can't just be *done* with your husband."

"Why not?" I shrug. "He is."

"I want you to know he's told every one of those girls he's here with his wife, and she's feral enough to bite."

I roll my eyes, fighting back the smirk that tugs at the corners of my lips.

Guess he knows me better than I thought.

"Can you just go talk to him?"

"No. He's the one that should be talking."

"As your friend and sister-in-law, I have to tell you, you're being a real butthole."

I gawk at her. "Rude."

"True."

I roll my eyes, turning to go get another drink. Maybe I'll just get a bottle this time.

Unfortunately, Bella has other plans. She catches my hand, tugging me back before I can walk away.

"Tell me what you're so worried about."

"I don't want to talk about this," I grumble, but she's got the grip strength of a pitbull, refusing to let

"You can never move forward until both of you lay it all out. Otherwise, it's just playing Russian Roulette every day you wake up. Wondering which day is going to be the day another lie is uncovered."

"I didn't *lie* . . ." I correct. "I evaded the truth."

She fixes me with a look.

"That's basically a lie."

I grab her drink, taking a sip. It's unfortunate that there's no alcohol in it.

"Drinking isn't going to make you feel better."

"Okay, Mom. What will?"

She smirks, nodding across the room.

"Do you think Talia will make a good sister-wife?"

"I must admit . . . I thought you were better than this."

I pause, turning to her.

"What?"

She shrugs. "Letting other women try to swoop in on your husband. I would have thought you would have put a stop to it by now. Especially since he's all you've been thinking about the last three weeks."

"That's not true." It is. "I've had plenty to keep me occupied." I haven't. Squaring my shoulders, I throw my chin up. "If he wants to see other women, then let him."

Bella snorts.

"Infidelity is not funny."

"No, but the fact that you can't see what's right in front of your face is." She waits for me to say something, and when I don't, she explains. "You love him. He loves you."

"It's not that simple . . ."

"Of course, it is. You're the only one making it hard. Well, him too."

I shake my head, crossing my arms over my chest and leaning back against the bar.

"There is so much baggage between us; I think we'll be tripping over it the rest of our lives."

"Every relationship has baggage. You've just got to be able to step over it to get to the clear path."

As if he knows we're talking about him, Christian looks up, his dark eyes locking with mine across the room. I can't read his expression, but a tingle of awareness slips through me under that thoughtful gaze. Like he's ready to accept whatever fate I've given him, even if it kills him.

I should be happy that he gave me the option to leave. I mean, look at everything he's done.

But . . . look at everything I've done, too.

A rush of confusing thoughts enter my head in that moment where we lock eyes. Like why I'm so concerned with the bruises that cover his body. Where he's been and why he was so exhausted when he came home.

Talia's gaze follows his, her eyes locking with mine in a challenge she's too idiotic to realize I refuse to take part in.

If I have to fight with another woman for a man, is he really mine at all?

She says something, but he doesn't respond, his stare burning through me instead.

"Mila," Paulina says, emerging from the shadows like *Batman*.

"Someone should put a bell on you," I grumble, but she flat-out ignores me.

"Go . . ." she urges quietly when a soft song comes on. "Go dance with your husband."

"I'd rather eat gum off the gum wall," I retort, but she's not listening to me. She and Bella both shove me forward, and I teeter in my heels, throwing them a glare over my shoulder.

As if this is a *Disney* movie and we're the unwilling prince and princess who just found out they're expected to wed in a fortnight, Levi shoves Christian towards me, and he jerks away from his grasp, ignoring whatever Talia says.

Yeah . . . really looks like a man in love to me.

"Go," Paulina urges quietly from behind me, and I grit my teeth. Fine. One dance to appease the masses, and then I'm going home.

Wherever that is now.

Christian stops in front of me in the sea of dancing, *happy* couples, his gaze indifferent. It doesn't even sweep over my dress. My chest tightens, but I let the anger cushion the blow when he reaches for me with a sigh, looking over my head, no doubt at Paulina and Bella with a glare.

He takes my fingers in his, and I stiffen when his hand comes around my waist. He moves me along to the music, but I can't bring myself to look at him, let alone lean into him.

It feels . . . foreign. This distance between us. Even when he was gone, he never felt this far away.

"I see you're still here," he mutters dryly, so quiet that only the two of us can hear. My chest tightens at the bitterness in his voice, my eyes stinging, but I refuse to cry. I didn't work this hard on my makeup to cry it all off.

"Would you like me to leave?" I keep my face neutral so even Talia Taylor couldn't spot the tension flowing through us.

I feel everyone's eyes on me. Like the entire room is waiting for the drop of a bomb.

It's human nature, isn't it? Wanting to watch other people's lives fall apart while never partaking in the act itself.

"I would have thought you would have run the moment the opportunity presented itself," he retorts, his tone clipped. Controlled.

He's not speaking to me like Christian.

He's speaking to me like a job. Like I mean nothing to him.

I don't know if his anger or his indifference is worse. Either way, I know there's a pit opening up in my stomach, threatening to swallow me whole.

"I'll leave the disappearing acts to you," I reply, equally as icy. If he wants to be a dick, so will I.

Out of the corner of my eye, I see his jaw tick, his hand tightening around mine almost instinctively.

"Yes, but I know your affinity for hiding things. I'd like to spare the poor souls who have to clean this place if possible."

"Wouldn't that be the perfect way to start this marriage?" I ask, my throat threatening to close. "Oh, right, how could I forget? We've been married for a year, and you just forgot to mention it to me. It's pathetic."

"Funnily enough, the happiest this marriage has been is when you didn't know about it."

"Fuck you, Christian," I growl, showing at his chest.

"In case you forgot, I've been there, and it's not that impressive."

I come to a stop, my heart cracking in my chest at the weight of his words. I finally look up at him, and I'm met with nothing but gray, cloudy indifference. Nothing of the man I loved.

I think it would hurt less if he'd slapped me in the face. Anger seeps through me, and tears gather at the corners of my eyes. I want to hurt him as badly as he hurt me.

"I wish I could forget you," I breathe, and his nostrils flare, his eyes darkening to midnight.

Turning, I hurry off the dance floor and out of the ballroom, my legs carrying me not to the bathroom like I had originally intended but straight towards the back door to pack my things.

I won't stay where I'm not wanted . . . no matter how much I don't want to go.

I suck in a breath in the night air on the walk up the back path to the mansnion, but it's painful, my throat closing up like all the air was sucked out of the room.

I won't chase you.

This is good, I tell myself. *Better now than later when he decides he doesn't want you.*

He tricked me into marrying him. Kidnapped me and brought me to a deserted island. Disappeared—again—and lied about why he'd been hunting me.

He has no one to blame but himself.

Then why does it feel like I ripped my own heart out of my chest and shoved it through a meat grinder?

I don't *need* Christian to survive. I made it on my own for months. If it weren't for him, I'd probably still be out there, traveling the States.

Starving yourself.

"Fuck off," I growl at the voice in my head.

He gave you your freedom. What are you still doing here?

—*I don't want to leave.*

He may be rude. He may have tricked me. He may have broken my heart.

—He also pieced it back together again after I was shattered. He bathed me when I couldn't do it myself. He made me feel like a human being for the first time in a year instead of a defective replication.

He's fucked up . . . but so have I.

I have spent the last three months fighting these feelings every step of the way. For what? To end up desperately in love with him anyway?

I storm through the front door and head straight towards the stairs, ignoring the aching sorrow building in my chest.

"*Mila.*"

The hair on the back of my neck rises at the volatile presence behind me, but I don't stop, hurrying up the stairs as fast as my heels will allow me.

"I'm going, Christian. You're getting what you want; why are you still following me?"

"We have unfinished business."

I push through the doors into the hall leading to his bedroom, scrubbing at the angry tears that slip down my cheeks.

"Like what?" I whirl on him, finding him only a foot away from me. "Like how I'm not enough? Not impressive? Not happy enough for you? Don't fit into your little protective box where you can lock me in your big fancy lodge in case you decide to show up?"

Shoving at his chest, I turn to storm away, but his arm wraps around my waist, tugging me back to his front and locking an arm around me. His hand covers my mouth, and I dig my nails into the skin, hoping to God it draws blood. He deserves it for what he said to me.

Leather, whiskey, and the forest coats my senses, and despite myself, my body yearns for him. To feel him the way he was last night. Dominating yet controlled. Needy, like I'm breakable, but his to break.

He turns me around, his hand sliding up to fist my hair and tug my head back at a harsh angle. His eyes consume me, his lips so close I can taste him. His lips skim mine, and we share each other's air. Neither of us moving.

Then he releases me, and I stumble away from him while he scrubs a hand over his face.

"Jesus fucking Christ," he rasps. "I can't fucking think around you."

Silence falls over us, bitterness coiling inside me like a venomous snake. His breathing is ragged, matching my own, and when his eyes meet mine, there's something dark and pissed off and bleeding.

And I realize he doesn't want me to leave.

In fact . . . he's desperate for me to stay.

"Why did you leave me in LA?"

"Mila—" he grits, trying to evade the question again.

"No," I growl through the tears in my eyes. "You married me. Then you left." My voice cracks, and his eyes come to mine, and his jaw ticks, his gaze flaring with heat before it's quickly masked by something else. Something dark and wounded.

That makes two of us.

"I loved you. I would have done anything for you. You made

me think you cared, and then you left like I meant nothing to you."

Still no answer.

"Goddammit, Christian, answer me!"

"You want to know why I left?" he chuckles darkly, and the bitter laugh sends a shiver down my spine.

"Yeah, I do."

"I left because your mother asked me to." I freeze, the weight of his words sliding over me. "Because she told me to stop Parker from marrying you off and I made sure no one would ever get the chance." He takes a step towards me, throwing his arms out at the sides. "You think I didn't care. But you fail to realize you meant fucking everything to me. Still fucking do."

I fall back a step. My mother . . . My mother made him leave.

Christian takes another step towards me. "You are the only fucking thing I have ever wanted," he growls. "Fucking *you*. You can think you care about me? I promise you've never been in this as deep as me."

I blink, and a tear slips down my cheek. Christian watches it's descent like he despises it.

"So, why did you marry me, then?"

"I don't know, Mila," he growls, throwing his arms out at his sides. "Maybe because I'm fucking in love with you?" My heart bottoms out in my chest, each heartbeat ticking like the hands of a clock. "Did you ever stop to consider that?"

I open my mouth to speak, but the words get stuck on my tongue.

"You can't mean that?"

"I can't?" he challenges, his voice rough like sandpaper. "You want to know the truth, Mila? I knew a man like me would never get a woman like you to marry him unless he found a way to cheat the system. So, I fucking did. Was it wrong?" He shrugs. "I don't fucking know. I know it kept you from a far worse fate and that's what I cared about."

Jessi Hart

"You were engaged—" I breathe, unable to finish the sentence.

He steps towards me, and I back up to the wall. His body cages mine and the heat rolls off him in waves, sending a shiver up my spine. His heavy scent is intoxicating as it slips over me, and my nipples harden to sharp points.

I'm suddenly acutely aware of how much I've been aching for him in the last three weeks.

"You have no fucking idea what you do to me, do you?" When I don't answer, he steps even closer, and the brush of his body against mine has heat gathering between my thighs. His fingers capture a lock of my hair, twisting the strands. Somehow, I feel his touch between my legs. "You think I could look at another woman while all I see is you? You and that soft fucking heart and those beautiful fucking eyes that make me feel like I'm losing my goddamned mind."

"Christian . . . I . . ."

"Do you know what I'd do to another man if I found out he'd touched you?" he asks, and my hands come between us, fisting the material of his button-up beneath his open suit jacket. "

"I'd start by cutting off each of his fingers for daring to touch what's mine. While he bled out, I'd let him watch me fuck you. Let him see how badly you beg for my cock in your pretty little cunt. Then when you were satisfied, I'd slice his dick off and feed it to him while he bled out at your feet."

I shiver at his admission, sucking in a shaky breath. He moves closer until his lips are at my ear, his breath tingling against the side of my neck.

God, I want him. I want him bad enough that my body feels like it's vibrating with need.

All our drama, baggage. None of it matters at this very moment because all I can think about is how badly I've missed him. How when he showed up in the bedroom last night, it felt like *home* had come to me.

Then leave . . .

With a rush of resentment, I shove him back. Harder than I would have thought I could.

He looks startled before the look in his eyes is replaced with a dark, searing warmth.

I shove him again, and this time, he catches me around the waist, the twist of a wry smile on his lips when he pulls me into him. And then, the moment our eyes meet, something in me snaps.

Lunging for him, I press my lips to his, and he tugs me against every inch of his hard body, the growl reverberating through him the most erotic sound I've ever heard.

His tongue licks into my mouth, the taste of whiskey, mint, and tobacco on his breath. My back hits the wall, and my arms wrap around his neck. He hoists me tighter against him, pressing my knees apart.

We're all nails and teeth and heavy breaths and absolute chaos as the three weeks we've been apart finally catch up to us.

He groans roughly, only breaking the kiss long enough to let me shrug his suit jacket down his arms. He reaches between us, popping the button on his dress pants and fisting his rock-hard cock in his hand. I grip the buttons of his shirt, and he stops me by ripping the remaining few away, scattering them on the hardwood floor.

I whimper, body on fire, and a desperate urge to feel him inside me consuming me. He fists my dress, hoisting it up around my waist, and takes my knee, locking it around his hip in a quick, fluid motion.

"Mine," he rasps against my lips. Then, his mouth is back on mine, and he's sinking two fingers inside me. My back arches away from the wall, my knee tightening around him. My fingers run along the bruises and tattoos that cover his abs and chest.

"Yours," I breathe, eyes half-lidded and hazy when he lines himself up at my entrance.

"Fuck, I've missed you."

And then he's sinking balls deep inside me.

"*Fuck.*" His head falls to my shoulder with a feral groan.

"Oh my God," I cry out, my head knocking back to hit the wall.

"Not God, baby," he rasps, lifting his eyes to meet mine. "Me. Only fucking me."

He fucks me like he's trying to brand himself on my soul. He doesn't realize he's already there. Our bodies meld together against the wall, his breathing rough and my heart pounding in my chest.

The sound of his hips against mine echo in the space between us as he fucks me with a brutal pace.

"Please, Christian," I moan, my nails digging into the muscles of his back.

It's not enough. It's never enough. I need to stake my claim on him as violently as he does me.

"Fuck," he curses under his breath, forcing my legs wider with his hips and powering into me. There's a reverence in the way he fucks me. Like touching me is as vital to him as breathing.

"Christian?"

The door to the suite opens, and I freeze, locking eyes with none other than Talia. She stands just inside the door, halted midstride, her eyes wide with shock and horror at the sight of Christian powering inside me.

He doesn't even look at her. In fact, one might go as far as to say he blatantly ignores her when he grabs my chin in a rough palm, forces my gaze back to his, and seals his lips over mine with a harsh groan.

Everything tightens with violence, the brush of his groin against my clit enough to make my eyes roll and draw a moan from my lips. He captures the sound, his tongue tangling with mine as he kisses me like it's the only thing he's ever wanted.

When I look up, our audience has vanished and the door's shut tight.

He breaks the kiss with a rough nip to my lips.

"You going to come for me?"

I moan in acquiescence, and he keeps up his brutal pace, fucking me until it feels like the walls will crumble around us.

"Come for me, Mila," he rasps, burying his face in the side of my throat, kissing his way up to my lips.

Heat swirls in my stomach, tightening viciously before it releases in a burst of fire. The orgasm crashes through me like a wave of fire, and I cry out, my knees shaking and threatening to give out.

I get lost in him, letting him own me in those few brief seconds where heaven and earth don't exist. Just Christian Cross and the miraculous things he can do to my body.

"Fuck . . . *Mila*," he groans with a ragged sound. "Just like that . ."

A convulsive shudder wracks through him, his entire body shaking with the force behind his orgasm. His cock jerks inside me, filling me until I feel it slip down my inner thighs.

When he lifts his gaze to mine, I don't have a second to react before he's stooping down, gripping me around the thighs, and hauling me up and over his shoulder. My ass is on display for God, the devil, and anyone else who happens to walk through our door.

I surge in his grasp, and his hand connects with my bare skin, making me yelp. Heat liquefies in my core, so intense it takes my breath away.

Or maybe that's just him.

"Where are we going?"

"Bed, Mrs. Cross," he grunts. My nails dig into his skin, but he doesn't stop. "I'm far from finished with you."

CHAPTER
Thirty-Eight

MILA

Christian steps into the master bedroom and hauls me back over his shoulder. Seconds later, I fall to the bed, bouncing on my ass. His eyes follow the movement of my breasts pressed tightly against the confines of my dress with each ragged breath I draw between my teeth.

His gaze is darker than I've ever seen it, like the deepest reaches of the ocean, dragging me down into its depths. Like a man on the brink of losing control.

Is it bad that I want to see what it looks like when that steel control finally snaps?

Leaning over me, his fingers trail under my dress, finding me and slipping inside. My head falls back into the mattress, and I fist the comforter with both hands, a whimper leaving my throat.

"You pissed me off earlier, little wife. What should I do with you?"

"You said I wasn't impressive."

His lips tip up at the corner in a dangerous grin.

"I meant perfect." He presses his lips to the side of my face over the tears streaming down my cheeks. "I live for your touch on me, Mila. I can't live without it."

He pulls back, looking down at me.

"I'm sorry I said it. I'm not sorry about the outcome."

He looks down to where his fingers enter me. I suck in a ragged breath, my eyes fluttering with my vision consumed by his.

"Fuck me," I breathe, wiggling to get closer to his palm. "Please?"

"I wanted to bend you over this very bed this morning and spank your ass. My cock was rock fucking hard thinking about it."

"You told me to leave," I whimper, tears stinging in the backs of my eyes despite the pleasure he's drawing from between my legs. It's maddening.

"You and I both know you'd never get far," he murmurs, and I could slap him if I wasn't so desperate for him. "You know I'd be right there with you, hiding in the shadows until you decided to come home."

"Christian . . ." I clench my eyes shut as my body threatens to explode.

"Look at me."

My pussy tightens at the command in his voice, and I force my eyes to his, the black of his iris bleeding into the blue.

He notices, his lips tipping up at the corner.

"Is that what you want? Me in control?" His fingers curl up to brush over the sensitive spot inside me. "You want to give me all your worries and let me spend the night buried inside my little wife? Making you come over and over again until all you have room for in that pretty little head is me?"

"God, yes." There's no use fighting it. Not with the way he's got control over my body.

What drives me over the edge is when he angles his palm to circle my clit. My eyes clench shut, my voice ringing out in a hoarse shout, and my legs clench around his hand.

"There's my good girl," he rasps, and my stomach flutters at his praise.

"On your knees," he commands when I float back down to earth, and I hurry off the bed, sinking to my knees on the floor in front of him.

His hand winds through my hair, and I take him in my palm, cutting off whatever else he was about to say when I run my tongue over the head of his cock.

"*Fuck*," he rasps, his head falling back to the ceiling with a slow blink of his eyes. "That's it, baby. Look at me." My eyes open and shoot to his, and his nostrils flare. "*Fuck*."

I moan in acquiescence, stroking him with my hand while feeding him between my lips. I swallow his cock, tasting his precum as I swirl my tongue around his thickness. His fingers tighten when I choke on half his length, pulling back to catch my breath.

"I love that I'm the only man to ever fuck you, sweetheart." His heavy gaze locks with mine, watching me slip him back into my mouth. "Only my cock has been in your pussy and your mouth. Soon, your ass."

We both know it's not exactly true, but the fact that he's erasing the touch of the monster that raped me brings a surprising sting to my eyes.

After the attack, I never thought I'd be normal again. I should have known Christian Cross would make sure of it.

He swipes the back of his knuckle through a tear slipping down my cheek, his touch surprisingly gentle compared to the savage way he's fucking my throat.

"There will be no part of you that I do not own, Mila. Just like you've owned me for the last six fucking years."

Maybe because I'm fucking in love with you . . .

I whimper around his cock, and he drives his hips forward an inch, testing me to see if I'll break. I breathe through my nose, swallowing as much of him as I can before pulling back.

"Open wide for me, sweetheart. I'm going to fuck your throat." He tightens his hold on my hair, wrapping it around his fist. "Think you can do that for me?"

I nod, though not very well, because of what he's doing to me. Opening my mouth wider, he takes control, his other hand coming to rest on top of my head while the one in the back pushes me forward to where he wants me.

I force myself to breathe through my nose, sticking my tongue out when he slides to the back of my throat, pushing past my limit and making me gag.

"Fucking hell, that's it," he groans, pulling back to push forward again.

I take everything he has to give me, my pussy throbbing at the steadily building brutality of his thrusts into my mouth. The size of him hitting the back of my throat and my lack of control. I like the fact that I don't have to worry. I like that I can focus on what he's doing to me rather than the voices swarming like a murder of crows in my head.

With a growl, he tugs me back by my hair, and saliva streams from my mouth before he shoves it back in.

"You going to swallow my come?"

All I can do is moan from where he's holding me, fucking my throat savagely and taking what he needs from me.

It's not long before he's growling, shooting his release into my throat and robbing me of what little air I have left in my lungs. I swallow everything he gives me greedily, my arousal dripping down my thighs.

"Up," he orders roughly, tugging me to stand before either of us has even gotten our bearings.

He grips me around the waist, hauling me onto the bed, and drops to his knees in front of me. Shoving my dress up to bunch around my hips, he tosses my heels to the rug behind him before his lips latch around my aching clit. He throws my legs over his shoulders, spreading me wide with a quiet growl.

His tongue swirls through my folds as he feasts on me. My head falls back to the comforter, my back arching and my hands gripping the sheets, his hair, my *own* hair—anything I can get my hands on to steady myself at the warmth slipping through my veins.

His fingers tighten to near-bruising strength when he slips his tongue inside me, fucking me with it.

He smirks, his eyes glinting in the darkness.

"You have thirty seconds to come, Mila. Count."

When I open my mouth to ask, he cuts me off.

"Count."

"One . . ." I stutter shakily, the sound cutting off on a moan when he drops back between my legs, sealing his lips over my clit and fluttering his tongue. His eyes lock on mine, pulling me into their depths and turning my brain to mush.

It's maddening.

Abruptly, he stops.

"Two . . . three . . ."

He resumes, his tongue slipping around my clit in circles. He slips his hand between us, sliding two fingers inside me while he sucks on my clit. I can feel my arousal seeping down my inner thighs, but he laps at it like it's honey. A deep groan reverberates through his chest, and my pussy clenches around his fingers from the vibrations.

The pleasure swirls through me, my legs shaking as the orgasm builds. Right before I reach the edge, a sharp sting on my clit has me gasping and surging against his mouth.

"Twelve!" I shout, my voice hoarse and my back bowing off the bed.

"That's it. Let me have it, Mila."

He fucks me with his fingers, curling the digits up to stroke some deeply buried part of me that only he seems to know, and I groan, throwing my head back against the comforter beneath me.

"Fuck, I need inside you," he grits through his teeth, dropping his gaze down the length of my body to watch his fingers enter me. "You going to come for me like a good girl?"

My pussy clenches in response, and I nod frantically, fisting the comforter on either side of me. "Twenty," I respond, and with a devilish glint in his eyes, he leans down, wrapping his arms around my thighs and spreading me with both thumbs and sucks my clit between his lips. His tongue flutters over the swollen bundle of nerves, and it's too much.

"Twent—Christian!" I scream, my back arching off the bed and my thighs threatening to close around his head.

White, hot light flashes behind my eyes, and my pussy clenches down on his fingers. I'm gasping, desperate for air, as the orgasm rips through me, leaving me a shaking puddle of need beneath him.

"Fuck, you're so goddamned pretty when you come," he grits against me, kissing his way up my body. My vision is spotty, my hair curling from his hands, and the sweat coating my hairline, sticking to my face. "Goddamn."

He climbs up on the bed, forcing himself between my legs and crowding over me.

"Taste yourself," he rasps, and I open my mouth wide. He obliges, spitting on my tongue before his lips find mine, and for the life of me, I can't figure out why I was so determined not to kiss him before.

Christian kisses with everything he has. Like he could rip my soul from my chest with a simple swipe of his tongue.

"You going to keep your lips from me again?" he rasps against my tongue and I shake my head. "Why?"

"Because I'm yours."

"Damn fucking right you are. Stay here."

Climbing off the bed, he crosses to the other side of the room, opening an antique writing desk in the corner and grabbing something out. What it could be, I have no idea, but my stomach lights with nervous tingles when he stalks back towards the bed, his gaze searing against my skin.

Standing over me, his cock straining under its heavy weight and glistening with precum. Shoving his dress pants down his legs and then pulling his shirt off, he looks magnificent. He climbs back up on the bed, kneeling between my legs, his hands sliding under my dress to pull it off. Once we're both completely naked and panting, I see what he'd gotten up to grab when rips the top off a permanent marker.

"What are you doing?" I ask, voice breathless, when he bends down towards my skin, slipping the marker along my flesh.

"Making sure you know who you belong to," he mutters gruffly. I look down to where he's marked me, and my eyes go wide, my heart stalling.

Over the words carved into my flesh, he's written *MINE* in big, bold letters over the word *whore*. Tears well in my eyes at the simplicity of it. The primal need for him to claim me despite my scars and baggage.

He moves higher, repeating the motion over *slut*. And then again, over a deeper scar on my ribcage.

"I'll tattoo them on you if I have to, but make no mistake, little wife. I don't give a fuck about your scars. I don't give a fuck what they say. You're my woman, and I'm your man. Nothing else fucking matters."

He shoves the cap back on the marker, tossing it behind him and taking his cock in his hand. Then, he enters me in one full thrust, his cock bottoming out halfway.

I gasp, shooting up the bed, and he leans back, taking my hips in his hands and dragging me back down.

"You cry so pretty for me, Mila." He leans down, capturing the tear on my cheek with his tongue. "So fucking sweet and innocent."

He groans, rolling his hips so his groin brushes against my clit. A moan claws its way from my throat, and my head falls back against the sheets.

I look down between us, watching as his cock slips between my folds until he's buried in me to the hilt.

"You like to watch?" My clit pulses with the rasp in his voice, but I don't have the good sense to be embarrassed. "I'll build a room of mirrors so you can see how fucking sexy you are."

Pulling back out, he slips forward, setting up a steady pace that has my body betraying me in every single way possible. When he pushes forward, his cock presses against my wall, and a lance of pain shoots through me.

His gaze runs down the length of my body, and he sits back, watching as he thrusts fucks me. I groan at the sting, and he brings his thumb between us, rolling my clit. My eyes flutter, heat slipping through me, forcing me to suck him in greedily.

"Oh my god," I breathe, spreading my legs to take him deeper. Needing him deeper. He thrusts harder, his hand coming up to slap the side of my breast. He rolls each one in his hand, grazing the nipple, and when he pinches, my back bows off the bed, craving more.

"You going to come for me again?"

"I can't," I growl, but I gasp when he thrusts inside me hard enough that his skin slaps against mine, his heavy sack hitting my ass.

"I'll be the judge of that."

He grips my knees in each of his hands, shoving them to my chest and making it hard to breathe. Picking up his pace, he powers into me, sweat dotting his brow and slipping down the hard ridges of his abs.

I don't even realize I'm moaning, rolling my hips to meet each of his carefully timed thrusts until his hand slides into my hair, fisting the strands and tugging my head back at a painful angle.

"That's my good girl. Show me how pretty you can come for me."

My back bows, my eyes screwing shut, and my pussy clenches

around his cock as the orgasm rips through me. I cry out, the sound echoing in the room as my body shakes underneath him.

"Christian," I whimper, tingles spreading through every nerve ending in my body as I fight the onslaught of pleasure. I'm overstimulated, spent, and covered in my own come, but he doesn't stop.

"*Fuck*," he shudders, his eyes falling closed and his head kicking back. "This pussy is so fucking tight. Just begging for my cock."

He grips my hips in his hands, rough enough that I'm sure I'll have bruises in the morning.

"You're doing so fucking good, Mila," he praises, and my stomach clenches from his words. "Look at you, taking all my cock like a good little wife."

Before I can say anything, he flips me over onto my stomach, hiking my hips up so my ass is in the air. He presses his hand to the back of my head, forcing the side of my face into the comforter while his hands tangle in my hair.

This new angle has his slipping deeper, fucking me harder. I cry out at the intrusion, clawing at the comforter beneath me desperately. He pins me beneath him, his deep grunts in between each thrust going straight to my pussy as he fucks me faster.

"Yes," I whimper when his fingers find my clit again, his cock stroking some deeply rooted part of me I never even knew existed.

My legs are shaking with the effort to hold me up. I'm covered in both our sweat and come, yet my body still begs for more.

God, who even am I?

Surging forward, he thrusts inside me hard and unforgiving. I cry into the comforter, desperate moans slipping free when the pressure builds low in my stomach.

"You hear that?" he rasps, the wet sounds of his body slapping against mine filling the room. "Hear how fucking wet you are for me? You were fucking made to take my cock."

"Please," I whimper, tears streaming from the corners of my

eyes. I'm sure if I come again, it'll be the death of me. I just know it.

"You can take it," he grunts, powering into me with each word. "You're my good little whore, aren't you?"

I nod, shivers rolling down my spine as he fucks me so fast, I couldn't speak even if I wanted to. He reaches under me, gripping me around the throat, and tugs me back to meet his gaze. He's so much bigger than me that I can see him over the top of my head as he fucks me, my vision consumed by his.

I'm going to come again. It's inevitable. Especially with the way he's stroking over that secret spot like he put it there. His fingers on my clit, mixed with his cock bottoming out in my pussy have me barreling towards another orgasm. How many times is he going to make me come before he releases me?

"You're so goddamned pretty when you're crying my name. You love my fucking darkness, don't you, Mila?"

I shiver, right on the precipice of collapsing into what he's doing to me.

His fingers tighten around my throat, restricting my air.

"Answer the question, little devil."

"Yes," I admit on a groan.

"Good fucking girl. Come."

He releases me, and I fall to the bed. Taking both my hips in his hands and powering me right over the edge. My body seizes in the most intense orgasm I've ever had, and my vision grows spotty. I'm not sure if I pass out, see God, or die, but I scream his name into the pillows, distantly registering his animalistic groan as he comes, pushing into me so deep, I feel it in my stomach.

"Fuck," he grits, a tremor moving through his hands on my hips. "Fucking hell, Mila."

When he rolls me over, he collapses over me, holding his weight on his arms so he doesn't crush me, and captures my lips with a soft groan. When he pulls back, he leans his forehead against mine, our hearts racing against one another in the darkness of our new room.

"You have no idea the things that I would do for you, do you?"

My heart beats unsteadily, the last bits of my soul surrendering to him and the sincerity in his gaze.

Leaning up, I press my lips to his gently, a shiver rolling through me from the aftershocks of my orgasm.

"Til death do us part," I whisper against his lips, and he chuckles darkly.

"Not even death could rip you away from me, baby. I'm a Cross. We don't give up what's ours."

I've always loved tracing the lines of the tattoos on Christian's skin. Staring at him while he sleeps, my fingers running over the smooth lines etched into his flesh, it's easy to picture the rest of our lives intertwined.

I know I'm breaking my own rules. Dreaming of him. Clinging to the idea that he can be something he's not. I mean, he forced me to marry him, but, like the idiot I am, I know I've fallen for him all over again.

And who wouldn't, after all? Fall for him?

He's the pinnacle knight in shining black armor, full of chinks and scuffs. Handsome as sin. Protective. He's everything every little girl with a broken past dreams of. Someone to wrap their arms around you until the demons can't reach you.

My chest aches, thinking of his words earlier when he gave me back my body by writing over the demented carvings of a madman because I think a part of me wishes I'd never met Christian Cross at all.

I was doing so well . . .surviving. Who were my nightmares hurting but myself? My silent misery living under my stepfather's rule? Why did he have to come in and show me that there was more to life? That I could allow myself things I didn't even know I was denying myself of?

Why did he have to make me fall in love with him?

Because now that I know what it feels like to have him, I don't want to give him up.

"Mila . . ." he murmurs quietly, stirring from sleep. It's two in the morning and he lays on his stomach, his head on the pillow, facing me, and I roll over to mirror his position. The moon shines through the bedroom window behind him, casting his tattooed back in shades of orange and gold and highlighting his stone muscles.

God, how is he real?

Without opening his eyes, he reaches for me, taking my hand and pulling it under his chest, bringing my knuckles to his lips.

"This tattoo?" I start, placing my hand over the raised edges of *MRC* on his chest. "It's our wedding date, isn't it?"

"It is."

"Am I allowed to ask a question?" I ask softly, lying perfectly still.

Finally, his eyes open and find mine, their deep blue depths stealing my breath away and stalling my heart.

"If you answer mine."

Fuck.

My stomach bottoms out, but even I know it's time. I've been hiding behind lies for so long I'm starting to forget the truth.

"Okay."

"What's your question?" he asks, neither of us moving.

"What happened while you were gone? Why are you covered in bruises?"

His jaw clenches, his eyes hardening. I expect him to tell me not to worry about it.

"We went to LA, first, to find answers regarding that night," he answers simply. "Found the house where you were held."

My stomach bottoms out, a sickness roiling through me. "You . . . found the house?"

"I did . . . I also torched it."

I suck in a deep, shaky breath, my heart ricocheting around my chest.

"And did you find anything?"

His gaze darkens, and he rolls onto his back, his shoulders stiff. I don't miss the way his tattoos ripple over the thick muscles despite spending the last hour drowning in him.

"Nothing that would answer any questions."

The blood rushes to my head, and the room spins around me. This is all too confusing.

"So, after the house was gone, we used the remaining time we had to hunt down anyone who would have any leads on who was behind that night."

"I have a feeling torturing then is more like it. Judging by your bruises and new scars."

"So you do notice?" he chuckles dryly.

"I . . . I've always noticed," I whisper, and his gaze finds mine.

He's silent for a moment, staring at me. His gaze slides over me, and even in the near darkness, my cheeks heat under his gaze.

It's ridiculous. The man just had his tongue buried inside me only an hour ago. I've got the word MINE written all over my torso, yet when he looks at me like that—like he's reading into my mind and reading my thoughts like the open pages of a book—it's impossible not to feel a rush of awareness.

"The first opportunity I had, I came back to you, Mila."

The air hums with electricity between us, the silence deafening. Somehow, I already knew that.

"And I had every intention of coming back for you a year ago."

"I know," I whisper so quietly I can barely hear myself. "I'm sorry you had to see . . . that."

My skin crawls just thinking of that hell hole.

"Stop."

Tears sting in the backs of my eyes, but I let him continue, even if I don't want to hear it.

"You are my wife," he murmurs. He leans up, hovering over me, his thumb slipping through the tears on my cheek. "I will do what I have to do to protect you."

I draw my bottom lip between my teeth, chewing on it, and he tugs it free.

"I . . . have something to tell you.'

He goes silent, leaning back in the bed to watch me, patiently waiting. Unable to lay down with the nerves swarming through me like a flock of birds, I sit up, pressing my back against the headboard. He follows suit, sitting up on the edge of the bed. His hand falls in my lap, and I trace the lines in his fingers so I don't have to meet his gaze.

"The night . . . I was attacked," I breathe, and a traitorous tear slips down my cheek. "They sent me a picture of you. You were bound to a chair and bloody, and they told me if I didn't come, they would kill you," I rush, knowing I have to get this out. All the while, I feel his gaze trained on my hands twisting together in my lap. "Of course, now I realize it wasn't you and just your twin . . ." Fuck, why is this so hard?

His gaze hardens, his back straight as a steel rod.

I force a breath through my teeth, a shiver moving through me.

"He told me he would come back, and they would go after my mother next. I wasn't thinking and thought if I was gone, maybe everyone would be okay. He had been stalking me for months. I should have known it wouldn't be that easy."

He's silent, processing the information while my chest feels like it's slowly turning to stone, suffocating me from the inside out.

Abruptly, he stands from the bed, pacing over to the dresser. He leans forward, gripping the edge and staring at himself in the mirror, the tension radiating through him palpable.

"You were being stalked?"

I nod, unable to answer through the lump in my throat.

"Why the fuck wouldn't you tell me?" His voice is rough and deep. I've pissed him off.

"Because I was scared," I whisper. "I still am. He could go after my family. What if he comes for you or your family—"

"*You* are my family, too," he grits, scrubbing a hand down his face, his hands visibly shaking.

The damn breaks, and tears slip freely down my cheeks. A quiet sob wracks through me, and I angrily wipe the tears away.

"If something happened to you, I'd never forgive myself."

Letting out a deep breath, he crosses the room, kneeling down beside the bed.

"I should have been there to protect you."

"You said you were. Why weren't you there?"

He grits his teeth.

"I was an idiot. After the falling out with your mother, I came back here to tie up whatever loose ends I could so I could come to you with the truth about our marriage. Be better. We'd just found out Dad was dying, and Paulina was in the hospital for surgery. I needed to be here for Bella. I thought everything was clear, and I planned to tie up all my loose ends and come to you with the truth, regardless of what your mother said. Of course, it was never going to be that easy."

Reaching up, he runs his thumb across my lip, tugging it from my teeth, his eye softening in the moonlight. "I'm sorry I wasn't there. I hate myself for it every day."

"It's not your job to save me," I whisper, shaking my head and blinking against the tears in my eyes.

He reaches for the nightstand, sliding the drawer open. He pulls out what I think is his ring; only when it catches in the light it's different.

"This says otherwise."

My gaze shoots back to his when he holds it up in front of me.

"You bought me a ring?"

A ring makes this marriage real. It solidifies ownership. A brand to let the world know I'm his.

My stomach twists uncomfortably, but it's the warmth in his gaze that settles it.

This man loves me. I love him. I may not understand it, but everything he's done has been to protect me.

"I bought it a year ago." I swallow heavily. "Another reason I came back here." His gaze meets mine, and for the first time in my life, I find what it looks like when Christian Cross is nervous. There's something oddly touching about the tremor that slips through his hand. "It's yours if you want it."

My tongue darts out to lick my lips, and I reach out, taking the ring from him and holding it in my palm. It's beautiful, from what I can see in the darkness of the room, but it doesn't matter. He could tie a dandelion around my finger, and I'd probably still say yes.

"Just know, if you put that on, it's never coming off."

"What if you decide you're done with me and want a divorce?"

He fixes me with a dark look.

"I've waited six years for you, Mila. This will never be over for me."

He's right. I've been the one running since I met him.

"On one condition." His jaw ticks at my words.

"Name it."

"You have to put yours on, too."

I reach for the chain on the nightstand, holding his ring, and he takes it from me. Without a second thought, he removes the chain, sliding it back into the nightstand, and slips the ring onto his finger.

"There's something else," I tell him, still holding my ring in the palm of my hand. "When things are bad, you have to tell me the truth. No more hiding things because you think it will protect me. It hasn't protected me so far. It's only created a wedge between us."

"Are you agreeing to be my wife, Mrs. Cross?"

"If . . . you meet my demands."

He chuckles dryly, taking the ring.

"I promise," he murmurs, his gaze locking with mine. A tremor moves through his hand on mine, so slight I barely notice it. "So long as you promise to always tell me when you feel yourself falling. I promise when you do, I'll be there to catch you."

God, for being a self-proclaimed atheist to romance, he's the most romantic man I've ever met.

"I promise."

Taking my hand, he slips the ring onto my finger, and I'm not surprised it's a perfect fit.

He reaches up, brushing a strand of hair back from my face, his eyes soft when they meet my own.

"You gave me freedom."

"I'm only sorry I didn't do it sooner . . . Come here," he murmurs, rising in front of me and pushing me back in the bed. He settles over me, pressing his lips to mine with a groan, a shudder moving through him when my fingers slip up his back.

When he breaks the kiss, his lips moving down to my throat, I'm nearly panting despite the million and one orgasms he'd given me earlier.

"By the way, Talia totally saw us in the hallway."

He smirks, and it does something funny to my chest.

"Do you think she enjoyed the show?"

I gawk at him when he raises back up. "You knew?"

"Of course, I knew. No one sees me fuck my wife without me knowing about it."

"Why didn't you stop?"

He runs a hand through my hair, fisting the strands and bringing my eyes to his.

"Maybe I want the world to know I'm yours as much as you're mine."

God, there's no way this man is real.

"You're bad," I tell him, though I can't fight my smile.

He lowers his lips back to mine, his response coming out as a whisper against my lips.

"You're perfect."

CHAPTER
Thirty-Nine

MILA

"Where are we going?"

"Keep your eyes closed." I stumble, giggling as I try to find my footing.

"You've got your hand over them."

"Well, then, don't even try. If you peek, I'll spank your ass."

"Maybe I want to peek now."

As punishment, his hand swats my denim-clad ass, and I yelp at the sting.

"Still think so, sweetheart?" he rasps, and heat floods through me, a shiver ghosting down my spine.

He chuckles darkly when I don't answer, drawing a shallow breath through my lips.

"I'll take that as a yes."

"Are we almost there yet?"

With my eyesight stolen, I'm acutely aware of every inch of him that presses against me as he leads me down a path into the trees. Heat slips through me, warming my blood against the cool October

Christian chuckles darkly from behind me, sensing the shift.

It's been two weeks since Founder's Day and two weeks of living a constant battle of wanting him or wanting sleep.

When we're awake, he's inside me. We shower together. Eat together. He holds me while we sleep.

I never thought it would be possible to crave another person this much. If I thought his coming home would lessen this . . . desire for him, I was wrong. It's only fed the addiction.

I have no idea where we're going, but I haven't been to this part of the property yet because the trees are thicker, and it's further away from the house.

"We'd get there faster if you'd walk."

"You try walking without your eyes."

In a rush, I'm lifted into his arms and let out a yelp when my feet leave the ground.

"Keep your eyes closed."

I can't help but smile when he starts back down the path, heading to God only knows where.

He walks for a few minutes before he comes to a stop, turning and placing me on my feet before he covers my eyes again and pulls me against his chest.

Once he's got me situated where he wants me, he leans down, pressing his lips at my ear. Goosebumps rise on my flesh at the brush of his warm breath in the cool, damp September air.

"Happy anniversary, baby."

I open my mouth to tell him our "anniversary" isn't for another two months when he removes his hands, and I fall silent.

The house looks like it was constructed with the earth. Like the land was built around it. If it weren't for the modern architecture and the glow of the warm light from within, I'd be sure it wasn't real.

I look up at Christian and find him watching me.

"You bought a house?"

"*We bought a* house," he corrects, taking my hand with my ring on it. His thumb circles the stone before he raises it to his lips.

"When did you buy this?"

"A few years ago. For all intents and purposes, I lived here, but we both know my life was back in LA. Think of it as a wedding present."

The way he says it like *I* was his life and not the job he did, makes my heart swell.

He watches me carefully, like I might run at any moment.

"You're the only woman who's ever been here, Mila . . ."

I wasn't even considering it, but now, I can't fight the surge of triumph that courses through me.

"It's ours?"

He nods once, slowly. "If you like it."

"Why didn't you bring me here sooner?"

"Because it wasn't ready."

I push away from him and make my way toward the warm, dark wooden door. He follows, his footfalls heavy on the front steps of the porch.

He doesn't let me get far, though, before stopping and hoisting me back into his arms.

"I can walk, you know?"

He smirks down at me.

"Isn't it tradition for the groom to carry the bride over their threshold?"

Heat blooms in my cheeks, and I roll my eyes. I can't hide the smile tugging at the corners of my lips, though.

"You're the most romantic, non-romantic I've ever met."

He pushes through the front door, carrying me inside. Inside is warm, lit with a low burning fire in the fireplace, and the scent of vanilla warms the air. It's everything I would expect it to be. Cozy and inviting. Like the cottage on Shipwreck Island if it had been constructed in the last hundred years. The walls of the living room are tall, reaching towards the ceiling with oak panels and a stretch of stone above a large fireplace.

The furniture is warm and something I'd pick out. Even the trees beyond the back are beautiful, adding to the space with the floor-to-ceiling windows that show off the Pacific Northwest wild.

"You can change whatever you want," Christian murmurs behind me. "And here," he stalks towards the windows on the far wall. "We can add a greenhouse since I know you liked the one on Shipwreck Island." He looks back out the window, and butterflies dance across my heart at the nerves radiating beneath his carefully composed exterior.

The only other time I've seen him nervous was when he asked me if I wanted to be his wife.

Tears well in my eyes, and I blink them back. This has to be a joke, right? A place we can call home. Actually, call home that's just ours?

It sounds like a dream.

"Phantom can run. We'll have our own space." His gaze shoots back to mine where I stand by the huge sofa, my fingers running over the soft material, his eyes wild and so blue they steal my breath away. "Did you see the kitchen? You could bake a horse in the oven."

God, I can never say no to those eyes.

"I love you."

"There's even a hot tub in the back."

"Christian," I stop him. I've seen enough. He pauses, his gaze studying mine. "I love you."

He freezes, seeming to finally register what I'd said. He closes his eyes for a brief second. And when he opens them, they're dark as night.

Slowly, he steps towards me, backing me up until my ass is pressed against the back of the couch. He leans in, his arms on either side of me, caging me in, and if I didn't know him better, I'd think he was pissed off. I can see by the slight tremor that runs through him, though, that it's something else entirely.

"Say that again," he rasps, his mouth hovering over mine. I smile softly, my tongue darting out to lick my lips at the heavy wash of his scent slipping over me.

"I love you," I breathe. "And I love this house."

He groans, the sound rumbling through our connected chests and settling between my thighs.

"Fucking hell, Mila," he grunts, his nose trailing along mine. "I love you."

"You don't have to sound so happy about it."

"You've got me by the balls," he murmurs darkly. "I'd stop the world spinning if you asked me to. You fucking own me, and you want me to be *happy* about it?"

My heartbeat flutters in my chest.

"Well . . . *I'm* happy about it."

"You really like it?"

His hands roam my body, reaching down to cup the swell of my ass.

I can't help but smile, tilting my face up to his. My heart stalls when I see the reverence in his gaze.

"Just shut up and kiss me."

He smirks, his fingers tightening on my ass. In a flash, he's lifting me into his arms, and my legs lock around his hips. He carries me towards a chair in the corner of the room, lit by the warmth of the fireplace.

When he settles down, me on his lap, his eyes latch onto mine, glinting wickedly.

"What was that you said earlier about punishing you?"

"Christian . . ." I warn, body tightening over his when his hands roam under the hem of my sweater. I'm not wearing anything underneath, and his fingertips graze my nipples. "I love you." Now that I've said it, I can't stop myself. I need him to know with every fiber of his being.

"Now, Mrs. Cross," he settles back in the chair, his hands

resting on either side of the armrests. "Be a good little wife and show me."

Christian Cross is the hurricane that completely destroyed my life.

He's also the man who put it back together again.

I'm in love with him. I know it. He knows it. Hell, the man on the moon knows it for how many times he's made me scream it in the last week when he's inside me.

He's everywhere. Inside me, all around me. He's claimed me body and soul, and I'm powerless to stop it.

I've fallen for him in the most depraved way, and not even an exorcism could bring me back now.

We spend a week in our house after that first night, falling into an easy rhythm. Out here, away from the hustle and bustle of the mansion, it's quiet. Peaceful.

He spends his days working—whatever he does—while I unpack with the help of Bella and Ava. I take walks with Ava and Phantom, and I even start baking again with Christian's encouragement.

I also help Bella out at the Lodge, organizing for her and doing whatever I can to help her and her fear of premature grey hair.

She even offered to hire me as an assistant of sorts, and I actually agreed.

Life has been crazy, but for the first time ever, it's good crazy. Not deadly crazy.

"I'm going to have to build a gym if you keep cooking like this," he says one night while he eats the lasagna I'd made for dinner.

I gawk at him.

"You don't work out?"

He shrugs, taking another bite.

"Never needed to."

"Figures," I grumble, rolling my eyes.

"Problem, little devil?"

My stomach dips at the warmth in his tone.

"Yeah, I missed you today."

"Want me to spend the evening making it up to you?" I can't fight the devilish glint in his eyes. It's too tempting.

"Maybe."

He chuckles darkly under his breath.

"Come here."

Standing, I think about walking around the table, but what fun would that be?

So, instead, I slide our empty plates out of the way and climb up onto the table, crawling across towards him.

He sinks back in his chair, his eyes lighting with a scorching heat as he watches the sway of my hips, and that's when I learn how much I *love* to make this man hot for me.

When I stop in front of him, sliding down to straddle his lap, his cock is hard against me, and his shoulders are stiff.

Turns out, my husband is just as addicted to me as I am to him.

"Is this close enough for you?" I whisper, throwing his words from years ago back at him.

He understands, smirking. He leans forward, brushing the hair off my neck and pressing his lips to that perfect spot below my ear. I bite back a sigh when tingles erupt from where he's touching me.

His hand comes up, pressing firmly to my back, and his other grips my hip, tugging me against his front before he leans forward and places his lips on mine. My arms come up to circle his neck, my nails raking through his short hair, and butterflies fill my stomach at his admission.

A low growl rumbles through his chest when I try to fist the short strands, and he breaks away, pressing his forehead to mine.

"You're impossible," I breathe. His jaw ticks, his lips pulling up at the corner.

"You're beautiful."

We also play a game of twenty questions every night over dinner.

I learn that he hates tight spaces while he learns that I have a slight fear of public bathrooms.

I learn that he played rugby in school—totally not surprised—and he learns that I was in the animal rights club—he wasn't surprised by that, either.

Life is simple and sweet. We spend the nights wrapped in each other's arms, and I spend the days counting down the hours until he comes home to me.

"You smell like heaven, baby."

His hands slide around my hips, tugging me back into his front, where I'm cooking at our stove.

"Fuck, I love coming home to you," he murmurs, pressing a kiss to the side of my neck. His lips slide over my skin, his breath warm, and a shiver moves through me.

With a soft laugh, I turn in his arms, letting him sweep me into him.

"New house rule. No clothes."

"Going to make cooking pretty dangerous. Or company uncomfortable."

"Okay, I'll amend it for cooking only and guests?" His eyes slide down my body before flicking back to mine with a scorching heat. "Fuck the guests."

Then, he cuts the burner off on the stove, hoisting me onto the island counter, and feasts on me until I'd be willing to sell my soul if it made him happy.

All in all, life is coming together beautifully.

There's just one problem.

—The fact that someone is still out there that wants us dead.

"I want to help."

"You are helping."

"Feeding you and fucking you every night is not helping," I argue when we're undressing for a shower one night.

I mean, what straight, hot-blooded woman wouldn't want to watch water run down Christian Cross's abs every night? Certainly, not me.

He smirks, his gaze sliding over me.

Maybe I shouldn't have started this conversation naked. It's only distracting him.

"You're more than that, and you know it."

"Then let me be useful. Maybe I can bring him out of hiding."

"You want me to offer you up as bait?"

"Well, when you put it that way," I grumble.

"Yeah," he grits, cutting on the shower. "He got to you once. I won't let it happen twice, Mila."

"He *won't* get to me, though," I urge, pressing my hands flat against his chest. "You're here."

He stares down at me, his eyes studying mine.

"Please," I try again, letting my hand slip down his chest and to the rock-hard abs beneath. "I want to help."

His jaw ticks, and he shakes his head.

"Jesus Christ," he grunts, pulling me into the shower. "No more arguing naked. It's not fair."

"Does that mean I get to help?" A rush of triumph slides through me.

But . . . he doesn't answer.

"Turn around," he murmurs gruffly, grabbing the shampoo. "Let me wash your hair."

By week four, post *I love you*, Christian and I are comfortable and this marriage *actually* feels like a marriage for once.

Like today, when I brought him lunch to the office in the family's lodge because I knew he would be meeting with a friend.

I don't know what it's about, but he ushers me out with a swat to my ass before I can ask, so I concede to bother him about it later.

I'm just starting off down the stairs when a cry stops me dead in my tracks.

"Help!"

The cry is muffled, but I jerk my head up on the stairs, pausing to listen.

"Help!"

There's no one around, so I dart back up the stairs, walking quickly towards whoever yelled.

"Hello?" I call out, but no one answers, save for one drawn-out cry for help.

Fuck. Where's an adult when you need one?

I look down at the wedding ring on my hand.

Oh, right. I'm an adult.

Worst decision I've ever made.

I follow the cries towards a hallway off to the left, a wing I've never been in, and slow my pace. At the end of the hall sits a closed door, and the cries are coming from that room.

What if it's a trap?

What if it's not, and someone needs help?

I groan aloud. Why couldn't I have just ignored it? I would take fourteen of Paulina's grapefruit over this, any day.

Pushing the door open, the room is dark, save for a single lamp in the corner. The light casts shadows around the room, showcasing a human-sized lump in the center of a large, four-post bed.

A man stares back at me like something out of a horror film. His skin is sunken, his hair thin and stripped of color. His arms are covered in bruises, and machines line the walls, keeping him alive. He doesn't say anything, and neither do I, so we both stay locked in our eerie staring contest.

Slowly, he reaches out a decrepit hand, beckoning for me to come closer.

I don't want to. I *really* don't want to, but I do, stepping through the dimly lit room and pausing at the side of his bed.

It smells . . . like death in this room.

His eyes rake over my face, up to my hair, and down to the wedding ring on my finger.

Oh my God . . . this is Christian's father.

"Are you okay?" I ask, my voice shaking. "I-I heard you yelling for help."

Still, no response.

Internally, I scold myself for being afraid of the man in front of me. He's clearly dying, and I'm sure the last thing he wants is to be locked in this room by himself all day and night.

"My name is Mila. Would you like a glass of water?" I reach for his cup on the nightstand, but at the last second, his hand darts out at an incredible speed for someone in his condition, wrapping around my wrist.

It startles me so much, I drop the cup, spilling water everywhere.

Time stands still while he stares at me with those dark, nearly black eyes.

—And then he laughs. A long, cackling, creepy laugh that sends chills through me.

"My son's going to kill you," he grins, his teeth garish and yellow.

I attempt to stumble back a step when his laugh rings out in the air, nearly falling to my ass when I run into the chest of someone standing behind me.

I let out a squeak, and Levi cocks a brow at me, shooting the dying man in the bed behind me a look that tells me everything I need to know.

He hates him as much as Christian does.

"Fuck off, you old ass," he barks at him, and his father has the good nature to at least stop laughing and release me, though his grin stays in place. "Come on, Mila."

Levi takes my wrist, leading me from the room. All the while, I get this sinking feeling that I need to keep my eyes on the man in the bed for fear that he might grab me and drag me down to whatever pit of hell he crawled out of.

"Stay out of there," Levi commands once we're out in the hallway.

"That's your father, isn't it?"

He doesn't answer.

"What's wrong with him?" I ask, shivering as the sound of his hacking cough comes from the room at the end of the hall.

"He's dying," Levi says, his stare hard when he finally meets my eyes. "Stay away from him."

A twinge of embarrassment washes through me, and I feel the need to explain myself.

"I wasn't going to hurt him. Contrary to popular belief, I don't go around shooting people every day."

"I never said *you* were going to hurt *him*."

I don't like the underlying danger in that statement.

"He's confined to a bed, and he was yelling for help. Was I supposed to ignore him?"

"Yes," he says, stalking off. Like the pest I am, I follow him.

"But what if he's hurt?"

"Good," Levi says without breaking stride.

"That's your father—"

He whirls on me, anger flashing in his gaze.

"He stopped being my father the moment he—"

A door behind us opens, and his gaze shoots over my head. I turn to find Ava standing there like a deer in headlights, staring straight at Levi like she's come face-to-face with an Anaconda.

"Stay out of there. Don't give Christian a reason to end his suffering sooner." He starts to walk off, his gaze still on Ava. "Fucker deserves what he's getting."

"What was that about?" Ava asks, stepping up beside me, her

cheeks flushed a deep pink. I look down the stairs where Levi had gone, to Ava, then back.

Oh, I can't *wait* to see how this plays out.

"No idea," I murmur, wincing at the cough from the end of the hall once more. "Let's go for a walk. I need out of here."

CHAPTER
Forty

CHRISTIAN

I sit at my father's desk in the main house's office, watching the cameras of home playing on the screen in front of me, when a soft knock sounds at the door.

"Come in."

I cut the screen off, getting one last fleeting look of Mila baking something in the kitchen and swaying along to the sound of music I can't hear when the door opens.

The sound of heels on the marble floor is loud when Talia saunters into the room, shutting the door behind her.

"Christian, it's been too long since we've gotten to catch up," she says, slipping gracefully into the chair in front of me. She's got her hair down and a Burberry coat unbuttoned at the top to show off her cleavage. She presses her chest out, her eyes flashing mischievously with a grin.

"After you practically ran out the other night, I thought it wise not to approach you when your partner was with you. I could see the effect seeing us together had on her.

"Wife."

"I'm sorry?"

"Wife," I correct her. "Mila is my wife."

"Yes, well. Semantics," she waves a manicured hand. "I must say, I was quite surprised you called and asked to see me. I was sure you weren't allowed. She knows about us, you know?"

I ignore the subtle dig at my wife for now, choosing to move on to why I called her here instead.

Standing from my chair, I cross to the window on the far side, looking out over the grounds to where the faint glow of Mila and I's house can be seen through the trees. It's not yet dark, but it will be soon, and I'm eager to get home to see what she's made for dinner tonight.

I swear the girl laces everything with cocaine.

Reaching into my pocket, I grab what I want and pull it out, turning back to Talia.

"Do you have something you'd like to tell me?"

Her brows furrow, a subtle smirk pulling on her lips.

"I don't know what you're talking about?"

"No?"

I place the phone down on the desk in front of her, and the smile falls from her lips.

She looks back up at me, her eyes widening with fear before she licks her lips and shakes her head.

"I don't know what that is."

"I must say, you always were a convincing liar."

Her eyes darken, her face growing red. She hoists her bag higher on her shoulder and stands, nearly sending the chair toppling.

"I didn't come here to be accused, Christian."

"Who's accused you of anything?" I reply calmly.

She scoffs and turns on her expensive heel, heading towards the door.

Only the moment she opens it she freezes.

"Not leaving so soon, are you?" Levi asks, stepping forward into the room. It forces Talia to fall back until she collapses into her chair.

She looks between the two of us, fear in her eyes hidden beneath the air of superiority she's always tried to flaunt.

"I found this in my room," I tell her, waving the phone in her face. "Seemed odd that my wife would happen upon it the day you arrived."

I don't want to outright tell her I know she planted it. I want to see what information she's willing to offer up on her own first.

Talia looks like she could vomit at my feet.

"Don't make me ask again."

"I just wanted to help her," she rushes out, her gaze ping-ponging back and forth between Levi and me. "She was so lonely and sad. I felt bad for the poor girl."

She dissolves into tears. Big, fake alligator tears that have her makeup running down her cheeks. Levi steps back, leaning against the wall and watching while I step around my desk.

"I'm sorry," she sobs. "I didn't know she wasn't allowed to have a phone."

I step behind her, and a sob wracks her shoulders, her head falling forward until my lips are close to her ear. The scent of her perfume is all wrong. It's not vanilla and honey, but lavender.

"Very good," I murmur, and a shiver rolls through her. "But I don't believe you."

Her head snaps up, tears instantly shutting off when I step back around to her front.

"Christian." She reaches for me, and I step away, putting some distance between us. "You have to believe me. I didn't have a choice."

I cock a brow, staring down at her tear-streaked face, and wait for her to continue. If she thinks the tears are going to work, it's just more proof of how little she knows me.

"You made sure Mila had this. Why?"

"You don't understand—"

"I understand that you put her in danger," I reply cooly. "I don't take lightly to that."

"Someone . . . threatened me . . ." she trails off, lowering her eyes to her hands. She twists them together in her lap. Levi's eyes meet mine over her head.

"Who?" She doesn't respond. "Who?" I bark, and she jumps at my voice.

"I don't know!" She scrubs a hand over her teary face. "I never saw them. They wore a mask."

"What kind of mask?" Levi asks, staring at the back of her head.

She sucks in a shaky breath, letting it out on a shiver.

"It was of a clown. An evil one." Her watery blue eyes meet mine. "He came to me the week before the wedding and gave it to me. He had pictures of my family. He told me he would hurt them."

"And yet, you didn't come to me. You took matters into your own hands and put my wife in danger."

She glowers back and forth between Levi and I. Levi nods at me only once.

"Get out. Don't ever let me see you in Seattle again." I dismiss her, stepping back behind my desk. Lighting up the screen, Mila's still in our kitchen, washing the dishes now, and my body aches to go to her.

"This isn't you."

Talia shoves to her feet, rushing around the side of the desk. She reaches for me, her fingers fisting in the material of my shirt.

"I *know* you. You still care for me; otherwise, you wouldn't have left."

That makes absolutely zero sense, but I don't care what she thinks. Not anymore.

"Christian, you wouldn't throw our friendship away. I know this is *her*. She's jealous. Please—"

Stepping into her, she falls back against the wall, her eyes wide with fear.

"What you fail to realize is there's nothing for her to be jealous of. You and I were over the moment she stepped into my life." She flinches as if I'm causing her physical pain. "What you think we had was fake. A ruse because of a lie you created. There will *never* be another but her."

"I hate you," she whispers, blinking back the tears clinging to her lashes.

She's not sorry she did it. She's only sorry she got caught.

I'm sorry I didn't see her for what she was before Mila got put in the middle of it.

"Stay away from my wife," I mutter. "This is your only warning."

Tears once again slip down her cheeks, but it does nothing for me. Not anymore. In fact, all I can think about is getting back home and spending the night buried in my wife. When night falls, no one needs me, and I'm free to take my time memorizing her.

"Get out."

Talia stares at me with hatred and hurt in her gaze, but I'm past caring.

I stopped the moment she put Mila's life in danger. No one may understand it, but my sanity hinges on her soft smiles and sweet voice. The way she laughs and how peaceful she is when she nestles into my side in her sleep.

That's my life, and Talia fucked with it. I don't take that lightly.

"If you do this, I'll never forgive you, Christian," Talia breathes.

I step back from her; any ounce of care I had for her gone in the blink of an eye.

"So be it."

Walking through the front door of our house, I find Mila taking dinner out of the oven, singing along softly to a song on the radio. She can't carry a tune to save her life, and I didn't even know the old built-in stereo under the cabinet still worked, but I know one thing for sure.

I'd sell my soul if it meant coming home to her like this for the rest of my life. My gaze rakes over her. Perfect ass in her leggings. Pretty curls piled messily on top of her head.

Striking gray eyes when she turns and finds me leaning against the kitchen doorway and lets out a slight squeak, nearly dropping the glass dish to the floor at her feet.

"How long have you been standing there?" she snaps, her cheeks flaming red when I step across the kitchen. She places the dish down, full of what I know is going to be the best fucking lasagna I've ever eaten.

"Not long." I take her face in my hands, pressing a kiss to her forehead, then her lips. She relaxes in my touch, her hands coming up to rest over mine. "Just long enough to know you won't be leaving me to become a famous pop star."

She gawks at me, her eyes shining with amusement when I pull back from her, and I know I made the right decision to cut Talia off.

She always was more trouble than she was worth.

"Ass," Mila grumbles, reaching for the two plates she's got set out on the counter.

I swat her ass on my way to the wine fridge to get a bottle for us.

"Brat."

I'm pouring our glasses when her question catches me off guard.

"Why is your father locked in a room by himself?"

She says it so nonchalantly that I have to wonder if I imagined it. She locks eyes with me, waiting, and I run through every person I need to fire so that doesn't happen again.

"Why were you in my father's room?"

She lets out a huff and sets the spatula in her hand down.

"Because he was crying for help, and he was all alone."

I grit my teeth, a sickening feeling in my gut.

"Stay away from him, Mila."

"Why?" she asks, rounding the corner of the island. "Levi made it seem like he murders kittens for fun."

"Levi knew you went in his room?"

She blushes, clearly realizing she wasn't supposed to say that.

"Well, he heard your father laughing at me and came to help. He'd grabbed ahold of my wrist and wouldn't let go."

Jesus fucking Christ.

I scrub a hand over my face, downing a good portion of the whiskey in my glass.

"What did he do, Christian?" she asks softly, using that fucking look that gets her whatever she wants.

I hate that fucking look.

"Stay away from him, Mila. I promise you, he's well taken care of. He has two nurses that come stay with him round the clock. He doesn't need your help."

"Well, he must need some better nurses," she grumbles. "He was alone."

"And that's how it will stay."

She goes to walk away, but I catch her hand, tugging her back.

"Promise me you won't go in there."

Her gaze softens when she looks up at me.

"I promise, though, I wasn't planning on it anyway. The whole experience was creepy. Not to be rude about your father's situation."

"Why?"

Her eyes dart away before coming back to mine.

"He just said something weird."

"Like?"

She lets out a deep breath, a tremor moving through her.

"Well . . . he laughed. One of those loud, cackling laughs, like some kind of creature of hell," she says. "Then . . . he told me you were going to kill me?"

Interesting . . .

"What else did he say?"

She shrugs. "Just that his son was going to kill me."

"And do you believe him?"

She rolls her eyes with a chuckle. "I think if you were going to kill me, you would have done it by now."

Reaching up, I take her chin in my hand, tilting her face up to force her to look at me.

"Don't go in there again."

"You aren't the boss of me."

"Please?"

She's so surprised at my request that she falls silent, her cheeks flaming for an entirely different reason. I remember she had a similar reaction when I asked her to lower the gun from her head nearly two months ago.

"Fine," she concedes. "But you better find a better nurse. Yours suck."

CHAPTER
Forty-One

CHRISTIAN

After dinner, I have a call to take, and when I return, I find Mila in front of the floor-to-ceiling windows in the living room. Snow falls from the sky, blanketing everything in a spray of white that glistens like fine glitter on the trees beyond.

I don't know what's fucking happening to me, but I know it's her fault. My chest hurts when I look at her. My cock throbs when she touches me. Fuck, she's all I can think about, even when she's lying in our bed beside me.

Is this what love feels like? Like cutting yourself open, time and time again, just for the off chance you'll get to see their smile? Hear their laugh?

It really was too simple. I was fucked the moment I saw her. Before her, I was merely existing. Living to work. Going through the motions of what everyone thought my life should be.

Now, for the first time, there's something greater to lose if I don't come home. Something far more important than my own life, and I'm learning, I don't have much control over it.

I'll live for her. Bleed for her. Fuck, I'd take another bullet for her.

Ask me to give her up?

Good fucking luck.

"It's snowing," she says softly when I hand her a glass of wine and sit down on the couch across from her.

"First snow of the year."

"I've seen snow once. When Marcus took us to Aspen for one Christmas."

Every day, I find more and more things that I want to show her. Experience with her.

Guess we have to add snow to the list now.

"Mom loved the snow," I murmur without thinking, taking a drink of the whisky in my glass and watching the large snowflakes fall outside.

"Christian . . ." she starts, staring at the wine in her glass as if it holds the secrets to life. "Why was Talia here today?"

Fuck.

Her gaze burns when it meets mine, and I know what she's thinking.

"I told her I never wanted to see her again."

Her head snaps up from where she twists her fingers in her lap, eyes narrowing on mine.

"Why . . . would you do that?"

I shrug. "Because she made you uncomfortable."

"That's it, then?" she chuckles dryly, shaking her head.

"Not all of it," I murmur gruffly. "Because I won't tolerate someone disrespecting you." Her gaze tells me everything I need to know. "Whether I'm around to see it or not."

"She was your friend, wasn't she? Bella said you two were close after your mother and brother . . . passed."

"We were, but that was then, and this is now."

Though I would normally love the possessiveness in her gaze, I fucking hate it right now. I hate that it was put there at all.

"I haven't touched her in years, Mila."

Her shoulders stiffen, and her eyes meet mine.

"I didn't ask," she counters, though the bite in her voice is gone."

"Talia and I grew up together. Our fathers were friends. We all used to spend a lot of time together. Over time, she started to view me as hers, and I started to view the world with a cold shoulder after Mom died."

"You . . . were in love with her?"

"Fuck no," I murmur under my breath, then I scrub a hand over my face, knowing how bad that sounds. "I guess, in a way, I loved her. I cared about her. Didn't want to hurt her. I suppose I loved her in a way you'd love a friend but nothing more."

"You were engaged," she points out.

"We were," I concede, finally meeting her gaze. "It was the worst mistake of my life."

"Why did you agree, then?"

Fuck.

"I didn't exactly have a choice," I admit, and she pauses.

"It was a marriage of convenience?"

"More like an engagement built on a lie. The night we had sex, I wasn't thinking clearly. I was drunk . . ." I don't know why thinking back to that night makes me feel sick to my stomach. "Anyway, after, she told me she was pregnant. Then, proposed we get married. When I found out it was a lie when I overheard her speaking to my father, I broke it off."

She shakes her head, tears brimming in her eyes.

"I need you to know, Mila."

I don't know why. Maybe because I don't want any more secrets between us, but also maybe because I've never told a soul, and she's the only person I think I'd ever want to say it out loud to.

"She raped you," she breathes, and I don't try to deny it.

440

"Hard to believe a man as big as me could be raped by a woman as small as Talia, but . . . shit happens, I guess."

"Christian—"

"I don't want your pity, Mila." I can't look at her. I fucking *can't* look into her eyes and see pity. "I just want you to hear me."

Carefully, Mila stands from the chair and crosses the room, her eyes on mine like she's approaching a wounded animal. I lean back on the couch, watching her, my chest aching with something bleeding and unresolved.

Reaching for my whiskey, she takes it from my hand and places it on the stand beside me before slowly sinking down to straddle my lap.

Her hands rest on my shoulders, her gaze soft on mine. I force myself to look at her. Really look at her because I've been avoiding it since I opened my mouth. Instead of the pity I expect, it's something else that makes a tremor slide through me. A burning desire to protect that I know all too well.

Her fingers come up to my cheek, brushing gently over the scar on my face.

"I hear you," she breathes, her eyes shining in the firelight. "I hate her, Christian, and it makes me sick what she did to you. I know you don't want to hear that, but I hope karma comes after her for what she did."

She falls silent, studying my face. I can only imagine the shit she sees there.

"When this is all over . . . If you want to, I'll let you leave, Mila. I won't force you to stay."

"And if I want you?" she asks softly, her fingers sliding over the tattoo on my chest with our secret wedding date and her initials. My skin burns at the contact. "If I want to stay?"

"Why would you want to?" I ask, not to drive her away, but to understand.

Her lips tip up at the corners, her soft smile going straight to my cock.

"Because maybe I've always been in this as deep as you have. You just couldn't see it."

Her hands slip over me. Down my arms and back. Up to my chest and over my heart that I know is beating fast.

Her breath catches in her throat, her eyes slipping from mine down to my lips and back.

"You once told me we've all got demons," she says softly. "But I don't want to think about them tonight. All that matters is us right now. Not my past or your past. I just want to be with you."

Fucking hell, how is this girl real?

A tear slips down her cheek, and leaning forward, I capture it with the barest brush of my lips. She tilts her face toward me, and I take the bait, closing the distance between us and

Our breathing grows shallow as the kiss starts out soft, bleeding into something desperate and hungry.

Lifting her, her legs wrap around my waist, and I carry her back to our bed, laying her on the sheets.

"So fucking perfect," I murmur against her skin, kissing over the flat planes of her stomach and then moving higher, slipping her shirt off as I go.

I strip her bare and take my time worshiping every scar, every curve and mark on her body that she finds so unappealing, but I find absolutely addicting.

"Please, Christian?" she begs, desperately trying to get me closer when I run my lips over her inner thigh, not touching her pussy where she wants me.

I've never been a man who makes love. It always seemed . . . boring to me. Now, with her underneath me, I know even if we're taking each other to the brink of insanity, it's never been just sex with her.

She moans into my mouth when I toss my clothes to the floor and settle over her. I drag my lips up the smooth column of her throat, to her lips, and my chest feels like it's going to explode when I push inside her, a rough groan rumbling through me.

"Christian . . ." she whimpers when I take her slow, as deep as I can, feeling every inch of her clench around me.

Fuck, it's not enough. It'll never be enough.

"Shhh . . ." I breathe against her lips, giving her everything we've both been asking for and fucking her slow and rough, my groin brushing her clit with every pass.

Her legs wrap around my hips, her arms holding me tightly as if she can't bear the thought of losing me and I don't stop, even after both of us comes.

"I love you," she breathes against my lips, and a growl reverberates through me.

Neither of us has said it since the day we moved into this house. It's been a no-fly zone since. Both of us tip-toeing around the phrase like it's an armed nuke.

"*Fuck*, I love you."

I want to tell her to stay. To give us a chance. That even if I've fucked up every step of the way, I want to be a better man for her. I want that little bakery she dreamed about. The kids running around the yard, and the quiet evenings at home nestled under the fire while the snow falls outside.

I want all that and more. Fuck, I want everything, but who knows when this shit will end. When we're free of the past and can move on to our future.

So I tell her with my body what I can't say with my lips. Stay. Live a life worth living with me.

Whether it lasts a minute or a lifetime is inconsequential. I don't give a fuck how much time we have.

I want to spend it right here.

"Did you buy another house?" Mila asks when I lead her out into our garage after dinner.

She stops short when she sees the black SUV sitting in our garage. Coincidentally, it's the same one she showed me a few months ago when I asked her what vehicle she'd pick if money weren't an issue.

"You tricked me."

I grin. "Did I?"

She jerks her hand back at the new SUV. "What is that?"

I step up behind her, pressing my lips to the top of her head. "It's yours."

"What?" she jumps, spinning around to face me, her eyes wide and her cheeks red. "You did *not* buy me a car."

"Of course I did."

"I can't accept this," she shakes her head, attempting to back away from me—key word, attempting. I don't let her, only pulling her closer until her front rests against mine. I walk her backward until her until her ass is pressed against the hood of her new SUV.

"Of course, you can. You're my wife. My money is your money. Which brings me to my next point." I reach into my back pocket and pull out the new card attached to our account.

"This is fast," she whispers.

I fix her with a look. "You've been mine for years."

I grip her ass and lift her to the hood to bring her closer to eye level with me.

"It's too expensive," she winces, and if she didn't look so damned sweet, I'd spank her ass for not seeing the value in her that I do.

The money is easy. I can come by more whenever I want.

Her, though . . . She's fucking irreplaceable.

"Mila—"

"Christian, I'm serious," she frowns when I take her face in my hands, forcing her gaze to mine.

Her pretty grey eyes are filled with guilt as if the money I spent on the new SUV could have solved world hunger.

"So am I." Dread, hope, or maybe even a bit of both makes my chest tight. I can't tell which. They both feel the fucking same. "I need you safe, Mila." I search her face, feeling her heartbeat racing under my fingertips when they slip down her throat. "With your new job at the lodge, I don't want you walking there on your own."

My chest grows tight when I pull back and take the last gift I have for her from my pocket, holding it up for her.

Her eyes go wide when she sees the phone in my hand.

"I don't want that."

"Mila—"

"We nearly divorced because of a phone only a few weeks ago, and now you're giving me another one?"

"This one isn't traceable." I hold it out for her, and tentatively, she takes it. "I don't want you to feel trapped, Mila. And I don't want to keep you from your family."

Her eyes widen, and her lips part over a quiet breath.

"Besides," I drop my hands, running them up her bare thighs to part them. Stepping inside them, my cock aches with her warmth pressed against me. "I want to spoil my wife, and it's time for you to accept that that's what you are."

She draws her bottom lip between her teeth, her eyes half-lidded and hazy as she stares up at me. Her cheeks are flushed, her eyes soft and full of apprehension and desire. Like she needs me as badly as I need her, and that concerns her.

Leaning forward, I run my tongue along the seam where her teeth dig into her lip, capturing it with my own and tugging it free. She lets me slip my tongue into her mouth, dancing it across hers and tasting the mint of toothpaste on her breath.

A quiet growl slips up my throat, rumbling through my chest, and finally, she opens for me, letting me in. Lazily, her arms come around my neck, her legs around my hips, and she kisses me back.

I've never given much of a fuck about kissing. Kissing my wife, though . . . fucking hell. Her lips may as well be laced with fucking heroin.

My hands slip into her hair, angling her head to where I want her, and the blunt ends of her nails scrape along the back of my neck, pulling me closer, her soft whimper in my mouth.

I can't stop the wicked grin from pulling in my lips at my little wife's neediness. How bad she wants me.

"Jesus, are you two done yet?"

Mila jumps away from me at the sound of Levi's voice behind us, but I don't move. I love the blush that lights her cheeks, like we're two teenagers caught in the act and not husband and wife in our garage.

I chuckle under my breath, brushing my lips across hers one more time before I help her down from the hood.

"What's got you in such a pissy mood?" I ask Levi as he stomps past us towards the house.

"Women," he grumbles before the door shuts behind him.

Mila stares after him, worry on her pretty face.

"Let me speak to him for a moment," I tell her, taking her hand with a chuckle to help her down. "Then, we'll take your car for a test drive."

CHAPTER
Forty-Two

MILA

"What did Lily have to say tonight?"

Christian walks me up the front walk to our house. We've just arrived home after we drove my new car into the city to have dinner with the kids from Home of Hope.

He drove, of course, because watching Christian drive is one of the hottest things I've ever seen, but we drove *my* car and that's something I never thought I'd get to say.

From living a life on the run to a homeowner, fancy SUV driver, and wife, all in the course of a year.

My mother would be proud.

And then it remember the phone burning in my pocket.

I want to call her. I just don't know if I'm ready to hear her voice. The disappointment I'm sure she feels because I ran.

How do you come back from that?

"She wants us to visit more."

He chuckles under his breath, his hand tightening around mine.

"She likes *you*, too," I correct him.

Christian pulls me to a stop on the porch of our house, reaching for me. He takes my face in his hands, pressing a soft kiss to my forehead.

"I have to go meet up with Levi before we go to bed. Go inside; I'll be in in a minute."

"Okay," I smile. "Don't be too long. I'm going to go start a shower."

His chuckle ends with a groan. He swats my ass, and I smirk at him over my shoulder, making my way inside.

The room is warm against my cool skin when I step inside, patting Phantom on the head when he trots over to me happily from his fancy new dog bed.

And Christian thought he was going to shoot him. The man's just as attached as I am now.

"I don't know," I muse, his bag of food in my hand. "Have you been a good boy today?"

He stares at me expectantly.

"Yeah, I guess you're right."

I feed Phantom and change his water before I head to the bedroom and grab some clothes. Then, I make my way into the bathroom and start the shower.

Tonight was fun, but my feet are sore, and I'm ready to curl up against Christian and read until we fall asleep. We're almost done with our book, and I think I'm going to read him *Dracula* or *Frankenstein* next because he'd like that.

Tossing my clothes into the laundry hamper, I step under the warm water and let out a sigh.

I close my eyes, slipping in further and soaking the top of my head, letting the water rush over me in droves while I think about tonight.

Things are starting to feel normal . . .

Except, when I open my eyes, everything is black.

I freeze, my heart stalling in my chest, the sound of the water impossibly loud in the silence of the night.

"Chri—" My voice gets caught in my throat. "Christian?"

No answer.

Just silence and darkness.

Fumbling for the water, I cut it off, listening to the sound of water droplets hitting porcelain and the hum of silence in the air.

Even Phantom is silent.

Swallowing over the heavy lump in my throat, I reach blindly for the towel I'd hung up beside the shower.

This is fine.

It's just a power outage.

Nothing to worry about.

Christian said he'd be in shortly.

Unfortunately, no matter how many words of comfort I hurl at myself, none seem to quell the panic rising in my chest.

I have to be careful when I step out of the shower, wrapping the towel around myself.

I quickly dry off as best I can and slip on my shorts and Christian's giant T-shirt before I attempt to venture out into the bedroom.

No way in hell, I'm dying naked.

Pressing my ear to the side of the door, I listen for any signs of movement from the other side, my heartbeat hammering in my throat.

I'm about to sink back and hide out in the bathroom until Christian comes home when heavy footsteps sound, and I breathe out a sigh of relief.

"Oh, thank God," I groan when I open the door. "That was terrifying—"

No one.

The room is dark, save for the little light emanating from the moon burning brightly outside. The moonlight shining through the window does nothing but illuminate everything in a glow, making the furniture look like sleep-paralysis demons waiting to claim my soul.

Stumbling back, I crash into the wall behind me, startling myself.

Okay, Mila. This is fine. You've been through worse.

Someone could be hiding behind the couch.

Shut up.

Someone could be hiding in the closet.

"Phantom?" I call out, my voice too loud for the tomb-like ambiance of the house around me.

I don't hear him, nor do I see his sleeping form on his bed in the corner.

Where the fuck could he have gone?

"If you're playing a joke on me, it isn't funny."

I could find the power box. I have no idea where the power box is.

I could run to the door.

What the fuck do I do once I'm outside? I don't even know where Christian went.

I could wait right here until someone or something reaches out from the darkness and grabs me.

Fuck that.

I don't have shoes, but I pad towards the door anyway. Anything to get out of this dark room and get to some sense of safety.

Only when I reach out and grab the handle . . . it's locked.

And then . . . someone reaches out for me.

From the dark, hands grab me around the waist, hauling me back until I fall flat on my ass. The scream gets stuck in my throat, all the air whooshing out of me when a large body falls over me.

From outside, I can hear Phantom growling and scratching at the door, but I can't move with the man pinning me down.

I jerk in his grasp, my hand connecting with his cheek and my ring slicing his skin.

"*Fuck,*" he curses in pain. "Fucking bitch." The back of his hand connects with my face, and my head whips to the side, my lip wet with either blood or saliva.

He falls off me, and I attempt to scramble away, but he's too fast. He grips my hips, dragging me back until I'm underneath him, this time on my stomach.

No. No. NO.

Panic wells in my chest, and I buck underneath him, my fingers grasping at anything I can reach, but there's nothing there but the rug.

I'm truly trapped.

"Christian!"

The man's hand presses into my back, pinning my face to the carpet beneath me while his other slips between us to try and drag my shorts down.

"Does this make your pretty little cunt wet?" he growls, and shame envelops me, my scars searing underneath my clothes.

With all my strength, I rip my head back, my skull connecting with his nose, and the sickening crunch of cartilage shattering fills the air. Blood drips down onto my bare ass, and he lets out a growl of fury, grabbing my legs and pushing all his weight on top of me.

"NO!" I thrash violently under his hold when he snarls through the blood in his mouth, ripping at my shorts. A lance of pain shoots up my side, but I don't stop fighting him, wrestling to get him off me through the chaos.

"That's okay, sweetheart," he taunts in my ear. "I like a little blood on my cock." His fingers fist in my hair, dragging my head back at a painful angle, and a strangled cry rips from my throat.

Oh fuck.

"Beg for me, huh? Maybe I'll take it easier on you if you cry a little harder."

He chuckles through the blood in his mouth, the sound sending chills down my spine. I let out a shrill cry when his fingers grip my ass, my throat clogged with tears and screams. I can barely breathe with all his weight on me.

His other hand clamps around my throat, his fingers digging into my flesh and cutting off my oxygen.

Distantly, I register the sound of a pounding at the door mixed with the feral growl of my dog outside, but the sounds slowly drift away as the corners of my vision grow fuzzy.

"Tell me, sweetheart," the man growls, but I'm fighting for oxygen. My limbs are growing numb as a sense of calm takes over. "Do you like pain?"

"Do you?"

For a moment, I lie there, sputtering as I suck in air, unable to move as all of the man's weight is lifted off me. My hands and legs tingle as blood flows back through them, and my eyes are blurry from the mix of tears and makeup clouding my vision.

I roll over, scrambling to my knees and falling back into the wall, my heart nearly beating out of my chest. Christian holds none other than Collin by the throat, pressing him up against the wall opposite me, his gaze darker and more potent with fury than I've ever seen it before.

He snarls, his fingers tightening around William's throat until his face takes on a blue hue from the lack of oxygen.

"Please," Collin manages to croak, fingers clawing at Christian's hands, but Christian's grip only tightens, his eyes wild and his face so blurred with rage that he's almost unrecognizable.

Christian shoves him back into the wooden wall, his arm shaking with the force of holding the grown man up off his feet. Collin chuckles, seemingly no longer concerned with begging for his life. He spits in my direction, a pool of blood landing at my feet.

Levi rushes into the room, and chaos ensues as two other men I've never seen before follow him. It's too dark for me to see much of anything, but a pain settles in my limbs, my breathing not quite returning to normal.

I reach out to pet Phantom's head, and a surprising lance of fire shoots through my hand when he whimpers from beside me, barking in my face.

"*Mila.*"

It's Levi falling down to his knees in front of me. He's got a flashlight, and he's shining it on my face, nearly blinding me while he looks me over.

Then his eyes go wide as mine threaten to close.

Why is the room tilting?

"I . . . can't breathe . . ." I mumble, my lips and fingertips prickling with numbness. Shivers ghost through me from head to toe, and I feel cold despite the sweat beading on the back of my neck.

"*Fuck!*" he grunts, launching to his feet. "Christian!"

"Get him to the fucking bunker," Christian growls from somewhere nearby, but I can't focus on anything.

Not even when Christian drops down in front of me.

"Baby, look at me."

I can't.

I can't open my eyes.

"Goddamnit, Mila, fucking look at me," he growls, but I can't. It hurts too bad to move.

And just as my consciousness starts to fade from the pain, I hear three little words that would seem crazy, were I not bleeding out on the living room floor.

"Call Paulina. She's been stabbed."

CHAPTER
Forty-Three

CHRISTIAN

"Get the lights!"

"On the table!"

I clutch Mila tightly to my chest, hoisting her from the ground while Collin is dragged from the house by a few members of our security team. The lights kick on, illuminating the dark, red stain in the grey material of Mila's shirt.

"What happened?" Paulina gasps when she rushes through the door, her gaze on my bloody wife in my arms. I'm not sure who called her, but I'm thankful she's here. I couldn't do this without her. Mila's head lulls against my chest, the knife in her side dripping blood onto the shining wood floor with every step I take. I hurry into the dining room, and Levi rushes ahead of me to shove the chairs out of the way.

"Fucking Collin," Levi growls.

"Collin?" Paulina gasps, but I cut off whatever she was about to say next.

"She's been stabbed." Mila's blood soaks through my shirt to

"Is she okay?" a small voice says from the doorway, and I turn back to find Ava watching the commotion with a look of resolute fear in her gaze.

I fucking hate it.

"Ava," Paulina rushes to the girl. "Take this. Call Toole. You'll find her in my contacts."

She shoves her phone into Ava's hand. Ava doesn't move, her eyes wide with fear as she stares down at Mila in my arms.

"*Ava*. Go," Paulina orders, and Ava's eyes snap to hers. "This is important."

Ava's eyes harden and she nods, turning on her heel and running from the room.

"Levi, tie her hands."

"No—I growl, but Paulina cuts me off.

"We can't have her ripping the knife out before Toole gets here."

"I can hold her."

"It's either this, or you run the risk of her dying," Levi snaps, and if I wasn't holding Mila, I know I would have punched him for the hell of it.

Paulina looks at me expectantly. I look down at Mila.

Fuck.

"Get her here quick," I growl. I place Mila on the table, and she stirs, big gray eyes fluttering to meet mine. I don't like how fucking pale she is. How her top is ripped, the knife breaking through the material of my T-shirt soaked in her own blood.

"Chris-tian?" she whimpers softly, and I brush a bloody thumb over her cheek.

"I'm here, baby. Stay still."

"It hurts." She arches her back, her eyes filling with red-tinged tears.

"I know. Look at me, Mila." Her hand reaches for the handle

455

of the knife sticking out of her side, and I grab her wrist, pinning it down to the table.

Her eyes widen, and she peers around at the chaos. I catch the towel Paulina throws at me from the other side of the room, nodding to Levi over Mila when he enters with two belts he must have gotten from our room.

"Do it."

Quickly, he wraps the leather around her wrist, then drags it underneath the leg of the table. Mila sees what he's doing, and her eyes grow large with panic. She tries to rip her hand away. But Levi keeps it pinned with his own, struggling to buckle the leather belt and hold her in place.

"No!" she screeches, and my chest tightens, listening to the agony in her voice. "Please!"

"Shhh . . ." I try to soothe her, but Levi rushes to the other side, grabbing that wrist from me, too, and repeating the motion until both her hands are secured to the side of the table.

Once she can't move, the panic sets in.

"Get her ankles," I growl. I press the towel in my hand around the handle of the knife, putting as much pressure on the wound as I can, forcing Mila's back to arch and a pained scream to rip through the air.

"Where the *fuck* is Toole?" Levi growls, struggling to hold Mila's feet.

"She's on her way," Ava rushes from the stairs, her eyes never leaving Mila.

"Ava, towels," Paulina orders without even looking at her, still rushing around the room to get things ready for Toole. Mila never stops jerking around, only causing me to move the blade in her side.

"*Fuck*," Levi groans when she manages to kick him in the side of the head, but he secures her feet, and Mila's wide eyes meet mine.

"Don't do this to me," she pleads, tears swimming in her soft gray gaze. It feels like I swallowed battery acid.

"Shh . . ." I stroke my free hand over the top of her head. "It's going to be okay."

She shivers, her lips quivering with each breath, and I fucking hate the fear in her eyes.

Her eyes flutter, and I know her consciousness is fading fast.

"Mila," I growl, tapping her cheek, and her eyes open only for a moment to meet mine.

Then, her head lulls to the side, and she passes out again.

The sound of Collin's cries fill the air when I enter the bunker hidden in the trees behind Mila and I's house two hours later, shutting the door behind me with a heavy thud.

Dr. Toole, a friend of Home of Hope and the only doctor I'd trust to call in a time like this, arrived right after Mila passed out and began the process of removing the knife. Luckily, Collin didn't manage to get as deep as I'd thought, and none of her organs were hit. If they had been, I'm not sure I'd be standing here right now.

I watch Levi punch Collin. Collin's lip is busted, his teeth tinged with the red of his blood. Unfortunately, for him, this is the best he'll look for the rest of his miserable life.

"What the fuck?" Collin spits a mouthful of blood onto the floor at Levi's feet. "He send baby brother to do the dirty work for him?"

I chuckle darkly under my breath, sticking to the shadows.

Oh . . . You're going to beg for what Levi's doing to you when I get to you.

"How's his little bitch? She bleed out, yet?"

Levi shrugs. "Why don't you ask him yourself?"

Stepping from the shadows, Collin's eyes go wide when he sees me stalking toward him.

"Wait—" he jerks in the chair, but it's bolted to the floor.

My fist connects with his cheek, knocking his head back in the metal seat.

"I've been dreaming of this day, Collin."

My knuckles fucking hurt, but I ignore them.

Collin's face is bloody, his eye swelling shut from what Levi's already done to him tonight.

He uses his one good eye to glare at me, and I almost wish he could see out of both, so he could know what I'm about to do to him.

"You touched my wife," I murmur, stalking around him. He rolls his neck, pretending like he's not shitting his pants, but I can see the tightness in his shoulders. He knows there's no way he makes it out of this room alive. "I really don't like when people touch my wife."

"I did what I had to do. I hope your little bitch dies from what I did to her."

I smile when I step back in front of him. His eyes flash with fear.

"We'll see who the little bitch is when I'm done with you."

"Why did you go after Mila tonight?" Levi asks, stepping forward. Collin spits at his feet in response.

I twist my knife around in my palm.

—Then, I sink it into his thigh.

"*Ffffuck!*" Collin curses, throwing his head back and gritting his teeth against the pain. I'm happy to see tears well in his one good eye.

"Now, we can't have that, dear Collin." I stoop down, running my thumb across his lashes and wiping away the tears that linger there. He glares up at me, his chest heaving through the pain. "I want you to *see* what's happening." I shrug, standing back. "You need to know what happens when you touch a Cross."

"Who the fuck are you working with?" Levi snaps, cracking his knuckles. They're already bruised and bloody.

"Fuck you."

"Unfortunately, I'm straight, but I know a few men that might be down," Levi looks him over. "Maybe if they couldn't see your face."

"What the fuck do you want?" Collin spits.

"Answers. You hurt one of us."

He laughs maniacally. "You should have seen what else I was planning for her."

I smirk, the blood roaring in my ears. I can feel my self-control threatening to snap, but that's what he wants. He wants me to lose control so we don't get the information we need.

Stepping back to the table across the room, I look over the instruments. Grabbing the bolt cutters made for industrial-style bolts, I step back over to Collin, laying them over my shoulder.

"Collin, I really don't have time for games tonight." I look at the clock. "My wife's asleep in bed recovering from what you did to her. You're wasting my time."

"What the fuck are you going to do with those, Cross?" Collin challenges. "You think you can kill me and get away with it?"

I look to Levi, who nods.

"Yeah, I think we can."

"How about this," I stoop down in front of him, resting my arm on the bolt cutters. "You tell me who you're working for, and I'll kill you quickly."

"Fuck. You."

"*Or* you continue to waste my time, and I kill you very slowly. You'll be in excruciating pain either way."

"Go to fucking hell."

I chuckle. Fucker can't say I didn't warn him.

"Look around, Collin," I look to either side of me. "You're already here."

I stand back. "Release his hands."

"What the *fuck*?" Collin thrashes in the seat, but Levi's bigger than him. He cuts the binds and drags his hands around to the front. He secures his wrists to the arms of the chair with zip ties, his fingers resting over the sides.

I take the pointer finger of his left hand, positioning the bolt cutters over the flesh, visions of my wife fading in and out of consciousness from the blade in her side flashing through my head.

"This is going to hurt."

"*Wait*—" Collin fights, cut off by the sickening sound of bones crunching fills the air milliseconds before his screams.

Blood pours from the wound, and his finger falls to the ground.

"That's one," I tell him. "One finger for touching my wife. Unfortunately, I'm not satisfied."

"Wait, I'll fucking tell you!" he screeches when I line the second finger up. I pause, still holding the finger in the cutters.

"I know you didn't do this all on your own. You've never been a leader. So . . . who *did* you do it for?"

"I don't know!"

Snap

Another finger falls to the floor, and blood splatters my jeans and boots.

Collin's wails echo around the room, but I'm so far gone I barely hear them.

He hurt my wife. Tried to take her away from me. That's not something I can stand by and let go unpunished. Collin's going to die soon. It'll just be as slow and painful as I can make it.

"Try again."

"I told you, I don't fucking know!" Collin thrashes in the chair, and Levi circles behind him, holding his head in place. Collin spits, but it drips down his chin, staining his torn shirt below while I line up for a third finger.

"I think you do," I smile wickedly, closing the cutters around the digit.

Jessi Hart

"Fuck!" he screams, trying to break the ties that bind his legs to the bottom of the chair but failing miserably.

"One more time, dear Collin," Levi chimes from beside me. "We can do this around the clock. Slowly cutting off more and more until you're nothing but a rolling torso and a useless head."

"Please," he croaks around Levi's arm, cutting off his airway. "Please stop . . ."

"I don't think you're being truthful . . . are you?"

"You know more than you're letting on," Levi says with a smile. "This is your last chance. Give us a name, and we'll stop. You don't," he shrugs with a smirk. "We'll start peeling layers." He flicks the knife in Collin's leg, and he screams in anguish. His head falls forward, blood oozing from his mouth and dripping on his pants.

Defeat is a harsh fucking mistress.

"Your father."

Fucking finally.

Snap.

"What the fuck!" he screeches, his face red and dripping with a mixture of his own sweat and tears. "I fucking told you everything."

"And now you're going to tell me more." I fist the short strands of his hair at the front of his scalp and rip his head back to look at me. There's real fear in his eyes. The same fear he put in Mila's eyes. "What did he tell you to do to her? Kidnap her? Hurt her? Kill her?"

"Answer the question, dickhead," Levi grits in his ear, tightening his hold.

I've got to say. Collin's a ballsy little fucker. He has the audacity to smile cockily, blue eyes flashing with malice.

"Told me to finish what he already started," he smirked, and my blood ran cold. "Do what should have been done in the first place. Listen to her little cries for help and carve her up real pretty for you to find. Only this time, I'd make sure you couldn't even sew her back together with what I was going to do to your pretty little wife."

Red clouds my vision, the hum of a thousand bees swarming at the edges of my brain.

My wife. My fucking wife.

Seizing him by the throat, I shove his head back, baring my teeth.

I don't even think. Everything goes black.

I rear back, smashing the bolt cutters into the side of his face, and Levi falls back. I swing the bolt cutters as hard as I can, over and over, until the sounds of Collin's faint cries of pain die.

Adrenaline courses through me, and the only thing that stops me is when there's a crater in the top of Collin's head, his eye gone and his face unrecognizable through the blood staining his skin.

I'm not nearly as satisfied as I want to be when I toss the bloodied bolt cutters to the floor, my chest heaving with each violent breath.

Levi and I lock eyes.

A phone rings, echoing in the silence of the room.

"Yeah?" Levi answers before he nods to me. "She's waking up."

I look back at what's left of Collin.

"Go. I'll take care of the body," he says, lighting a cigarette despite the blood on his hands.

I nod to him, and head towards the door.

Mila's stirring when I step into our bedroom. Paulina is brushing a wet washcloth over her face, her expression grim.

"She's stable," Toole says, nodding to the knife on a tray in front of her. It's broken and jagged. Probably the only thing that saved her. "But she'll need a few weeks to heal. She can't be on her feet, or she'll risk breaking the stitches open."

I nod, watching the steady rise and fall of Mila's chest.

She's alive. She's fucking alive.

"I would like to stay here tonight," Toole says. "I want to be close."

I nod towards the hall. "Through the living room. The second door on your left. Should have everything you need."

"Good. Wake me up if anything happens. If she's in pain, give her one of these." She hands me a bottle of pills, and the rattle echoes throughout the room.

"Thanks," I murmur, knowing it's not enough for what she did. "For saving her."

"She saved herself. I just did the stitching."

She walks away, leaving me alone with Paulina and Mila. The silence is filled with my racing thoughts when I stare down at my wife.

"Chris-tian . . ." Mila breathes, her eyes hazy when she squints at me.

"Go to sleep, baby," I brush the hair back from her face. "I'll be right here when you wake up."

She doesn't respond, her head lulling to the side, and I know she's fallen asleep again.

Paulina moves to stand. "I'm going to get fresh water and bathe her."

"I'll do it. You go to bed."

She pauses, an odd expression crossing her face. As if she can't believe I'd like to take care of my wife.

She doesn't say anything, though, and instead nods, leaving the bowl on the nightstand in front of me.

"Is he . . ."

"He's dead," I respond, knowing her question before it even leaves her mouth.

She's silent for a moment, looking back at Mila.

"Good."

Alone with Mila, I stand and grab the bowl, crossing over to the bathroom. I wash my hands and refill the bowl with warm water and soap, grabbing a fresh washcloth and heading back to Mila.

Pulling a chair up beside her, I start to wash her face, then the blood that's on her arms, and finally, her stomach that's not covered by the thick gauze covering her wound.

"I'm sorry, baby," I whisper, even if I know it doesn't make up for what happened to her. "I'll make it right."

When she's cleaned up, I dump the bowl and stoop down to press a soft kiss to her forehead. Then I pull the chair closer and sit down, closing my eyes to try and get a few hours of sleep.

Unfortunately, I have a feeling it'll be plagued with the sound of Collin's voice uttering *that* name.

Reaching for Mila's hand, I hold it in mine, pressing my lips to the ring on her finger.

If something happened to you, I'd never forgive myself.

Gritting my teeth, I pull my pistol out and place it in my lap before I lean back and close my eyes.

Tomorrow, I have some tough decisions to make.

Right now, I focus on the feel of her skin against mine and quietly plot my revenge.

CHAPTER
Forty-Four

MILA

I'm underwater.

At least . . . that's how it feels when my consciousness slips in, my mind waking up before my body.

I'm no longer in the dining room I remember from flashes of my memory. I'm in our bed.

Opening my eyes, I blink against the rush of nausea pooling in my stomach. My side is sore. My back and limbs ache. I feel like I rolled down a mountainside.

A soft whimper comes from beside me, and I raise my head when Phantom nudges my fingers, big brown eyes lit with worry.

"I'm okay, buddy. I survived."

Unfortunately.

My body hurts when I pull myself up to sit. Looking around, everything's the same as when I left it. The only difference is it's empty, with no sign of my husband anywhere.

Odd.

I let out a quiet groan when I move my legs to the edge of the mattress before the reality of what happened dawns on me.

Oh. Right. Of course, I'm sore. I got stabbed.

My legs don't want to move, but I force them, climbing to my feet. I'm shaky, my body threatening to give out, but I've got to pee like crazy.

Shuffling toward the bedroom door, I twist the handle, pulling it open, only to freeze at the sound of voices nearby.

"She doesn't need to go to a hospital," Christian growls from somewhere nearby. "Do you know how easily accessible she'll be?"

"She wasn't easily accessible with you?" a woman's voice argues back, and my heart bottoms out in my chest.

I know that voice.

"Exactly, and look what the fuck happened? In case you forgot, this is partially *your* fault. Need I remind you of the little temper tantrum you threw when I married her?"

"I told you to stop it, not marry her," she scoffs.

"And yet, you did nothing to stop it from your end. I did what I had to do. You're not the victim in this situation, Monica."

Her voice is cool when she responds. "You're going to kill her."

"I'm keeping her alive," Christian fires back when I round the corner from the bedroom, stopping dead in my tracks when my eyes land on the woman standing at our kitchen table.

"M-mom?"

She's not real.

This isn't real.

It's just another dream my mind created to torture me. My mother is in LA. She doesn't know I'm still alive, and she doesn't know that I was stabbed.

But . . . when she steps closer to me, and the familiar, comforting scent of her perfume wafts over me, tears sting in the backs of my eyes.

Awfully realistic for a dream.

Her eyes go wide when she sees me, and my first thought is how

I must look. A rush of emotion takes over and I sway on my feet, but Christian is there to catch me when I take a stumbling step back.

"You're supposed to be in bed," he grits through his teeth, holding me against his chest.

"I . . . heard you guys."

"Mila," Mom breathes, her eyes filling with tears. She holds her arms out, crossing the kitchen, but at the last second, Christian puts his arm in front of her to keep her from hugging me.

"Stitches," he mutters darkly, and she concedes, pressing a kiss to my forehead instead. When she pulls back, her blue eyes are soft, filled with all the pain of the last six months. Pain I caused her.

"You're really here," I breathe, and she smiles through the tears in her eyes, taking my face in her hands.

"My baby," she whispers, sucking in a ragged breath, her thumb stroking my cheek. "My God, how I've missed you."

"What are you doing here? How did you find me?"

She pauses, looking over at Christian, and warmth slips through me.

He called her. Of course, he called her.

"I have so much to tell you." My voice sounds far away like I'm sinking beneath the surface of the rough waves again.

Mom smiles, releasing me. "We'll have plenty of time for that later."

I nod, thankful that sleep is in my future. Now that the adrenaline has worn off, all I want to do is sleep.

I attempt to pull away and hug her, but the room sways around me, and Christian growls under his breath, stooping down to lift me into his arms.

I don't want to be carried, but I fear I have no choice. I'm not sure I could take another step on my own.

Christian takes me to the bathroom first, unfortunately standing guard while I have the longest pee of my life. When I'm done, he carries me back into the bedroom.

He lays me in the bed, and I suck in a shallow breath through my teeth, the pain in my side stronger than ever.

Grabbing a bottle from the nightstand and a glass of water, Christian hands me a little white pill before forcing me to drink the entire glass of water.

"Get some sleep. If you need to get up, I'm right outside."

"Mom—" I start, but Christian silences me with a kiss on my forehead.

"She's not leaving anytime soon," he murmurs before pulling away too quickly.

He tucks me in, covering me with blankets up to my chin, and it's then that I finally get a good look at him. He looks exhausted. Like he hasn't slept in days. There's a fine stubble growing on his cheeks, and his eyes are ringed with purple.

Reaching out, I catch his hand, and he stalls, looking down at me with indecision. I don't want him to go. Especially not when he looks like this.

"Please . . ." I whisper, knowing once I get him into bed, he'll fall fast asleep. "Just until I fall asleep."

His jaw ticks, and I think he's going to refuse me, but in the end, he lets out a sigh, scrubbing a hand over his face. As if I'm made of glass, he slides onto the bed beside me, overtop of the covers.

"Only until you fall asleep," he murmurs, his voice gruff. "I've got work to do."

"I know," I say softly, forcing a smile to my lips. Relief floods through me when he nestles beside me and lets me put my head on his shoulder, soaking up his warmth and the scent of him I've become addicted to.

The moment of tenderness strikes me, but when I close my eyes, breathing deeply, he presses his lips to my forehead, his kiss lingering on a quiet groan.

"What happened to Collin?" I ask, but I'm not sure he heard me.

"I took care of it," he says quietly, his knuckles brushing down the side of my face. "I'd do anything for you."

I want to open my mouth and tell him I love him, but my mind and my body are not working as a team. Sleep is pulling me under, my brain growing foggy. Even still . . . I don't miss his quiet voice rising above it all.

"Sleep, Mila. We'll be here when you wake up."

"I can do it, Christian."

"So can I."

I growl at him under my breath, sliding from his arms into the bed. He situates me against the pillows, propping one up behind me so I can watch the TV he had installed last week. Stepping back from the bed, he covers me up, tucking me in like a child.

"Better?"

"I can walk myself from the bathroom."

"And I can carry you."

Asshole.

"Is this how it's going to be if we ever decide to have children?"

"There's no deciding anything. You'll have all my babies whenever this shit is over."

My cheeks flame, and my heartbeat pitter-patters in my chest.

"Enough," My mother scolds, rushing to the other side of the bed. "You'll stress her out. Let me brush your hair, Mila."

"I'm stressing her out, am I? You can't brush curls," Christian scoffs. "Everyone knows that."

Yep. This is my life now. I can't decide who's more of a helicopter nurse. My mother or my husband.

"Can both of you back up, please? My show is on."

"Look," Mom snaps at Christian. "You've gone and gotten her addicted to television."

Rolling my eyes, I throw the comforter over my head. Neither one notices. They don't notice anything unless it has to do with their daily pissing match.

"She's not addicted. She's a grown woman who was stabbed. And in case you forgot, my wife."

"Stabbed under *your* protection," Mom fires back. "And forced."

"And she has the option to divorce me at any moment."

Mom scoffs. "How noble of you."

"Honestly, you both suck right now," I grumble from under the covers, but neither listens to me.

I may as well be mute.

Deciding I've had enough of listening to the two people I love most in the world rip each other to shreds, I grab the remote, steadily turning the TV up higher until they're forced to fall silent.

Both stare at me in annoyance and disbelief.

I stare at the TV.

It's been four days since I was turned into a kabob, and my side hurts. My head hurts from listening to Christian and my Mom. My back hurts from lying in the same place for so long.

. . . my pride hurts because I have to be carried to and from the bathroom, and painkillers are hell on your system. I haven't had even a spare second worth of privacy, and it's driving me insane.

Great way to really break in a new (to me) marriage.

Now that I have their attention, I turn the TV back down.

"We need to talk," I start, and Mom's already cutting me off.

"You need to relax—"

"You need to shut up for five seconds and fucking listen."

Mom's mouth clamps shut.

Christian hides his smirk by brushing a thumb over his lips.

470

"Sorry," I wince. Did I mention painkillers make me cranky? "Look, I love both of you, but you're smothering me."

"We're just trying to do what's best for you," Mom says, and Christian shoots her a look, which she shoots right back.

I feel like I'm in the middle of an old-west showdown.

"What's best for me right now is just rest. I can't do that if I'm worried about you two at each other's throats."

"You can rest when we get home," Mom says, and ice slips up my spine.

"Excuse me?"

She blinks.

"When we get back to LA . . . You *are* coming home, right?"

Is she serious?

"I'm not leaving."

"It's not safe here, Mila."

"In case you forgot, I was raped and beaten half to death in LA, Mom. Nowhere is safe."

She winces at the mention of what happened, her eyes growing pained. I've always tiptoed around that night, but if there's anything being stabbed taught me, it's that you can't hide from the pain.

Sooner or later, it'll find you, and when it does, it'll reap hell on your emotions if you bottle up for long enough.

"I know you're still struggling with this, Mila, but I want—"

"What about what I want?" I ask, and a hush falls over the room. Christian leans back against the dresser, his eyes on the floor in front of him and his shoulders stiff.

Mom, on the other hand, has nothing to say.

I do, though.

"I'm not leaving. I'm staying . . . with my husband"

Christian's eyes snap to mine. As if he actually thought a knife to the stomach would be enough to send me packing.

At this point, I'm not sure a nuke could tear me from his side.

"But Savannah and Mason . . . Hannah, they miss you."

"They can visit her here when she's ready," Christian says, pushing off the dresser. He crosses the room, stopping at the side of the bed. I miss him. I've slept alone for the last three nights because he refuses to lay beside me for fear of hurting me, and I miss the scent of him on my skin in the morning.

Bending down, he places a kiss on my forehead, his lips lingering like he's memorizing my scent.

"I've got a meeting. Will you be okay until I get back?"

"I'll be okay," I say softly, my heart rolling from the softness in his eyes. "I love you."

"I love you," he says, brushing his knuckles down the side of my face before he pulls away and steps out the door, leaving Mom and me alone.

Mom sighs heavily and falls down in the chair beside my bed.

"I can't believe he would go to a meeting right now," she grumbles.

"Can you stop?" I snap, my temper flaring, and in turn, my side cramps too.

Mom just glowers at me like a scolded child.

"Why are you being so hard on him?"

"Because he abandoned you—"

"Because you told him to," I snap, interrupting her.

She falls silent.

"Christian married me to keep me from being forced into marrying one of Marcus's friends. You know, because you allowed him to auction me off."

"I asked him to stop it. Not marry you."

"Call it toxic or a mistake or a violation," I shrug. It hurts. "I don't care. It's between Christian and I and no amount of nasty comments hurled his way will change the outcome."

"You can't tell me you're *not* considering a divorce. At the very least, an annulment?"

I shake my head.

"At first . . . I wasn't sure. Then I realized, even if he had asked me, the outcome would be the same. I love him, Mom."

She purses her lips, and I know she wants to argue. That's just who my mother is.

I sigh, leaning my head back against the pillows. One thing about being a human pincushion? Sudden bouts of exhaustion.

"We've both made mistakes, Mom. You have, too. What matters is how we move forward."

She purses her lips, looking at the television. A commercial for bridal gowns flashes across the screen.

"You didn't get that, Mila," Mom says quietly, her eyes settling with tears. "I know he loves you. I know you love him, I'm just . . . sad all of that was taken from you."

So that's what this is about. Her own feelings of guilt.

"Who's to say I even wanted it?" She pauses, looking at me like she's finally seeing me for me and not a replica of herself.

"What do you want?" she asks carefully, and I shrug.

"Christian," I answer without thought. "A family. A comfortable home and to feel safe." I scratch Phantom's head, where he lays beside me on the bed. "I wanted a dog, and I found one."

"That's not a dog," Mom says warily, eyeing him like he might turn ravenous at any second. Phantom eyes her back, cocking his head with sass. "That's a creature of hell."

"Don't listen to her, sweetheart," I coo, petting his head. He lays his chin on my leg, closing his eyes. "He saved me, in a way. Kind of like I saved him."

"Well, I suppose he does love you."

"Christian saved me, too."

She sighs.

"He's like one of my kids," she grumbles. "He just pissed me off. Took my baby from me."

I can't help but laugh.

"I'm not a baby anymore, Mom. I'm twenty-four."

"You'll always be my baby. Big, scary husband or not."

CHAPTER
Forty-Five

CHRISTIAN

It's been three weeks since Mila was stabbed and three weeks with no news on the whereabouts of Sebastian. I've been hunting nearly every day and night, scouring the internet and calling in favors with old "friends", but there's been no trace of him.

Between that, the presence of my mother-in-law up until last night, and missing my wife, I'm on edge all the time. There's not a moment that goes by that I'm not either thinking about killing the man who hurt her, or searching for him.

"You really think Collin was telling the truth?" Levi asks out of nowhere when we get back to my office. We just went through Collin's room and other than a few pictures of my sister that pissed us both off, we found nothing that would give us any leads.

"I think he had no choice."

Levi's gaze snaps to mine, confused.

"What does that mean?"

I lower my voice, listening for the sounds of Mila in the house. She was reading in the nook of our bedroom across the house when last saw her.

"It means he's running out of options. You don't stay hidden for this long and whoever's doing this . . . it's personal."

"Could be someone you put away."

I shake my head. "There are too many similarities. It doesn't add up."

"And what are you going to tell Mila? When this is over?"

"The truth. She needs to know."

"Pretty fucked-up truth."

"Got any better ideas?"

He chuckles under his breath, straightening.

"She's tough. Scrappy. She can handle it."

"Better not let her hear you say that," I muse.

Just last night, at dinner, he'd called her scrap and I thought she was going to smash her plate over his head.

I can't say it wouldn't have been funny. Just that our dining room table has seen enough blood for the next hundred years.

"It's her mother I'm worried about," he grimaces. "That woman may as well lead our army. She's got the balls for it."

I chuckle. That sounds like Monica Parker.

"She's hard to get along with," I concede. "But she means well, in the end."

"You really think we can do this?" Levi asks, looking out over the map. "Pretty big warehouse for two men."

"I want to help."

Both Levi and I freeze, staring at the doorway where Mila stands, looking back and forth between the two of us.

"No."

Her gaze narrows and she opens her mouth to argue, but I don't have time for it. Crossing around the front of the desk, I reach for her, but she steps back.

"It's not happening."

"You're going after him, aren't you? My stalker."

"Mila," I take her by the shoulders. "I don't have time for this."

I step past her, checking my watch. I've got half an hour before I have a meeting in the bunker.

"You've been hiding out in that bunker for days, avoiding me."

"I'm not avoiding you."

"You don't come home."

Guilt washes through me, but I shove back at it.

I'm doing this for her. I'm doing this to protect her. Once he's out of the picture, we'll have our whole lives to argue over stupid shit. Right now, I just need her okay.

Unfortunately . . . my *wife* is not one to be dissuaded.

I step out the back door and stalk down the path towards the bunker while she trails after me, practically running to keep up.

"I want to help."

"Mila, I said, no."

"Why?"

Jesus fucking Christ.

"It's not safe."

"Neither is jaywalking. Do you plan to keep me locked up for the rest of my life?"

Thought's crossed my mind . . .

"If I have to."

"Then, I'll leave."

I stop so fast, she runs into my chest when I spin on her.

She glowers up at me, her lips twisting together.

"Want to run that by me again?" She doesn't respond, so I take a step towards her, forcing her to back up towards our house. "Because I could have sworn you just threatened to leave me."

Crossing her arms over her chest, she meets my gaze head-on.

"I'm not a puppet, Christian. You had your shot to figure it out alone, but I'm done hiding. I have *sat* in the *house* for months and I'm sick of it."

"Sick of a goddamned roof over your head?" I counter, shoving my hand at the house behind her. "Sick of baking or painting your nails or lounging with the dog all damn day?" She jerks back like I'd slapped her. "Sorry, I didn't realize it was so damned hard to lay low while I figure this shit out."

A tear slips down her cheek and I look away. It's not fucking fair that she can say whatever she wants, but the moment I see a single tear on her cheek, I'm ready to rip the world to shreds.

"Isn't that why your father took your mother to that cabin?"

Fuck.

"I'm going home," she says with finality when Levi steps out of the bunker, his gaze locking with mine over the top of her head. My eyes flick from him back to her. "I'll leave it up to you whether you can find the time to join me tonight."

Turning, she marches back up the path towards the house. Levi joins me when she pushes past him and both of us watch as she disappears inside.

Levi blows out a breath.

"Take it there's trouble in paradise," he muses, a hint of amusement in his gaze.

"Never," I lie. "Everything's perfectly fucking perfect."

"Sounds like a conundrum."

"You'd be correct."

"Should you go after her?"

I shake my head. I know Mila better than anyone. More than even her mother. When she's pissed off, she needs time to herself.

Turning away from the house, I resume my way towards the car.

"She'll cool off," I murmur when Levi follows me.

—I hope.

I'm sitting at my desk in my office when the call comes in.

Looking down at the unknown number on the screen, I can't stop the sinister laugh that leaves my lips.

I've been waiting for this call.

"Hello . . . *brother.*"

"I'll fucking kill you," he growls immediately. I lift the phone from my face when he spews a string of explicatives my way, and lean back in my chair.

A smile pulls on my lips.

Game on.

"I'm afraid you'll have to take a number."

"Where the fuck is it?"

"Your dick? I'm afraid you weren't born with one. The doctors said there was nothing that could be done.

"You think you can keep me from what's rightfully mine?" he scoffs. "You would have nothing without me."

"You *are* nothing." I sit forward, watching my wife asleep in our bed on the screen, her hand outstretched to my side.

"You're going to rot for what you've done. I'll make sure to bring Mila to your trial. Would you like that?" he sneers. "How about if I put a pretty little collar around her neck and walked her naked through the lodge? Think the guests would like that?"

"I heard they have homes for people like you. A place where you can get the help you need with your delusions. But . . . of course . . . you would know all about that, wouldn't you?"

"What do you want?" he grits, and I can hear him shaking through the phone. He's pissed.

Good. I am, too.

I can't help but smirk.

"Retribution."

"You know I'm going to find your pretty little wife, right? No amount of guards or money can keep me away. I could walk through your front door right now if I wanted. I'll make what happened to our mother look like child's play when I'm done with her this time."

"You would know all about what happened to our mother, wouldn't you, Sebastian?"

"And I'll enjoy doing the same thing to your whore when I find her. Tell me, does Mila still think about me?"

Violence slips through me in waves.

If he were here right now, I'd rip his throat out.

"You want to know the difference between you and me, Sebastian?"

"Aftershave?"

"While you're sitting in your little rundown warehouse, contemplating how you can get everything I already have . . . I'm plotting your death while Mila's asleep in my bed.

He's silent on the other end of the line, and I can't help but smile wickedly because I know the fucker's getting redder and redder by the moment.

"That what you want to hear? The way I fuck her every night? The way she clings to me as if she can't get enough?"

"When I find her, I'll make you regret the day you stole from me," he says, voice dark and malignant. "And my only hope is for you to live long enough to watch me pass her around to my men. Hard to find good whores nowadays."

I chuckle darkly, scrubbing a hand over my jaw.

"What you fail to realize is that as long as I'm alive? You'll never get the chance."

Click

I look to Levi across the room.

"Did we get it?"

He smiles a toothy, wicked grin.

"Got him."

CHAPTER
Forty-Six

MILA

I t's after midnight when Christian comes home. He takes one look at me, sitting in the living room, dressed in a silk robe, and crosses through to the kitchen.

Old Mila would sit and stew in our argument, but new Mila stands from her place in front of the fireplace and follows him. In the kitchen, I find him pouring a glass of whiskey before he plops down at the kitchen table.

He doesn't look up when I enter, but his spine stiffens like someone's jammed a steel rod down his shirt.

"If it's a fight you're after, I'm not in the mood, Mila."

"Me either."

It's not a lie. I'm not in the mood to fight with him.

Reaching back to the little stereo under the kitchen cupboard, I cut it on, and the soft sound of music floats through the air, the singer's voice filling the room.

Christian stares up at me, his gaze dark when I place my hand on his chest, pushing him back until he plops down in the kitchen

front of me.

"You pissed me off earlier," I murmur when his hand catches my thigh. Amusement lights in his gaze for a brief moment before he downs the entire glass of whiskey and pulls me forward.

"Is that so?" He pulls me to stand between his legs, his hands sliding up my bare thighs to the hem of my silk robe. I stop him, pushing his hands back, but he catches me, pulling me into his lap.

His hands feel so good on my skin that I almost forget all about my plan and beg him to take me to our bed. He's been so worried about hurting me, he hasn't fucked me since before I was stabbed.

I think I'm starting to lose my mind.

"Punishing me, little devil?"

"Something like that," I breathe, my legs on either side of his, straddling him while his hands come up to my hips. I can feel the hard ridge of his cock in his jeans where it presses against me, and I resist the urge to grind against him.

It's been three weeks without him and three weeks of feeling like I'm losing my mind. I never thought I would go from hating the touch of *anyone* to being starved for the touch of a single man that makes me feel like the only woman to exist in the world. Like I'm a coveted priceless artifact that he's sworn his life to protect.

"I'll take your punishment over your pain any day."

I narrow my gaze, agitation winding through me.

"I'm not a child, Christian. I've survived far worse than a stab wound."

"You have," he agrees, his eyes full of something akin to pride. "You're the strongest fucking woman I know, and that scares me."

I scoff. "Bullshit." Christian's not scared of anything.

"I saw you in a coma, Mila." His words hang heavily between us. "I saw the scars when they were fresh. I saw the stitches. Heard your screams of terror every night in your nightmares . . . you think that was easy?"

"And hiding me will only drag this out for eternity." I suck in a breath, willing myself to calm down. If I can't reason with him in words, I'll use . . . other methods. "I understand your desire to keep me safe, but you also have to let me live, Christian. I can help."

"It's not a desire. It's a fucking need," he says, not moving from the chair.

God, he looks like a damn King on a throne.

"And you are helping."

I roll my eyes. "What, by letting you fuck me?"

"By being the sole reason I live and breathe."

My breath catches in my throat at his words.

I step away from him, but he catches me around the waist, tugging me into his lap. I fight in his hold, but he only tightens his grip, his fingers digging into my chin to force me to look at him.

"You don't have to be anything other than what you are."

My heart flutters in my chest when he presses his forehead to mine and sucks in a deep breath.

"Let me handle the chaos. You worry about what I'm going to do to you when I get you to my bed."

My clit throbs at his words, heat filling me until I shudder. He chuckles low under his breath, his tongue rimming the shell of my ear.

In the silence, his phone starts vibrating on the table between us, *Levi* flashing across the screen.

I never knew his brother would be such a cock block.

"I have to take this," he says, his eyes searching mine.

"Right now?" I ask, but he's already answering the phone.

I move to stand, but his hand holds me in place when he answers, his gaze pinned on mine, daring me to move.

Alright, *Mr. Cross.* Have it your way.

Deciding my sole purpose in the moment is to be a menace, I slip my hands up his chest, reveling in the way his abs draw up under my fingers and the way his heart beats harder.

His gaze narrows on mine, but whatever Levi is saying must be important because he, otherwise, doesn't acknowledge me.

So . . . I take it a step further.

Leaning into him, I press my lips to the pulse fluttering in the side of his throat. I trail higher, running my tongue over the shell of his ear before dragging my teeth over it.

I nip and suck at his flesh, and a rumble reverberates through him, vibrating against me on his lap.

His hand tightens on my hip when I continue to move my hands over him, marking him with my teeth and tongue until I'm sure there will be bruises on my hips from his fingertips tomorrow.

No matter. He started this war.

I'm going to finish it.

Sliding my hands down his sides, I tug his shirt free of his jeans, and he lets me, his gaze flashing in amusement.

"Interesting."

What's interesting? I want to ask, but instead, I continue to slip my hands over him while his brother unknowingly distracts him on the other end of the line.

Grabbing what I want from his pocket, I slip off his lap and step back from him, holding up the pair of handcuffs I'd stolen from his back pocket.

"Do you trust me?"

His jaw ticks, his gaze flicking from the handcuffs in my hands then over the length of my bare legs underneath the hem of my robe.

"I'll call you back," he murmurs, voice thick. The heaviness settles between my legs. "I have something to take care of right now."

Hanging up the phone, he places it on the table beside him, leaning back in his chair and kicking his feet out in front of him.

God, he looks like a king on a throne.

There's a moment where my throat closes, and the room buzzes around me.

"What's your game, little devil?"

"Do you trust me?" I repeat. He'd said the same thing to me

months ago, and I'd fallen blindly.

I take a step towards him, and he stiffens but doesn't move, watching me with a hint of darkly satisfied amusement in his gaze.

"If you wanted me at your mercy, all you had to do was ask, baby."

I shake my head, sliding my hands up his chest and over the inked skin sticking out from under his button-up.

"We both know that wouldn't work. You would find a way to control the moment." I press my lips along the side of his throat. "I want this," I breathe in his ear.

Then Christian chuckles darkly, slow and menacing.

"Do you trust me?"

I lean over him, running my hands up his hard chest, teasing, and a tremor moves through him under my touch.

"Fine, little wife." His arms circle the back of the chair, his hands held tightly behind him. "Do your worst."

Bad idea, Mr. Cross.

Trailing my fingertips down his arms, I reach for him, leaning in once again to press a kiss to the side of his neck. A quiet groan slips through his lips.

This is dangerous, but . . . then, again, I seem to get off on danger.

"Don't worry, baby. We all have our weaknesses," I whisper in his ear, sliding the cuffs onto his wrists.

—And then I lock them.

Slowly, I step back from him, my heartbeat racing in my chest. He looks deranged. Like a man whose control has all but depleted, and now, he's not even seeing me.

He's seeing prey.

"You think these are going to hold me?"

I take another step back, my pussy throbbing from the threat in his voice.

Carefully, I reach back and turn the music up just a notch, and the deep vibrations settle in my core. Maybe it's the fact that we argued earlier, or maybe it's my newfound courage, but either way, I know if I think about what I'm about to do, I'll chicken out.

"I'll take my chances." I am as surprised by the strength in my own voice as he is. Slipping my hand down over my stomach, I pull the silk rope holding my robe closed and let it fall from my arms to pool at my feet.

His nostrils flare when he sees that I'm wearing one of the silver lacy pieces of lingerie he bought me.

"Uncuff me. Right fucking now."

His eyes glint almost black in the light. He's fucking terrifying.

I tilt my head to the side.

"No."

I can tell he wants to punish me by the dark, caustic look in his eyes. Part of me wants that, too, so I continue, seeing just how far I can push him until he breaks.

He's been so careful with me lately as if I might break from the touch of his hand. I miss his roughness. His desire.

"I wanted to prove to myself that I'm not what everyone says I am tonight. Scared . . . helpless . . ." I step around him in slow circles, the sounds of my bare feet padding across the floor. I slip my finger across the tight line of his shoulders, loving the way the muscles ripple under my fingers. "But then I realized," I lean down and press my lips to the side of his neck, and his entire body vibrates under my touch. "I can make one of the most dangerous men in the world fall to his knees with my touch. As helplessly addicted to me as I am to him. That's real power if you ask me."

He chuckles when I step back around to his front, circling him. For once, *I'm* the predator. Not the deadliest man in the room.

"Do you feel powerful right now, little devil?" There's no sweetness in his tone. Just pure, uninhibited darkness. I hate that my clit throbs at the imminent danger in his voice because it's just as he said.

I get off on his darkness.

Slipping my fingers over the lace on my stomach, I stop at my hips before moving back to my breasts. It has the desired effect because his eyes follow the movement, his stare dark as night. His jaw clenches, and his muscles pulse like he's seconds away from breaking the cuffs and fucking me into a pile of rubble on the same dining room table I almost bled out on nearly three weeks ago.

"Knowing your cock's hard right now. How badly you wish you could touch me? Yes," I breathe. "It does make me feel powerful."

"Is your pussy salivating for my cock, Mila?"

"Yes," I murmur. There's no use in hiding it. He can read me like an open book.

Leaning down over him, I place my hands on the chair and swivel my hips slowly, sensually to the low beat of the music. Each pulse of the bass is like a heartbeat in my clit until my core throbs.

Christian's tongue runs over his teeth as his eyes drop down the length of my body, not even bothering to hide the desire in his eyes as he watches me dance for him.

"Am I doing a good job, baby?" I ask sweetly, knowing that nickname is like playing with fire. Christian isn't the type to be called baby. His lips tug back in a snarl like he can't wait to rip my throat out.

"So fucking good," he says as he watches me. I run my hands over my stomach, twisting to slowly sink down to my knees. His breathing is tight and heavy as I follow the movements of the music.

Dancing for Christian may as well be sex. Raw, uninhibited sex.

I arch my back, bending over for him, and he hisses out a breath through his teeth that goes straight to my pussy.

Between his legs, my hands slip up his stomach, over the hard plains of his abs to his shoulders. I climb into his lap, my legs on either side of his and his erection against my pussy.

"Maybe I'll keep you like this. Climb on top of the table and touch myself. Keep you here wanting and watching." I tease, slipping my fingers back down, delighted in the feel of his muscles rippling under my touch. "You've been avoiding me. Hiding from me," I whisper, a devilish smile pulling on my lips. "I *was* going to ask you if you'd give me something, but now I don't know if you deserve it."

"Mmm . . ." he hums, his tongue running over his teeth. "You can try. I promise you won't like the outcome."

My lips hover over his, our shallow breaths mingling in the space between us.

"Maybe I want you to fuck my ass," I breathe, voice drawn tight over the lump in my throat. His eyes go blacker than night. "Maybe I want you to replace his touch with your own. Show me how good you can make it feel and chase away my nightmares."

"You've got one minute before I'm breaking this chair. Then I'm breaking you."

My pussy clenches at his words, but the heavy weight of his stare is intoxicating. I place my hands on his shoulders, lighting trailing my nails up his neck while I roll my hips. I arch my back, and when my panties brush up against his cock, he lets out a growl between his teeth.

"That what you want? Want me to show you that every piece of you belongs to me? That you were made to take my cock and mine alone and that anyone else who touched you was nothing more than a thief trying to steal from me?"

The hard notch in his jeans presses against the silk covering the apex of my thighs, and I bite back a whimper at the friction of his erection digging into me.

"Do you think I'd make a good dancer?"

"No." His voice is raspy, his eyes moving from my nipples pressing against my top to my pussy before he finally meets my eyes. "Hard to be a dancer if all your customers keep coming up missing."

He rolls his hips up, the brush of his cock against my clit, causing my head to fall back with a quiet whimper.

"That want you want, baby? Want to see me gut any man who

dares to see you like this? Fuck your ass in front of them, so they know it's *my* cock you beg for?"

"Would you?" I taunt, shifting and drawing a sharp sound of lust from between his clenched teeth. "Would you defend my honor, baby?"

"Honor? Fuck, no. I'll take it. Tie you to the bed and fuck your sweet cunt until there's no fucking doubt in your mind who you belong to." The thick bands of his arms flex, the chair creaking under the strain. "Your moans, your breathless little whimpers, the way you cry my name like you're calling out for God—it all belongs to me."

A shiver rolls through me at his words. A fever blooms from where we're grinding against each other ruthlessly. I'm not even sure this really counts as a lap dance anymore. His hips jerk underneath me, and I realize there's not a thing I could do to keep this man still.

"No one will ever make you feel the way I do," he says tightly. I hardly even recognize his voice. "You can run—I'll find you. You can hide—It won't matter." His tongue darts out, rimming the shell of my ear, and I moan at the tingles slipping up my spine, my eyes screwing shut, and my nails digging into the back of his neck. "At the end of the day, you'll still end up right here, riding my cock like a good little wife."

"Christian . . ." I whimper. Perspiration clings to my skin, my body shivering with the need to feel him inside me.

"You have five seconds to undo these cuffs, Mila." His voice is calm in my ear. Deadly.

I pull back, brushing the hair out of my face. To the outside world, he would appear unbothered. Maybe a little pissed off. To me, though, I can see the vein bulging in his forehead. The way his abs are drawn tight. The way his eyes are darker than the Marianna Trench.

God, he looks terrifying. Hauntingly handsome but terrifying.

"I don't think that's a good idea."

I knew handcuffing him to the chair would piss him off. I knew he would strike like a venomous snake. I just didn't know how.

Now that the time has come to pay the piper, I'm finding I'm not sure if I can handle Christian Cross truly unhinged.

"There's nothing to be afraid of, right?" The soft, gentle way he says it makes me think there is *definitely* something to be afraid of. "You've got one of the most dangerous men in the world willing to fall to his knees for you."

Three seconds pass where everything seems to hang in the balance of chaos and calm. I count them with my racing heartbeat as the world seems to move in slow motion.

"Last chance, Mila."

He's offering me up a Hail Mary before he takes what he wants anyway.

It's . . . unnerving.

So is the dark chuckle that rumbles through his chest when I don't move, and he holds the cuffs up for me to see them broken right at the center.

Oh, shit.

"Remember, you're my wife, and I love you."

"Why?" I ask breathlessly, and his lips tip up with a menacing smile.

God, that's terrifying.

"Because when I catch you, I'm going to fuck you like you're my whore."

CHAPTER
Forty-Seven

CHRISTIAN

S he runs as fast as she can, barely making it halfway down the hallway before I catch up to her. Stooping down, I hook my arms around her waist and haul her over my shoulder.

"Christian, please . . ." she begs breathlessly, and the dry chuckle that leaves my lips is nothing but deranged.

"What's the matter, baby? I thought you wanted to play dirty?" My hand connects with her bare ass, and she jerks in my arms. Unfortunately for her, she can't escape me.

I haul her into the bedroom and drop her on the bed, my eyes taking in the way her tits bounce with the impact in the smokey set of lingerie I got her.

I knew she'd look beautiful in it. I just wasn't planning on how much *I'd* like seeing it on her.

"I was going to go easy on you tonight," I murmur, stepping over to the dresser and grabbing what I need. I'd already gotten everything we need for tonight a few weeks ago, since we first talked about this. "Now you've pissed me off."

Her pretty eyes widen when I hold up the handcuffs in my hand.

Handcuffing her is the last step in gaining her trust. Her doing it to me first makes it even sweeter.

"What are you doing?" she asks when I cock my head at her, watching the unsteady rise and fall of her chest. Her lips part over her breath, and her cheeks are flushed. She's never looked more beautiful. Messy hair, soft pouty lips.

"Do you trust me?"

"Yes," she swallows heavily.

Fuck, my chest aches just looking at her.

"Turn over."

"Wait—" she starts in a panic.

"I won't ask again. Bend the fuck over."

She swallows, shivering as she slowly spins over, pretty fucking ass in the air begging for me.

I step up behind her, my eyes tracing over the curves of her hips, her ass, her back.

Fucking made for me.

My fingers trace the wet silk covering her pussy, and I hiss out a breath through my teeth.

"Did you like me at your mercy, baby?" I ask, my voice rough. My cock pulses when a shiver slips down her spine, and the need to bury myself in her roars in my veins. "Did you like knowing you were in control?"

"Yes," she breathes, her eyes screwed shut. She moves her hips from side to side, attempting to lessen the pressure, but I don't let her. My hand connecting with her ass causes her to yelp before the sound dissolves into a moan, and I bite back a grin.

"Give me your hands."

Surprisingly, she doesn't hesitate, and I bite back a grin, locking the handcuffs around her wrists at the center of her back.

"Fuck, Mila," I breathe, my hands roaming over the lace straps at her waist. "You look so fucking pretty like this. Waiting for my cock. Do you remember your safeword?"

"Always."

"Good girl."

I slip the material of her panties to the side, gritting my teeth at wetness between her legs.

"I'm going to fuck your ass, but first, I need inside you," I murmur. I step back, kicking off my shoes and jeans, and slip back on the bed behind her. My knees press hers further apart, and she hisses through her teeth as I push her even further.

"Keep them here," I order, my hand gripping her hip while the other strokes my cock slowly.

Leaning down, I press a kiss to her spine, right over the scar. I take my cock out of my jeans, fisting it in my palm and biting back a groan at the friction.

"You've always been strong, Mila," I tell her, aligning my cock with her entrance. "You just needed to prove it to yourself."

And then I'm driving inside her.

She screams, her hands reaching for something, but she can't move. Not when I've got her cuffed and trapped underneath me, my cock buried halfway inside her tight, wet heat. I surge forward, fucking her rough and fast. Giving her everything we've both been fucking aching for since we left for that godforsaken party.

The headboard bangs against the wall, but I don't give a shit. I'll rebuild the entire fucking house if I can fuck her on every single surface I can think of. Anything I can get before I'm gone.

I drive inside her, bottoming out in her pussy, and she lets out a groan at how deep it goes. My cock pulses as her pussy clenches around me, begging me to fuck her until she's shaking, but I stave myself off. I want to enjoy this. I want her to feel me inside her for days.

"Feel how tight you are, just begging for me?" I taunt, twisting the rubber around in a full circle. She jerks forward, and I chuckle, slipping it out before pushing it back in. "Fuck, you're so ready for me."

"Christian," she mewls, clutching at the comforter.

My balls slap against her clit, and I lose myself in the feel of her soft skin beneath mine. I pull her harder against me, the sounds of our bodies filling the room as her eyes roll back in her head. Her knees buckle as the first orgasm rips through her. Her muscles pulse around my cock, and I let out a sharp hiss at the tightness.

"That was one," I say in her ear, and she shivers, whimpering as I keep the same brutal pace. "Let's see how many we can get."

Grabbing the lube, I pop the cap and pour some along the curve of her ass. It glistens in the moonlight streaming through the window.

"Breathe out for me, baby. Let me feel you."

She sucks in a shaky breath, then releases it. I slip my fingers through the lube, slowly fucking her with my cock still inside her pussy, and press against the tight ring of muscles. She tenses, and I run my other hand up her back to calm her.

"Keep breathing, Mila. Let me in."

A shiver moves down her spine, and her breath hitches, but I move slowly, working my finger into her tight heat.

"Fucking beautiful, sweetheart," I rasp, groaning at the way she accepts me. I work my finger in and out of her, loosening her up before slipping back to add a second. Her body struggles against the sensation, so I strum my fingers over her clit in slow movements, matching the rhythm of my cock in her pussy. "How do you feel?"

Fuck, I'm going to come if I don't get inside her.

"Good," she trembles, her nails digging into the bed beneath her.

"Does it hurt?"

"A little," she purrs, her words ending on a breathless sound when I twist a third inside.

"It's going to be uncomfortable, but you'll crave it by the time I'm done with you."

I roll my hips into her, fucking her ass with my fingers and her pussy with my cock. I clench my teeth, my balls drawn up tight.

Forcing myself, I pull out of her pussy, removing my fingers before replacing them with the head of my cock.

"Talk to me, baby." My voice comes out a rasp, dark and depraved with savage need. I drizzle more lube on her ass before coating my cock, thrusting in my hand around the touch. "Tell me how you're feeling."

"I . . ." she breathes, but it ends on a sharp breath when I push inside just the smallest inch.

Fuck. Me.

She clenches, and my fingers slip underneath her to roll her clit in slow circles while I pull out and push back in.

"*Mila.*"

"It burns," she hisses through her teeth as the muscles protest and stretch around my cock. "It's too much."

I let out a dark chuckle that sounds insane, even to my ears.

"My cock was made for you, sweetheart." I push all the way in, picking up my pace until both of us are trembling. "Whether it's making you come buried in your ass or your pussy, you have always begged for me."

"Christian," she whimpers, a tear slipping down her cheek over the flushed skin.

Fucking hell.

Her breath catches when I slip deeper, feeling her body pushing back against mine as she accepts me inside her. Her cries dissolve into moans as my fingers continue to work her clit.

Fuck, this is like some really fucked-up endurance test.

"Fuck, that's it, baby," I grit through my teeth, heat traveling down my spine until I feel like I'm going to fucking bust. "Open wide for me. Show me how bad you want to please me."

I close my eyes at the moan that slips free from her lips. Methodically, I work myself inside her until there's nothing left for me to give, a tremor moving through me.

It's not lost on me that she thinks I'm replacing the parts of her that she lost. She still thinks I'm the good guy. Her knight in shining armor, even if we both know it's a lie. I'm a monster, just not one that has his sights set on hurting her.

I want to own every part of her. Body and soul as she does me, and I'll stop at nothing to get what I want.

Slipping my hand up from her hip, I wrap my fingers around her pretty little throat, lifting her back until my lips press against her ear while I fuck her. She groans, her fingers fisting at the sheet underneath her while my hips slap against her ass.

"I was the first to fuck your pussy," I grit, my voice betraying how close to fucking snapping I am. "Then, your mouth." She arches her back more as her arousal coats my fingers. "And now your ass. You know why those men who took from you don't matter?"

"No . . ." she chokes, and I know this angle has her feeling me in her stomach.

My tongue darts out to capture a stray tear on her cheek.

"Because they were just men," I growl. "Men stealing an angel from the devil's grasp. I'll rid the fucking world of them for daring to touch what's mine."

"Oh my God," she moans, her voice choked as I pull back, thrusting into her faster. I set a steady pace. One that makes me feel like I'm going to lose my fucking mind. Her ass grinds back against me, her back arching to take me deeper. She spreads her legs wider, granting me better access to her clit, and moans when I circle the tight bud faster.

"There's my perfect little wife," I praise. "So fucking greedy. How's it feel, baby?"

"Good," she breathes, voice cracking with desire.

"You want more?"

"Yes," she pants, sweat dotting her hairline and her face bright red as she screws her eyes shut.

"*Fuck,*" I growl fucking her deeper. Faster. She jerks in my grasp, so I press my palm to the back of her head, keeping her shoulders pinned down and her ass in the air for me. "Feel how deep I am, Mila?"

"Please, Christian . . ." She moves her hips back against me as much as she can with the angle we're in, and I meet each of her thrusts. Both of us completely lost to the pleasure as I fuck her faster. Her spine arches and desperate cries spill from her pretty lips as I tighten my hold around her throat, stealing her breath as she steals mine.

The sounds of our bodies meeting fill the room, and my fingers strumming her clit feel like they're going to fucking fall off, but neither of us stops. Sweat slips down my abs and back, heat gathered in the base of my spine to stave off coming for as long as possible.

"You going to come for me?" I nip the line of her jaw, my tongue darting out to lick the perspiration off her throat.

Fuck, I love that I can get her like this after everything. Her nails digging into my abs, her hands cuffed behind her as she gives herself to me fully. Trusts me fully. Frantic little moans spilling from her lips with each thrust of my cock bottoming out inside her ass.

"Yes . . ."

"Ask me to make you come, Mila," I order, rubbing her clit faster. "Show me how pretty you can beg for me.

"Please, Christian, make me come!" she cries, and I damn near break at her pleading.

She sputters when I tighten my fingers, crowding over her until my front is completely molded to her back. She sputters, her face growing red as I suck the air from her lungs and bring her body to the breaking point.

Her throat works to swallow underneath me, and when I tighten more, cutting her oxygen off completely, her eyes roll into the back of her head, and a choked gasp leaves her lips. Her ass clenches around me as the first waves of her orgasm crest, and wetness coats my fingers, but I don't stop.

I release her throat the moment her eyes roll back into her head, and she nearly collapses in my arms. I'm not ready to come yet, but she feels too fucking good. I shove inside her, milking my cock with her ass as I set a brutal pace.

"*Fuck, Mila,*" I grind through my teeth, my head falling back as the orgasm steals every little bit of fight I had left in me.

A rough growl slips from me, and I press my mouth to the curve of her shoulder, biting down on the flesh as my cock fucking explodes. My entire body tightens, my cock shooting inside her as her ass continues to milk me as I come. I freeze, everything in me drawing to a sharp point as my ragged heartbeat pounds in my chest.

"Fuck," I grit, fucking tremors rolling through me when I slowly slip out of her.

I've never come that hard in my fucking life.

Unfortunately, watching my come leak from her ass only makes me want her more.

I bend down, placing a kiss on her shoulder right over the mark where I bit her. She'll have a bruise there, and I like the image it paints in my head. At this point, I'm thinking of tattooing it on her so everyone knows she's mine.

Mila shivers beneath me, little aftershocks moving through her when I slip from the bed and immediately go start the shower. When I return to the bedroom, I find her sagging against the sheets, her eyes closed, and her breathing still heavy.

"Baby, let me see." I uncuff her hands, rubbing the red marks on her wrists, and she whimpers as the blood flows back to them. I press my lips over the marks and then slip my arms under her to carry her to the shower.

A bath would be better, but judging by how heavy her eyes are, I know she needs sleep. Stepping into the shower with her, I gently place her on her feet and work on cleaning her off. She shivers under the spray, and I pull her into me to hold her up. I press my lips to each part of her I wash, giving her little praises as I go because I know how much she likes it.

"You did so fucking good, baby. So good."

She looks up at me, smokey eyes boring into my soul. I expect tears like the first time I fucked her pussy, but instead, she's looking at me like at me with something I know I don't fucking deserve. Trust. Adoration. Like I hung the fucking moon.

She still thinks I'm a good man. Despite my actions, she still thinks I won't break her heart.

She doesn't realize I've never been a good man, and when the time comes, she'll hate me for what I'm going to do. She deserves better than me, but it won't matter in the end.

She'll never have to be afraid again . . .

After tomorrow, she'll never have to be afraid again.

No one prepares you for what love really feels like.

The maddening obsession to watch another person be happy. Safe. The knowledge that there's a single person walking around with your heart inside their chest, and at any moment, someone could snatch it away.

I've never been a sentimental man. I couldn't be. I've never needed another person to survive.

Until now.

If loving her makes me weak, I don't care. I'd gladly do it all over again to see the way her eyes lit up when I first told her I've loved her for the last five years.

Looking at her asleep on the bed, her lashes cast shadows over her cheeks. Her lips part over her soft, even breathing. It's not lost on me the difference in her now versus when I first came back into her life. How timid she was. Scared of her own shadow.

I'm also not forgetting how fucking numb to the world I was before I came back into her life. How I didn't give a shit what happened to me.

After everything, she's still the same soft, bright, shining light, eating away at the darkness that surrounds my heart.

Except now she's also mine.

Mila stirs in the bed, blinking her eyes open to find me sitting in the chair in the corner of our room, a glass of whiskey in my hand.

After I fucked her, I cleaned her off in the shower and brought her to our bed, where I held her until she fell asleep. Then, I forced myself to finish getting everything ready for tomorrow. Now, it's after three in the morning, and though I need to sleep, I find myself in the chair, watching.

Neither of us speaks when her soft gray eyes meet mine. Mila blinks at the room around her, looking at the darkened window behind her before her eyes find mine again.

"Come to bed," she says sleepily.

Fuck.

I don't move.

"I have somewhere to be tomorrow. I won't be here when you wake up."

Her eyes widen slightly, and realization crosses over her delicate features.

"Where?"

I shake my head. "That's not important."

She bolts up in bed, and the sheets slip down around her waist. My gaze slips over her, and I want nothing more than to climb back into bed with her and spend the night worshiping her, but we need to talk.

"You're going after him, aren't you?"

"I am."

"Christ—"

My patience flares. "Mila, I need you to listen to me."

Her mouth clamps shut at the sternness in my voice. Her cheeks flame and her thighs press together, and I resist chuckling at the need in her gaze.

"Our account information, the deed to the house, the titles to the cars . . ." She shakes her head, but I continue. " . . . are all in the safe in my office. My will is in there, too."

"I don't want any of it." Tears slip down her cheeks, and they burn in my veins.

"Mila, if something goes bad tomorrow, I need to know you'll be taken care of. My share of the lodge goes to you. All of it goes to you."

"None of it matters without you in it, though," she snaps, and a vehement need rushes over me. "I'm our lady, and you're my man, right? Let me come with you."

"No."

She jumps at the bite in my voice, defeat crossing her features.

I soften at the despair in her gaze but refuse to let her anywhere near this. "You need to stay here tomorrow. Understood?"

Slowly, she nods, and her eyes finally meet mine.

"I'm scared," she breathes, and it feels like she's punched me in the chest.

I stare at her for a beat, emotions swirling in my gut. Finally, I place my glass on the table beside me and stand, crossing the room back to our bed.

She lets me pull her into my arms and lay back against the pillows, crying softly against my chest.

This life we've built, it's everything I've ever wanted. The thought of leaving it behind tomorrow with no knowledge of whether I'll ever return makes me sick to my stomach,

It has to be done, though.

I press my lips to the side of her face over the tears streaming down her cheeks. My arms tighten around her as if I can shield her from whatever happens tomorrow.

"I'm going to fix this, Mila."

"Just come home to me," she whispers, burying her face in the crook of my neck.

"Always."

CHAPTER
Forty-Eight

MILA

W hen I wake in the morning, I'm alone in bed.

The house is quiet, save for the tap of Phantom's paws on the hardwood floor when he follows me out to the kitchen to start getting ready for the day.

I don't know how to navigate this . . . ache in my chest.

The uncertainty of not knowing whether or not he'll come home. I feel empty.

He held me while I cried last night and then let me get lost in him until the first light of dawn hit the horizon. He was different, like he needed to brand himself on me before he left and that scares me.

I may have marks from his hands, his teeth, his lips . . . I may have a delicious ache between my legs, reminding me he was there.

Hell, I even have his last name.

—None of it makes a goddamned bit of difference if he's not here.

They can have the money, the house, and the cars. I just need him, Phantom, and maybe our little island. Everything else is

I go through my morning, getting ready for work. I apply makeup, hoping it will give me a pick-me-up.

It doesn't. I still look as miserable as I feel.

I do my hair, though I know it will be frizzy and a wild mass of curls as always by the time I come home.

And then it strikes me.

When will he come home? A few hours? Days?

"God, this sucks, Phantom," I grumble through the toothpaste in my mouth.

The cock of his head tells me he agrees.

By the time I make it to the lodge, I've thought of every possible outcome of today's events, and I'm numb to everything but the anxiety swirling in my stomach.

—A feeling that's made worse when I walk through the back door to the lodge and find Paulina running around like doomsday is upon us.

"Where *have* you been?" she snaps, her eyes flaring with that fiery temper she conceals so well.

"I, uh . . . wasn't due in until ten."

She pauses, guilt flashing across her face.

"Right. I'm sorry, Mila. Have you seen Bella?"

"Bella? No. Not since last night."

"She isn't in her room, and she didn't come in this morning. I've been trying to juggle everything, but I *need* her."

"Okay." I lead her away from the front into one of the offices. "Let me call her."

"I tried that. Six times, to be exact."

"What's going on?" Ava asks, coming into the room.

"Have you seen Bella?"

Her eyes flash between the two of us, and she winces. "She left with a man this morning around five."

"What did he look like?"

Ava shrugs. "It was dark. He had dark hair. Kind of tall. I think it was that man she's been seeing."

Paulina pinches the bridge of her nose between her thumb and forefinger, letting out a breath.

"I swear, all of you are going to age me beyond my years."

I dial Bella's number, but it goes straight to voicemail, so I text her instead.

Mila: Need you to come in. Paulina is laying an egg. A big one. Send help.

"It looks like her phone is off, but I texted her."

"That's what I was trying to tell you."

"Paulina, why don't you go take a break? I can handle things for a bit."

"I admire your courage, Mila, but have you ever run a lodge before?"

"No, but I have common sense, which is basically the same thing."

I'll let Christian deal with the monsters. I'll hold down the fort at home.

Paulina studies me for a moment, uncertainty in her gaze.

"If I don't do a good job, you've got full rights to fire me."

"You'll do fine," she grumbles. "I'm going to take a nap. *Something* kept me up last night," she glares pointedly at Ava, who blushes a deep shade of crimson. "If you need anything at all, come wake me."

"We'll be fine," I urge her, lightly pushing her towards the door. "Scout's honor."

"Christian and Sebastian were Boy Scouts for two years," she grumbles. "It was the most stressful time of my sister's life."

She goes, leaving Ava and me alone, and that's when the jitters start back up.

"Mila, you're shaking," Ava points out, and I nod through the deep breath passing through my lips.

"Just nervous."

She stares at me for a moment, then her face pales.

"They're going . . . aren't they?"

I swallow past the lump in my throat.

"They already left."

She lets out a heavy breath, shaking her head and wrapping her arms around her middle.

"God, I never knew caring about someone would be this difficult."

My gaze snaps to hers. She blushes even brighter.

"I knew it."

"Knew what?"

"You and Levi."

She scoffs, her mouth falling open, but she can't form a coherent sentence.

"That's-that's not . . ."

"Your secret is safe with me."

She shoots me a look, but when I can't help but grin at her, she grins back.

"It's strictly platonic."

"So are Christian and I."

With the absence of Bella, the lodge doesn't run nearly as smooth as I would have hoped. It's easy to see now why she was so frazzled before.

I'm approached with a thousand and one questions about the art of folding towels, guests with complaints, guests with compliments, and problems I never would have thought existed in a lodge as grand as this.

Like a missing bazooka. Apparently, it's worth thousands,

though I'm willing to bet, judging by the sly grin on the dad's face when the kid is telling me about it, he threw it out.

It's not until two that I'm able to check my phone when Paulina comes back, looking well-rested and a thousand times more chipper.

I slip into the employee bathroom to take a well-deserved pee break and check through the messages. There are a grand total of zero because all of like three people have my new phone number, plus my mother.

There's still no news from Christian, but I push those thoughts aside.

The last thing I need to do is have a meltdown while I'm at work.

There are also no updates from Bella. I try to call her again, but it rings straight through to voicemail like the first time.

I chalk it up to needing a break and wash my hands in the sink while I stare into space and contemplate life as I know it.

My husband is going to catch the man that raped me, who just so happens to be my brother-in-law. My best friend is falling in love with my *other* brother-in-law, and my sister-in-law is missing.

Add on the fact that I'm going to start my period soon, and you've got yourself a very emotional Mila.

My phone buzzes, making me jump, and I look down to see Bella's name on the screen.

I blow out a breath. I'm really not in the mood right now, but I reach for it anyway, answering it on the last ring.

"Hello?"

"Hello, Mila."

Ice slips down my spine at the familiar edge to the voice on the other end of the line.

My scalp prickles and my scars burn under my clothes like they've been dipped in molten lava.

"I've got a proposition for you."

I swallow down past the lump in my throat, my hand shaking

where I'm holding the phone.

No, no, no . . . this can't be happening.

Forcing myself to meet my own gaze in the mirror, my grey eyes are clouded. Alive with fear.

"What do you want, Sebastian?"

CHAPTER
Forty-Nine

CHRISTIAN

"Where the fuck is this place?" Levi asks, scanning the buildings around us.

I silence a call from Paulina on my phone and pull up the exterior shot we were able to find online. She's called three times already, but I don't have time for whatever bullshit is happening at the lodge right now. I know Mila's safe. The last time I checked on her, she was getting ready in our bathroom.

"Jenning's Paper Company," I grunt. "It's supposed to be right fucking here."

My phone buzzes for the fourth time, and with a rough exhale, I give up, answering it.

"What?" I snap.

"Hello, Mr. Cross. My name is Mr. Trilliam. I'm the accounts manager over here at the Seattle Bank. Do you have a moment?"

"What is it?" I ask, irritation coiling inside me. "I'm in a bit of a rush."

"Of course. Your wife is here, sir," he says, audibly wincing on the line. "Requesting to withdraw a sum of two million dollars from your shared account. Because it's such a large sum of money, we need your authorization as well."

My hand tightens around the phone. The blood rushes in my ears.

Levi, curious, peers over at me.

"Two million?"

"Two million," Trilliam answers. "Sir . . . she's a bit . . . frantic."

I scrub a hand over my mouth, my eyes on the road in front of us, but I'm not really seeing it.

"Let me speak to her."

"Sir—"

"I will pull every one of my accounts there immediately if you don't let me speak to my goddamned wife."

"Yes, sir."

"Seattle Bank," I tell Levi, who stares at me perplexed. It's in the opposite direction of where we're going. "Now," I growl, and immediately, he pulls to the curb and flips the car around.

"Fuck," Levi curses. "We're more than two hours away."

"Your husband, Mrs. Cross." Trilliam's voice is muffled while he hands the phone to Mila. Silence greets me from the other end of the line. There's a barely audible intake of breath, and a visceral rage slides through me.

"Mila. What are you doing?"

"Christian . . ." she breathes, and I can hear the change in her voice.

Something's wrong.

"Are you leaving me?"

I fucking hate the way the words taste like battery acid on my tongue. The desperation in my chest, knowing that there's another person out there just walking around with my heart inside their chest and the ability to rip it to shreds at any moment.

"Mila, talk to me. What's wrong? Was it last night?"

"No," she says softly. "I just . . . it has to be this way, Christian."

Why are you doing this to us?

It has to be this way, Mila.

"Mila, whatever it is, we can fix it together."

"We can't. We can't fix this. Just . . . please. Let me go . . ."

Fuck.

FUCK.

Let her go? Are you fucking serious? After everything?

My hands shake when I run my fingers through my hair. I feel like my skin is too tight. Like all the air was sucked out of the vehicle.

First, Sebastian fucking us over, and now my wife is on the run again.

Something isn't adding up.

"Mila, I'm coming home. Just wait for me."

"I just don't want to be with you anymore," she snaps, and I think I'd rather take a bullet than hear her repeat those words.

A dark chuckle slides up my throat, and burning, bitter rage slips through me.

"You're just going to go? Just like that? Sebastian is still out there looking for you."

"I'm-I'm going home, Christian," she says, her voice cracking with emotions I know all too fucking well.

Home. She's going back to LA.

What about me? She *is* my fucking home.

My heartbeat is in my throat, and tension radiates through me that I can't break. Like the night I'd found out she was attacked.

How the fuck can she expect me to go on and pretend like none of this happened? Like my goddamned heart doesn't belong to her, no matter where she's at in the world?

"Fuck . . . *Mila* . . ."

"I'm sorry, Christian . . . I'll," her voice catches, and I hear the pain in her voice—the pain I caused over two years of this pathetic excuse for a marriage.

Things have been so good lately I'd forgotten how bad I actually fucked up. Even if I'd chosen her, she never really got the chance to choose me. Not without some kind of curse over her head.

"I'll always love you," she whispers, and a cold clarity slips over me, numbing every nerve ending in my body.

This is really the fucking end.

Who the fuck am I kidding?

I told her I'd always find her. I'm a man of my word.

"Can Trilliam hear me?"

"Yes," she exhales.

"Give her the money."

"What the fuck?" Levi snaps, running a red light in our race towards downtown.

"Mila—"

"Goodbye, Chrisitan."

The line goes dead, and I curse, banging my hand on the dash so hard my knuckles burn.

"*Fuck!*"

"What the fuck is going on?"

"Change of plans. Mila's at the bank withdrawing two million from our bank account."

"Is she running?"

I open my mouth to tell him she's leaving me. Before I can respond, my phone lights up with a new message.

This one has my blood running cold.

It's from Bella, and it's a picture of her. Bound and gagged to a chair.

"No," I grit. I don't know whether to be elated or fucking terrified. "She's going after Bella."

CHAPTER
Fifty

MILA

I pull to a stop at the old rundown warehouse in the middle of the Mount Baker National Forest.

The building is crumbling around me, the ceiling boasting large holes that allow what's left of the sunlight outside to seep through. The floor is wet and covered in a bed of moss, and a faint scent of mildew hangs in the air.

I cried the entire way here. Hearing the pain in his voice. Christian called me three times after our initial conversation at the bank, where I told him I was leaving him, but I ignored each one.

Now, my phone sits dejected and silent in the passenger seat, nearly dead.

I look down at my wedding band on my finger. The one he carried with him when he left me for three weeks. I want to believe this will work out and it won't break us, but I know better.

Our marriage has been fragile since the moment it was conceived. Hearing those words . . . I can't imagine what it did to him.

I force a deep breath through my lips. This is what I have to do. I can't allow another person I care about to get hurt because of me.

I suck up the pain, letting the fear of what might happen to Bella take its place. There's no room for tears right now.

Forcing my legs to carry me out of the car, I step out onto the muddy concrete, my sneakers scraping when I stand.

Looking around, it doesn't appear that another person has been here in a hundred years. An eeriness hangs in the air like I'm being watched but not by something of this world.

Something inhuman.

That means *he's* here.

"Hello?" I call, searching the shadows around me, but it's too dark.

I'm met with silence. Deep, harrowing, *echoing* silence.

A shiver rolls through me, and I pull my jacket tighter around myself.

"Bella?"

I can't mistake the sinking feeling that this is just like last time. That he's lured me out here, and now he's going to hurt me.

He won't get the chance, though. I'm smarter this time. Stronger. I'll fight to the death before I ever let him touch me again.

"You have five seconds before I'm leaving, asshole."

It's a lie. I refuse to leave without Bella, but it has the desired effect.

"Are you alone?"

The voice makes me jump, and I suck in a deep breath, swallowing past the thick lump in my throat.

"Yes."

I'm met with silence.

Nothing.

"Where's Bella?"

"Where's my money?" he counters.

"Let me see her, then I'll let you have it."

"In case you forgot, you aren't in charge here," Sebastian growls. "If you want to see my precious baby sister again, I suggest you get me that money."

Fuck.

"Fine." I open the trunk, grab the two heavy bags, and pull them out.

Who knew two million dollars would weigh so much?

"Drop them."

Gritting my teeth, I do, dropping them to the dusty floor on either side of me.

"Now, step away with your hands held up very slowly. "

"That wasn't part of the deal."

"I KNOW WHAT THE DEAL IS!"

I jump at his echoing voice ringing in my ears and fall silent.

"Do as I say, Mila. You really don't want to piss me off."

Bile rises in my throat, remembering the feeling of his hands on my body. The sound of his voice mocking me. For a second, I'm back in that basement, and he's the demon lurking in the corner, waiting to strike.

"Give me Bella, Sebastian. She wasn't a part of this. She's innocent."

"Is she, really? Innocent? Are any of you? My father locked me away in that putrid asylum. His visits were like bread crumbs while they had his full attention."

"Your father is a bad man. He didn't deserve you. I know you're hurting. People have been horrible to you. But you're better than this. You deserve to be happy."

He actually deserves the electric chair, but at this point, I'll say anything if he doesn't hurt Bella.

He's silent for a moment. And time stands still while I listen to the sound of my own heartbeat.

"Please?"

Nothing.

"Mila?"

I spin, finding Bella behind me, her eyes wide and full of tears. Her lip is busted, and there's a bruise on her cheek, but otherwise, she looks unharmed.

—Except for the gun pointed at her head.

"Talia . . ."

She rolls her eyes.

"As if you didn't figure it out by now. Ratting me out with that stupid cell phone."

I fucking knew it.

"Mila . . ." Bella whimpers.

"Just let Bella go." Fuck, I don't like how her finger is hovering over the trigger.

"Or what? You're going to tell Christian?" Talia giggles—like a real, *I will eat your heart* giggle and presses the barrel of the gun tighter against Bella's forehead.

"Talia," I say, trying to keep my voice calm when all I really want to do is grab Bella and bolt. "Think about this. That's his sister. You shoot her, he will *never* forgive you."

"Christian never cared about me. Not the way he cares about you," she sneers. "But Sebastian does. Sebastian made me feel whole when Christian left me high and dry when we were supposed to get married."

Because you drugged him, raped him, and lied about a fake pregnancy . . .

"I saw the way he chased after you at the banquet. It was pathetic."

Bella's eyes flick to mine, and I nod my head ever so slightly. She stares at me a beat before her eyes widen, then very carefully, she adjusts her footing.

"It's you he wants, Talia. He married me because he had to. Because he was forced." I *hate* saying those words, but I can see by the vengeance in her eyes that it's working. "If you deliver Bella to him, what kind of chance have I got?"

She cocks her head, grinning from ear to ear.

She thinks she's won.

It's at that moment the crunch of glass sounds behind me, and I only have a second to react.

"Bella, run!"

Bella stomps on the toe of Talia's expensive riding boots and bolts right as someone grabs the back of my head and drags me back.

"Hello, Mila," Sebastian fucking Cross greets, a wicked grin on his face that looks so much like my husband's, it's instantly unnerving. "Miss me?" He rears back, a syringe in hand, and bites the cap off.

"NO!" I screech, ripping at his hand in my hair, but he manages to sink the needle into the side of my neck, and an instant warm sensation washes over me.

Oh, fuck. This is bad.

Sebastian drops me to the ground, and the earth spins around me, the ceiling overhead coming in and out of focus.

"That should shut her up."

"I was enjoying the screams," Talia says, stepping closer. A tear slips down my cheek. My tongue feels weightless, and my legs won't move. Whatever he gave me, it's a whole lot stronger than what Christian had used. "What about Bella?"

"Let her go. Let her crawl back to her family and tell them I've got her."

"And the money? I thought we were just taking the money?"

"Change of plans."

Sebastian looms over me, smiling wickedly.

"Starting to kick in now, isn't it, sweetheart?"

I open my mouth to tell him to go fuck himself, but nothing comes out but a choked breath.

Fuck, I can't focus.

The last thing I see before everything goes black is Sebastian lifting his hand and waving his fingers.

"Night, night, little whore."

And everything goes black.

CHAPTER
Fifty-One

CHRISTIAN

"You put a tracker on your wife?"

Correction.

I put two.

"You try sleeping in a car for six months."

"Touché," He muses, jerking the car to a stop outside the lighthouse beside Mila's car. The front door is open, greeting us like an old friend while the waves crash against the rocks below.

I try not to think about the two months I spent with Mila here, but the moment I see it, all the memories come flooding back.

I was able to follow the tracker on both her wedding ring and her car once we got back to town. We came straight here, but the sinking feeling in my gut tells me we're already too late.

I keep my gun drawn, motioning for Levi to follow me and he nods, circling around to the other side of the closed front door.

The place is a fucking wreck. I've had cameras out here, but I haven't checked them in the last few days with everything going on. Inside, silence looms from the darkness as if it's taunting me.

Reminding me that my deranged and murderous brother managed to kidnap both my sister and my wife and now I'm on the verge of losing my fucking mind.

"One . . . Two . . . Three . . .'

Stepping forward, Levi kicks the door open, and I storm inside, gun drawn—

—At nothing.

The place is empty.

"Fuck," Levi curses.

My chest fills with lead, but I force my legs to carry me, stopping just a few feet inside the door.

The knowledge of what I could find inside is fucking terrifying, and my mouth fills with saliva when I see the jagged note written and left on the table.

History always repeats itself.

Gritting my teeth, I rip open the closed bathroom door, nearly dropping to my knees at the tear-stricken face staring back at me.

"Jesus Christ, Bella," Levi growls, dropping down in front of her to untie her. She's been bound and gagged, and she stares up at us through big, wide eyes. Other than a few bruises on her face, she looks physically unscathed.

Mentally, it's a different story.

The moment Levi removes the gag from her mouth, she's throwing out the details a mile a minute.

". . . he showed up I my room with a gun. Why is he alive? I thought he was dead? And then Mila," her eyes lock with mine. "Christian I'm so sorry. I didn't know. He threatened to kill me. And Talia's working with him—"

"Where is she?" I rasp, the pit in my chest opening up further and further until it's nothing but a black chasm.

She looks like she might break down. Guilt crosses her features, and she grimaces through her tears.

"She . . . she . . ."

"Bells, tell us," Levi says, rubbing her back in soothing circles.

Unfortunately, I'm not feeling very soothing right now. Not with my wife still missing.

Bella looks right at me, a tear slipping down her cheek.

"He took the two million Mila brought to save me . . ." she breathes "Then he took her, too."

My wife has been missing for three hours, and I'm losing my fucking mind as the sun starts to set over the horizon. My chest aches with a hollowness I've never known. Like someone ripped my heart out and threw it in a goddamned meat grinder, then laughed in my face about it.

I'm unsure how to get rid of the irritable, edgy sensation slipping through my muscles, like death by a thousand cuts.

Why did she have to fuck up all my plans?

I was comfortable. I was good at my job. Helping the helpless. I never felt like anything was missing because my life was complete with my work.

Then she waltzed into my soul with her pretty gray eyes and that blonde hair and the softest heart and fucked everything up.

Now, everything is incomplete.

I'm incomplete.

Pain is easy.

Emptiness is what's fucking hard.

I'm exhausted. Sore. Pissed off and growing more and more desperate with each passing moment.

Everyone is gathered around the house. Paulina helped Bella clean up, and they've been speaking quietly in the spare bedroom since. Ava is here, looking grim in her spot by the fireplace, and Levi's been calling in favors left and right. I've even spoken with Logan, who's gotten in touch with his FBI buddies in Seattle. I've searched her cell phone. The car. Fucking everywhere.

No one can find her.

Her fucking ring was left in the car. The tracker I'd had installed inside is useless to me if she's not fucking wearing it. If I get her back, I'll make sure she wears it to bed, to shower, to the fucking bathroom.

I haven't received one text or call apart from the picture of Bella. I also haven't moved from my spot on the front porch where Phantom sits at my feet, watching me with sad brown eyes while I pet his head.

On the outside, I'm calm. Resolute. On the inside, though, I'm on fire. Burning from the inside out with flames I can't extinguish. I can't shake the awful visions swarming in my head, like that video playing over and over again.

Mila is innocent. Whatever happens to her is because of me. Because I'm in love with her, and my brother will do anything to take that from me. Just as he did our mother.

His hate is potent, mixed with his delusions. He's a walking time bomb. One I thought died when he lit that cabin on fire sixteen years ago.

Until my girl is safe and sound in my arms again, I'll light the fucking world on fire, and not a soul can fucking stop me. Hell will look like a tropical vacation spot by the time I'm done with this goddamned state.

"You need to eat."

"Fuck off."

Bella, never one to be swayed, steps out on the front porch anyway.

"Doing whatever . . .*this* is, isn't going to bring her back. You should be out there, searching."

"I'll let you know when I need advice from someone who was

just kidnapped hours ago."

She lets out a deep breath like she's composing herself.

"I'm going to let that go because I know you're hurting. I'm also going to tell you that you won't be able to find her if you're dead, and right now, you're looking close to it."

"I'm fine."

"Will you just stop being a stubborn asshole for two seconds?" she snaps, that carefully composed calmness gone in the blink of an eye.

Good, that makes two of us.

"Listen to you?" I snort, rising from the chair. Her eyes go wide as if she thinks I might hurt her. "Why the fuck would I want to listen to what you have to say?"

Storming inside, Bella follows me, hot on my tail. I ignore her, grabbing the bottle of whiskey from the cabinet in the kitchen and flicking the lid off.

—Only for it to fly at the wall a moment later when that pissed-off rage takes hold.

"What the fuck is wrong with you?" she snaps, and Levi takes one look at the scene, his eyes going wide before he jumps off the couch. He places a hand on her shoulder, trying to wrangle her in, but she's not one to be persuaded. "Your wife is missing, and you've been staring at your hands for the last two hours like she'll magically appear? And now you want to get *drunk*?"

I stand to my full height, my chest bumping hers and knocking her back into Levi.

"What the fuck else do you want me to do?" I growl, and Levi yanks Bella back from me. "I've got surveillance teams all over the fucking country looking. I've got the goddamned cops *and* FBI involved. You want the fucking president next? Want me to send up smoke signals? I can't fucking find her, and this is *my fault*!"

Paulina steps out of the room, her eyes glistening. Her tear-streaked face means nothing to me. She may as well be the shattered whiskey bottle lying in pieces on the floor.

The room is silent, everyone having stopped what they were doing to look at me, currently losing my fucking mind.

Great. The more, the merrier.

In a rush of anger, I whip the barstool beside me at the wall, watching it splinter. The fragile wood is a replica of my self-control.

Then, because that felt so damned good, I threw the next one too.

Fuck those stools. I've always hated them, anyway.

My head spins at that moment, and I stumble back a step, falling to my knees on the hardwood floor. The blood rushes in my ears, my heartbeat a pounding drum in my throat. Sweat coats my skin, and for the first time since my wife went missing, I realize what the feeling in my gut is.

It's fucking hopelessness.

"This is my fucking fault," I breathe, and no one says a word. I'm not even sure anyone even breathes. When the man who's always in control finally snaps, shit tends to get volatile.

As expected, Bella is the one to speak up.

Wrenching away from Levi, she drops down to her haunches in front of me, her light blue eyes flashing with tears.

"Then fucking find her."

And then it clicks.

"The cabin."

Everyone stares at me, no one understanding what I'm saying.

Except Levi.

One look at him, and he understands.

"The fucking cabin."

I surge away from Bella and climb to my feet. Levi races towards the door.

"Where the hell are you going?" Bella barks, following after us. When I grab the shotgun, I keep it loaded in the closet by the front door, her eyes go wide as saucers.

"Paulina," I point to her in the doorway on the front walk. "Keep Bella here. There's a gun in my nightstand. Grab it. Don't open the door for anyone."

"Your father—"

"Fuck him," Levi groans from the driver's side of the car.

I nod to Paulina, who looks back and forth between the two of us with both despair and confusion. Today's been a day of revelations for her. Finding out Sebastian's dead. A missing Bella. Now, a missing Mila. I'll deal with her later. For now, I need to get my wife.

Bella chases after me when I storm towards the car, still wrapped in a throw from inside. "Christian—" she starts, and because I know she's going to ask to come with me, I pull her into a hug.

Her spine stiffens, and she freezes, but eventually, she hugs me back.

"Please . . ." she can't say the words.

All I can do is nod when I pull away.

I'll get her back or die trying.

Because without her, what else have I really got to lose?

"Don't leave the house."

CHAPTER
Fifty-Two

MILA

The first of my senses to return is, unfortunately, smell.

The air *smells* like death. Bleeding, pungent death. Like a body burnt to a crisp.

I groan as pain blooms behind my eyes, my skull throbbing and my head groggy. I try to sit up, tugging on my hands that are bound to a metal chair.

Fuck! Bella!

My eyes snap open, peering around the space.

I'm no longer at the cottage. I'm in a house. Or what's left of it. The walls are burnt to a crisp, the old wallpaper peeling and stained with years of rain leaking through the hole in the roof.

Tears fall from my eyes as the panic takes over. Am I in the cabin where Christian's mother died?

This is not *happening.*

"CHRISTIAN!"

"Screaming won't help."

I freeze, my blood running cold at the voice behind me.

"Sebastian . . ."

His lips tip up in a smirk.

"Hello, Mila."

He steps forward into the light, his gaze unfeeling as he watches me struggle against the chains that bind me. It's like looking at a replica of my husband, only with the knowledge that something isn't right.

"What do you want, dickhead?"

"So feisty. I can see why my brother was so obsessed with you. He always did think with his cock." His gaze roams over my body in a sick, sadistic way.

I stare at him in confusion, tears welling in my eyes.

"Was?"

He chuckles under his breath, grinning from ear to ear.

"Oh, you didn't know? Shame."

Please . . . anything but that.

"It seems he couldn't survive two more gunshot wounds to the chest." He shakes his head. "If only I knew that the first time."

"He's . . . dead?"

I refuse to believe it. Not my Christian.

"You should really be *so* proud of him. The idiot thought he could save you." My heart feels like it's being ripped in two. This can't be real.

Sebastian steps around the circle of light, his hands in his pockets as he examines me like an experiment. His cold gaze is demeaning as it rakes over me, from my sneakers up to the mats in my hair.

"So young to be a widow," he asks, shaking his head. "It really is unfortunate that I had to be the one to do that to you."

"What did you *do*?" I lunge for him, a growl ripping from my throat, only to fall to the floor when the chains rip me back. "What did you do to him?"

Sebastian's gaze is unfeeling as a sob wracks through me. He kneels in front of me, his face so much like that of the man I love that it's haunting.

It's not the same, though. They may be twins, but Sebastian doesn't have the scar down his cheek like Christian. He doesn't have the fire in his eyes or the rough growl of his voice. He doesn't smell the same, and his eyes aren't the right shade of blue, like the ocean glistening off the rocks of Shipwreck Island. He'll never be half the man Christian is.

"You're pathetic," I grind. "You are *nothing* compared to him."

"You sound so much like my dear, sweet mother," he sneers. "She used to hate me. Compare me to Christian at every chance she got. I was the smaller twin. The twin who preferred books over sports. Do you think she loved me?"

"I think it would be hard to love a sadistic psychopath."

He smiles.

"Tell me," he stops, kneeling in front of me. "Do you know where we are?"

My stomach turns at the deeply disturbed look in his eyes.

"No? Well, look around you. My mother took her last breaths in this house." His gaze flicks down at the damaged floor. "Right where you're sitting. You should feel honored I'm letting you go out the poetic way." He brushes his fingers along my face, and I bend away from his touch. "Sadly, you won't be the first, and you definitely won't be the last."

My mouth runs dry as everything falls into place.

I blink through the tears clinging to my lashes, a year's worth of questions finally getting answers.

"You did this because you hate him . . . didn't you?"

He stares at me for a long moment.

Then, a broad, shark-toothed grin spreads across his face, sending my heart plummeting.

"Very, very good, Mila." He claps his hands, the sound echoing in the container. "Now, ask me the plan so I can tell you. It's a good one."

I look up at him through watery lashes, wishing that I could wrap the ropes binding my hands around his neck. I've never wanted to kill another human being until this very moment. "Fuck you."

"Oh, we'll get to that. I always did love the sound of your agony." He shrugs. "Maybe you'll find a purpose in life after all."

He shakes his head, continuing his earlier pacing.

"It's really quite simple; I can't believe you haven't figured it out yet."

"What's it matter?" I shrug. "You're going to kill me anyway."

He rolls his eyes, his shoulder slumping.

"Oh, come on," he growls. "Where's that fight? You wouldn't want Christian to think you've given up, have you?"

If he's safe, I don't care what he thinks of me.

Ironic, huh?

"You made him think you were dead. For years, he's thought it was his fault, but no, it was you, wasn't it?"

"Oh, semantics." He waves a hand. "My dear big brother. The golden child. You know, everyone thought he would do big things."

He comes to a stop in front of me, crouching down.

"Sadly, this time, I don't think I'll be able to keep you alive." His eyes roam over my body, disgust entering his gaze. "You smell like him."

"He's going to kill you," I breathe. "You won't live long enough to revel in your revenge."

He smiles, a big toothy grin.

"You're assuming he survived."

My chest aches, but I refuse to believe that Christian is dead.

"You're assuming he didn't."

A silence falls over the air between us, and his eye twitches. I can see I've gotten under his skin, so I push a little further.

"Christian is stronger, isn't he? He's survived your bullet before. He'll do it again. That's why he's the golden child." I scoff. "You could never live up to him. That's why your mother didn't love you as much as she loved him. And Sebastian . . . well, you know what they say about twins? One's always a dud."

His dark, evil laugh sends chills down my spine when his phone vibrates in his pocket.

"Seems your time's run out, dear Mila." Stalking away from me, he grabs a fiery red gas can from somewhere behind me. With a maniacal grin, he holds it up for me to see.

Oh, this is bad.

"You know, I've got to say, I'm glad he chose you. You're turning out to be a great sister-in-law."

"Can't say the same," I grit through my teeth when he rips the top off the jug.

Oh, this is really bad.

"Shame. I've always preferred blondes."

The smell of gas burns the inside of my nose.

Sebastian splashes it around the room and the old, broken structure seems to sway around me.

"Christian . . ." I cough from the smell of the fumes when he raises a lit match into the air with a feral smile.

"Bye bye, Mila. Give my mother my blessing."

CHAPTER
Fifty-Three

CHRISTIAN

The moment he tosses the match, I'm on him, tackling him to the ground.

Mila screams as the entire room erupts in flames, and I grunt with a blow of Sebastian's fist to the side of my head.

Rearing back, I punch him, hitting him so hard, blood seeps from his nose.

"You going to kill me, Christian?" Sebastian grins through red-tinged teeth. He scrambles to his feet, but I'm stronger, grabbing him around the throat and hauling him to his feet.

He took my mother. He tried to take my wife.

"Christian!" Mila shouts from somewhere behind me, and I falter only long enough for him to bash his forehead into mine. I stumble from the impact, shaking my head and dropping him from my hands.

He falls to the floor in a heap, and I grab him by the ankles, dragging him towards me and shoving him to his back.

End this.

hands around his throat, cutting off whatever bullshit was about to come out of his mouth.

When I thought about all the ways I would kill him, I wanted it to be slow. Excruciatingly painful.

Now, I just want him dead.

I don't give a fuck how we get there.

I watch the light drain from his eyes, his lashes fluttering over the tears that seep through his vision.

The house around us is burning, but this problem can't wait.

It's either now or a lifetime of the same cat-and-mouse game.

I growl through my teeth, snarling with the burn in my veins while my brother chokes underneath me. My twin. The same person I shared a womb with.

All our earlier years flash through my mind, but instead of happy memories, I now see them for what they were. He was always different. A little fucked in the head. I just wish I'd seen it sooner.

"CHRISTIAN!"

That's all it takes. One single second and, a gunshot rings out over the roar of the fire surrounding us.

Instant pain blurs my eyes, and Sebastian manages to thrust my hands away from him, sucking in oxygen. He attempts to scramble out from under me, but we've come too fucking far to lose him again.

Ignoring the blistering pain in my chest, I grab his ankles when he stands, sending him flying to the ground. Both of us are wounded, but the one thing he doesn't have is the sheer fucking will to keep going.

He thrashes in my hold when I wrap my arm around his neck, securing the handcuff to his wrist and then the radiator attached to the concrete beneath him.

"You fucking—" he sputters, shock in his eyes while he fights with its hold. Sweat drips down my face and back, and my vision grows spotty, but I've got to get to Mila. She's tied up. I have to get her out.

Dragging myself to my feet, I immediately fall back to the ground.

"Fuck," I curse, blinking as the room sways around me. "Mila?" I call but can't see her through the smoke and flames reaching up the walls.

Sebastian lets out a maniacal laugh across the room from me, his eyes glinting in the wickedness of the inferno.

"Looks like it's just you and me, brother."

Just let her get out . . .

I press a hand to my chest where I've been hit, gritting my teeth at the pain. I attempt to stand again, but I'm fucking weak.

"Christian!"

Surely, I fucking imagined that.

"Mila, go!"

The fire roars, bright and blinding, but through the haze, I see her at the same time she sees me. She rushes for me, falling to her knees beside me.

"Mila, get the fuck out of here," I grit when she reaches for me.

"NO," she growls, trying to slip her arms around me. "I'm not leaving you here."

"*Mila—*"

"Shut the fuck up and help me."

Gritting my teeth through the pain, I raise on shaking legs, letting her help to steady me. Up in the smoke, it's hard to breathe, and we both cough, trying to suck air into our lungs, but none comes.

Sebastian looks shocked, looking back and forth between us before he starts screeching.

"Talia!" he screams, but she doesn't come.

Looks like her inherent selfishness won out, after all.

"Looks like it's just you . . . brother."

Sirens sound outside, but there's no way in hell they'll be able to get him out of here now.

"Mila," Sebastian tries, tears slipping down his cheeks.

She takes one look at him and starts forward.

"Mila, please?"

"Go to hell."

Sebastian's screams of pain tear through the night sky as sirens draw near.

Mila and I stumble out onto the clearing, sucking in air through the smoke in our lungs.

My chest heaves with the force of each breath and is rippling with pain, but I ignore it when we both fall to the ground, panting.

Immediately, Mila throws herself into my arms with a soft cry, and for the first time since I made her my wife, I realize I fucking did something right.

"You came," she whimpers, burying her head in the side of my neck while I hold her.

Fuck, I never thought I'd get to hold her again.

"Where's Bella? Is she okay?" She pulls back to look at me through the tears in her eyes.

"She's okay. Levi's got her."

"I'm sorry I didn't tell you," she rushes, and I take her face in my hands despite the agony radiating through me. "I couldn't. He was going to hurt her."

"Mila," I try to focus on her gaze, but the world is spinning around me. A dozen blue and red sirens race up the path, but their lights go in and out. Like a poorly-timed dimmer switch. "I love you."

Her eyes widen, filling with tears, and she closes the distance between us, pressing her lips to mine.

"I love you," she whispers against my mouth, and I groan in satisfaction, holding her tighter.

The pain in my chest takes on a sharp edge as the adrenaline wears off, and I pause, feeling a sickening sensation rise in my gut.

Fucking hell. Not again.

Mila's eyes widen when she pulls back, looking down at the

front of my shirt.

"Christian . . ."

"It's okay, little devil."

Fuck, if I die, at least I can die knowing she's safe. My brother will take care of her. Paulina. Her family.

"You've been shot," she whispers, her fingers roaming aimlessly over me, shaking with fear. "Help!"

My head spins, and she slides from my grasp, no matter if I try to hold onto her.

Fuck . . . I just want to hold her.

"He's been shot," I hear her whimper when I lay back on the ground, looking up at the cloudy sky overhead. I've been expecting it to rain all fucking day, but none has come.

Levi looms over me, then Bella, their faces grim.

"Fuck, Mila. Press this on his chest. The ambulance is almost here."

"Hey," I reach for her when she presses Levi's shirt to my chest. "It's okay."

"Stop saying that," she growls, placing pressure on the wound.

Ironically, it's on the other side of my chest this time.

"Mila . . . look at me." The light from the fire is fading, but I can still see the panic in her gaze. My wife. My fucking everything. "I love you."

"Stop it, Christian Cross. You aren't allowed to die. You're unkillable," she growls, tears mixing with the blood on her face.

I open my mouth to tell her I'm not and that this bullet hurts a whole lot fucking more than the last one, but I can't speak.

Come to think of it, I can't even feel it. All I can do is watch her as the moon darkens above me, my last vision of her with tears in her eyes, screaming at me to stay awake when all I can do is close my eyes and fade out.

CHAPTER
Fifty-Four

CHRISTIAN

E verything fucking aches.

That's the only way I know I survived.

My chest is on fire, and a dull pain spreads throughout my body when I first open my eyes to a steady beep filling the room.

That shit's annoying.

My vision is blurry, but I reach around for whatever's making the noise with every intent of throwing it at a wall.

Sleep.

I just want to sleep.

"No," a soft voice says, gentle hands taking mine and laying them back at my side. I'm too fucking weak to fight them as sleep threatens to drag me back under.

And then I remember what happened.

"Mila . . ." I breathe, my voice hoarse and sore.

"I'm here," she says softly from above me. My eyes threaten to drift shut, but soft gray ones loom over me, peering down at me with a tenderness that makes everything hurt worse.

Fuck, maybe I did die.

Maybe this is my hell. Knowing she's here but not being able to hold her.

"Shhh . . ." she soothes, and I hadn't even realized I was speaking until her finger presses to my lips. Tears pool in her gaze, and she leans in, pressing a kiss to my forehead I can't even feel.

Fuck, this must be some kind of sick joke.

"Go to sleep . . ." she whispers, and I try to fight it, shaking my head, but before I can tell her I love her, I slip into the inky blackness, fading off into unconsciousness once again.

The second time I wake up, it's because I have to piss like fucking crazy.

I groan when pain erupts throughout my chest when I attempt to roll over, struggling against the hands that try to push me back to the bed.

"Stop fucking moving, dickhead," a voice growls, and instantly, I know who it is.

When my eyesight focuses, Levi is staring down at me, his eye bruised and his mouth set in a grim line.

"You'll pull something."

Feels like I already did.

Looking around, I'm in the hospital with monitors and screens lining the wall, all offering an insight into the fact that I'm, somehow, still alive. An IV's in my arm, and I tug it out, not even feeling the pull of the needle leaving my skin.

I fucking hate needles.

"Mila?" I know she was fucking here. Where the hell did she

go?

"She's asleep in the chair behind you, and I swear to God, if you wake her up, I'll put a *third* bullet in you," Levi grumbles. "Poor thing's been a nervous wreck."

I grit my teeth, shoving his hand off my shoulder, and force my legs to stand from the bed. I'm shaky and weak, and my head's spinning the moment I'm on my feet. I would never admit it to him, but I'm actually glad when Levi wraps his arms around me because, without him, I would have fallen on my fucking face.

"What the hell are you doing?" he growls, shuffling with me like we're two elderly patients out for a stroll.

"Going to piss. Is that okay?" Why can't he shut the fuck up? I don't want Mila to wake up and see me like this.

"I'll help you."

I start to snap back and tell him I can do it myself, but I know I can't, so I let him help me to the bathroom.

"I don't need you to hold it for me," I grit, and he holds up his hands, turning back to the room.

I'm supposed to be the older brother. The one always in control. I'm supposed to be stronger than this, but yet, here the fuck I am, pissing—with a lot of fucking difficulty—while my brother waits to walk me back to bed.

Pathetic. My only saving grace is that Mila isn't awake to see me struggling. Weak.

"You're a fucking dumbass," Levi grits the moment I'm back in bed. He takes the chair beside me, his gaze softening when he looks to the corner chair behind me. I haven't looked at her yet. Some part of me feels like if I do, I'll realize she's not real, and this was all some fucked-up dream.

"How is she?" I ask quietly. I can deal with it if she's pissed off and hates me when she wakes up. We're already married, which means it'll be hell for her to get away from me.

I wasn't lying when I told her I'm not a good man. She's mine, and I'm hers. Now that I've got her, there's not a fucking judge in the world that will take her from me.

If she's broken, though . . . If I broke her again, sent her spiraling back down into that dark place she was in when I first found her almost three months ago . . . I don't know that I'll ever be able to forgive myself.

"You don't deserve her," he says after a moment, his stare hard. "She is the best thing that fucking happened to you—"

"You're right."

"—and you throw it all the fuck away—" he pauses when he realizes what I'd said, cocking a brow at me. "What?"

"I don't deserve her . . . but she's mine. I'm not giving her up."

"Well, you almost died. What the fuck were you thinking?" he grits, working hard to keep his voice low.

My jaw clenches, my stomach unruly from all the meds they've been pumping in me through that damned needle.

"I was thinking that the man who killed our mother, raped my wife, and then thought he could kill her wasn't going to get the chance to try every again."

"Jesus fucking Christ," Levi grumbles, scrubbing a hand over his face. "He could have killed you."

"But he didn't."

He lets out a huff, but he doesn't fight back, though I can see he wants to. I get it. He's mad because he was scared. Levi doesn't get scared.

"I've got to hand it to her. She's a fucking badass," he murmurs, his gaze on Mila behind me.

I finally allow myself to look at her, and when I see her, my chest aches. She's sleeping, her lips parted over her soft, even breathing. There's a bruise over her cheek that I fucking hate, a cut healing on her lip, but otherwise, she looks peaceful.

"She punched the fuck out of Talia before the cops arrived. When they were loading you in the back of the ambulance."

I look back at him in disbelief, then look at my wife.

Nothing would have surprised me at this point. At least . . . nothing but my gentle, sweet, way too fucking kind wife.

He nods, amusement in his eyes.

"Surprised me, too."

"And Sebastion? Talia?"

"Sebastian died," he murmurs darkly. "They found him stuck in the house, nearly burnt to a crisp."

"And Talia?"

"She was arrested," a soft voice says from behind me, and my spine fills with cement.

Both Levi and I look to Mila, who's now sitting upright in the chair, her eyes tired and her expression guarded.

Fuck, I never thought I'd see her again. The urge to hold her consumes me, but Levi opens his mouth, cutting me off from asking for her.

"Turns out, you were right. She and Sebastian met when they were both at the asylum, and she was just heartbroken enough after her little stunt with you that she let herself get drawn into his shit."

"Guess her father couldn't save her from this one."

The room falls silent, and Levi looks between Mila and me, giving her a slight nod. "I'll give you two some alone time."

"Levi—" I start, but he stops me.

"Tomorrow," he murmurs, glancing at Mila in the corner of the room.

He turns to walk towards the door, stopping to place a hand on Mila's shoulder. "Fuck him up, scrap."

The moment the door closes behind him, the room falls silent. The air hums with all the unspoken shit neither of us is saying. The pain, the anger. The love.

"Mila." I'm surprised by the rasp in my own voice.

Fuck, there's no way she's really in front of me right now.

Her gaze burns into mine, and I k now what she's thinking.

Everything Talia and Sebastian did. We were just pawns to their manias. Their real obsession was themselves.

She's quiet, studying my face. I can only imagine the shit she sees there.

"You took out your IV," she says quietly after a long moment, staring at the thin trail of blood slipping down my arm. "The painkillers won't work without it."

"I don't need it." Pain is inevitable. Hiding from it will only make it hurt worse in the end.

"Do you need . . ."

"Mila," I sigh, cutting her off. I can feel myself getting tired again, but I refuse to fall asleep without her in my arms, where I know she's safe. "I just need *you.*"

She swallows, pulling her bottom lip between her teeth and staring down at her hands in her lap.

I think she's going to deny me, but after a long pause, she nods, almost to herself, before climbing out of the chair and crossing the distance to the bed. She stops in front of me, and I sit up, gritting my teeth and ignoring the pain in my shoulder.

"Mila, talk to me, little devil," I whisper, chest on fire. Maybe I went too far, and she's come to realize what I've known all along. That she's too fucking good for me, and she'd be better off without me. She's still too far away from me for me to wrap my arms around her like I want, so I settle for taking her hand instead. "Tell me what's going on in that pretty little head."

"I watched you almost die again," she whispers, her eyes finally meeting mine and brimming with tears. The sound of her voice breaking makes my chest tighten. "I'm sorry for the things I said to you. I never wanted to hurt you, but I had to make you let me go . . . for Bella."

"Baby, I know."

She shakes her head, wiping a tear that slips down her cheek. I take her other hand, pulling her closer despite the pain that emanates from my shoulder.

"And I'm sorry you had to kill your brother. I'm sorry it happened in that house, and—"

"Mila." I search back and forth between her eyes, my heart in my throat. "They say love makes you a better man," I murmur, brushing the curl back from her forehead. "Loving you just made me fucking ruthless."

"I . . ." she breathes, and I pull her between my legs, wrapping my arms around her waist and leaning my head against her shoulder.

Fuck, she's really fucking here.

"I love you," she whispers, pressing her cheek to the top of my head. "Every piece of you. Even the broken parts."

"Fuck, Mila," I rasp, pulling her to my lap. "Come here."

She tries to be careful, slipping into my lap, but I drag her closer, cradling her to me. I crush her body to mine despite the burn in my bruised ribs and my shoulder, and she wraps herself around me.

"Please stay."

I don't know what makes me say it, but I feel like I need to. The desperation may be from what just happened, or it may be from a lifetime of watching people disappear, but I don't care. All that matters now is that she's here.

"I love you," she repeats, burying her face in the side of my neck and pressing her lips there. A groan of satisfaction rumbles up my throat. "You're my husband. I love you. Wherever you go, I go."

That's all I needed to hear.

"Fuck, I love you." I press my lips to hers before pulling back and leaning my forehead against hers. "You are my heaven and hell, little devil. My end and beginning. My perfection, and I will spend an eternity creating a paradise for you if you say you're mine."

"I'm yours," she whispers, eyes closed and tears on her cheeks drying. "Always."

"Always," I repeat.

I'm not sure how long I hold her, but when she yawns, I realize

I'm fucking exhausted too. Whatever bullshit they have me hopped up on is threatening to knock my ass out.

"Nope," I murmur when she attempts to climb from the hospital bed. "You're staying here with me."

"Are you forgetting you were shot?" she cocks a brow at me, all fire, and I fucking love it.

"Got a matching bullet in the other shoulder." She groans, and I chuckle under my breath, pulling her down to the pillows. As if her body is agreeing with me, she yawns.

"What if I hurt you?" she asks when I pull her into my side. She nestles her head on my shoulder, and I suck in a breath of relief.

Home. This is home.

"You won't." I open my eyes to find her watching me.

"Don't ever do that again," she whispers, and I don't need an explanation to know what she's saying.

"Never." I press my lips to hers, drinking her in, and despite the bullet in my chest, the meds still wreaking havoc on my consciousness, and everything else we've been through in the last couple days, my cock twitches in my sweats.

She breaks the kiss when I slip my tongue into her mouth, laying her head back down.

"By the way, Doctor Roberts said no sex for at least eight weeks."

Doctor Roberts can suck a dick if he wants to keep telling her shit like that.

"Doctor Roberts is dramatic." I press my lips to her forehead. "Give me twenty-four hours, and I'll have you underneath me."

She raises a brow. "We'll see about that."

"Yeah, we will . . . *wife.*"

CHAPTER
Fifty-Five

CHRISTIAN

William Cross looks like death contained in human cells. Like a corpse and not a living, breathing human being.

Or . . . as close as you can get when you're as fucked-up and twisted as he is.

Levi stands on one side, Mila on the other, while Bella and Paulina stand behind us. I would have preferred if Mila hadn't seen this, but after I returned home from the hospital a few days ago, she's refused to let me out of her sight.

I can't say I mind.

"I see you managed to live," my father croaks out through the oxygen mask, pumping air that should go to someone else who needs it. Someone who deserves it and not the bastard in front of me.

"I see you're still alive, somehow."

"Christian," Bella admonishes quietly from behind me, and Levi shoots her a look, silencing her.

She just doesn't understand yet what kind of monster he really is. She was always protected as a kid, whether by Levi or Mom or me.

That ends today.

"Let's start at the beginning." I take a step forward despite the pain in my shoulder. I shouldn't be up right now, but this can't wait.

Every second I know he's here, being waited on hand and foot is another second that passes where I think about killing him. Slitting his throat in his sleep and watching the life drain from his eyes.

"You sent Mom away to the lake house earlier than us because you thought the lodge would go to you in the event Mom died."

"What?" Bella snaps from behind me. I continue.

"You knew she was planning to divorce you and that you had no claim to Mom's money, so you set up your son to kill her. Didn't you?"

William doesn't answer.

That's okay because I have more.

"You knew how twisted his mind was, and you also knew it wouldn't take much to convince him that she needed to be dealt with. So, you had them ride up there together, and when he got her alone . . . he murdered her. When he was done, he burnt the place to the ground, and conveniently, we were far enough behind them that by the time we got there, the bodies would have been unrecognizable."

I hear Bella gag, and Paulina lets out a deep breath. There's a heaviness in the air, but of course, there always has been when he's around.

"Glad to see you finally figured it out," William smirks, though it lacks any of its usual heat with the tubes all around him. "Only took you fourteen years."

"After it was done, you made us believe Sebastian had died because you knew he could tell everyone what you made him do. So, you shipped him off to Saint Peter's and left him to rot in that asylum. That is . . . until he met Talia after I called off the engagement and the three of you devised the plan to get rid of us. You promised Sebastian and Talia the lodge would be theirs in your will. But of course, it wasn't yours to give away, was it?"

"Is this true?" Bella asks and I don't have to turn around to know she's crying. She steps forward to the edge of our father's bed, tears streaming down her face while she looks down at him. "Is this *true?*"

William ignores her, looking straight at me instead.

"Your mother did nothing for this place," he wheezes. "While I was working late nights, she was at home with the children she *had* to have. This place belongs to *me.*"

"Wrong," I tell him, holding up the documents I'd had in my hand since the moment we walked in. "This was hidden in the safe down in the basement along with Mom's death certificate. It's her will, and it states the property goes to her children. Which means Levi, Bella, and I are the owners." I toss the papers in his lap. "You never owned anything except that cancer that's slowly killing you."

He glares at me, reaching out with a feeble hand to grab the papers.

"And before you think about ripping those up, just know that's a copy. You're only wasting what little energy you have left."

"This document proves nothing."

"On the contrary," Paulina finally speaks. "It proves you've committed larceny. You kept the lodge from it's rightful owners."

William laughs from the bed.

"When you found out I was onto you, you sent Sebastian to hurt my wife, didn't you?"

William's gaze flicks to Mila, and I step in his path. Fuck that. He doesn't get to scare her again.

"You sent him there to kill her in the hopes that I'd fly off the handle; only your plan backfired when she proved to be stronger than what you could do to her, so you sent your hounds to find her. That night on the rooftop, you planned for Sebastian to kill me, but . . ." I shrug. "He's never been a good shot. Guess I fucked that plan too."

"You were supposed to die," he croaks, his eyes glinting in anger in the dim lighting of his room.

"*Then*—and this is the most laughable part—after you learned I was alive, you found out you had cancer and wouldn't be around to inherit the lodge, anyway. You were pissed off, so you sent Collin to my house, but that failed. You lost control of Sebastian, and he kidnapped my wife because you told him with me out of the picture, he would be welcomed back into the family. That failed, too."

"What are you going to do? Kill me?" he challenges, a wicked grin on his face. It's all the more creepy with the oxygen mask over his lips. "Please. I'm already dying. You'd be doing me a favor."

I open my mouth to speak, but Mila takes my hand. When I look down at her, she gives a subtle shake of her head.

"He's right. Killing him is what he wants," she says softly.

Fuck.

I'd come to the mansion with every intention of putting him in the ground tonight, but looking down into her soft gray gaze, I know she's right.

"How could you do this?" Bella asks, tears clogging her throat. She backs up when he holds a hand out to her—he's always had a soft spot where she's concerned. "You killed mom? Had Sebastian *rape* Mila? He *carved* nasty things into her skin and you *sent* him to do that to her?"

When he doesn't respond, she turns on her heel and storms out of the room.

"Let's not forget the other shit you've done over the years," I murmur, and Levi's shoulders stiffen. "My siblings and I are finding it hard to move on with you in our lodge."

"You can't move me," he croaks. "I'd be dead within a week."

I shrug. "Quite frankly, I don't care. You'll be moved to a care facility with enough funds to cover your very basic needs." I look down at his fancy oxygen machine keeping him alive. "Once that runs out, well . . . I guess you'll find out the rest when it happens. I know you love a good show."

"This is my home," he growls, attempting to look menacing

when he sits forward. Unfortunately for him, a stiff breeze would take him out. "You will *not* throw me out."

"If I had my way, I would have thrown you in the ocean," I murmur darkly and Mila's hand tightens around mine. "You can thank her for the rest of your miserable life."

I pull Mila towards the door, and Levi follows. Paulina stares at my father for a long moment before she joins us in the hall, shutting the door on a hacking cough that rings out behind us.

"I'm so sorry," she whispers, tears shining in her eyes. "I never knew—"

"None of us did," Levi interrupts her, wrapping an arm around her shoulder. "You've been the best damn aunt to a bunch of unruly kids. We owe you everything."

She smiles, but it dissolves into tears.

"You guys are going to make me cry."

"Too late," I chuckle, and Mila releases me to give her a hug.

We start back down the hall, Levi walking beside me and Mila with Paulina up ahead. I'm slow due to the bullet hole in my side, but I'll be damned if I roll around on one of those electric scooters like Mila suggested. Can you picture a six-foot-three man crammed on a motorized scooter? I fucking can't.

"I'm leaving," Levi says quietly so the women won't hear.

To be honest, I expected it. He's been here long enough. The lodge has never felt like home to him. Only a prison.

"When?"

"Now."

"Job?"

"Something like that," he shrugs.

All I can do is shake my head when Levi's jaw tightens.

"Keep an eye on her."

I don't have to ask who the *her* is that he's referring to. I can see it even if he can't. As if on cue, Ava walks out of her room up ahead of us, her eyes going wide when she sees us. She looks between Levi and me before she turns away with a flush to her cheeks.

"Don't run from this place because of him," I say, stopping at the door to my office. I have the task of finding the shittiest nursing home I can find to shove William Cross into for the remainder of his days.

Bonus points if there are fleas.

Levi pauses, his hands in his pockets. His jaw tightens, and he looks away.

"You should have killed him."

"No . . ." I start, my eyes landing on Mila, where she stands at the foot of the stairs, hugging a crying Bella. "Think I've killed enough for one lifetime, don't you?"

"It's what we're good at," he shrugs. "Besides . . . he tried to kill Mila. He tried to kill *you*."

"Don't you know?" I cock a smile. "I'm unkillable."

"Hey . . ." Mila says, stepping out onto the back porch of our house where I'm sitting and watching the sun fade behind the trees. "I couldn't find you. I got worried."

I hold out a hand for her, and hesitantly, she comes to me, sinking into the bench beside me and nestling into the crook of my arm. She's so careful; it's like she's afraid that if I make one wrong move, I'll break.

"Just needed to think."

"I'm sorry," she says softly, her head resting over my heart. "About your father. I know it must be hard."

I shake my head. "No . . . he was the easy part. He was dead to me the moment I was born. He never knew how to be a father."

She's quiet for a moment, studying me. Abruptly, she sits back and takes my chin, forcing my gaze to hers.

"You aren't him. You'll never be him."

"No?"

"Christian Alexander Cross," she scolds softly, raising up on her knees to face me. She cups my cheeks in her hands, the soft scent of her perfume washing over me.

Fuck. Dr Roberts at the hospital is a dick for telling Mila I had to wait eight weeks to have her. It's been one, and I'm already pissed off.

"You may be an asshole sometimes. You may leave the toilet seat up too often, and you may have almost died—I'm still mad at you for that, by the way—" She shoots me a look that has me chuckling under my breath. "—But you're also so intuitive, sometimes I wonder if you can read my mind. You saved my life. You saved so many others from an even worse fate. You're . . . everything."

I reach up, despite the pain, and capture a tear that slips down her cheek.

"I told you if you wanted your freedom, I would give it to you," I murmur quietly, running my fingertips over her wet cheek.

"You already did. In return, I want to give you everything."

"So, where do we go from here?" I repeat the same words to her she used when I came back from hunting whoever tried to hurt her. Back when I didn't know Sebastian was still alive, and before I knew, the people responsible were right here under my nose.

Mila smiles softly, leaning in until her lips hover over mine.

"To bed."

"Fucking finally."

"To recover, Mr. Cross."

I slip a hand up her thigh, and she shivers at the contact.

"We'll see about that, *Mrs.* Cross."

Jessi Hart

CHAPTER
Fifty-Six

LEVI
3 Weeks Later

The mansion my family lives in is quiet when I step through the back door. It's three in the morning, so I know they're all asleep, as I quietly pad down the hall towards the staircase.

It's been three weeks since I left, and every day, I've been quietly plotting. Stewing.

Making my way upstairs, I pass my sister's room, then *hers*. Finally, I pass Paulina's, and the room at the end of the hall beckons to me like an old friend.

Like it knows why I'm here.

The machines around the four-post bed in the center of the room beep quietly in the night. It smells like a hospital past the door, and my chest fills with disgust. I've always hated the scent.

He's asleep in his bed, but when I rip the cord keeping the machines on out of the wall, it only takes a moment before his eyes open. He reaches for the oxygen tube in his nose, confusion on his face.

"It won't work," I say from the shadows, and his eyes go wide

I step into the moonlight. He stares at me in shock, and I grin.

There's nowhere to run, now.

I've been waiting for this day all my life. From the moment he put his hands on me, I've envisioned what it would be like to put a bullet in his head.

Now that we know he kept my brother locked away and alive, knowing that he murdered my mother, almost had my brother killed *twice,* sent Sebastian to rape and torture his wife . . . fucked with *her.* . . there's nothing that could stop me.

My family will never be free, so long as he's alive.

He's already dying. I'll make sure the fucker makes it to hell a little early.

He opens his mouth to speak, but without his precious oxygen tube, nothing comes out but a raspy breath. Stepping forward, I grab a spare from the end of the bed, wrapping the tube around my hands while I approach.

"Christian wants you to suffer. Tomorrow, you would have been moved to a new facility where you'd probably be kept alive for another few months." I shrug. "I think that's too kind."

And then I lunge for him. We struggle, but I'm bigger than him now. Stronger. Wrapping the tube around his throat, I pull it tight until it's cutting off what little oxygen he can get.

"Le—"

"Shhh . . ." I tighten my hold on the tube, silencing the sound of his gurgling cough, begging for air.

It won't come, though.

It's time for us to move on. Be a family.

Looming over him in the darkness, his eyes are wide with fear and pain.

Good. Now he'll finally know what it feels like to wonder if you're going to die or not.

He struggles feebly underneath me, his hands clawing at my wrists to pry me off, but it's no use.

"I always liked Mom better," I murmur, though I'm not even sure he hears me. His hands fall away from mine to the bed with a thud, his eyes glazing over. I listen to the sound of his wheezing breath until it fades, and even then, I don't let go.

Now, I won't stop until he's dead.

When I'm sure he's gone, I release my hold, cracking my knuckles in the silence of the room. The machines keeping him alive start to beep frantically, and I take that as my cue to leave.

With one last parting look, I can't help but feel a sense of relief wash over me.

William Cross signed his own death warrant the moment he hurt my family.

I'm only sorry my sister will be the one to find him.

EPILOGUE

I stop at the foot of the tree house nestled high in the top of the old oak tree behind our house.

"You know you can't stay up there forever, right?"

Slowly, a blonde head with bright blue eyes peeks out over the edge at me, the rest of her face hidden behind the shelter of the tree hut.

"Says who?"

I cock a brow at her. One thing having kids teaches you is patience. And how to limit your use of the word fuck.

"Says your mother."

She shakes her head, leaning out further. There's a split second of panic in my gut when I think about her tumbling over the side, but it quickly dissipates.

Kid's a fucking spider monkey.

"That's a lie," Lily points out with a cheeky grin. "Mom wouldn't say that."

"Then, I said it." I take hold of the rope ladder, holding it steady.

"How about I make you a deal? You come out for an hour, and if you aren't happy, you can come back here."

She stares at me for a beat as if she's trying to pick out the catch in my statement. There isn't one. I know my wife and daughter well enough to know sometimes shit gets overwhelming, and they need a moment to themselves.

"Did Mom make chocolate cake?"

I smirk.

"She did, though, I did see Uncle Levi eating a *big* piece before I came out here. It might be all gone."

In a flash, she scrambles towards the ladder, swinging down until she falls flat on her feet in front of me.

She's getting bigger. Healthier. She's always been small for her age and still is, but at least now, there's a new light behind her eyes.

After a year in our family, she's come a long way. When we first adopted her, there were some difficult moments. We worked through them as a family, and now, it's like she's been here her entire life.

Except for those times when she needs to hide.

"Going to be getting colder soon. We'll have to cover this place up."

Lily frowns, following me back towards the lodge.

After everything happened, we turned it from a socialite's dream mountain venue to a family lodge with more affordable prices. Surprisingly, it was Mila's idea, and Bella's been far happier now that she's not running herself rampant to organize the finest caterers and decorators.

I like the lodge now. Fuck, it's home. I like being able to raise my family here without worrying about what kind of life they're growing up in.

Now, instead of formal banquets and expensive garden parties, we're having slip-n-slide contests with the other families and scavenger hunts.

It feels . . . real, now.

Something I can leave behind for Lily and whatever other kids Mila and I have.

This will be my legacy. Not wealth.

"What's wrong, Lily?"

"Nothing," she lies.

I side-eye her.

"You're quiet."

"Do you think they'll like me?" she asks after a long pause.

"Why wouldn't they?"

"I'm different," she points out.

Another part of being a father I never expected? This infinite urge to not only protect but to let life happen. Learning to control your overbearing tendencies fucking sucks.

I pull Lily to a stop at the edge of the party.

Mila's entire family is here. Mine too. The last time we were all in one place was when Mila and I had a *real* wedding over a year ago. Once everything died down, I wanted to give her the choice. A real choice to marry me and spend the rest of her life with me.

Luckily, she accepted. I'm not sure what I would have done if she hadn't.

Kneeling down to her level, I force her to look at me and not the people milling about, getting ready to sit down to dinner.

"Everyone's different. It's what makes life exciting. If we were all the same, there would be no love. No joy. Nothing. Just emptiness."

"You think?" she asks, biting her lip.

Sometimes she's so much like Mila it scares the shit out of me.

"I know so," I correct, and she looks back at the party. Across the way, I see Mila watching us, her brows furrowed together. "Remember our deal?"

"One hour."

"Yep."

"When does the clock start?"

I chuckle under my breath and stand. "As soon as you sit down to eat."

I steer her towards the party, and Monica opens her arms for a hug. Of everyone, Monica's the last person I expected to be so open to Mila and my decision to adopt Lily. She takes her role as grandmother seriously, and she's already spoiled her.

Lily beams and runs into her arms while I join my wife on the opposite side of the table. I lean into her, wrapping my arms around her stomach, and press a kiss to her cheek.

"Everything okay?" she asks quietly, turning to face me.

My chest tightens at the look in her eyes. That mother bear instinct is firing on all cylinders.

"As long as there's chocolate cake."

Mila laughs. "Then, I guess you're lucky I made two . . . do you think they're okay?" she asks, her brows knitting together in worry.

"They'll be fine," I murmur, pulling her towards our seats. "We pay them to handle it. They'll handle it."

She still looks worried, so I stop her and pull her to me, pressing my lips to her forehead.

"I'll text Baxter and make sure when we're done eating."

She breathes out a sigh of relief and finally takes her seat.

Mila had spoken about opening her own bakery for years. When we decided to change the lodge into a more family-friendly resort, we made that dream come true. Today's their first day since it opened a month ago without her, and I'm glad she's finally getting a break.

With the addition of the bakery, the spa Bella added, and a few new upgrades, everything is finally coming together.

Looking around the table at our family and friends, it seems surreal to think about where we were two years ago. My family, with Levi and his wife. Bella and her new fiancé, Sam. Paulina and Rudy, though they'd never admit there's something between them. On the other side is Mila's family, with Monica and Bob. Savannah and Logan fawning over her pregnant stomach. Charlie and Bailey with their two kids. Bailey's best friend, Andi, her husband, Jake, and their son. Mason, Hannah, and Luke.

Shipwreck Island feels like it's across the world and not an hour away, nestled into a forgotten corner of the world. We've hired a young couple to look after the place now that it's served its purpose.

Looking at Mila, I know those four walls brought her back to me. I'll forever be grateful for the magic that place holds, and maybe it can do the same for someone else.

"What are you looking at?" she asks, smiling coyly while passing me the mashed potatoes.

My hand slips up her bare leg under the table, and she almost drops the bowl in her hand.

"I'll show you later."

She blushes but doesn't swat my hand away.

"I think you need to focus on your mashed potatoes, Mr. Cross."

"I'd much rather focus on yours."

"Nana, what is the mile-high club?" Lily asks out of nowhere, and both Mila and I freeze, our heads snapping to look at Monica. Monica handles it in stride without missing a beat.

"It's for people who use the bathroom on a plane."

"Why is there a club?"

"Because I suppose they feel important about it." She winks at me and continues onto a new topic while Mila hides her laugh behind her drink.

Over her head, Levi catches my eye, nodding once, his wife completely oblivious beside him. I nod back, something unspoken passing between us.

We've come a long fucking way from losing our mother. From our father to Sebastian, all the way down to this very lodge where our family is having its first-ever combined cookout in the front yard of Mila and I's house.

Life may have taken a turn neither of us ever expected, but when

Mila lays her hand down over mine, I know I wouldn't have it any other way.

Her eyes meet mine, pretty gray glinting like silver in the sunlight overhead.

Fuck . . . those eyes. Even after three years married and eight years in each other's lives, she's still got me wrapped around her fucking finger.

"Keep looking at me like that, Mrs. Cross," I warn quietly in her ear, and a shiver rolls through her.

"I love you," she whispers, her fingers tightening around mine.

"I love you, too," I murmur, pressing a kiss to her cheek. "Always."

I'd once wondered what God did to men who stole angels from the heavens.

Now I know we'll never find out.

Mila made me the man I was meant to be. I may not deserve this life, but who cares? I'm never giving it up. I'll spend eternity chasing after her, and somehow, I know it'll never be enough.

She was made for me, and in the end, the devil better be prepared to pry her from my hands because there's no way in hell, I'm ever giving her up.

The End

Thank you so much for taking the time to read Never Fall for an Angel. If you enjoyed reading this book, please consider giving it a review on the platform(s) of your choice.

Reviews are like tips for authors, and let us know how we're doing, as well as spread the word of our work. Your opinion matters.

Love,

Jessi

<u>JOIN</u> THE <u>CLUB</u>

If you want to follow along for future updates, secrets, or just want to read the ramblings of a tired, book-crazy writer, click the link below to sign up for my newsletter.

Love Always,

Jessi

jessihart.com

Tiktok: jessihartauthor

Instagram: jessihartauthor

Facebook: jessihartauthor

ALSO BY JESSI HART

ABOUT THE AUTHOR

Hey everybody! I'm Jessi Hart, writer of contemporary and dark romance stories that will probably make you fall in love, cry, laugh, and want to throw the book across the room, all in a few chapters.

I like my hero's grey and my heroine's sassy and full of wit. My characters are human with human flaws that might make you angry, sad, or maybe, relate to them a little more than you thought you would. In the end, though, you can't help, but love them. Because even if they're just on paper, they're real, just like you and I.

-Jessi Hart lives in Ohio with her partner and dogbaby, Rylie. When she's not daydreaming up the perfect scene, you can probably find her gaming, binge-watching a spooky show or pranking her partner, Nick.

Made in the USA
Monee, IL
23 December 2025

40227681R00321